Shamrock Green

'Let me change your dressing.' Her voice was soft, even softer than Sylvie's. 'Come on, Private McCulloch, big brave chap like you. What would your wife think of you, scared of having your bandages changed?'

He did not deny that he had a wife, but he did not confirm it either.

To appease her, he said, 'All right.'

The dressing came away from his face in one piece. Cold morning air pressed against his lids. His eyes were a mess. He knew they were a mess. He kept them shut. He could see threads of colour, though, and the darkness was no longer white but black. He felt the icy solution dribble down his cheeks.

'Open your eyes.'

He opened his eyes and saw natural light and in the light the nurse's face, solemn and sallow and drawn with concern.

'Can you see me?' she asked.

Beautiful, he thought, she's quite beautiful. But all he said was, 'Yes.'

About the author

Born in Glasgow, Jessica Stirling is the author of
twenty-two heartwarming novels, many with
Scottish backgrounds.

Shamrock Green

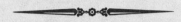

Jessica Stirling

CORONET BOOKS

Hodder & Stoughton

Copyright © 2002 by Jessica Stirling

First published in Great Britain in 2002 by Hodder and Stoughton
First published in paperback in 2002 by Hodder and Stoughton
A division of Hodder Headline
A Coronet paperback

3

A CIP catalogue record for this title is available from the
British Library

ISBN 978 0 340 81848 0

Typeset in Bembo by Palimpsest Book Production Limited,
Polmont, Stirlingshire

Printed and bound by
CPI Group (UK) Ltd, Croydon, CR0 4YY

Hodder and Stoughton
A division of Hodder Headline
338 Euston Road
London NW1 3BH

In Memory of my Grandfather
Private David McNair
7th Battalion Gordon Highlanders
Hazebrouck, 14th April 1918

and
For Theresa, of course, with Love.

PART ONE

Sylvie

Chapter One

She met him first late in the afternoon of a Sunday in July only days before the war began. She was outside feeding the chickens when the Hudson appeared in the street on the far side of the arch and, tilted on two wheels, swerved into the alley. The alley appeared too narrow to accommodate the broad, black motor-car and for a moment she thought the wings, lamps, even the fender would be torn away and Turk Trotter, who was perched on the running board, would be smeared against the wall, then the car straightened and shot, roaring, into the yard.

The hens scattered and the rooster flew up in the air like a fighting cock. Maeve was seated on top of the coal box. She jerked in her legs and tumbled backwards, giving the strangers a glimpse of her stockings and little girl's garters, but the men were on fire with the day's events and had no interest in little girls or their garters. Turk leaped from the running

3

board. He pranced away from the motor-car, plucked Maeve from the coal box and spun her round.

'By Gad, ay-hay, we taught them a lesson today,' he chanted. 'Did we not march, my sweetheart, straight into Dublin town, the first Irish army to do so in a hundred years?'

Sylvie paid no attention to Turk's prattle. She stood by the kitchen doorway, cornmeal running in dusty little streams through her fingers, and peered into the window of the motor-car at the stranger in the back. His head was resting against her father-in-law's belly. His coat, a long, grey, threadbare ulster, was wrapped around his knees. His fists were tucked between his knees and his body drawn away from her as if in shame or shyness. It was a small, pale face that topped the collar and the collar was fastened with a stud not a pin and the tie was like a string a dog had chewed. There was a leaf-shaped splash of blood across the breast of his shirt and fresh blood on the folds of the overcoat.

'What happened to him?' Sylvie asked.

The young man in the front seat beside Charlie leaned over and said, 'Pull yourself together, Fran, for God's sake. You're scarin' the woman.'

'He's bleeding,' Sylvie said.

The young man in the front seat was younger than Charlie who was hardly much more than a boy. At times it was hard to remember how young they all were and that she herself was still some years short of thirty.

Turk came up behind her. He wrapped an arm about her waist and squeezed his wrist against her breast. It didn't matter to Turk that she was Gowry McCulloch's wife. Old or young, pretty or plain, married or single, it was all the same to Turk Trotter for he was the younger son of a Wexford cattle broker and still had the rough manners of a country man.

'I think he took a bullet,' Turk said.

Daniel McCulloch laughed. Nervous laughter was her father-in-law's response to most things. If he had been a slender young woman instead of a fat old man he would have been a giggler.

He said, 'Sure now and we all know he took a bullet.'

'Bullet or not, he's bleeding,' Sylvie said. 'Bring him into the house.'

'No,' Charlie said. 'If he's going to die he'd better do it in his own bed.'

'His own bed?' said Turk. 'Is he still lodged at the college?'

'He has not been lodged at the college for years,' said Charlie.

'Take him home to his wife then,' Turk said.

'Wife!' said Charlie. 'If you mean Maureen, she threw him out.'

'Well,' Sylvie said, 'you can't just leave him there.'

Charlie had silky hair and protruding ears. He shrugged his thin shoulders.

The young man was also a country boy. He had

the same tanned, ruddy look they all had at first, scared of nothing.

'Have we not more important things to do than fuss with the likes of Fran Hagarty,' he said.

Turk detached his arm from her waist and glanced at the piece of Sperryhead Road that was visible through the arch.

The sun had already begun to sink towards the west. The shadow on the wall of Watton's warehouse was slanted towards the eaves and the back of the hotel was all in shadow. Charlie opened the driver's door, leaned out and looked back at the archway and the sunlit cobbles.

'Did we shake them off?' he asked.

'Sure and we shook them off,' Turk said. 'The peelers ha'n't got time to chase us, not with corpses strewed all over Bachelor's Walk.'

'Corpses?' Sylvie said. 'Dead corpses?'

'They fired on the crowd,' Turk told her.

'The soldiers,' Charlie added.

'The King's Own,' Turk said. 'They're not after us, the bastards.'

'We don't know who they're after,' Charlie said. 'We shouldn't sit round here waitin' to be caught red-fisted.'

The wounded man's head was resting against the leather seat. Her father-in-law had slid away, groping for the door handle. There was no sign of blood on the man's lips but his eyes were lustreless, as if the stuff of life were seeping out of him.

He looked up at Sylvie.

'Leave me,' he said. 'I'm fine where I am.'

'Damned if you are,' said Sylvie.

And yanked open the passenger door.

Daniel McCulloch, her father-in-law, was secretary of the Brotherhood of Erin, Charlie an active member. When Gowry was off on trips they met Turk in the back bar of the Shamrock and jawed the night away. Sylvie had no interest in secret societies or the tangle of Irish politics. She left all that blathering, time-wasting stuff to the menfolk. She had been to only one big parade, at Bodenstown, and only because Maeve had been keen.

Maeve could twist her mam and daddy around her little finger when she set her mind to it and since Daddy was driving a charabanc hired from Flanagan's by the brotherhood why couldn't Mam and she go too? Sylvie had no great desire to hear the speeches and the bands but with the threat of war hanging heavy in the air she felt it was time to discover what all the ranting was about and why her in-laws were prepared to die for an Ireland that seemed to her perfectly fine and dandy just the way it was. But when she had arrived in Bodenstown and marched beside Maeve in the parade she had begun to experience a little of the national pride that so excited her daughter. Gowry had stayed on the omnibus, feet up, cap pulled down, eating cherries from a paper bag, reading *Tit-Bits*, pretending that none of it mattered to him.

For Sylvie it had been a surprisingly good day, a day away from running the hotel, from feeding hens and frying bacon and making sure that Jansis swept the stairs. And she was pleased to see her daughter enjoying herself. Only in hindsight did she realise that marching in the parade at Bodenstown had prepared her for Francis Hagarty.

Turk guided him through the kitchen into the house.

He was too proud to allow them to take his legs and swing him between them. He leaned heavily on Turk and kept his hand down between his thighs, pressing his knees together, walking with mincing steps like one of the comic turns at the Tivoli. Blood followed him down the corridor to the sitting-room, pattering on the linoleum like the spoor of an animal. Maeve trailed him, mopping up the spots with a newspaper and when Mr Hagarty slumped into the armchair by the fireplace she stuck a wad of newspaper under his feet to protect the rug.

Turk stood back, frowning, then went out into the hall where Charlie was pacing restlessly up and down.

Sylvie heard Charlie say, 'Where's Gowry? Where's my flamin' brother?'

'Dad's out with the bus,' Maeve answered. 'He's driving Sunday trippers to the lakes. He'll not be back before nine.'

'Thank God for that,' said Charlie, and disappeared.

The sitting-room was at the front of the house. The curtain had been drawn to keep sunlight from fading the furniture. The room was sombre, brown and still. A table, four chairs and the two big armchairs that flanked the fireplace were reflected in the oval mirror above the mantelpiece.

Sylvie knelt at the stranger's feet. 'Where are you hurt, sir?'

'Don't call me "sir",' he said quietly. 'I'm Fran Hagarty.'

'Are you now?' Sylvie said. 'Well, Mr Hagarty, show me your hand.'

'It *is* my hand,' he said, 'and a bloody mess it is, too.'

He drew his fist from between his knees and held it out. Blood dripped sluggishly on to the newspaper. He did not look at it. He stared at the crown of Sylvie's head and her soft inarticulate curls.

'Are the fingers gone?' he said.

She touched the flesh. 'Have you no other injury?'

'Is one not enough? It's my hand of truce, my hand of friendship. Let me talk to your commanding officer, says I – and they shot me. How many fingers are left?'

'All of them,' Sylvie said.

'And the thumb?'

'And the thumb.'

He drew in a breath and let it out again. 'It's not so bad then?'

'No, it's not so bad,' said Sylvie. 'I'll wipe it clean and you can see for yourself. There's a man in a house round the corner who keeps stitching needles. He does for the dockers when there's an accident.'

'Bugger the needles,' Fran Hagarty said. 'I could do with a drink, though.'

'Tea?'

'Whiskey. Powers preferred.'

The bullet had scored the pad below his left thumb but she doubted if there was anything broken. She could feel his blood leaking into the palm of her hand and was reluctant to release him yet.

She turned her head and called out, 'Maeve, bring the gentleman a glass of whiskey from the bar. And some water from—'

'No water,' Fran Hagarty said.

'Some warm water from the kettle in a clean bowl, gentian from the cabinet, lint too. And my sewing scissors. Maeve?'

'I hear you, Mam,' Maeve answered. 'I'm on my way.'

'Ah, it's a good girl you have there,' Fran Hagarty said. 'An obedient girl.'

'When it suits her.'

'Are there more children in the house?'

'Just Maeve.'

He eased himself forward and studied the wound. He was half her age again, forties. He had the worn sort of shabbiness that was not uncommon in the commercials who lodged in the Shamrock, but none of their affability. He was puffy about the gills and his greying hair needed trimmed. His sad brown eyes were filled with resignation, not self-pity.

Outside in the corridor there were thumps and bumps.

She could hear Turk cursing and her father-in-law's nervous snigger.

Fran Hagarty said, 'How many rooms are in the house?'

'Ten, in addition to domestic apartments.'

'How many are occupied?'

'Five,' Sylvie answered. 'Are you looking for lodgings? We charge one shilling and sixpence a night for a bed and a meat breakfast.'

'You're Scottish, aren't you?'

'I am,' she said. 'From Glasgow.'

'I did hear that Daniel had relatives in Glasgow.'

'I'm only related to the McCullochs by marriage.'

She was tempted to blurt out the whole story, to tell him that she was Forbes McCulloch's rejected lover and that only Gowry's kindness had saved her from going straight to the dogs after Forbes had abandoned her. Imparting such information went beyond the pale of first acquaintance, however, and she doubted if Mr Hagarty would be impressed by her history.

'Only one child?' Fran said. 'What does the priest have to say about that?'

'It is none of the priest's business,' Sylvie said. 'We're not Catholic. But I imagine you knew that already, Mr Hagarty.'

'I did,' he said. 'I did, and I forgot.'

'What are they doing out there?'

'Hiding the tackle.'

'Tackle?' Sylvie said.

'Guns.'

'My God!' Sylvie tossed his hand back at him. 'You can't dump guns in my house. My husband'll have a fit if he finds weapons here.'

'Are there no empty rooms upstairs?'

'That's beside the point.'

Sylvie spun round as Maeve breezed into the sitting-room carrying one of the big wooden kitchen trays. She was tall for her age, already gawky, not at all like her dainty, doll-like mother. She had Sylvie's curls, though they were glossy brown like ripe horse chestnuts, not fair. Her eyes were alert to everything that was going on and she often seemed too knowing and bold for her age, a precocious quality that Sylvie recognised and feared.

'Powers,' the girl said, 'in a clean glass. Gentian and lint and water.'

'Thank you, dearest,' Sylvie said, a little more sweetly than she would have done if Mr Hagarty had not been there. 'Put the tray on the table, please.'

The girl set the tray down carefully, then, turning, stared at the man in the armchair. 'You're the chap who writes for the papers. I've heard of you.'

'Ah, but have you read anything I've written?'

'Only the stuff in *Scissors & Paste*.'

'Where I'm usually quoted out of context.' He seemed grateful to have found an admirer, even one as young as Maeve. He said, 'I'll not be taught on the syllabus at your school, I'm thinking?'

'Aye, but you are,' said Maeve. 'Mr Whiteside reads *Scissors* to the class. He thinks you're funny.'

'Do you think I'm funny?'

'I don't understand what you're on about half the time.'

'Heresy,' Fran said. 'Sheer heresy.'

'What does that mean?' said Maeve.

'It means you'd better make yourself scarce,' said Sylvie.

She got up, crossed to the table, picked up the whiskey glass and carried it back to the man in the armchair. He reached for it with his good hand, took in a great gulp and blew out his cheeks. He looked at Maeve and winked then straightened his shoulders and tilted up his chin. With the stoop gone and a smile on his face Sylvie realised that not so long since he must have been handsome.

'Tell your grandfather and Charlie to stop what they're doing,' Sylvie said. 'I'll not have them dumping guns in my house.'

'Guns, is it?' Maeve said. 'I thought it might be.'

'Mausers,' Fran said.

'Where did you get German weapons?' Sylvie asked.

Fran drank again and held out the glass.

'Fetch the bottle,' Sylvie told her daughter and when the girl had gone out of the room, said, 'Is this the war they've been talking about for so long? Is this the start of the – the *thing* itself?'

'Would that it were,' Fran said. 'No, it is not the start of the rebellion but it will give the government something to think about.'

'Isn't there a law against gun-running?'

'Oh, indeed there is,' said Fran. 'But no effort has been made to apply it. It will be a different story now, after what's happened on the quays.'

'Is that where you got shot?'

Sylvie carried the tray to the fireside and placed it on the rug at Fran Hagarty's feet. She knelt again and anointed his wound with stinging violet liquid. He made no complaint save a little hiss and, sipping from the whiskey glass, watched her work on his hand.

'Bachelor's Walk,' he said. 'Before that it was all pretty smooth and easy. For those in the ranks it was just another Sunday route-march out to Howth. Only a handful of officers knew what was going on.'

'And what was going on?' said Sylvie.

It felt odd to be crouched on her knees in her own parlour, doctoring a stranger's hand. The wound was closing, blood congealing. She cut a strip of lint with her scissors and then, to be safe, another. She bound them tightly over his thumb and around his wrist with clean linen bandages. He talked on, pausing only to sip from the glass now and then, and seemed oblivious to her ministrations.

'Fifteen hundred Mausers purchased with American money and brought in by yacht. What a cheer there was when the lads saw what she was carrying. Only the firmness of the officers stopped them spoiling things with their eagerness.'

'What were *you* doing there?'

'Observing.'

'Observing – with my father-in-law, Turk and Charlie?'

'Daniel got wind that something big was about to take place and invited me to go with them in the motor-car.'

'I don't believe you,' Sylvie said.

'Do you not now?'

'I think it was the other way about. I think you took them there with you.'

'Well, perhaps you are right, Mrs McCulloch.'

'Sylvie.'

'Sylvie; perhaps you are right.' He paused then went on, 'It wasn't until we reached the entrance to the Dublin Road that we met fixed bayonets.'

'Were you marching with them, Mr Hagarty?'

'I am not the marching sort. I was riding in the motor-car behind the column. When we met the bayonets there was scuffling and fisticuffs but no shooting and many of the men managed to scatter, taking the guns with them. We rounded up Charlie's friend and gathered about thirty guns for safe-keeping.

We slipped away and headed back into the city – and that's where I got shot.'

'In Bachelor's Walk?'

'The Walk was crowded,' Fran Hagarty said. 'Women and children mostly. They were just jeering at the soldiers who were marching back to barracks. Then the order was given to fire on the crowd. I had just got out of the motor-car to look for a clear way. I was not in the fray, not in the thick of it. I had just held up my hand to show my peaceful intentions when the soldiers started shooting.'

'How many were killed?'

'I was in no fit condition to count. I saw several, many in fact, go down just before Charlie bundled me into the motor-car and got us away.'

'Why did you come to our house, Mr Hagarty?' Maeve asked.

Man and woman glanced round. They had been so intent upon the narrative and upon each other – Sylvie's forearm on Fran's knee, his hand resting on her shoulder – that they had failed to notice that Maeve was loitering in the doorway.

'We thought we were being pursued,' Fran answered.

'Couldn't you have gone back to Towers, to my granddad's place, and hidden the tackle there?' Maeve said.

'Young lady,' Fran Hagarty said, 'that is a very sensible question. I will tell you the answer. We couldn't hide the guns at Towers because the brewery's one of the first places the inspectors will look when they start hunting down the caches.'

'What does that mean?' said Maeve. 'Catches?'

'Stop asking so many questions,' Sylvie said. 'What's Charlie doing? Why has it gone so quiet?'

'They're in the bar, having a glass and waiting for Mr Hagarty.'

'What have they done with the – the tackle?' Sylvie said.

'Left it upstairs, I think,' said Maeve.

'Well, we'll have to see about that,' Sylvie said and removed Fran's hand from her shoulder.

She was dressed in a drab cotton dress and a soiled apron and looked like a common skivvy. She wished she'd had warning that an important person like Francis Hagarty was about to arrive at the Shamrock, for then she would have dug out one of her pretty dresses from the chest in the attic and put it on, along with lip rouge and the pink powder that Gowry said made her look like a trollop. It had been years since she'd done herself up to please a man. She had remained true to Gowry since the moment they had set foot on Irish soil, for she had been big with the baby inside her and grateful for the hasty civil ceremony that Gowry had arranged to give Maeve a name and a father.

She was hurt by the fact that she had not impressed Mr Francis Hagarty however, or had not impressed him enough. She got to her feet. He rose with her, protecting the whiskey glass with his bandaged hand.

He seemed, she thought, recovered. He was not vital. He was languid. But that, she guessed, was how he always was. He wasn't even looking at her. He was looking at Maeve who was posted in the doorway with a little scowl of concentration on her face.

She waited for Maeve to start flirting with him but the child, though precocious, was not so advanced as all that.

'Cache,' he said softly, 'is a word derived from the old French. Cash-ay. It means a hole in the ground, a hiding place.'

'Cash-ay,' said Maeve. 'Cash-ay.'

'There you are now, young lady,' Fran Hagarty said. 'You have learned something new, so the day has not been wasted.'

Then, lifting the whiskey bottle, he ambled out of the sitting-room to join the other rebels in the bar.

Chapter Two

Gowry had always looked well in uniform. In Glasgow he had chauffeured for the Franklin family and had worn a leather topcoat, quilted motoring cap and elbow-length gauntlets whenever he'd called upon her on his brother Forbes's behalf. She had been so blindly, stupidly in love with Forbes, however, that she had hardly noticed Gowry at all at first. Now, in the blue-black, high-collared tunic and braid-trimmed cap of Flanagan's Motoring Company he looked so military that he had often been spat upon by urchins and corner boys too ignorant to tell an omnibus driver from a British officer.

Now and then Gowry would be employed to drive one of Flanagan's handsome limousines to a wedding or a funeral but usually he was hired out to drive charabancs filled with drunken football supporters or severe, if not always sober, committee men to rallies and parades in far-flung rural townships.

In summer he collected parties of tourists from the big hotels, stiff-necked English ladies, sentimental Americans and a fair sprinkling of well-off Italians who tipped generously. In fact, the local gentry were no less generous and a good deal less patronising and a bus full of racing gentlemen with a skinful of brandy inside them was like money in the bank.

Rallies and race meetings often kept Gowry away overnight and in the tripper season he could be away for the best part of a week while, unknown to him, his father and his brother's pals made hay in the bar of the Shamrock.

Maeve kept quiet about what went on when her father was out of town but she carried his timetables in her head, the way the daughter of a fisherman carries knowledge of the tides, and would warn her grandfather or uncle when Gowry was due back. She saw no harm in dividing her loyalties, for nationalism was taught like holy writ at Sperryhead school and her teacher, Mr Whiteside, was forever preaching the benefits of home rule. She helped Jansis empty ashtrays and mop up spillings after the men had gone and would polish sticky fingerprints from the beer handles and the lid of the piano.

It was Turk who played on the bar piano. Turk Trotter, with his Ottoman colouring and big fat fingers, could coax from the battered instrument melodies both rousing and sweet and after a dozen pints of stout would lift his voice in song and sound, Maeve thought, just like the Harp of Erin.

When Daddy, not ten minutes back from the lakes and still in uniform, shouted, 'What in God's good name is this?' Maeve had no ready answer. He held the cartridge up between finger and thumb and pushed it towards her the way a beau might offer a flower. 'Tell me the truth. Has Trotter been here again, or Charlie, and who did they bring with them this time?'

She would have bolted for the front door or out through the kitchen into the yard but she was so scared she couldn't move.

'I – I don't know.'

He crouched, bending from the waist. He had a longish face and a furrow down each side of his mouth. He had grown a little moustache when he'd worked in the Dublin ship repair yard and she'd liked his little moustache, but the job in the repair yard hadn't lasted long and he was always close-shaven these days. He had shaved somewhere that evening, for she could smell the faint soapy tang off him and see a fleck of lather dried behind his ear.

'Do you know what this is, Maeve?'

'Nuh.'

'Don't lie to me.'

'It's a bullet.'

'It's a cartridge, a live round. Where did it come from?'

'Du-dunno.'

'Turn off the waterworks, girl,' her father said. 'I'm not impressed.' He continued to hold up the cartridge, aimed at the ceiling. He put his hand on her shoulder so she couldn't run away. 'Have you heard what's been happening over on the quays?'

'Nuh.'

'Has Mr Dolan or Mr Pettu not told you?'

'Ha'n't s-seen e-either of them,' Maeve stammered.

To her mother she might seem much older than ten but to her father she was still a little girl of five or six, trusting, innocent and loving. She wouldn't have lied to him then. She would have been incapable of lying to him then. He cursed the influences that had made her so furtive and deceitful.

He said, 'Well, one poor woman and two men are dead and the whole town's buzzing with government officials looking for someone to blame.'

Maeve said, 'It was the soldiers, the soldiers are to blame.'

'So,' her father said, 'you *have* heard about it. Where are they?'

'What?'

'The guns. Sure and they're here, are they not?'

She pursed her lips to stifle tears. She wasn't fey the way her mother had been once. She was stubborn. Gowry felt a tiny prickle of pride in his heart at her defiance even though it was he himself she was defying. He was Irish enough to respect her courage but he scented danger in what had happened in the quays, more so now that a war was boiling up in Europe.

'What if they are?' Maeve said. 'I'm not the one to say they are, but what if they are? Are we not the martyrs to the foreign rule just like – just like Belgium?'

'What's this?' Gowry said, still crouched, still holding her by the shoulder. 'Where have you been hearing such nonsense?'

'It is not nonsense,' Maeve said then, her nerve breaking, tossed back her head and bawled at the pitch of her voice, *'Mam. Mam-eee.'*

He straightened, cupped his fist over the shiny cartridge he'd found glinting under the slant of the stairs where Turk or Charlie had dropped it, and released his daughter. She was off in an instant, darting out through the kitchen into the enclosed yard, and he felt again the panic that he'd felt so often before, the terrible clawing fear that something bad would happen to her, something he would be powerless to prevent.

Sylvie appeared from the dining-room. No one had shown up for dinner that evening, not even Mr Dolan. Gowry wondered where Dolan had got to. He was a milk-and-water old nationalist and unlikely to venture out into the streets when trouble was brewing.

'What's wrong? Where's Maeve?' Sylvie said.

'She's gone out the back.'

'Has she? Why?'

'Because I showed her this': the cartridge erect in his fingers. 'Because I asked her where her granddad had hidden the guns.'

'Guns?'

'Don't *you* start, Sylvie,' Gowry said. 'I know there's tackle here. Do you want me to tear the place apart to find it?' He didn't wait for her reply but went on. 'My dada was here this afternoon, wasn't he? Was Charlie with him?'

'I have no idea what—'

'Sylvie, waken up,' he snapped. 'If the peelers find smuggled guns under our roof they'll shut down the hotel and drag me off to the Castle. Do you suppose my father or Charlie will step forward and confess? Not them. They'll let me take the blame without a qualm of conscience and mourn only because the shooters have been lost. What did they bring and where have they hidden it?'

'You're not going to turn them over?' Sylvie said.

'I won't turn them over. I just want to know what they brought.'

'I won't let you turn them over.'

'You've no say in the matter.'

'The Shamrock's mine. You said it was mine.'

'Licensed in your name, Sylvie, paid for with our money.'

'Forbes's money.'

For the first time in years she had uttered Forbes's name. She thought Gowry would be shocked to hear it again from her lips, to be reminded that she had been bought off with money enough to purchase the goodwill of the Shamrock's previous owners and the remainder of the lease.

Once the name was out she felt guilty. Truth was that she could hardly remember Forbes McCulloch or the intensity of her feelings for him. Even so, the sensation of reliving something that had happened before was strong and connected her to what had taken place that afternoon in the sitting-room when she had held Mr Hagarty's hand and felt his blood drip into her palm.

'All right,' Gowry conceded. 'Forbes's money. It's immaterial now.' He put the cartridge into his pocket and glanced upstairs. 'What is it, guns?'

'Yes, it's guns,' Sylvie said. 'You'll have heard what went on today?'

'I have,' said Gowry.

'They were desperate.'

'Who was it – Charlie?'

'Daniel and Charlie and Turk.'

'Is that all?'

'A boy, just a boy, was with them, and a man. I don't know who he was.'

'Had they been out at Howth with the volunteers?'

'I think they had, yes.'

Gowry said, 'I might have known my old man would be mixed up with gun-running and wouldn't rest happy until he got me tangled in it too. Where did he stow the tackle, Sylvie?'

'I don't know. I haven't been upstairs since they left.'

Gowry grunted and headed for the stairs.

Sylvie switched on the electrical light that would guide him to the first floor. Above that there was no wiring and he would have to light one of the oil lamps that were set out on a long whatnot on the second landing. She watched him swarm up the stairs two at a time and, after a moment, followed him, prompted by the fear that he would find out that Fran Hagarty had been here.

She followed the oil lamp to the top floor. There was no wallpaper on the walls only bare boarding. The rooms were small as closets. She watched the distortions of the lamplight as Gowry went from room to room. He even peered into the attic, though it contained nothing but a few dusty trunks and the water cisterns. He came back to the head of the stairs. Sylvie trailed down floor by floor after her husband while he flung open bedroom doors, poked into closets and looked under beds.

'Who's in this room?'

'Mr Rice.'

'Where is he?'

'In the bar along with the others. They've been out walking together, I think, seeing the sights.'

'Some sights!' said Gowry. 'Who else is booked in?'

'No one,' Sylvie said.

They were on the second floor now. The corridor was tee-shaped and one window looked out into the road. The rooms here were long let to Mr Pettu, who worked for a Catholic wine merchant, and Mr

Dolan, who existed on a meagre pension from the port authority. He had been a harbour pilot until his eyesight had failed. He had no living relative left in the world. He had been here when the McCullochs had taken over the hotel and in all likelihood he would die here.

Gowry paused. He glanced at Sylvie at the stair-head. She shook her head and shrugged. Gowry knocked on Dolan's door.

'Mr Dolan, Mr Dolan are you there?'

There was a smell of smoke from the lamp but no other smell, save the dry, summer-night odour of the house itself. It was still daylight outside, twilight, but the window at the corridor's end did not admit much light. Gowry gave the lamp a shake, making the oil in the base slop and the flame run up the wick.

'Mr Dolan?'

Gowry rattled the door handle.

'Go away.'

'Mr Dolan, what're you doing in there, sitting in the dark?'

'Go away.'

'You've not had your dinner, Mr Dolan,' Sylvie called out. 'Are you sick?'

'Go away.'

From the pocket of her apron she fished out the key that opened all the bedroom doors. She walked along the corridor and gave the key to Gowry. He handed her the lamp. She held it in both hands and watched Gowry stoop and fit the key and turn it.

'Mr Dolan, I'm coming in.'

'Ah no, ah no, ah no,' the old man moaned. 'Ah no, my dear God, no.'

Gowry opened the door. Sylvie held out the lamp.

Mr Dolan was hunched in the half-light on the side of the bed, his feet propped on the boxes. He looked not cross but terrified. He wore woollen stockings and an undershirt and his braces hung slack on his shoulders. In a frame above the bed was a print of the Sacred Heart and on the dressing-table a small plaster statue of the Virgin.

'So this is where you've been hiding yourself, Mr Dolan?' Gowry said. 'And what's this you have for a footstool? I don't recall having put in any new furniture.'

'Oh, God! Oh, Mother of God!'

Sylvie had never seen a man so terrified. His ancient yellow eyes stared out of his head, popping with the fear in him. His legs and arms twitched and his head flew back and forth on his leathery neck, denying the obvious. He was afraid of Gowry, Sylvie realised, of her husband's denunciation, his anger.

'Ah now, and it's all right,' Gowry said gently.

'They told me, they told me not to tell you.'

'Sure and what else did they tell you?' Gowry said.

'It was for Ireland, they told me, for the sake of the country.'

'And so it was,' Sylvie heard herself say. 'So it is, Mr Dolan.'

Gowry was on one knee, hands flat on the lid of the box. It looked, Sylvie thought, as if he were praying over the coffin of a child.

'Did they tell you what's in the boxes, Mr Dolan?' Gowry said.

'For Ireland, they said. For Ireland.'

Gowry drummed his fingers on the wood. 'Well, I'll be taking them away, if you've no objection. There is no room for them here.'

'You'll tell. You'll tell them. You'll tell him I told you.'

'Nah,' said Gowry. 'Nah, nah, Mr Dolan. It'll be our secret. You go on downstairs now and Mrs McCulloch will see you fed. When you come back, or soon after, there will be nothing here.'

'They said . . .'

'Who said: my father?' Gowry, standing now, asked.

'Him. He came up with them afterward.'

'Who did?'

'Mr Hagarty,' said Mr Dolan. 'He told me it was for the good of the mother country. He gave me the drink and money for the drink and he told me not to tell you the tackle was in my room – and now I have.'

'Hagarty?' said Gowry, frowning. 'Who the devil's Hagarty?'

He glanced round at Sylvie. She shook her head.

She put the lamp on the floor, came forward and, reaching over the boxes, took Mr Dolan's hand and lifted him up.

'Come,' she said. 'Mr Rice is downstairs. You like Mr Rice, do you not? And Mr Pettu will be in from church any minute. He'll tell you what's been going on. Come on, Mr Dolan. I've stew in the pot and it'll spoil.'

He rose reluctantly, trembling still, and clambered over the boxes with the German words stencilled on the sides. Sylvie supported him while he hoisted up his braces and groped for his boots. She was annoyed at how poor Mr Dolan had been used by Fran Hagarty but at the same time she was impressed by the soft-voiced, insistent ruthlessness that had bewitched an old man and led him willy-nilly into abetting a cause he did not fully understand.

'What are you going to do, Gowry?' she asked from the doorway. 'You're not going to hand them over, are you?'

'No, not that,' Gowry said. 'I'm going to hide them, hide them where they won't be found.'

'And where might that be?' Sylvie asked.

'Never you mind, dearest,' Gowry answered. 'Ah no, never you mind.'

First thing in the morning as soon as breakfast was over Sylvie put on her straw bonnet and best jacket and set off for Amiens Street railway station.

The day was soft but hazy and there were thin strands of cloud that might turn to rain later. Newspaper billboards shouted out the massacre. In town there was a queer drone in the air like a beehive about to swarm. In the streets and in the railway station the police were much in evidence, burly-looking officers from the Royal Irish Constabulary. Around the ticket-office and the platform gate were little parcels of soldiers with carbines slung over their shoulders. She bought a ticket to Malahide and boarded the train just three or four minutes before it pulled out. She sat with her hands folded, small as a child, her shoes hardly touching the floor and listened to the chat in the compartment about what had happened to the poor innocents in Bachelor's Walk.

She listened to the talk jabbering back and forth, and said nothing. Today it was a different sort of nothing, though. Today she listened intently to her fellow-travellers' opinions and thought how easy it would be to jump in and tell them a tale that would shut their gobs quick enough and how they would regard her then not as a neat, pretty little woman in a cheap straw bonnet but as someone involved, a friend of the great Fran Hagarty.

Nine miles the line ran, the train stopping now and then. When it came out on the flat land with the sea on the right Sylvie looked out at the sea for a moment or two then inland while the train jogged past Towers, a couple of miles short of Malahide. Away across the barley fields were the whitewashed walls of the brewery and, sheltered by elms, the two-storey cottage where Gowry's father lived with his wife Kay and the remnant of their brood.

She got off the train at Malahide and, ignoring the gigs at the pavement's edge, headed out of town on foot. There was no breeze to speak of but the waves broke in creamy arcs across the sand and out to sea the sails of the water wags were full. Children, bright and tiny, played at the water's edge. She walked quickly and soon left the trippers behind.

She had been to Towers only three or four times, for Gowry's mother, Kay, who had been born a Franklin and who spent much of the year in Glasgow staying with Forbes, had never made her welcome. There had never been enough coming in from brewing hardly to feed them, Gowry claimed, and certainly not enough to satisfy his mother's aspirations and pay off the debts his father accrued by betting on three-legged horses. These days Charlie and young Peter kept the brewery ticking over while Daniel messed about with the affairs of the brotherhood.

Sylvie had no desire to confront her mother-in-law and slipped past the cottage into the lane that squared the gable of the brewery.

She was tense with expectation. She hoped that Charlie might have brought him here in the American motor-car. Common sense suggested that he was probably somewhere in town scribbling his account of the massacre for one of the ratty under-the-counter newspapers that Gowry called nationalist trash. She wondered how well writing work paid and why the college and his wife too had thrown him out, whether it was drink or adultery or the writing itself that had brought him so low that he would bleed all over a stranger's carpet and let a woman he had never seen before bind up his wounds.

She walked through the cooper's yard, past barrels and bottle crates, all empty. It seemed quiet to her, too quiet, for she was unaware that mashing and brewing were done mostly in winter months.

'Charlie,' she called out. 'Charlie, are you there?'

The air was sour and wisps of steam escaped from a vent high on the windowless wall.

'Charlie?'

Peter came out of the open doorway. He was stripped to his undershirt and licked with sweat. He was only sixteen or seventeen and had the long neck and unformed features that Gowry must have had before he matured.

'What are you wantin' here?' Peter said trucu-lently.

'Charlie,' Sylvie said. 'I have to talk to Charlie.'

'Sure an' he's busy.'

'Fetch him here at once. If you don't, you'll be in trouble.'

'You can't make trouble for us,' Peter said.

A man had appeared behind the boy, a big, ugly fellow with a barrel chest and a ponderous belly. He carried a long-handled wooden spade across his shoulder. He stood in the cut of shadow in the doorway and peered out at her.

'I can't,' said Sylvie, 'but the peelers can.'

'What's this about the peelers?' Peter said.

'I'm not giving my news to boys. Find Charlie. Tell him I'm here.'

In the split second it took her to shift her gaze from Peter to the doorway the man with the spade vanished.

Half a minute later Charlie emerged from the doorway, walking very quickly. He wore a brown suit, a stiff paper collar, paper cuffs, and a necktie. He carried his jacket across his arm. He brushed past his brother and came up to her. He glanced behind her then round at the whitewashed walls, up at the gulls on the roof, then at her again.

'What the hell are *you* doing here, Sylvie? Has something happened?'

'It has,' she said. 'Gowry found the guns.'

'Did you—'

'No, I did not.'

'Was it Maeve? Did the kid blab?'

'No, she did not. He found a bullet on the floor and guessed the rest.'

'Is he for turning us over?'

'Why did you put the boxes in Mr Dolan's room?'

'The old boy's one of us.'

'One of you,' said Sylvie. 'He's one of nothing.'

'Has Gowry gone to the castle?'

'No,' said Sylvie. 'He's taken the guns off with him.'

'What's this you're tellin' me? Taken them where?'

'To hide them properly.'

'How did he shift them?' Charlie asked.

'He brought the charabanc round from Flanagan's early this morning, packed them into the back and off he went.'

'He didn't move those crates by himself,' said Charlie.

'Maeve helped.'

'Jaysus!'

'I helped too.'

'Who saw you?'

'Nobody saw us. It was too early. We didn't have to lug boxes. Gowry opened them last night and we carried the guns downstairs two at a time. The bullet boxes we carried between us,' Sylvie said. 'If anyone did see us they didn't mention it at breakfast.'

'What does Gowry intend to do with the tackle? Where will he hide it?'

'Somewhere safe, he said.'

'Nowhere is safe, not today. If he gets caught . . .'

'Gowry won't get caught.'

'Those guns were paid for with blood as well as cash,' Charlie said. 'They're irreplaceable.'

'You should have thought of that yesterday,' Sylvie said.

Charlie glanced behind him.

Peter was hunkered in the doorway, smoking a cigarette and spitting. Peter had never visited the Shamrock. Charlie had tried to keep him clear of involvement with the brotherhoods but to judge by the hard, ugly look on his face Peter would be into it soon and then there would be no holding him back.

'You should have thought of that before you stowed those boxes in Mr Dolan's room. Why did Mr Hagarty have to do that?'

'Expediency,' Charlie said. 'Do you know what that word means?'

'I'm not ignorant,' Sylvie said. 'I'm educated.'

'All right, all right,' said Charlie. 'Where's Gowry now?'

'Gone to the west coast, driving a party from Jury's. They wanted out of Dublin today so he's taking them to Bunratty Castle and the sea-cliffs at – somewhere or other.'

'Moher,' said Charlie, 'in County Clare?'

'Somewhere.'

'He won't be back this night, I'm thinking.'

'No, nor tomorrow,' Sylvie said. 'Three days this trip.'

'Are you telling me he took the guns with him to Clare?' Charlie tossed his jacket from one arm to the other. 'We've arranged to collect them tonight. Dada's in town setting up the transport right this minute.'

'Where's Mr Hagarty?'

'Fran? What about Fran?'

'He'll know what to do, won't he?' Sylvie said.

'Nah, nah.'

'He knows everyone, doesn't he?' Sylvie persisted. 'Why don't you call him on your telephone and ask his advice?'

'I don't need his advice.'

'I'm not having a lorry turn up at the Shamrock and your boys creating trouble because there's nothing there for them to take away,' she said. 'What sort of a stramash is that going to cause in the Sperryhead Road with half my neighbours out on their doorsteps looking on?'

'I can't call him on the telephone,' Charlie said. 'Fran doesn't have a telephone. God, he barely has a shirt to put on his back.'

'I thought they were his guns?'

'They're not his guns. They're our guns,' Charlie said. 'Keep your nose out of it. It's no business for a woman.'

'Is it not now?' Sylvie said. 'Did I not hear that a woman died in Bachelor's Walk yesterday?' She tapped her bonnet on to her curls and turned away. 'Oh, well! Suit yourself!'

He darted after her, caught her by the sleeve. 'Why *did* you come here?'

'To help,' Sylvie said. 'If you must know I came because I think Gowry's hiding those guns from you, not the authorities. He doesn't want you to have them. He doesn't believe in what you're doing, Charlie. He's against bloodshed.'

'I know that. By heck, do I not? He's told me often enough.'

'Gowry reckons he knows why you hid those guns in our house.'

Charlie's eyes narrowed. 'Does he now?'

'He reckons you're stealing guns from the volunteers because you've found another use for them.'

'My brother has a big mouth.'

'I think you're going to wait until the English are fighting the Germans then you're going to make it hot for them in Dublin. Am I not right?'

'What if you are?'

'You need those guns. You also need to stop your boys calling at my house tonight. I think the man to do that is Mr Hagarty.'

'Do you now?' said Charlie.

'I'm going back to Dublin shortly. If you want me to deliver a message to Mr Hagarty I'll be pleased to do so.'

Charlie grunted. 'Charmed you too, has he? Aye, well, you wouldn't be the first, but I never thought we were so transparent that my brother's wife would see through us. Hagarty's a lot more than a scribbler, Sylvie. You don't want to underestimate him or what he can do if he puts his mind to it.'

'Where does he live?'

'Endicott Street. Up by the Mountjoy.'

'Near the prison?'

'No, not so far. He's in the tenements.'

'Which tenement?' Sylvie said.

'The last on the left facing the canal. He has a room on the top floor.'

'What shall I tell him?'

'What you've told me,' Charlie said.

'And will he know what to do?'

'He will.'

Sylvie nodded, turned again, her business done.

'Wait,' Charlie said. 'I'll have Peter hitch up a cart and drive you to the railway station.'

Sylvie glanced at the boy hunkered in the doorway, smoking and spitting.

'No thanks,' she said. 'I'll walk.'

It was only a short walk from Amiens Street across the Summerhill Parade. There were still fine houses there, but between the prison and the Liffey branch line poverty was all too apparent. In all her ten years in Dublin Sylvie had never ventured into this quarter, though she had heard of the awful conditions north of Parnell Street and how slums bit into the Georgian magnificence at every point.

Endicott Street was split by a narrow lane. On the steps of the ruined mansions were shawled women, ragged children and mewling babies, while on the corner, outside the pub, men lounged in their usual grand fashion. On the canal side of the lane four tenements rose like pieces of opera scenery and the street became a broad, dark funnel. Many tenement windows were thrown open to let in a gasp of air or let out the gases that ten or twenty sleepers had released in the night. The stench of fried fat, boiled cabbage and overworked drains reminded her of certain streets in Glasgow, near where she'd lived when she'd been Forbes McCulloch's lady-love, before Gowry rescued her and carried her off to Dublin.

The doorway of the last tenement was a high squared-away portico that led to a hallway out of which a rusty iron staircase spiralled to the floors above. In the hall a young woman cradled a tiny infant wrapped in old newspapers. A boy of eight or nine squatted on the stairs. He was naked save for a pair of stained breeks. He had a penny whistle in his hands and picked out a tune on it while the woman swayed to the music as if it had charmed all sense out of her.

The boy didn't look up when Sylvie asked where she might find Mr Hagarty. He jerked his head and went on playing the imperfect melody, one note at a time. Sylvie stepped around him and climbed the metal stairs, her heart beating fast. She hadn't felt like this since she'd waited for the sound of Forbes's key in the lock of the apartment in Glasgow. She wondered why she should be so excited at the prospect of meeting a man she had met only once before. She was excited because she didn't know why it mattered or what would come of it or if after she'd seen him again the feeling would go away. From the top landing Sylvie looked back down the stairs. The iron banister was wound as tightly as the coil of a dynamo and far below the boy gaped up at her, open-mouthed.

She stepped forward and knocked on Fran Hagarty's door.

'It's open,' he said.

There was no handle, only a thumb-latch.

She pressed the latch and went into the room.

It was a very small room, square-shaped, neat and spartan. On a small table by the window were a typewriting machine, a pile of copybooks, a shaving lamp and a bottle of whiskey, half full. On the bedside table were a ewer and basin and a candle in a tin holder. There were two chairs in the room, both wooden, both upright. The bed-end pointed at the door.

Fran was lying on the bed on top of a brown patchwork quilt. He wore only trousers and a white cotton undershirt. His feet were bare. He was propped up on a bolster flanked by two feather pillows. His left hand, bandaged, was behind his head and he was smoking a cigarette.

He looked at her for a moment without moving then rolled on to his hip and dabbed the cigarette into the base of the candleholder. He rolled back and put both hands behind his head.

'Well, Sylvie,' he said, 'that didn't take you long.'

'What didn't?' Sylvie said.

'Finding me again,' Fran Hagarty said, and grinned.

Chapter Three

There was a time when Sylvie would have considered the appearance on her doorstep of three plain-clothes detectives as something of a joke.

Before Bodenstown, before Fran, she remained ignorant of the threat she posed to law and order. It hadn't occurred to her that the Shamrock had become a meeting place for subversives, mainly because the subversives were relatives. It was impossible to regard her father-in-law as much more than a comic opera Irishman, big-bellied and bluff and none too agile in the brains department, difficult to imagine Turk or Charlie grasping the reins of power with the same enthusiasm with which they reached for a glass of stout; yet there they were, Detective Inspector Vaizey and two other detectives from the Special Crime Branch framed in the doorway in the mid-morning light.

Jansis opened the door. She was a tall, angular

woman, not much more than thirty, but with a long, sallow, horsy sort of face and a lugubrious expression that suggested she was already reconciled to spinsterhood. Though the men weren't in uniform Jansis recognised their trademark raincoats and snap-brimmed hats immediately. 'We're full, so we are,' she said. 'Sorry.'

She made to close the door but a heavy welted brogan slapped down on the draught-rod to prevent it. She stepped back into the hall, stuck her fists on her bony hips, spread her elbows and with a truculence honed by years of serving breakfasts to commercial travellers, snapped, 'Cards.'

The moist moustache that clung to Vaizey's upper lip twitched. He raised a hand, clicked his fingers. One of the men, a head taller than Vaizey, thrust an identity card under Jansis's nose.

'Metropolitan Police,' he growled. 'If you know what's good for you, woman, you'll be lettin' us enter wi'out makin' a fuss.'

'Oh, so you're a copper, are you?' Jansis said.

She turned her head and spat drily over her shoulder.

Vaizey said, 'Get rid of her, Ames, please.'

The burly copper strode into the hall, lifted Jansis up by the elbows as if she were a large flowerpot and placed her clear of the doorway. Before her feet touched down, Jansis was shouting, 'Raid, it's a raid, Missus 'Culloch. Raid. Raid.'

From the stairs came the cry, '*Brutes*,' followed by

a shower of stale water from a ewer, followed by the ewer itself, then a packet of candles that split when it struck the floor and sent waxy missiles skittering about the officers' feet.

'*Mam, Mameee, it's the peelers,*' Maeve shrieked, and galloped off upstairs with Ames in hot pursuit.

'She's a child, a kiddie, are you for shootin' her too?' Jansis said.

Vaizey ignored the servant. He gestured again. A second detective, no less muscular than the first, flung open the door to the dining-room, then, finding the room empty, lumbered down the corridor opening one door after another. Under the skirt of his trench-coat he carried a holstered revolver.

Scuffling and shouting came from above. Ames appeared out of the gloom holding Maeve, kicking and squealing, in front of him, his arms about her waist. Sylvie was right behind him, beating at his shoulders with a dustpan. When he reached the hall he flung the girl from him, then, rounding on Sylvie, caught her wrists, broke her grip on the dustpan and swung her down into the hallway too.

'Good morning to you, ma'am.' Vaizey lifted his hat. 'I apologise for the intrusion but I'm afraid we have our duty to do and cannot be hindered in doing it.'

'Duty?' said Jansis. 'Terrorisin' women and children, do you call that duty?'

Vaizey addressed himself to Sylvie. 'You know what we're looking for, of course. We have good

45

reason to believe you are hiding illegally imported arms.'

'Hah!' Sylvie exclaimed. 'So that's it, is it?'

She helped Maeve to her feet and put the girl behind her. There was the clatter of utensils being tossed about in the kitchen and a draught around her ankles indicated that the door to the yard had been opened. She remembered everything that Fran Hagarty had told her yesterday in the room in the tenement in Endicott Street and she was alarmingly calm, possessed not by a sense of outrage but of engagement. She said, 'You'll find no weapons in my house.'

She was relieved that Gowry was not at home. Gowry would have admitted the officers straight away and condoned their right to search the premises, would, in other words, have co-operated. She was also relieved that Mr Dolan had toddled off for his daily survey of the harbour, for she knew that weakness was more dangerous than principle when the peelers got on your back.

'I have no guns here and no truck with men who use them,' Sylvie heard herself say. 'I'll thank you to inform your bully-boys that if they lay another finger on my daughter I'll complain to the commissioner in person.'

Vaizey said, 'We're empowered to inspect your premises, you know.'

'And manhandle young girls?' Sylvie said. 'Maeve, stop crying.'

'*Brutes!*' Maeve shouted. '*Bastards!*'

'For a young girl,' Vaizey said, 'she has a nasty mouth. You' – he pointed at Jansis – 'take the girl and yourself into that room and wait there until I call you.'

'I will not be taking orders from—'

'Do as he says, Jansis,' Sylvie told her. 'I'll deal with these people.'

Muttering under her breath the servant led Maeve into the sitting-room and closed the door. Sylvie glanced along the shiny river of linoleum into the kitchen. There were pans on the floor, a bucket, a broom and a mop. Through the open door at the back she could make out a detective poking about in the hen-run.

'I hope he's not interfering with my chooks,' Sylvie said.

'Chooks?' said Vaizey.

'Chickens,' Sylvie said. 'My hens.'

'He's just doing his job. He won't harm your – chooks.'

Vaizey took her by the elbow. She was tempted to yank her arm away but, capitulating, let him guide her to the alcove under the stairs.

'Look' – Vaizey's breath smelled of tobacco – 'it gives me no great pleasure to have to descend on you in this manner, Mrs McCulloch, but we've received a report that a crate of rifles from the landing at Howth is hidden here.'

'Do I look like a gun-runner to you?' Sylvie said. 'Well, do I?'

'Where's your husband?'

'Out earning an honest living.'

'He drives for Flanagan's Motor Company, does he not?'

'Why ask me questions when you already know the answers?'

'How many resident boarders do you have at present?'

She told him, 'Two.'

He nodded. 'Have any strangers stayed here this past weekend?'

'No strangers, only three salesmen who've stayed here often enough.'

'I'll be needing their names.'

'They're written in the guest-book,' Sylvie said. 'I'll get it for you.'

'No.' He touched her elbow again. 'Wait.'

She could hear the creak of floorboards as Ames searched the upper floors. She was unsure exactly what branch of authority the men represented. Fran would know. Fran would have them labelled.

'We know what your husband is and what he does,' Vaizey said.

'Then you'll know he's no nationalist.'

'His father is.'

'We see little enough of Daniel McCulloch here, thank God,' Sylvie said. 'When Gowry and he get together all they do is squabble.'

'Still, blood *is* thicker than water.'

'Not in this house it's not,' Sylvie told him.

'Have you ever met a man called Hagarty?'

'I don't think so,' Sylvie said. 'I'd have to check my guest-book to be sure.'

'You're a Scot, Mrs McCulloch, aren't you?'

'Aye, of course I am.'

'It'll hardly be your fight then.'

'My fight? What are you talking about?'

'It would be a sin to lose everything for a cause that doesn't concern you.'

'Is that, by any chance, a threat?'

He was standing close to her, knee brushing her apron. He was not tall enough to have to bend his head to fit into the triangular space beneath the stairs.

He said, 'My own mother, God rest her soul, was Scottish. She came from Ayrshire originally.'

'Did she really?' said Sylvie flatly.

'Francis Hagarty? Are you sure you've never met him?'

'I told you, not to my knowledge.'

'What about Charles McCulloch and Eamon Trotter?'

'Yes, they drink here now and then when my husband is out of town.' Sylvie paused. 'Who is this man, this Hagarty you're looking for?'

'We're not looking for him,' Vaizey said. 'We know where he lives.'

'Ah,' Sylvie said. 'So it's his connections you're after. Well, there are no rebel connections in this house, and no guns.'

'The guns *were* here, were they not?'

'No, they were not.'

'Sunday night, when you were asleep, perhaps Charlie McCulloch—'

'I'm a very light sleeper,' Sylvie said.

Vaizey was clearly enjoying himself. Sylvie wondered what sort of things a man in his position might do in the name of the law.

'We can close you down, you know,' he said, smiling.

'Is that a threat?' Sylvie said.

'It's a warning,' Vaizey said. 'I've nothing against you personally.'

'Then why are your bully-boys raking through my cupboards?'

'Mrs McCulloch,' Vaizey said, 'you have an enemy.'

'An enemy? Who?'

'Anonymous,' Vaizey said. 'No name given.'

'You mean somebody *told* you there were guns in my house?'

He drew her closer. 'It would be wise not to let your father-in-law and his cronies drink here for a while. I take it you *can* bar your door to them.'

'The Shamrock is my property. I can do as I like here.'

'Better safe than sorry, Mrs McCulloch, especially in troubled times.'

'Who was it? Who told you there were guns in my house?'

'Some malicious trouble-maker too cowardly to give his name,' Vaizey said. 'Trouble-makers are ten for the penny in Dublin right now.'

'Are you telling me someone has it in for me?'

'For you, or your husband,' Vaizey told her. 'I haven't the foggiest idea who the person is, Mrs McCulloch, but I'm keen to find out.'

'Not as keen as I am,' Sylvie said.

They were still tucked under the stairs, still intimate and conspiratorial. He seemed a far cry from the usual broad-shouldered, dignified gentlemen of leisure whom Dublin Castle dressed in plain clothes in the fond belief that it would make them any less obviously policemen. There was an edge to him, a rough sexual edge that she found both exciting and repulsive. She realised with a jolt that he might even be the political arm of the Metropolitan and was pleased to think she had come so far so quickly, far enough to constitute a threat.

'If you do happen to find out . . .' Vaizey shrugged.

Sylvie lowered her voice. 'I suppose you'd like me to tell you?'

'I would,' he said. 'Indeed I would.'

'Don't you usually pay your informers?'

'Oh, now, I'm not asking you to inform,' Vaizey said. 'Fact is, we don't have to pay our informers. Not everyone in Ireland is a nationalist.'

'Oh, I know *that*,' said Sylvie. 'My husband isn't.'

'And there are thousands, hundreds of thousands like him.'

'So,' Sylvie said carefully, 'if I do happen to find out what's become of those stray crates you wouldn't be interested?'

'I didn't say I wouldn't be interested,' Vaizey told her. 'I just said I'm not prepared to pay for the information.'

They had been standing as close as lovers and when the shadow fell across them Vaizey stepped back quickly. He turned, half tripping, to find Ames lurking in the hall behind him.

'Well, Boris,' Vaizey snapped, 'did you find anything?'

'Nothin', sir, not one damn thing.'

'Where's Rogers?'

'Out'n the back.'

'Fetch him,' Vaizey said. 'We're leaving. There's nothing here. It was just another wild-goose chase.'

He walked out of the alcove, glanced up the staircase then at the closed door of the parlour. There was no sound from within, though Maeve and Jansis would no doubt have their ears plastered to the woodwork.

Vaizey went to the street door and opened it.

Down at the kitchen end of the hallway Sylvie heard Ames's coarse shout, 'Wally, Wally, will you be for comin' now. Boss says we're leavin'.'

Moving swiftly she went after the man and caught his arm.

'Who are you?' Sylvie said. 'At least tell me your name.'

'You've no need to know my name.'

'If I don't know your name how can I get in touch with you?'

'In touch?'

'If some interesting bit of information comes my way.'

He cocked his head, hesitated, then said, 'You'll find me at the Castle.'

'And the name, your name?'

'Vaizey,' he said.

'What are you – a sergeant?'

'Inspector.'

The officers lumbered past her into Sperryhead Road. They exchanged a few words with Vaizey then all three turned towards the docks.

From the doorstep Sylvie watched them go, her heart in her mouth. Neighbours were out in fair number, innocently beating carpets or pretending to scrub doorsteps. Sylvie stepped on to the pavement and looked left. She watched the detectives pass the row of terraced cottages further down the street.

Honeysuckle and clematis and waves of ivy spilled over the railings of the front gardens. Beyond the cottages, before the drab walls of the warehouses closed in again, Sperryhead Road was joined by Parish Lane. Out of the lane came Mr Dolan. He walked slowly, eyes down. He wore a thick tweed jacket and a woollen cardigan, for he felt the cold even on warm days. He had his little stick with him, a cane that seemed too slender and jaunty for a man of his years. He didn't see the officers at first and was almost abreast of them before he lifted his head, stopped dead in his tracks and flopped against the ivy-clad railings.

The detectives closed around him. Sylvie could no longer see the old man, only the broad backs of the detectives, raincoats tight across their shoulders and Vaizey, in half profile, smiling his thin, unfriendly smile. Leaning on brooms or raised up from their knees on the doorsteps, the neighbours watched too.

Ames's laughter boomed out. Vaizey patted Mr Dolan's shoulder, then the officers left, walking fast, three in line, around the corner and out of sight.

Mr Dolan leaned on the ivy, hand to his chest, but when, looking up and squinting, he spied Sylvie on the pavement, he gave himself a shake, straightened his cap and with the stick hung on his forearm came shambling on up the Sperryhead Road towards her as if nothing had happened.

Sylvie stepped back indoors. 'You can come out now, girls. They've gone.'

Maeve and Jansis burst out of the sitting-room into the hallway.

'Were they lookin' for you-know-what?' said Maeve, breathlessly.

'They were,' Sylvie said, 'but they didn't find anything.'

'Thanks to my clever daddy,' Maeve said.

Sylvie nodded. 'Yes, thanks to your dear old dad.'

*   *   *

Orange peel, apple cores and cigarette butts littered the floor under the seats. Gowry, tunic off and sleeves rolled up, had to dig for the litter with the back of the brush or kneel and scoop out the mess with his bare hands. Once women had been employed to do the cleaning and he would have been able to walk over to the kiosk behind the office block, turn his keys and his petrol log over to Frank Roddeny, the late-shift manager, and be on his way home with a pocketful of tips and two or three little bags of sweets to keep Maeve happy.

At the time of the strike, a year ago, however, John James Flanagan had paid off most of the casual labour and informed the drivers they must leave their vehicles 'tidy' at the end of each duty. The drivers had held a meeting on the gravel where the charabancs were parked but Flanagan had sent men round to break it up and had even turned up himself, just as the drivers were dispersing, to issue his ultimatum. All his life, it seemed, Gowry had been faced with choices that were no choices at all but, like Flanagan's law, boiled down to 'Take It or Leave It.' He needed the work, though; he needed the wage. He couldn't even politicise the issue or carry the case to the union headquarters in Liberty Hall, for Flanagan was no government lick-spittle but a good God-fearing Dublin businessman who made generous contributions to the national-ist cause.

The sun had gone down behind dark bands of

cloud and tomorrow there would surely be rain, and trippers bound for Tara would have a misty wet ride and see little of the fabled landscape. Gowry didn't care; wet or dry, he would be paid.

The electric lanterns that Flanagan had installed cast wan shadows on the gravel. Gowry was last man in. The other drivers had done their bit with brush and bucket and had trotted off to the pub.

He leaned his brow on the window and stared out at the backs of the houses across the pad, at the faint glow in the sky that the city released like a gas. He had no particular desire to go home, except that, with luck, he would have Maeve's company at supper and a grateful kiss for the sweets he had brought her. He had no urge to get back to Sylvie, though. In the past year or so the Shamrock had become less of a home to him than the houses in which he lodged when he was on the road. There he was known, liked, and made welcome as only Irish folk can make you welcome.

Sighing, he put on his tunic, shouldered the brush, hoisted up the bucket and went down the aisle to the door. He put one foot on the gravel. Someone grabbed him and slammed him against the side of the bus. He flailed out with the bucket, then, recognising his brother, sagged back.

'For God's sake, Charlie! Are you for scaring me to death?'

'Is the tackle still on board?'

'She told you, did she? I thought she would.'

'Never mind who told me,' Charlie said. 'Where is it?'

'That,' said Gowry, 'is for me to know and you to find out.'

His brother was coiled tight as a watch-spring and for an instant he thought Charlie was going to punch him.

'What have you done with our bloody guns, Gowry?'

'They're safe.'

'Where?'

'Where you can't get your paws on them.'

'Why are you doin' this to me?'

'I'm not doin' it to you, Charlie,' Gowry said. 'I just don't want you or the old man usin' my wife's place as a dump for arms.'

'Sylvie didn't object.'

'Did you give her a chance to object?' Gowry said.

He had argued the toss with Charlie and the old man often enough in the past but this was the first time he had really taken a stand. He was well aware that nationalism had become a substitute for all the things the family had never had or that the old man had frittered away, all the things he'd been told were unworthy of decent Irishmen when, in fact, they were not unworthy at all, merely unattainable.

'You're lucky it's me,' Charlie said. 'If they'd sent Turk he'd have cut you up by now.'

'Cut me up? Cut me up for what?'

'Stealin' our weapons.'

'Weapons you stole from the volunteers in the first place?'

'You haven't sold them, have you?'

'No, of course I haven't sold them. What do you want with rifles?'

'What everyone wants with rifles,' said Charlie. 'To claim back what's ours. You know the old saying: one Protestant with a rifle is better placed to express his opinion than a Catholic without one.'

'You're not a Catholic, Charlie.'

'Home rule, without partition, is what I mean.'

'I see,' said Gowry. 'Are you willin' to pay for freedom with your life?'

'If necessary, yes.'

Charlie jerked his hands from his pockets and waved them about. Any moment now he would pepper the night air with clichés that Gowry had heard a thousand times before.

'I threw them into the sea.'

'You did *what*?' Charlie shouted.

'Off the cliffs, into the sea.'

'Ow, ow, Jaysus, Jaysus!' Charlie hopped like a flea on a griddle. 'What've you done, Gowry? Jaysus, what have you done?'

Gowry laughed. 'No, I didn't throw them into the sea.'

'You pig, you bastard!'

'They're hidden where nobody will find them.'

Charlie had always been a bad-tempered tyke and lacked a sense of humour.

'Tell me then, tell me now or I'll send Turk to—'

'When the time comes, Charlie, when the time comes.'

'The time's now.'

'The time is not now,' said Gowry. 'My God, man! We could all be at war with Germany before we're much older.'

'You're a damned Tory swine, Gowry. You always were. Tell me where you've hidden those guns or—'

'Or what?'

'I won't be able to answer for your safety.'

Gowry said, 'Is it a threat I'm hearing now?'

'It'll be more than threat if Turk has his way.'

'This is not the time to go baiting the British government.'

'You know nothing about what's going on behind the scenes.'

'Do I not? Well, this I do know: there will never be enough compromises to satisfy you. Dear God, Charlie, don't you ever get tired of bargaining for more and more concessions?' Gowry said. 'To hell with politics. I'm going home.'

'All right,' Charlie said. 'How much?'

'How much for what?'

'How much will it cost for you to tell me where those guns are hidden?'

Surprised, Gowry said, 'I'm not in the business of selling weapons, Charlie. I removed the guns from the Shamrock because I don't want you or the old man doing something you'll regret afterwards.'

'There'll be no regrets,' said Charlie. 'We're not all cowards.'

'Aye, you've called me that often enough,' said Gowry. 'Look, I've told you a thousand times, I'm tempted to support you with my heart but I can never support you with my head.'

'Just tell me where the guns are, Gowry?'

'The guns are safe. They'll stay hidden until you give me a valid reason for handing them back.'

'Is that your final word?'

'That's my final word.'

Gowry started off towards the kiosk.

In the window of the box Roddeny's big round face was buttery in the overhead light. Roddeny was a Sinn Feiner and his dislike of Protestants legendary. There was never a cheery goodnight from Frank Roddeny for Gowry. Charlie, however, would linger and blow off steam to Roddeny before he left and tomorrow it would be all over Flanagan's that he, Gowry McCulloch, had come out in his true colours at last.

'He said this is what you'd do,' Charlie called out.

Gowry stopped, turned. 'Who did? Dada?'

'Never you mind who,' Charlie said. 'He's got your measure, Gowry, and he says for to tell you there are plenty other ways to skin a cat.'

'I don't know what you're blathering about, Charlie.'

'You'll find out soon enough,' Charlie said. 'You'll live to rue the day you ever crossed the brother-hoods.'

'I doubt it,' Gowry said, grinning.

Then he turned in his keys and logbook and went home.

On that first afternoon they had done nothing but kiss. There had been no intrusive tongue, no roving hands. He had seated her on the end of the bed and had leaned forward and kissed her on the lips. His lips, though tasting of whiskey, were dry. He had kissed her three times, letting the last one carry the message of his intentions, so that when she came again she would know what to expect.

She was trembling when she climbed the spiral staircase for a second time. She knew that he had put the onus on to her and had already transferred any guilt that might accrue, even, she thought, the manner in which she would yield to him, the speed, the tempo at which she would plunge into an affair that would probably end in tears.

The door was ajar.

She could hear the clash of the keys of the typewriting machine, a furious noise, like a factory loom. When she pushed the door open and said, 'It's me,' he stopped typing. He lifted his hands from the keys and held them high the way the concert pianist at the Tivoli did when he finished a difficult piece.

Fran didn't look at her. He continued to stare down at the paper that curled over the bar-lock, smiling to himself, though whether the smile was for her or at what he had written Sylvie had no way of telling.

She took off her bonnet and cape.

They were pearled with the rain that had come sweeping in over the hills that early morning and that fell steadily now, sifting down upon the city. The room smelled differently in the rain, not dank but musty.

'What are you doing?' she said.

'Waiting for you.'

He took a cigarette from an ashtray and inhaled smoke. He lifted a glass and finished the whiskey in it.

'You look lovely,' he said.

'Thank you,' Sylvie said.

The paper curled over the bar-lock was covered in dense paragraphs. There were other papers on the table, thin sheaves tabbed with steel paperclips. The whiskey bottle had hardly been touched. Fran wore a collarless shirt, sleeves folded back and crimped with broad rubber bands. The bandage on his left hand was grubby and a little frayed.

'Is it raining still? Are you wet?'

'I am,' she said. 'My hair.'

'Ah, the rain has a lot to answer for,' Fran said.
She seated herself on the end of the bed.

She watched him open a small cupboard under the cabinet. He moved briskly as if the act of typewriting had restored lost energy. He brought out a towel, thick-pelted and spotless. He opened it across his hands and offered it to her.

'You do it,' she said.

'May I?'

'Yes.'

Many men had tried to woo her into bed. The commercials were forever at it, especially when they had the drink on them. They would croon to her, make goo-goo eyes, beg her to go upstairs with them. Some were fine-looking men, handsome in a shabby way, others big, red-faced and vigorous. She had laughed them all away. She was not unsatisfied with Gowry.

In the hope of making another child he had kept her going, beating away on her with metronomic regularity. Gowry was a silent lover and not as ardent as Forbes had been. When Gowry was inside her she seldom got carried away. With Gowry there were no surprises, only the same monotonous little signals that would end with him upon her – and hardly a kiss now, hardly even a kiss.

She shivered when Fran touched her.

He brushed the towel across the fine hair at the nape of her neck. She could feel his fingers through the nap of the towel, touching her as lightly as a mayfly lands on water. He moved behind her and knelt on the bed. She could feel the springs yielding, hear their pliant little plaint. He slid the point of the towel downward under the collar of her blouse.

She shivered again and said, 'Yes.'

He uncoupled the hook from the eyelet and, flattening his fingers, traced the line of her bare shoulders. He pressed against her, chest, thighs, his chin touching her curls. 'I hear the detectives came to see you yesterday?'

'Yes.'

'One with a grey moustache?'

'Yes.'

'Vaizey: he's the boss.'

'They found nothing.'

'I didn't expect them to,' Fran said.

'Someone told them there were guns in my house.'

'Ah, that's how it is these days. Nobody's safe from wagging tongues.'

'Was it you?'

'Me?' He was amused, not offended. 'Why would it be me?'

'To bring me back. To frighten me.'

'Are you frightened?'

'No.'

'Were you frightened when Vaizey turned up?'

'No.'

'Where did your husband take the rifles?'

'He won't tell me. He won't tell anyone.'

'I expect he won't,' said Fran Hagarty. 'He has his reasons, no doubt.'

She felt his fingers work the row of four small buttons that dropped below the stitching of the collar. She wore only a summer camisole beneath the blouse. He opened the back of the blouse and touched her again, his thumbs pressing her spine.

'Is your wound healing?' Sylvie asked.

'I haven't looked.'

'I will look later.'

'Aye,' he said.

'I'll change the dressing.'

'Please.'

'Later.'

'Yes, later will do.'

He slid the blouse from her shoulders. He slipped one hand beneath the camisole and caressed her breasts. She had small, sensitive breasts and felt them stiffen as he continued his expert fondling. She lay back against him, head on his chest, and his fingers found her, nimble fingers that sparked sensations as dazzling as the charges of current that crossed the wires above the tramway lines.

She reached back with her arm and brought him down, his mouth upon her mouth, his tongue touching hers. He pressed his lips together, formed a small, moist bud from his tongue and rubbed it against her lips. He pulled her back along the length of the bed and pushed her arms out by her sides, then, pinning her in that position, kissed her openly again, and again.

'I won't hurt you,' he murmured. 'I promise I won't hurt you.'

'Please,' she said. 'Please don't.'

But somehow she knew that he would.

Chapter Four

Complacency might have set in earlier if it hadn't been for the war, the war and the character of her lover, Fran Hagarty, who was too complex and inconsistent to permit her to take her pleasures lightly. He was a writer by profession but trailed behind him – much as she did – a chequered history of foolishness in dealing with the more obvious aspects of reality.

For a man whose work was so secretive Fran was remarkably liberal with information about his achievements and Sylvie soon realised that he was no ordinary hedge-schoolmaster with a flair for fancy phrases. College educated, he had taught at university until his philandering or his politics had become too much for the governors. He had travelled to America several times and was undoubtedly a man of the world. He had dined in the Old Irish American Club in Philadelphia with Judge Cohalan and other founders of the Clan-na-Gael and even had meetings with O'Donovan Rossa, a legendary rebel, who lived in retirement on Staten Island.

'Land hunger,' Fran told her, 'is at the root of it, at the root of everything. Even so, national pride should not be put down as a crime. He was married three times, you know, the old scallywag.'

'Who are we talking about now?'

'Rossa, of course, old O'Donovan Dubh, the arch Fenian himself.'

'What happened to his wives?'

'Oh, they died young, two of them at any rate.'

'And you, Fran, what about your wife?'

'Who told you I had a wife?'

'Charlie let it slip.'

'True, it's true. There was a wife. There *is* a wife.'

'And children?'

Just for a second he looked almost sheepish. 'Three sons,' he said. 'Fine boys: Jack, Ross and Hugh.'

'Where are they now?'

'Far away across the sea.'

'Do you not see them at all?'

'No.'

'Do you support them?

'Alas, I have no money to support them.'

'Where is your wife?'

'Huddersfield.'

Sylvie did not have the gall to enquire what Mrs Francis Hagarty was doing in Huddersfield.

The fact that Fran was so loquacious relieved her of the need to explain herself. He went on and on about everything and anything that interested him and asked her very little about herself.

She was well aware that he still regarded her as a smart little simpleton. For this reason she refrained from informing him that she had been thoroughly well educated at one of Glasgow's top schools for which her birth father, Tom Calder, had paid the fees. She might truthfully have claimed to be a girl with *two* fathers but wasn't sure how to explain the triangular nature of her upbringing. She had been fostered out to her father's sister Florence soon after her mother had died, raised by Florence and Albert Hartnell, turned religious and under Albert's guidance had collected in public houses and gambling dens for the Coral Strand Mission Society. Florence and Albert had creamed the takings and before she was seventeen Sylvie had acquired a taste for alcohol, tobacco and footloose gaiety, though there was precious little gaiety left in her now.

Naturally she did not mention Forbes, not even when Fran tentatively enquired where she had learned her bedroom tricks. She certainly hadn't learned them from Forbes who had been even less imaginative than Gowry.

She was intrigued and sometimes bored by Fran Hagarty's education, intelligence and loquacity.

'Tell me,' he said, as they lay side by side in bed, 'has your husband got more hair than I have?'

'On his head, do you mean?'

'I meant in general; everywhere.'

'He isn't lacking in hair, no,' said Sylvie.

'He's young, of course, younger than I am.' Fran lifted his hand and brushed the greying locks that sweat had pasted to his brow. 'After a certain age a man can expect to give a few hairs to fortune, I suppose.'

'You're not going ba— not so bad,' Sylvie said, trying to make light of his concern. 'You're not old. I mean, you're still in your prime.'

'He'll have more hair on his chest than I have, I expect.' Fran lifted the sheet and, chin tucked in, earnestly studied his breastbone. 'I've never had much hair on my chest. My brothers used to jag me about it all the time.'

'Brothers? I didn't know you had brothers.'

Refusing to be sidetracked, he lifted the sheet higher.

'What d'you think, Sylvie? Tell me honestly.'

His skin was as pale as paper and mottled with little veins like watermarks. Three or four individual hairs sprouted feebly from the centre of his chest. The rest was bare, hairless down as far as the belly button, sparse beyond. Gowry was well endowed with hair, a lean-muscled, vulpine hairiness that put poor Fran to shame. Constitutionally Fran was so unlike Gowry, in fact, that she felt a little wave of astonishment pass through her that she had actually climbed into bed with him.

'You're fine,' she said. 'Absolutely fine.'

'I don't suppose you've seen a lot of men without their clothes on.'

'No,' Sylvie said. 'Hardly – I mean Gowry, just Gowry.'

'Hmm!' He flicked the sheet to one side and stared down at himself, sad-eyed, fishing not for compliments but reassurance. 'What about the rest of me?'

More cautious than embarrassed, she leaned across him and, smothering her distaste, laid a hand on his thigh and peered at his parts. He was different from Gowry in that department too. Forbes had been similar in shape and size to Gowry, as far as she could recall, and the thought strayed across her mind that perhaps it wasn't just ears and noses and the colour of eyes that family members shared. There was something almost comically brutal about Fran's parts, something curiously unfinished too, as if the ends had not been knotted properly. She was filled with a vague, milksop distaste, not at what she was doing but at what she was doing it to.

She touched and made to kiss him but he pushed her away.

'I can't,' he said, 'not again, not so soon.'

'There's no shame in that,' Sylvie said.

'Shame, who said anything about shame? I'm not ashamed of it.'

'Nor should you be,' she said. 'Not after what—'

'What?'

Piqued that he had revealed his weakness, he

inched away from her, folding his arms behind his head. She had too much sense to try to rouse him. She turned on her side, crossed her arms across her breasts and looked up at him: 'I'm glad.'

'Glad,' he said. 'For what?'

'That you've had enough.'

He glanced at her, frowning.

Sylvie said, 'I'm quite worn out, you see. You've quite worn me out.'

'Have I?'

'Yes, darling, you have.'

He turned towards her, a smile on his lips, slid beneath the sheet, put an arm about her and nestled her against his cold, white, hairless chest.

'You're only saying that.'

'I'm not. I mean it.'

'Well!' he murmured. 'Well!' and kissed her.

'Do you think it will be making much difference?' Jansis asked.

'What? The war?' said Sylvie.

While she had been making love to Francis Hagarty the parliament of Great Britain and Ireland had been leading the nation into war.

'Aye,' Jansis said. 'The war.'

'Certainly it will. How can it not? Look what's happening already.'

'They say it'll be over by Christmas.'

'Kitchener doesn't think so,' said Maeve.

'What do you know about Kitchener?' Sylvie said.

'It's all over the *Progressive*,' said Maeve.

'Why are you reading that rag?' said Sylvie. 'You didn't buy it, did you?'

'No, I didn't buy it. Mr Pettu gave it me.'

'Mr Pettu? Well, I am surprised,' said Jansis. 'I thought he'd more sense.'

'He's not a revolutionary,' said Maeve. 'He buys it for the racing results.'

'I didn't know Mr Pettu was a betting man,' said Jansis. 'And him so staunch in his faith too.'

'He has an occasional flutter,' said Maeve. 'Won four bob the other day.'

'You've become very pally with Mr Pettu all of a sudden,' said Jansis.

At one time Jansis had cherished a notion that the little widower might take a shine to her, court and even wed her, no matter that he was thirty-odd years her senior, but Mr Pettu had remained indifferent, not cold but disinterested. After his wife had died and his last surviving daughter had entered a convent, he had sworn a vow of strictest chastity – or so he told Jansis. Having no evidence to the contrary, Jansis believed him and refused to consider that little Mr Pettu with his peaky white face and bootlace moustache might be veering towards hypocrisy.

'We got talking, that's all,' said Maeve.

'Not up in his room, I hope,' said Sylvie.

'No, not in his room,' said Maeve, 'though I can't see any harm in—'

'Listen to your mother,' Jansis said. 'You can't trust any man.'

Maeve blinked her blue eyes and shook her chestnut curls.

Sylvie studied her daughter warily. She had no idea what Maeve knew of life, of men and how they related to women, or if she understood that youth and innocence were no protection against predatory nature but rather an enticement to it. In four or five years, if they were spared, she would no more be able to hold Maeve back than Charlie McCulloch could hold back his brother Peter.

It had been a hectic spell in the Shamrock and she could have filled the rooms twice. Whatever else Dubliners might say about the war it had brought trade to the city. Bank holiday visitors had been replaced by country lads lured to town by rumours that the ship repair yards were taking on apprentices and the government opening factories to supply the British army with everything from woollen drawers to pork-meat. Every traveller in Ireland seemed to have descended on Dublin, for on a buoyant market the commercials were first to reap the benefit.

From one of the salesmen Sylvie had purchased six good, cheap lengths of curtain material to improve the top-floor rooms and in the quiet of the afternoon Maeve, Jansis and she were in the sitting-room sewing them up.

Sylvie had felt like a traitor slipping off to Endicott Street when the Shamrock was so busy, had felt like a fool standing outside Fran's door, knocking desperately upon it even after it became apparent Fran was not at home. She had been engulfed by disappointment and annoyed by his indifference but by the time she'd picked her way down the spiral staircase to the street, she had calmed down. After all, she reasoned, Fran had important things to do and she could hardly expect him to be lying in bed all day long, awaiting her arrival.

She had called in at the butcher's on the way home and had left a large order with the green-grocer next door. Back in the Shamrock she had helped Jansis iron sheets and Maeve change beds and, in a charitable mood, had served Mr Dolan a bowl of soup in his room where the old chap spent most of his time these days. Now, in the quiet part of the afternoon, the women and girl were alone.

'Can't you trust Daddy?' Maeve, busy with the needle, said.

'Daddy's different,' Sylvie told her.

'What about Charlie?'

'No, you have to be careful even with Uncle Charlie.'

'Careful, what d' you mean "careful"?'

Jansis and Sylvie exchanged a glance over the swaddle of curtain material.

'Just,' Sylvie said, 'careful.'

'Not to let him take liberties, you mean?' said Maeve.

'Has Charlie done that, has he tried to—'

'No, no,' said Maeve. 'He hasn't done anything.'

'What,' Jansis enquired, 'about Mr Trotter?'

'Turk? Nah. He knows Charlie would kill him if he did,' Maeve said.

Sylvie cleared her throat. 'If he did — what?'

'Kissed me, or tried to,' said Maeve.

'Kissed you, is that all?' said Jansis.

Sylvie frowned and shook her head in warning.

'I know what you're talkin' about,' Maeve said.

'Do you now?' Sylvie said. 'What are we talking about then?'

'Huggin'.' In spite of her precocity a faint pink blush appeared on Maeve's cheeks. She took refuge in sewing. 'You're not allowed to let a man hug you.'

'Not unless you're married,' said Jansis.

'Is it a mortal sin then?' Maeve asked.

'It — aye, it is a sin, though maybe not mortal.'

'Have you ever been hugged, Jansis?'

'What like a question is that to be askin' a respectable woman?'

'Have you?'

'No, indeed I have not.'

'Never?'

'No. Never.'

'Wouldn't you like to be hugged?'

'Maeve, that's enough,' Sylvie said. 'Go and brew

76

us a pot of tea. We could all be doing with something before the knockers come to the door.'

'I'll do it,' Jansis volunteered. 'I'm weary of stitching anyway.'

The servant left the sitting-room and padded down to the kitchen.

Sylvie noticed that the house had a different smell today, richer and more exuberant, as if an influx of guests had added texture to the air.

She snipped a thread with her teeth and tied off the loose end.

'Was he not there, Mam?' Maeve said. 'Is that why you came home early?'

'Who?'

'The person you go to see every day, the man?'

'Man? What man? What are you blatherin' about?'

'Is it him? Is it Mr Hagarty?' Maeve said.

'Mister – no, of course it isn't Mr Hagarty.'

'Who is it then?'

'I go to the market for provisions.'

'Every day?' Maeve said. 'I mean, every day for three hours?'

'Has Jansis been complaining about the extra work?'

'Jansis complains all the time.' Maeve scraped her chair across the floor and brought herself knee to knee with Sylvie. 'You can tell me, Mam. Is it really Mr Hagarty? It is, isn't it?'

'Mr Hagarty is far too busy a man to bother with the likes of me.'

'So you have seen him again?'

'I didn't say—'

'Then how do you know he's so busy?'

'Maeve, dearest, you shouldn't jump to conclusions.'

'Is it for the huggin' you see him?'

'Maeve! Enough!'

'If I was your age an' Mr Hagarty gave me the eye—'

'The eye? What is all this nonsense?'

'Jansis says—'

'Jansis, is it?' Sylvie said. 'Jansis had better watch out for her job.'

Maeve sat back, head cocked. Curls bobbed across her cheek but the blush had gone. She looked, Sylvie thought, remarkably like the sort of girl she'd been at that age. There was a photograph in one of the tin boxes in the attic, in fact, a studio picture; she, dainty little Sylvie, seated on a rickety little chair, her foster-father behind her, a hand on her shoulder, his thumb tucked into his waistcoat pocket; she with such a knowing expression on her face that her foster-father had never dared show the picture to her aunt.

'It isn't Jansis's fault,' said Maeve. 'I saw you.'

'Saw me?' Sylvie's mouth went dry and the hair on the nape of her neck rose as if an icy wind had blown through the room. 'Saw me where?'

'I followed you for a piece.'

'F-followed me?'

'You went up across the Parade. You should've tooken a tram.'

'How dare you? How *dare* you!' Sylvie hissed. 'Spying on your own mother.'

'It is where he lives, isn't it? Endicott Street?'

'If you ever – if you *ever* follow me again—'

'Charlie told me: Endicott Street: Mr Hagarty,' Maeve said. 'I think it's awful brave of you, Mam.'

'Brave?' Sylvie felt as if her tongue were frozen to the roof of her mouth. 'Brave, for d–doing w-what?'

'You're doing it to save Daddy, aren't you?'

'Doing what?'

'Meeting Mr Hagarty,' Maeve said. 'Charlie told me it was Mr Hagarty told him not to put Dad on the spot 'cause he took those guns away.'

'When did you talk to Charlie?'

'He came round the other day, Tuesday, the day the war started.'

'Why didn't you tell me?'

'He said for me not to tell you.'

'Where was Jansis?'

'Makin' beds upstairs. Where's the spot, tell me?'

'It doesn't mean – it isn't – it's not a place.'

'Daddy shouldn't know, should he? About the spot, I mean?'

'No, dearest, no.'

In the kitchen the big kettle with the whistling spout sang.

Sylvie felt as if she were melting away. She wanted to clasp Maeve to her and rock her in her arms, assure her that it was all just silly grown-up nonsense but she guessed that Maeve wouldn't swallow the lie and that the insidious process of corruption had already begun.

'Daddy shouldn't know you've been talkin' to Mr Hagarty, should he?'

'No.'

Maeve nodded sagely. 'He has his pride, I suppose – Daddy.'

Sylvie paused then said, 'I won't be visiting Mr Hagarty again.'

'Why ever not?'

'Because it – he . . .'

'Does he not like you?'

'Yes, but . . .'

'And you like him,' said Maeve. 'I like him too. He saved Daddy's bacon.'

'Is that what Charlie told you?'

'Aye.'

'Maeve, is Mr Hagarty one of the brotherhood?'

'I don't know what he is,' Maeve said. 'I just think he's awful nice.'

'He's awfully clever,' Sylvie said. 'I'll give him that.'

'Does he hug you?'

'No.'

'Doesn't he want to?'

'I don't know. We just – talk.'

'About what?' said Maeve.

'Things.'

'About the guns? About Daddy an' the guns?'

'Yes,' Sylvie said, establishing a plausible lie. 'Yes, it's all to do with Daddy and the guns.'

'I thought as much.' Maeve gave a little sigh, signalling relief that her mother's secret was not more adult. 'I think you're into it now, Mam, I really do.'

'Yes, dear, I think you may be right,' said Sylvie sadly, just as Jansis brought in the tea.

There was hardly an Irish newspaper he hadn't written for at one time or another. Even when he had been tutoring at the university he had always found time to dash off articles as well as his regular reports to the Clan. Nothing had ever stopped him writing, not even tumbling down the back stairs in McKinstry's one wet Friday night and breaking his wrist. He had written under so many pen names that he couldn't recall them all and when he added in all the false names he had given to all the girls he had bedded, there were times when he thought there could be nothing left of the original Fran Hagarty.

Sometimes when he wakened on the floorboards, sick with the drink and chilled to the bone, he would have to work hard to select one name for himself from the host of inky ghosts, for he wanted to be not one but all of them at once.

Until Sylvie entered the picture, though, he had no intention of allowing himself to fall properly in love, especially not with a Dublin landlady. But when he wakened he found himself dreaming of Sylvie McCulloch and before he rose to pee or to boil water for his breakfast tea, he would lie quite still and repeat her name over and over again. McCulloch: he pronounced it in the soft-boiled, slip-off-the-tongue accent you could still hear spoken in the vales of Glendalough: *M'Cullow* it was, all lip and tongue, with the stress on the *mick* and the *cull*.

He brooded about Sylvie when he should have been planning his escape. God knows there was enough going on in the world, let alone Dublin, to claim his full attention. What rash moves might the brotherhoods make next? If conscription were forced upon the Irish would there be rioting in the streets and would he have to unmuzzle Turk Trotter to beat the daylights out of the bus-driver and force him to hand back the stolen guns, or at least enough of them to get the job done? How would he explain *that* to Sylvie? Then, unaccountably, he would find himself at the window peering down into Endicott Street, waiting for her to arrive, and would see her pass below dressed in her prim little cape and funny straw hat and would feel pity for her, pity for himself too, at tragedies in the making, tragedies which, if he hadn't loved her, he would simply have laughed away.

'Sylvie,' he would whisper, leaving his breath upon the glass. 'Sylvie,' before he scrambled on to the bed to greet her, pretending to be heartlessly masculine, with no thought for anything but the tricks and the tickling.

When word came through that a secret meeting was being convened in Cork he knew he would have to leave her. He didn't dare send her a letter – letters were always dangerous – and had no one he trusted enough to carry a message. He simply had to pack and go. It was his duty to report upon all meetings between the brotherhoods, and the Clan would expect a full account. He could not let them down, not when he might need their protection in the not too distant future, but duty was an intrusion right now and he felt so bad about abandoning her without warning that he even performed a little war dance of frustration before he packed his razor and one clean shirt and set off to catch the train to Cork.

Chapter Five

Dry mash and clean litter had built a healthy flock of fowls. They provided eggs even in the depths of winter and white meat all year round. Sylvie couldn't bring herself to do the killing, though, and left that side of it to Jansis who had no compunction about despatching chickens. 'Born to die,' Jansis would say. 'Born to die, that's all they are, poor things,' as she stretched out a feathery neck and tugged.

The coop was well ventilated but did not get quite enough light and every morning Sylvie opened the wire gate to let the birds out into the courtyard. That particular morning the weather was breezy and bright. Chimney cocks whirred on the roof of Watton's warehouse, small white clouds scudded across the sky and gulls soared restlessly overhead. The holidays were over and Maeve was back at school. The commercials had breakfasted and gone their separate ways and Mr Dolan was off, albeit nervously, on a tour of the harbour. There was a war going on in Europe but Sylvie was too locked in on herself to dwell on it.

She was angry with Fran, resentful of the fact that he'd left her in the lurch and that she hadn't heard from him for the best part of a week. Beneath her resentment, though, lay fear that he had come to harm or that now he'd had what he wanted from her he had thrown her over and she would never hear from him again. She had just filled the water basins and scattered fresh grit when, looking up, she saw him in the archway. He had on the long overcoat, collar turned up, but he wore no hat and the breeze toyed with his hair.

'Fran?' she said, under her breath. 'Fran, is it you?'

He was too far off to hear but when she turned towards him he started down the lane and raised a hand in greeting and she felt her heart open like a flower. Putting down the basin, she wiped her hands on her apron, ran a few steps and threw herself into his arms.

'God,' she said. 'Oh, God, I missed you.'

He hugged her against him. He felt strong, so strong, stronger than Gowry had ever done. She did not know what words or gestures would explain what he had come to mean to her during the days they had been apart but uttered instead a little *uh-uh-uh* of pleasure when he pressed his lips against hers.

He drew back. 'Is it safe?'

'Yes,' she said. 'Yes.'

'Where's Maeve?'

'At school.'

'And the girl, the maid?'

'Shopping.'

He did not ask about Gowry.

Sylvie laughed, kissed him again, took his hand and led him into the kitchen.

Breakfast dishes, newly washed, gleamed in the sunlight. Three small saucepans glinted on the stove. She could hear the crackle of new coals and smell the smoke that leaked from the iron stove in windy weather. She had the taste of him on her lips, the relief of knowing that she was not alone in loving after all.

'Can we go some place?' Fran said. 'Is there somewhere safe?'

'Have you eaten? Have you had your breakfast?'

'Yes, yes, I've had my breakfast. Don't you want to?'

'It isn't that. I just—'

'Upstairs, can we not go upstairs?' He frowned. 'Is it not convenient?'

'Convenient?' Sylvie said. 'What sort of a word is that? Yes, it is convenient, dearest. It will never be more convenient. Come.'

She pulled him along the corridor. He moved jerkily, as if he had forgotten how to give in to impulse. They paused on the first landing. He put his arms about her and pressed himself against her. She tilted back her head and let him kiss her cheeks,

87

her brow and, lifting up her hair, her ear. He cupped her breasts and sighed as if holding her again removed the pain of being Fran Hagarty.

They stumbled noisily into a vacant bedroom.

And closed the door.

'See,' Sylvie said, 'you were hungry after all.'

'It's true,' Fran admitted, 'but one appetite overcame another.'

She gave him a nudge with her elbow.

They were seated at the long table in the kitchen while he ate the bacon, eggs and sausage that she'd fried for him after they'd come downstairs. She sat close to him, teapot and milk jug pushed aside, her chair drawn up so that she could lay a hand on his thigh now and then and lean against him with her shoulder.

'An appetite?' Sylvie said. 'Is that all I am to you?'

'Hung-gurrr,' he said, growling. 'Hung-gurrr.'

'I've never seen you eat before.'

'It's not a pretty sight,' Fran said.

'Oh, I don't know. I've seen worse.'

'I can't even claim I'm not used to breakfasting at noon – for I am.'

'You're dissolute, that's what you are,' said Sylvie. 'Plain dissolute. If you were married to me I'd soon sort you out.'

'What if I don't want to be sorted out?'

'Fatten you up then.'

'Like a lamb for the slaughter?'

He chewed thoughtfully while Sylvie buttered him a slice of bread. He mopped up egg yolk with it and put it in his mouth.

She said, 'You don't have to go, Fran. You can stay all night if you like.'

He shook his head. 'It wouldn't be right.'

'Gowry won't be home until tomorrow afternoon. He's driving recruits to the barracks at Tipperary.'

'Tipperary?' Fran said. 'What recruits are they?'

'How would I know?' said Sylvie.

She poured tea, a half-cup for herself. She wanted to take nothing into herself yet, to keep what was in her undiluted for a time longer, but her thirst was insistent and the tea refreshing. She held the cup in both hands, leaning snugly against him while he finished his breakfast.

'Why didn't you tell me you were going away?'

'It was a sudden thing.'

'And secret?' Sylvie said.

'And secret,' he said, and then gave a little shake of the head. 'No, there's little enough secret these days. An Irish division has been granted government sanction and recruiting has begun in earnest. All those farmers' sons and corner boys who are ignorant about the true state of affairs are bound to be dazzled by the flash of the bayonets and the guns. Soon they'll be so confused in their loyalties they'll forget what patriotism means and be whisked off in

Flanagan's charabanc to die for a country that isn't their own.'

'Gowry says joining the fight against the Germans is the only way of making sure the English keep their promises.'

'Keep their promises to whom?' Fran said. 'It's an impasse now and it'll be an impasse even when the war's over. Dying for England won't win us our freedom.'

'How can you be sure?'

'I can't.' There was more argument in him, more prophecy and pessimism, but he would not burden her with it. He pushed away his plate and put a hand on her arm. 'We are born fighting men, we Irish. The warrior strain is in our blood and the English will exploit it. I can't say I blame them.'

'I thought you'd gone and left me,' Sylvie said.

'No,' he said. 'I'm not sure I could even if I wanted to.'

'That's a comforting thing to hear. Will you come back tonight?'

'It wouldn't be right,' he said again.

'You can come back after dark.'

'I wouldn't be wanting your daughter to hear us.'

'We'll be quiet as mice,' Sylvie said. 'Besides, Maeve likes you.'

'No,' he said again. 'No.'

'Is it because I have an enemy?'

He paused, then said, 'It is.'

'Have you no idea who it might be?'

'None,' Fran said.

'Is it Gowry they're after, Gowry and the guns?'

'I don't know what they're after, or who they are.'

'If I could find out where the guns are hidden . . .'

'Keep out of it, Sylvie.'

'How can I?' she said.

'I'm sorry,' he said. 'I should never have done this to you.'

She laid her fingers lightly against his lips.

'*Sssh!*' she said. '*Sssh!* What's wrong with making me fall in love?'

'Is that what's happened?' He answered his own question. 'Aye, that is what's happened, I suppose.'

'Will I try to persuade Gowry to tell me where the guns are?'

Fran rubbed his lips with his forefinger. 'I couldn't ask you to do that.'

'I will,' said Sylvie. 'I'll do anything I can for you.'

'It wouldn't be for me.'

'I know, I know: it would be for the cause.'

'You mustn't confuse the two,' Fran said. 'I'm not what you think I am. I'm not a good man raised up by a just cause.'

'You're a good man in my book, whatever your politics.'

'Politics! God, but I wish it was just politics.'

'What is it then?'

He would not, or could not, answer.

91

She put down the cup. He took her hand and kissed her fingers. No one had ever kissed her fingers before. She told herself that she must expect no more of him. His profession was words and he surely knew how to weave words into lies. There would be no *I love you* from Fran Hagarty; a kiss was more honest and sincere.

Maeve breezed in through the back door.

'Hello, Mr Hagarty,' she said, unsurprised at finding her mother's friend in the kitchen, holding her mother's hand. 'I thought you were still in Cork with my granddad.'

'I was but, as you can see, I'm back.'

'Is that where you were? Cork?' Sylvie said.

'Secret meeting,' Maeve said. 'Very hushy.'

'Some secret!' Fran detached himself gradually from Sylvie as if it were the most natural thing in the world for a married woman and a man who was not her husband to be spooning at the kitchen table.

Maeve slung her school satchel on to the dresser and, crossing to the stove, lifted the lid of one of the pots. 'Where's me dinner, Mam?'

'Ten minutes,' Sylvie said. 'It's soup and tinned salmon.'

'Tinned salmon! Ugh!'

'There's nothing wrong with a bit of tinned salmon.' Fran patted the chair that Sylvie had just vacated. 'Sit here, Maeve, and tell me what else your grandfather told you about our meeting in Cork.'

'He said he would bring me something nice.'

'Ah well, a promise is a promise,' Fran said. 'I'm sure he will.'

Maeve folded herself into the chair, an elbow on the table, her thin legs crossed under the pleated green skirt. Even in school clothes she looked older than her years. 'I hope he brings me ribbon. Mr Whiteside says girls my age should not be putting up their hair. Is he not wrong then?'

'I would say he's wrong,' Fran answered, 'in practice if not principle.'

'Mr Whiteside says the government will force all our young men to join the British army for to fight against the Germans.'

'I would say he's wrong on that score too.'

'You wouldn't go fighting against the Germans, Mr Hagarty, would you?'

'Not I,' said Fran. 'I'm far too sensible.'

'I wouldn't neither.' Maeve twisted a strand of hair about her finger, cocked her head and gave Fran a look that was unintentionally coy. 'I would fight for Ireland, though. I'd fight for Ireland in a minute if she needed me.'

'Ah well now,' Fran said, 'perhaps she will – in time.'

Jealous and unaccountably afraid, Sylvie planted the round tin and a wicked-looking opener on the table before him. Obediently he opened the salmon and tipped the pink meat out on to a saucer.

'Will you be staying with us now, Mr Hagarty?' Maeve asked.

'No.'

'Are you not staying here tonight?'

'Would you mind if I stayed here tonight, Maeve?' Fran asked.

'I wouldn't mind at all,' Maeve said. 'And I wouldn't tell.'

'Tell?' Sylvie said.

'Daddy,' Maeve said, innocently.

'And why would you not be telling your daddy?' Fran asked.

'Because,' the girl answered him, 'my daddy's not one of us.'

In accordance with Army Council instructions and with the approval of His Majesty King George V, the 16th Irish Division was formed to supply the British army with cannon fodder or, as some would have it, the finest fighting soldiers in the whole wide world.

The lot that Gowry collected from the recruiting base in Dublin did not seem like warriors, however, more like survivors of a drunken spree. They had been paid a bit of bounty on making their marks and, still in mufti, guzzled bottled beer and sang, not battle songs or songs of yearning but the rebel songs their fathers had taught them. After a while, though, the lads grew boisterous and bottles flew and the sugary tenors were drowned out by barnyard noises so rude that Gowry pulled his cap over his ears and switched on the big wiper to drown out the worst of the racket.

He was glad to see the mountains rising up blue and grey under the rain-cloud and to come down into the Golden Vale.

He drove through the town and steered the vehicle through the barrack gates and braked in front of the guardhouse. He counted the recruits out as if they were sheep and had one of the regular warrant officers sign his logbook. Five hours would take him back to Dublin, but he wasn't due to pick up another batch of recruits until one o'clock tomorrow. Once he filled the bus with petrol at the army taps, he would drive off to his lodging, not in Tipperary but out in the Galtee mountains, his home away from home.

Roddeny had first suggested that farm lodgings were cheaper than those in town. That first night, two years back, Gowry had steered the bus through a maze of sheep walks and wooded tracks until he had come to a low, isolated cottage on the plain under the ridge of the Galtees, close to the Limerick border. By that time he had been cursing Roddeny, for the night had been dark and the track rough and there was sod all by way of habitation except that one lonely cottage clinging to the foot of the mountains.

He'd had no choice but to climb out of the bus and knock on the door.

The glimmer of a lantern had showed in the tiny window, and a voice had asked, 'What is it you want here?'

'A bed for the night, that's all.'

'Are you lost?'

'Aye, I'm lost. I'm down from Dublin, driving a Flanagan's bus. I need a place to sleep until morning.'

'How many are with you on the bus?'

'None. I've dropped my passengers at the Imperial where I will collect them tomorrow at half past nine, after they've had their breakfast.'

'Why did you not put up there too?'

'Because I'm not a rich tripper, only the driver.'

She had stayed safe behind the door.

The wind had made odd noises, he remembered, lonely noises in the tussocks and he could see saplings behind the cottage swaying against a starless sky. He had smelled turves and ponies, wood smoke, cooking, and had thought she would turn him away. He wouldn't have blamed her if she had, a woman alone in the wilderness. When she opened the door, however, he found no fair colleen but a big, bluff, brown-faced woman not quite as old as his mother. She was holding a storm lantern in one hand and a revolver in the other.

'You've nothing to fear from me,' he'd said.

'Why are you out here? Why are you lost?'

'I was looking for a cheap lodging.'

'Are you a Dublin man?'

'I am.'

She'd lifted the lantern and inspected him thoroughly.

She had on a smock, like the old-style smocks his mother had worn years ago when they'd been scrambling to make ends meet but, unlike his mother, the woman before him had had a kindly face and soft brown eyes.

'If you have no accommodation . . .'

'I have,' she'd said. 'I have beds.'

'How,' he'd hardly dared ask, 'how much?'

'Sixpence.'

'And for a bite of supper?'

'All for sixpence,' the woman had said.

'I would – that would be fine.'

'Come in then,' she'd said. 'Come in and be welcome.'

The revolver was army issue and not loaded. She had lost her husband in the campaign in South Africa, for he had been a regular with the Connaught Rangers. He had died not of battle wounds but of some malevolent disease that had claimed more soldiers than bullets or spears. She had also lost a son to the sea. He had gone out with the mackerel fleet from Dunmore and had been washed overboard in a spring night storm. All that tragedy, all that loss had not hardened her, though, for she was a woman of character and counted herself fortunate to have one son still alive – he was a sergeant with the Connaughts – and two daughters in Boston in America, both married to policemen.

Her name was Maggie Leonard and she proved to be a sound, practical, down-to-earth Catholic woman with no liking for nationalists. She farmed the fifteen acres that soldiers' pay had bought, and bred compact little Connemara ponies that she showed around the fairs. She was one of the most contented women Gowry had ever encountered, with a big flouncy bosom and sturdy bare calves and a soft, soft, wind-whispering voice.

He lodged with Maggie whenever he possibly could, for he badly needed her sixpence worth of optimism to keep him going. He soon became her friend, a close, affectionate friend. Indeed, if Maggie had been younger and he had been free he might have swapped driving buses for the pony trade and thrown up everything to live with her. When he told her how he felt, however, she just laughed and said he was far too much a town-boy for her taste and even if he had been a bold bachelor and she not a good God-fearing Catholic woman, she wouldn't have entertained his proposal, for she was satisfied with the single life and would never find another man as loving as her husband had been.

Gowry reached the cottage just as dusk was falling. Cloud had cleared from the tops of the mountains and the colours of autumn were vivid in the last watery gleam of sunlight. Ponies were bunched behind the birch fence and a curlicue of smoke rose from a hole in the cottage roof – the place so old and peaceful and romantic that Flanagan's bus seemed totally out of place there.

Maggie waited in the open doorway. She had flour on her hands. She had been baking bread and the aroma of bread was warm in the air. She baked in a tin oven on the stones in the hearth and the dirt-floored kitchen was hot with the flames of the fire and the candles that burned in dark corners.

'I heard they were bringing down more recruits and I thought you might be doing the driving,' she said.

He gave her a hug and followed her into the kitchen, watched her kneel before the tin stove on the grid over the stones.

She was a strong woman, large in scale, not so much stout as solid. He loved that about her, that granite strength. If there had been other women whom he loved – Maeve was the sole exception – he would not have been here at all, would not have had to submit himself to the melancholy truth that something had gone wrong somewhere in his life.

'Why are you looking so glum, Gowry?' she said. 'Are the soldiers getting you down again?'

'Well, they are a rowdy lot,' Gowry said, 'but you can hardly blame them. If they knew what they're in for they would be singing all the louder and drinking even more.'

'Ah, it's a priggish man you are, Gowry McCulloch,' Maggie said. 'There will be those on your bus today who will be thinking they've died and gone to heaven when they reach the barracks.'

Gowry took off his tunic and hung it on a chair back. In a canvas satchel were his nightshirt, a clean shirt and his razor. He hung the satchel on the chair back too. The woman poured him a glass of

Guinness. He drank it slowly, letting the tensions of the day ease.

He said, 'It will be heaven some of them will wind up in before this war is much older, I'm thinking.'

Maggie took the loaves from the oven and put them on a wicker board to cool. The bread was brown on top and smelled delicious. Gowry supped a mouthful of stout. He lifted his shoulders when the woman touched him as she passed on the way to the tub to crank the pump that brought water up from the spring beneath the house. The house had been built around the spring. After heavy rain or snow melt you would hear the gurgle of it under the dirt floor and the water would come gushing out of the spout of the pump in a great, cold, crystal splash, so cold that it made your teeth ache to drink it.

'Think where they might be coming from, those passengers of yours,' Maggie said. 'How bad their lives might be at home. The army has been the making of many a young man. The army will feed and clothe them and give them a bed to themselves and will train them to be useful.'

'At the killing,' Gowry said.

'I can't deny it,' Maggie Leonard said, 'at the killing too.'

'Ah, you are too stoical for me,' said Gowry.

'Are you not going to argue with me?' Maggie said. 'I haven't had a good argument since the last time you were here.'

Gowry laughed. 'I'll argue with you only after

I've something in my stomach. I've been on the road since before dinner time and I'll not have a nice sergeant-major waiting to serve me a big fat juicy steak.'

'Hoh!' the woman said. 'Will I not be doing as well as a sergeant-major?'

'Every bit as well,' said Gowry.

He finished the stout, took the glass to the tub and rinsed it. He was shoulder to shoulder with her. He would have liked to put his arm about her and hug her again but didn't dare. It was a queer kind of love he had for the woman. He could imagine himself lying next to her in the big double bed at the back of the house but could not imagine entering her. He lifted his tunic and satchel and headed for the ladder that led up to the loft.

Maggie said, 'The tackle is safe.'

'I wasn't thinking about the tackle.'

'I have put blankets over the boxes, for there might be frost soon.'

'It's too early for frost,' Gowry said. 'Besides, what harm will frost do?'

'It makes the bolts contract.'

'Who told you that? Your son?'

'My husband,' Maggie said. 'Mind you, that was in the days of the old ball muskets. Mausers will be a different kettle of fish from the weapons Joseph was used to. Still, it will do no harm to keep them snug.'

'No,' Gowry said. 'I suppose not.'

He moved towards the stairs. He had to make

himself small to go up them, eight steps, head bowed, elbows tucked in. Up there he felt quite close to the husband buried in Africa and the son who had been lost at sea. There was something about a lonely cottage on the plain that transformed you into a dreamer, Gowry thought, whether you liked it or not.

Maggie brought him a lighted candle in a wooden holder and he carried it upstairs to the loft where he would spend the night, sleeping beside the guns.

Turk had been at the drink all afternoon but he had a head for it and a belly like cast iron and was no more than flushed when he strolled into the bar of the Shamrock about half past eight o'clock. Charlie arrived hot on Turk's heels but there was no sign of Daniel, for which small mercy Sylvie was thankful. She would have barred the brothers from her house and threatened them with the constables but Maeve was there and six commercial gentlemen who knew Turk by name and reputation, and she could not bring herself to do it. Besides, she refused to be intimidated by Vaizey's threats.

She pulled on the handle of the engine.

'Is that for me, my sweetheart? Ay-hay, but I'm in sore need of it.'

Turk swept the glass from the bar and swallowed the contents. He wiped his mouth with the back of his hand and put the empty glass back on the counter.

'Another on the slate. One for me an' one for Charlie.'

Charlie had no taste for black stout, which was strange in a man who manufactured the stuff. He was drinking whiskey and water. There was profit in every glass that Sylvie sold and there would be a great fat bag of silver and copper to lug to the bank tomorrow. She remained puzzled as to why Gowry refused to live on her profits instead of working for Flanagan, a man he despised. Perhaps he still resented the fact that it was Forbes's money that had set them on the road to solvency in the first place.

The bar room was small. The piano occupied more space than it justified but she knew the regulars would howl if she got rid of it. They were all in the bar that weeknight. Mr Pettu had dropped in to partake of a drop before he went upstairs to do his books and even Mr Dolan had given up brooding and had slipped into the bar on Mr Rice's coat tails. Sylvie waited for Fran to appear, but the big, round wall clock *tocked* away the minutes and minutes ran into an hour and she had almost given up hope that he would show that evening. She cleared tables, washed glasses in the alcove, racked them below the bottles and from the corner of her eye watched Maeve nudging Turk towards the piano.

Turk tickled the girl, his big, sausage-like fingers trailing over her waist and narrow hips. Maeve's shrill, pizzicato giggle made the men at the tables smile. Though it was long past Maeve's bedtime, Sylvie was reluctant to order her daughter to go upstairs to bed. A crowded bar was no place for a young girl, but at Maeve's age she had been trailed round many a Glasgow pub by her foster-father and had loved every minute of it. Frowning, she watched Turk pull out the piano stool with his foot. Arm about Maeve, he drew the girl on to his knee, lifted the piano lid and struck from the yellowing keys a great solemn chord that had all the men in the room, even prim Mr Pettu, nodding approval.

'What'll it be then, me lads?' Turk roared.

'"The Lass o' Skibbereen".'

'Nah, nah, nah: give us "Denzil's Delight".'

'Not with ladies present,' Mr Pettu objected. 'How about "Ave Maria"?'

'"Ave Maria"?'

'Get away wit' you!'

Turk pulled Maeve closer. He whispered in her ear. She uttered another giggle, wriggled, put out one hand and covered the range of keys that Turk Trotter had indicated. On his nod, she struck down on them and the men, every one, shouted out, '*The Glories, The Glories*,' and with Maeve still riding on his knee, Turk began to sing.

Sylvie leaned on the counter in the smell of the stout and looked through the haze to the door. There in the dark of the corridor was Fran. He wasn't smiling but had a wistful sadness on him as if the song touched him too. He looked haggard, though. Sylvie wondered if what they had done that morning had wearied him. No, it could hardly be that. He flicked his eyes at her, did not smile. Like a ghost in the dark of the hall he was, and she knew then what it was he would have her do and she was not afraid of him or any of them for they were all marked men and she would surely be marked with them.

They sang with Turk, not the last chorus but the whole verse. She saw Fran's lips move, as if he were uttering a prayer. The song finished to shouting and the slapping of palms on tables.

Sylvie called out, 'Charlie,' and when her brother-in-law glanced up she nodded in the direction of the hall. Turk looked round too. When he spotted Fran all the merriment went out of him. He tightened his arm about Maeve's waist, lifted her from his knee, held her for a second or two, close and protective, then with a roar he bounced up from the stool and headed for the door.

'Nature calls, nature calls,' he said and hurried after Charlie into the hall.

'Is it settled then?' Charlie said.

'No, it's far from settled,' Fran said.

'Is he not coming then?' said Turk.

'Aye, he's coming on Sunday to his country estate at Aughvanagh.'

'What for?' said Turk.

'A holiday,' said Fran.

'Now he's done his worst in Westminster, he

needs a bloody holiday!' said Turk. 'Him and his bloody recruiting drive. How could he commit us all to fight for the British government without even consulting the brotherhoods?'

'Will we take him at Aughvanagh?' said Charlie.

'No, at Woodenbridge,' Fran said.

They were in the yard at the rear of the house. The kitchen door was open and the long corridor stretched empty to the door of the bar.

'Sunday,' Charlie said, 'doesn't give us much time.'

'Do you want to quit?' Fran said.

'Quit?' said Charlie. 'We haven't started yet.'

'Woodenbridge?' said Turk. 'What's the old devil doing at Woodenbridge?'

'Passing through on his way to his estate at Aughvanagh.'

'You already told us that,' said Charlie.

'But,' Fran said, 'he'll break his journey to inspect a parade of the Irish volunteers at Woodenbridge.'

'I know Woodenbridge well enough,' Turk said. 'There's plenty of cover and good back roads. Are you sure it is he'll stop there?'

'He'll stop,' said Fran. 'John Redmond's a politician and can never resist an opportunity to make a speech and, by God, it will have to be some speech to justify the fact that he promised Irish help in the war without consulting any of us.'

'How does Redmond know there's a parade at Woodenbridge?' said Turk.

'The schoolmaster told him,' said Fran.

'The schoolmaster?'

'MacSweeney, the leader. He's been a friend of Redmond's for years.'

'Did you get this information from my father?' said Charlie.

'No,' Fran said. 'It's reliable.'

'Is Redmond to be shot?' said Turk. 'If he is, then I'll—'

'He is not to be shot,' said Fran. 'God, Turk, would you have us branded as murderers? We're not murderers. Besides, we've no copyright on martyrs and Redmond would be a martyr before his body struck the ground.'

'A martyr for the English,' Charlie said.

'Exactly,' Fran said.

'What will it be then,' said Turk, 'a wounding?'

'Shots, just shots fired into the air, a volley or two,' said Fran.

'Ay-hay, that'll make the volunteers think twice about joining up, I'll wager. They'll run like bloody rabbits at the first sign of shooting,' Turk said.

'There are many brave men among the volunteers,' said Charlie. 'I'll not hear a word said against them, even those that side with Redmond.'

'We'll be seeing who's brave come Sunday,' Turk said. 'How many guns do you have and how many will be needed?'

'Two,' Fran said.

'Just two?' said Turk.

'Where will we be gettin' the guns?' said Charlie. 'Don't tell me my bloody brother has relented?'

'He has not,' said Fran. 'I have the guns.'

'Rifles?'

'Mausers,' Fran said.

'From the stolen lot?' Charlie snorted. 'Very clever, Francis, to have the foresight to keep back two rifles from the batch you left at the Shamrock.'

'What's so clever about it?' said Turk.

Charlie said, 'Vaizey knows guns were delivered here. He'll come clattering down on Gowry and this time he'll not take *no* for an answer. That'll teach my bloody brother not to meddle in our affairs.'

'Is that how you planned it from the beginning, Francis?' Turk asked.

'How could it be?' Fran Hagarty said. 'I didn't know Redmond would promise the English that the Irish volunteers would fight for them against Germany. However, we may as well use the guns now as later. Will the boy come in with us?'

'He will, that he will,' said Turk.

'Charlie, the motor-car?'

'It'll be my pleasure to drive your Hudson.'

'Turk,' Fran said, 'you and the boy can go down by train on Saturday afternoon. Take food and drink with you, find yourselves a place to lie up in the woods near the road. Charlie will drive down in the early part of Sunday morning with the rifles. He'll hide them in the ferns by the roadside south of the big field and mark the spot with a scarf draped on the bushes.'

'And we'll pick up the guns while the parade's assembling?'

Fran nodded. 'Charlie will park the motor in one of the farm roads nearby. When he hears shooting he'll come for you. Make for the road to the south of the field. It's not far, two or three hundred yards at most.'

'Do we bring the rifles out with us?' said Turk.

'No,' Fran said, 'wipe them clean and toss them away.'

'Do you want them found?' said Turk.

'Sure an' he does,' said Charlie. 'So Redmond will think there's a traitor in the ranks. If we're stopped we'll be pure as driven snow with a plausible story to cover ourselves. We'll tell them we're in Wicklow to buy a barley crop.'

'Hah!' said Turk. 'I like it. Now, where are the two Mausers?'

'On top of the coal box right behind you,' Fran said.

'By Gad, you've thought of everything,' Turk said.

'What's my father's role in this?' Charlie said.

'There is no place for him, I'm afraid,' said Fran.

'Do you not trust him to keep his gob shut?'

'No, I do not,' said Fran.

'No more do I,' said Charlie.

'An' where will you be yourself, Fran, on Sunday afternoon?' Turk asked.

'I'll be right here in the Shamrock,' Fran answered, 'in bed with the gunman's wife.'

★   ★   ★

Gowry lay on the bed listening to the wind sighing along the ridge and the saplings rushing to shed the tenacious little leaves that would not depart the bough. He lay on the narrow bed listening to Maggie moving about below and, thinking of Sylvie, wondered how he had lost his way.

His mother it was who had insisted that he follow Forbes to Scotland to carve a niche for himself. He might have been in Scotland still if Forbes had not taken up with Sylvie and treated her so badly. Had he ever loved Sylvie, or had he only felt sorry for her? Perhaps it was only spite that had driven him to steal her from Forbes and bring her to Dublin. She had been a sprightly little piece then, not nearly as silly as Forbes had supposed; after Maeve had been born she had become very balanced and shrewd indeed. The truth was that he didn't understand Sylvie, did not understand women, though he didn't dismiss them, as many men did, as good for nothing but cooking, copulating and bearing children.

He lay with his hands behind his head listening to the wind and the sounds below. When Maggie called he got up and went downstairs, seated himself at the table, ate the food she'd cooked for him and sought the sixpence worth of optimism that he badly needed at this time.

'I hear there's been serious fighting in Flanders,' Maggie said.

'Aye, two or three weeks of it.'

'With horses?'

'Cavalry against cavalry.' Gowry was relieved to be distracted by talk of the war. 'Do you think the horses suffer much?'

'It's not the horses I grieve for, it's the wives an' the sweethearts.'

'Did you see any of the fighting on the veldt?'

'No, I chose to remain in Ireland.'

'Were wives not encouraged to travel with the regiment?'

'To South Africa? Aye, some went with their men. I did not.'

'Why not?'

'The veldt was no place for women. I didn't want Joseph to see me unhappy.'

'But if you loved him . . .'

'I could love him as well here as there.'

'Didn't you ever think that he might not come back?'

'No,' Maggie said. 'He was with me then and he has been with me ever since. No matter that I can't see him. I tell him how much I love him every day and I know he loves me – wherever he is.'

'Still in Africa, buried on the veldt?'

'There,' the woman said, 'or elsewhere.'

'You believe in heaven then?'

'I do.'

'I wish I did,' said Gowry.

'Ah now, it's a great pity that you do not.'

'Perhaps if I'd been born a Roman Catholic like you . . .' He shrugged.

'Heaven is there for all comers,' Maggie said, 'even Protestants.'

'I don't like to think of it,' Gowry said.

'Of what?'

'Of you going to heaven before I do.'

She nodded, neither flattered nor put out by his confession. He wondered if she felt sorry for him, or if she regarded him as a hopeless case.

Maggie said, 'You mustn't talk like that.'

'Like what?'

'Wishing your life away.'

'Is that what I'm doing?' He smiled ruefully. 'Aye, I suppose it is.'

'Doesn't she love you, your wife?'

'I don't know.' He made a little pop with the air in his cheek. 'I think Sylvie has found another man.'

'Another man?'

'Someone else.'

'Are you sure?'

'Not certain, no.'

'Who is he?'

'A rebel, a writer.'

'Perhaps it will blow itself out,' Maggie said, 'if it is happening at all.'

'Perhaps it will,' Gowry said. 'As it is, I feel nothing much, not even disappointment. Isn't it sad, Maggie, not to be hurt by my wife's infidelity? That's not love, is it?'

'How long have you been married?'

'Eleven years.'

'Long enough.'

He wanted consolation not agreement. He felt sulky for a moment. He was irked by her apparent indifference, for he had traded in pity himself and understood its workings all too well.

She got slowly to her feet, pushing herself up with her hands. Until that moment he had seen her as soft but now he realised that she was burdened by age and the manner in which she moved was cautious, not patient. He shouldn't have picked up her question about Sylvie. Love was no fit subject for a grown man. What he felt for Maggie Leonard was probably not love at all but some odd distillation of all the things he had never found elsewhere. Perhaps, he thought, shaken, he was using Maggie selfishly just as Sylvie had used him or – if it were true – as the man, Hagarty, was using Sylvie.

He got to his feet too. 'I'm sorry, Maggie,' he said. 'I am, truly.'

'For what now?'

'Burdening you with my woes.'

She smiled, put down the plates she had taken from the table, placed an arm round him and hugged him.

'That's what you come here for,' Maggie said, 'is it not now?'

'It is,' said Gowry, sighing. 'I'm afraid to say it is.'

*   *   *

At eleven she closed the bar. Turk and Charlie had gone and Fran had not returned. Mr Dolan and Mr Pettu had long since gone to bed. Mr Rice and two of his traveller friends remained and would have gone on drinking half the night if Sylvie had not called a halt to it. They were not rowdy except in the clumsy way drunkards have of banging into things and laughing in great coarse shouts. Maeve would sleep through it. Maeve had been disappointed when, on his return, Turk had sung just one more song, a silly music-hall thing, before going off with Charlie.

Sylvie tapped three pints of stout and carried them to the table under the window where the men were. She unloaded the tray, put the glasses on the table and swept up the empties.

'On the house, gentlemen,' she said.

'Ish – is thish a hint, m' darlin' lady?'

'It is, Mr Rice.'

'Well, yoush – you've t' be thankit for your gen – generoshity.' He bowed his head, a gracious nod that turned into a waggle.

She pulled the iron gate up from beneath the counter and fitted it into the slots, bolted the half door and put out the lights, all save one. She fixed the guard over the coal fire, though it was nothing much but ash now, and told the men not to make a noise when they finally came to bed.

They wished her goodnight and she went out

into the hallway and climbed the staircase to Maeve's room, opened the door carefully and looked in.

In the arrow of light from the landing she saw that Maeve was fast asleep, the sheet pulled up and wrapped around her head so that only her face peeped out. Sylvie kissed her fingertip and touched it to her daughter's cheek, then tiptoed out of the room and along the corridor to the big bedroom that she and Gowry shared. She paused outside the door, heard a guffaw from downstairs and then, in the ensuing quietness, all the other small sounds that men make in the night, the clink of a jug, the clank of a chamberpot, a lion-like yawn, an explosive snore, the creak of springs as someone turned over in bed. Then, tired and unaccountably depressed, she entered the bedroom.

The flicker of the match flame made his face seem ghastly white.

'My God!' Sylvie exclaimed. 'What are you doing here? I thought you'd left with the others.'

'I came back,' Fran said. 'Are you not pleased to see me?'

'Of course I am.'

He pulled back the covers and put one bare leg out of the bed.

'I'll be going if you wish; just say the word.'

She shook her head vigorously. The sight of him naked in her husband's place in bed had fired her blood. She turned the key in the lock of the door, the door that was never locked when Gowry was at home, then walked forward to the bed. He was ready for her. Had he been lying here thinking of her, excited to be in Gowry's bed, her bed, under her roof, waiting for her as if she were a bride and he the groom?

She bent forward and kissed him on the mouth. He scooped at her skirts, bundling them about her hips, reaching up until his hands were above her stockings. He clasped her, cupped her and, in a rasping whisper, said, 'Sylvie, Sylvie! God help me, I can't get enough of you.'

She moved closer, let him untie her drawers. Closer still, tilting her hips.

He let out a groan when he slipped into her.

'Ah, God! Ah, God, Sylvie!' he said. 'You'll be the death of me yet,' then gasped as she smothered the words within him once and for all.

Chapter Six

He had made the round trip of almost two hundred and fifty miles three times in the week and he was weary, bone weary, on the last homeward run. Behind him the empty bus jolted over ruts and potholes, the headlamps so feeble that he steered more by instinct than sight. His shoulders ached and his eyes itched and he felt as if the road between Tipperary and Dublin would never end.

The depot was deserted when he reversed the bus into the last slot. He climbed down from the driver's seat, stretched his arms wide, rolled his neck, heard the *crick-crick* of little bones adjusting and felt the muscles in the small of his back ease. He tossed his cap on to the seat and went round to unhook the lid of the compartment where the brush and shovel were kept.

It was a murky night with an autumnal fog seeping in from the sea. He had been smelling clean wet earth and fresh-fallen leaves all day and the Dublin air tasted rancid. He dug out the brush and, unbuttoning his tunic, returned to the front of the charabanc only to find John James Flanagan leaning on the bonnet.

Flanagan never looked anything less than prosperous with his swallow-tail moustache and black eyebrows and the best-tailored clothes that money could buy but it was his smugness that really stuck in Gowry's throat.

'Well now, if it isn't my favourite driver come back from far-flung places.' John James rocked on the balls of his feet. 'Leave the brush, McCulloch. I'll take your logbook, though.'

'You, sir? Where's Mr Roddeny?'

'Gone home. It's late, you know.'

'Oh, I know that, Mr Flanagan,' Gowry said.

There must be a catch to it; John James Flanagan didn't drag himself away from the dinner table just to greet a driver. Gowry put the brush aside and reached for the logbook that was tucked under the driver's seat. He had been scrupulously careful about log entries and had purchased three gallons of petrol out of his own pocket to cover the extra miles he'd driven that day.

John James took the log and slipped it into the pocket of his overcoat.

'If that's all, Mr Flanagan . . .'

'Not quite,' John James said.

'Something wrong, sir?'

'Are you game for the weekend?'

'Game, Mr Flanagan?'

'Saturday night, through Sunday.'

'I've had a hard week, Mr Flanagan. Can't some-one else do it?'

'They'll all be on parade. It's a big day for parades, you know.'

Ah, Gowry thought, so it's a punishment for not being one of them. God knows he'd done enough Sunday work, standing in for men who had some religious duty to perform or some obligation to the nationalists.

'Is it more soldiers?' Gowry said. 'More recruits?'

'No, a funeral party.'

'On a Sunday?'

'We're not providing the hearse. The deceased is elsewhere. You'll be running a small party down in the limousine on Saturday afternoon and collecting them for return to Dublin late on Sunday.'

'The limousine?' Gowry said.

'Two passengers, sons of the dear departed, I believe.' Flanagan smiled, more smug and unctuous than ever. 'There'll be a little something extra in your wage packet, Gowry, if you do me this favour. Shall we say five shillings?'

The bribe explained everything. Obviously he would be ferrying some great and glorious chieftain to a secret meeting and Flanagan preferred not to use one of the regular drivers in case it aroused suspicion. There was no funeral, of course, no corpse. In the foggy half-dark at the back of the garages the conspiracy seemed so ill conceived as to be almost laughable.

'I'll do it,' Gowry said. 'Where is the — ah, deceased?'

'Woodenbridge,' Flanagan told him.

She was not so much sore as tender and the weariness that clung to her all day long eliminated any longing for Fran. In any event she was reconciled to not seeing him over the weekend. He had told her he had much writing to do and must apply himself to catch up on his deadlines.

If the other guests thought it odd that Fran Hagarty had spent the night in the Shamrock they kept their observations to themselves. Some of them were in no fit state to observe anything, of course, for an excess of black stout had taken its toll.

Sylvie got through the routine chores with Jansis's help, went to bed in the quiet of the afternoon and slept like something dead.

It was almost dark when she wakened.

She lay motionless in the bed where she and Fran had made love and thought how deceptive appearances could be, how she had misjudged him. For a man who had the reputation of being rather burned out, Mr Francis Hagarty had acquitted himself exceptionally well.

'Mam?'

Maeve was leaning over the bed-end.

Sylvie sat up quickly, her head swimming.

'Are you all right, Mam?'

'What time is it?'

'After six. Dinner time.'

'Is your father home?'

'Nuh.' Maeve gave her the wisp of a smile. 'Not yet.'

'When do we expect him?'

'Tipperary?' Maeve calculated. 'Half past nine.' She leaned closer. 'Is Mr Hagarty stayin' again tonight?'

'Mr Hagarty's gone home.'

'Why'd he stay last night?'

'He was dr— He took a drop more than was good for him.'

'I thought he went before Turk.'

'Well, he didn't.' Sylvie was puzzled by her daughter's complicity, if indeed it was complicity. 'Tell Jansis I'll be down soon. I'll need to change the sheets.'

'I'll change the sheets.'

She was too soggy for guilt to take hold. She threw back the bed covers, adjusted the throat of her nightgown to cover her breasts and, with effort, swung both feet to the floor.

'No,' she said, firmly. 'Go and help Jansis lay out the supper things.'

'Done,' Maeve said. 'All done.'

'Has Mr Dolan come downstairs yet?'

'Nuh.'

'Knock on his door. Tell him supper in twenty

minutes.' She was still woolly-headed, leaden limbed. 'How many casuals do we have in?'

'Four.'

'Who booked them?'

'Jansis. I helped.'

'Suppers?'

'Five – and Mr Pettu if he's back in time.'

'I'll be downstairs directly,' Sylvie said.

She waited for her daughter to leave but Maeve remained, elbows on the bed-end, chin resting on her knuckles. She seemed fascinated by the sight of her mother in her nightgown at six in the evening and smiled the enigmatic little smile that she, Sylvie, had once had down to perfection.

'Stop staring at me,' Sylvie said, testily. 'Go away.'

'Aye-aye, sir,' Maeve said and snapping off a military salute, marched out of the bedroom and galloped downstairs.

'What is it, Gowry? What do you want with me?'

'You know what I want with you.'

'I don't feel like it. I'm not – not right.'

'You weren't right a fortnight ago. Is something wrong with you?'

'Nothing is wrong with me,' Sylvie said.

'If something's wrong, you should see a doctor.'

'I don't need a doctor. I drank too much port last night, that's all.'

'Who with?'

'Oh, they were all in,' Sylvie said, 'having a sing-song.'

'Who bought you the port?'

'Mr Rice; you know what he's like.'

'Who was singing?'

'All of them.'

'Including Trotter?'

She had drawn away from him under the sheets. The sheets still had a stiff, unfolded feel to them and the faint, sawdust smell of the cupboard. She felt closer to the sheets than she did to Gowry. She wanted only peace, silence, sleep, and would do nothing to encourage the routine signals that would end with him on top of her. She would only give him what he wanted if there was no other way to stop him asking awkward questions.

She sighed. 'How could I keep him out?'

'Charlie was with him, I suppose, and my father?'

'Not your father, just Charlie.'

Gowry shifted from her and crossed his arms over his chest in a position that reminded her of the effigies of dead kings.

'What did they want?'

'Nothing,' Sylvie said. 'A drink and a place to meet, that's all.'

'Did anyone else turn up?'

'No, just Turk and Charlie – and the commercials, of course.'

'I don't want them drinking here. Let them drink elsewhere.'

Jessica Stirling

'They always pay the slate, Gowry. They're good customers.'

'They are not good customers,' Gowry said. 'They're not good anything. Was Hagarty with them?'

Fran's name on her husband's lips shocked her. It was all she could do not to sit bolt upright and cry out: *Who told you about Fran? What have they been saying about me?* Controlling herself as best she could, she lay like a stone in a river and let cold fear ripple over her. If Gowry had learned from one of the commercials or, say, from Mr Dolan that Fran had stayed overnight and she denied it then he would know she was hiding something, and even staid, unimaginative Gowry would surely deduce what it was.

'Have you ever read any of the stupid articles he writes?'

'Some folk don't think they're stupid,' Sylvie said.

'Aye, Maeve thinks he's wonderful.'

'Maeve?'

'It's Whiteside, her teacher. He shouldn't be filling young heads with that republican nonsense. Damned propagandist. Pettu has been giving her newspapers too. Unsuitable material for a young girl,' Gowry said. 'What chance does the child have of developing a mind of her own if this goes on?'

'If what goes on?' Sylvie said.

'This systematic corruption.'

'Oh come, Gowry, it's hardly corruption.'

'What is it then?'

'Politics, just politics.'

'Aye well, it's politics that's killing men in Flanders, is it not?'

'Dearest, I'm tired,' Sylvie said. 'Please don't rant on. It's not my fault the country's in the state it's in. If you still want to . . .' She touched his thigh.

'No,' he said. 'No, I don't.'

'I thought you did?'

'I was just being polite.'

'Polite?'

'You know what I mean.'

'I don't know what you mean,' said Sylvie.

'I don't think you even *want* another baby.'

'Oh!' she exclaimed, surprised. 'Babies, is that all?'

For once she had failed to follow the little jumps and rabbit hops of her husband's reasoning. Had he been thinking of babies when he put his hand upon her, or had it been a manoeuvre to catch her off guard? No, Gowry wasn't devious. It was the sort of thing she might expect from Fran, but not from her husband.

'Soon,' Gowry said, 'you'll be too old for babies.'

'I will not. I've years left yet, years. I'm not trying *not* to have babies, you know,' Sylvie said. 'It isn't my fault.'

And then it occurred to her that all the energy, all the passion that she'd put into coupling with Fran might jog nature into doing what it had been reluctant to do before. If she became pregnant what would she tell Fran? What would Fran do? How would he react? Cold fear rippled over her once more.

'What is it, Gowry?' she said. 'What's really troubling you?'

He gave a cough and a grunt. 'Flanagan. I'm working at the weekend.'

'Oh!'

'Toadying to that bloody hypocrite is beginning to get me down.'

'Will . . .' Sylvie said, 'will you be away overnight?'

'Saturday,' he said. 'Back home Sunday, late.'

'Is it soldiers again?'

'No, a funeral.'

'At least you'll get to drive the limousine,' said Sylvie.

'That's some consolation I suppose,' Gowry said and, grunting again, butted the bolster with his fist and settled down to sleep while Sylvie, fretting and wide awake now, lay like a stone at his side.

Flanagan had ordered one of the latest Benz limousines during his last visit to Germany. There had been great excitement among John James's drivers when the car had arrived from the docks, for somehow they had got it into their heads that what was being delivered was a 'Blitzen-Benz' racing car akin to the one that had set the world record at a hundred and twenty-five miles per hour. Disappointment ensued;

the limousine, though handsome, was clearly built for passenger comfort rather than out-and-out speed. Gowry was less disappointed than most. The high, elegant vehicle reminded him a little of the Lanchester he'd driven for the Franklins, though the Benz was no bone-shaker and could do fifty even on poor roads.

On Friday evening he suggested to Roddeny that it might be sensible to come home on Saturday night, but Roddeny would have none of it. The log had been filled out, the route planned and, damn me, wasn't he being paid enough of a bonus? Gowry didn't argue. Once he dropped the clients he would be free until Sunday afternoon. Woodenbridge was forty-five miles from Dublin, Tipperary a hundred and ten. He could cover sixty-odd miles in a couple of hours in the Benz and be at Maggie's cottage in ample time for supper.

On Saturday afternoon he picked the clients up outside the Vincentian RC church at Phibsborough. He had brushed his uniform, sponged his cap, polished his boots, for even if the status of the men meant nothing to him and he was opposed to everything they stood for, he wanted no complaints leaking back to J. J. Flanagan.

The men were waiting on the pavement. He didn't have to ask if they were his hire. They wore heavy tweed overcoats and flat caps and had black crape armbands on their sleeves. They were youngish chaps, early thirties. One was bearded, the other clean-shaven. Both had the damp, sullen eyes of slaughter men, though, and Gowry didn't dare inspect them too closely for fear of giving offence.

He opened the door of the passenger compart-ment. They climbed in. They said nothing, not even good afternoon, gave him no instruction and spoke not a word throughout the length of the journey to Woodenbridge or, rather, to the gates of the Nugget Hotel between the Bridge and Avoca, where the beard, knocking on the glass partition, told Gowry to draw up.

The men climbed out of the Benz and stood by the roadside.

The gates of the Nugget were open. The drive-way, about a quarter of a mile long and flanked by oak trees, was deserted.

The men loitered, hands in pockets.

They had no luggage.

Gowry waited in the cab.

'What's wrong wit' you?' the beard asked.

'What time will I collect you tomorrow, sir?' Gowry said.

The beard glanced at his companion. 'Three o'clock?'

'Three o'clock it is, sir,' said Gowry. 'Where?'

'Here on this very spot.'

'I'll be here at three tomorrow, gentlemen,' Gowry said. 'Good-day to you.'

He touched his cap, threw the big lever to put the Benz in gear and drove off along the road to Woodenbridge, heading out towards Arklow and hence by Waterford and Clonmel to Maggie Leonard's cottage in the hills.

The kitchen was filled with steam. She had decided to serve the guests a dish of creamed salt cod and had forgotten just how 'niffy' cooking fish could be. She had only made enough for six. Being Saturday many of the commercials had gone out and would not be back for supper. She was stirring egg whites and parsley into the big saucepan when Fran came into the kitchen.

Maeve was in the dining-room setting out cutlery, Jansis lighting the little coal fire in the bar. Sylvie held the empty saucer over the pan and wafted at the steam with her free hand.

'Fran?'

'Here I am, in the flesh.'

He looked better than he had three days ago. He had some colour in his cheeks and seemed somehow fatter. She guessed that he had been at the bottle and when he kissed her she smelled whiskey on his breath. Though he was far from intoxicated, he had a liveliness on him that amounted almost to impudence. He even had the temerity to pinch her bottom.

She giggled and slapped away his hand.

'Is there some of that for me?' Fran said.

'Some of what?' she said.

'Whatever's in your little pot.'

'Not so much of the little pot.'

'Big pot then,' he said.

'Give me that spoon,' Sylvie said.

'This one?' He held the spoon out, erect. 'This one?'

'Don't play the fool, Fran,' Sylvie said, laughing. 'I need to stir.'

'I'll stir. I'm a grand man for the stirring.'

'I know you are.' She snatched the spoon from him. 'But you'd be wasting your talents on a piece of salt cod. Are you staying for supper?'

'I am,' he said. 'For breakfast too if you'll have me.'

She stirred the sauce, beat it gently for a moment or two, then pulled a hot dish from the oven and poured the cod into it.

Hands on hips, Fran watched her work.

His shabby black coat had been replaced by a new Ascot with Italian lining and a velvet collar. He wore a roll-collar shirt with a neat little bow tie in spotted silk. He'd had his hair trimmed and looked, Sylvie thought, like a well-to-do poet or a successful playwright.

'How did you know about Gowry?' Sylvie asked.

'What about Gowry?'

'That he'd be gone all night?'

Fran was not languid tonight. He looked ruddy and jovial and when Maeve bounded into the kitchen, he spread his arms and sang out, '*Tra-la!*'

'I thought I heard the voices,' Maeve said.

'Never admit to hearing the voices. Joan of Arc

heard the voices,' Fran told the child, 'and look what happened to her.'

'She burned,' said Maeve. 'See, I know about Joan of Arc.'

'All little girls do,' said Fran. 'She's a heroine to little girls.'

'I'm not a little girl.'

'Young ladies. I mean young ladies.'

'Wonder what they sounded like, them voices,' said Maeve.

'Like this, perhaps.' Cupping his hands to his mouth, Fran uttered a hollow stage whisper. 'I'm huuun-gery, Joan. I waaa-nt my dinnn-ner.'

Maeve laughed.

Sylvie laughed too, her question concerning Gowry lost in the general merriment and the promise of the night to come.

It was one of those lovely autumn twilights with the moon not just big but huge. In the cool evening air the scents of farmlands and pinewoods were heady beyond belief. At the wheel of the German limousine, Gowry sang to himself as he drove past Mockler's Hill and through Cashel and came within sight of the graceful peaks.

He sang sweet songs, not war songs or the coarse songs that had been dinned into his head at the Tivoli music hall where Sylvie and Maeve dragged him whenever they could manufacture an excuse. He sang without words, lips pursed, shoulders bowed, hands light on the wheel and he spared no thought for the men he had dropped off at the Nugget.

He prowled the car up to the front of the cottage. He hoped that Maggie would come out and say, 'Gowry, what's this?' as if the elegant motor-car belonged to him and he had brought it to her like a trophy.

There was no sign of Maggie but a man came around the gable lugging a hay-bag over his shoulder. He wore a khaki shirt, puttees and good leather boots: Maggie's son, the Connaught Ranger, Gowry guessed, and felt the excitement go out of him. He clambered from the cab and introduced himself.

Sergeant Maurice Leonard grinned broadly, slung the hay-bag against the wall and in a deep, hearty voice said, 'McCulloch, I'll be bound. Gowry McCulloch. Is my mother expectin' you?'

'No, ah – I thought I'd surprise her.'

'Fine motor. Damned fine. Benz, isn't it?'

'Aye.'

'Give Jerry his due, he knows how to build motor-cars.' The sergeant came forward and shook Gowry's hand. 'You'll not be delivering rookies to the Tip in this, I'm thinking.'

'No, mourners for a funeral party.'

'Ah! Ah-hah! Well, come along inside. My mam *will* be pleased to see you. She speaks very highly of you, Mr McCulloch.' With a wave of the arm he ushered Gowry into the cottage where Maggie, all flour as usual, was putting the lid on a beefsteak pie. She looked up and beamed.

'Gowry! I didn't hear the bus.'

'No bus today, Mam,' Maurice said. 'A German limousine, no less.'

Dusting her hands on her apron, she came forward and clasped him to her bosom. 'Ah now!' she said. 'Both of you together. Isn't it a grand thing to have both my boys together in the house at once?'

And Gowry, with a hollow feeling in his heart, agreed.

Turk was up for it. Turk was always up for it. He had brought six bottles of stout and a half of whiskey down with him inside the knapsack, wrapped in the thin blanket that would keep out the chill of the night. He didn't expect to sleep. The boy, Kevin, had come equipped like one of Teddy Roosevelt's rough riders with a bedroll and groundsheet, packets of tea and sugar and several tins of baked beans.

They had walked from the railway station to the inn that overlooked the confluence of waters where the Aughrim flowed into the Avoca. They had tramped up and down for a piece before they found the field, the only possible field, where John Redmond would meet not only with the Irish National Volunteers but with a hail of bullets that would give the bastard something to take back to bloody Westminster with him – so Turk said, rubbing his hands in glee.

Above the field was a wooded hillside with several steep faces and enough cover to hide an army but the road that ran along the margin of the river offered scant protection. The road, that Saturday evening, had been cluttered with cart traffic and folk tramping back from the little towns, and once they had marked the line of the road Turk and the boy had cleared off into the woods above the field.

Hidden by trees and faded ferns they had hunkered under a shelf of rock. It was a fine place to camp, Turk had said, and had opened his knapsack and dug out the bottles. Kevin had been all for lighting a fire to heat the beans but Turk would have none of it and they had eaten the beans cold, washed down with stout.

It had been a long, damp night, though there was no rain.

Turk had talked and talked, his voice low and confiding in the darkness. He had told the boy all he could remember of the wild disturbers, led by General Holt, who had engaged the king's forces, horse and foot, in this very glen and who, being steadfast and disciplined for once, had routed them and sent them trailing back to barracks with their tails between their legs.

Before the tale was halfway done, Kevin had fallen asleep.

Back to the rock, Turk draped the thin blanket about his shoulders and kept watch, dreaming and muttering, keeping himself warm that way. And by the time the sun filtered through the trees and the mist rose from the river, Turk was up for it. By God, was he not!

The mountains seemed higher in the morning light, Gowry thought, as he stepped, blinking, out of the cottage door.

The sergeant had been up for hours by the look of him, though he had drunk twice as much as Gowry and had not gone to bed until well after two. They had sat up talking, the three of them, seated round the fireside with the bottle going back and forth and the sergeant as relaxed as any man Gowry had ever seen, lying in an old rattan armchair with a glass in his hand and his pipe in his mouth, his long legs stretched out, big bare feet toasting on the hearth.

Gowry had seldom talked so openly or listened with such rapt attention. There was no heat in their discussion, however, for they were all agreed that politics was a mug's game and was it not a crying shame that politicians controlled the fighting men and not the other way about. When Gowry finally went to bed he had slept like a baby, falling off the cliff of consciousness with the woman's voice and the sergeant's rumbling laughter drifting up from the room below.

'Top o' the mornin' to you, Gowry,' Maurice called out. 'Sleep well?'

'Aye, like a baby,' Gowry said. 'And you?'

'Never a dream to trouble me,' Maurice said. 'How long will you be with us?'

'I'll need to be off about half past noon.'

'Bound for Dublin?'

'No, for Woodenbridge.'

'For the parade?' Maurice said.

'Parade? What parade?'

'The volunteers parade on Sundays in the field by the river. I've heard John Redmond, the MP, will be stopping by today to address them.'

'Well, I've no interest in hearing what Redmond has to say.'

'I thought you supported his policies?'

'I do,' said Gowry, 'but that's no reason to want to hear him spout.'

'He'll need to make a damned good speech to justify himself,' Maurice said. 'If we don't muster enough recruits for the regiments the War Office won't send us to France. It would be a helluva shame if the Rangers were denied an opportunity to fight because of a few hot-heads.'

'Are you training men for France?'

'We would be delighted to train men for front-line combat,' Maurice said, 'but we've no weapons and no sign of weapons, so it's just drill, drill and more bloody drill.' He tossed the hay-bag into the shed. The ponies stood in the big paddock, their tails to the breeze, all sturdy and patient. From across the plain a church bell announced an early mass. Maurice put a hand on Gowry's shoulder and clapped him as if he were a pony, or a homesick recruit. 'If you do happen to bump into old Johnny Redmond at Woodenbridge this afternoon,' he said, 'tell him from me that the Irish brigades are ready and willing to fight but that we need proper weapons to do it. Tell him to convince the English that we need arms.'

Gowry laughed. 'Sure an' I will,' he said, then, linking arms with the affable sergeant, went back into the cottage to eat.

There were more flat caps than bowlers in the field by the river and a multitude of dogs sniffed about the legs of the volunteers. There were two or three officers in uniform with lanyards and sheathed swords but not a revolver among the lot of them that Turk could see. Only a handful of the rank and file had rifles and when he wriggled closer Turk saw that most of them were dummies. There were pikestaffs here and there but nothing sleek enough to be hurled across the river or into the wooded slopes. The parade was casual and disorganised, not at all like the Dublin parades Turk had marched in; the Woodenbridge volunteers looked like what they were, farmers pretending to be fighting men.

Squinting down at the gathering Turk felt vague distaste for the job he had to do; the men below might have been his cousins or his uncles and, in spirit at least, he was one with them. He focused his attention on the officers, those tools of authority with their braid and swords and strutting manners.

Crawling on his belly through the yellowing ferns, he searched for the best angle from which to place his shots.

Kevin was back in the woods loading the rifles. They had picked up the rifles from the roadside without a hitch and so far Fran Hagarty's plan was working.

Turk felt a lot better now he had the rifles and was on the move.

He studied the field carefully. Rank and file faced the river. He would fire over their heads. One officer – MacSweeney? – kept fishing out his pocket watch and glancing anxiously towards the high road; Turk reckoned that Redmond must be due to arrive very soon.

The field had been mown and was covered with tufts and tussocks and the officers in their tall riding boots hobbled and lost balance now and then. The men were steady, though, as they formed up and squared off into platoons. There were a hundred or more spectators gathered round the perimeter of the field, old men mostly, and boys in knickerbockers and stiff collars, all thoroughly enjoying themselves on that fine Sunday afternoon.

Turk found his spot, a stubbly hump in the midst of the ferns, the crown worn bare by rabbits. He eased himself on to his backside, cross-legged like a tailor. He braced his elbows against his hips and aimed an imaginary rifle. There would be no killing; Fran had been adamant about that. By Gad, though, would it not be a joy to pop off an officer or two and see their sabres spin away and their heads burst open when the bullets struck?

He sighted on MacSweeney, shaped a soundless little '*pah-pah-pah*' with his lips, then, grinning, blew away invisible smoke just as Johnny Redmond's lackeys appeared on the path from the high road and MacSweeney marched across the grass to greet them, drawing his ceremonial sword as he went.

'Yes,' Turk said, under his breath. 'Yes,' then retreated backward through the ferns to fetch young Kevin and the guns.

Chapter Seven

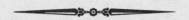

They brought him into Dublin Castle through the gateway at the top of Cork Hill; Dublin Castle, that dismal pile of brick and stone disposed around two courts at the top of Parliament Street. He had never been inside the castle before, for he was not the sort of man who kept company with government officials and he had no interest in visiting the state apartments. His father had told him about the horrors of the place, however, the Devil's Half Acre, where in the old days rebels had been flogged and tortured and thrown into prison.

He was sweating heavily inside his uniform, his hands so knotted on the steering wheel that he could scarcely make the lock that brought the limousine into the courtyard. He was scared all right and when the detective, Ames, poked him with the barrel of the revolver he almost jumped out of his skin.

'What is it now?' Gowry said, shrilly.

'We can't go any further,' Ames told him. 'Stop here.'

Gowry braked, slewing the rear wheels on the damp cobbles.

They had entered under the Bedford Tower, under the statue of Justice, but he didn't expect to find much justice here. The detective hunkered beside him. In the back seat were another plainclothes copper and two RIC constables.

He yanked on the handbrake, turned off the engine and waited, sweating in the cool evening air.

Ames poked him again: 'Out.'

Gowry climbed from the seat and lowered himself to the cobbles.

The constables went out through the side door, batons unsheathed.

At least they hadn't cuffed him. Perhaps they would do so now.

When they'd pounced on him outside the Nugget he'd assumed they would impound Flanagan's motor-car and jail him somewhere in Wicklow. Instead they'd shoved him back into the driver's seat and told him to head for Dublin.

'What am I supposed to have done?' he'd shouted. 'You can't just go lifting me for no reason. I've passengers to collect.'

'Passengers, is it?' Ames had said. 'Where are they then, these passengers?'

'I – I don't know. Maybe they're up at the hotel.'

'Aye, and maybe they've fled wi'out you.'

'What do you mean? Fled?'

'Done a bunk,' the cohort had said. 'Run off.'

'They were brothers, two of them, attending a funeral.'

'Brothers, were they?' the cohort had said. 'I don't doubt it.'

'Attending your funeral, McCulloch,' Ames had said, and laughed.

'*What's going on? What the hell is going on?*'

But they had parried all his questions and wouldn't even tell him what crime he was supposed to have committed, or where they were taking him.

He had heard of this happening to mysterious figures in the secret societies, to militant socialists and those suspected of being in league with the Germans, but he had chosen to believe that everyone who was lifted and imprisoned without a fair trial was guilty of sedition in one form or another. It was not a point he'd dared argue with Charlie, though, for Charlie knew everyone who was anyone in the organisations and Charlie, God help him, still believed in martyrdom.

Ames grabbed his arm and jerked him round to face the arch that led to the lower court. Gowry resisted. 'What'll happen to the limousine? I'm supposed to be responsible for Mr Flanagan's motorcar.'

'You've more to worry you now, McCulloch, than Flanagan's motor-car,' Ames said and steered him beneath the archway and across the lower courtyard to the Ship Street gate.

Ship Street: Sheep Street: lambs to the slaughter: heads around the walls: the old tower towering over him: before him the oldest part of the city, narrow alleys and streets, mostly dark and dirty, tenements inhabited only by the poorest classes. Gowry knew that the story of the city was contained therein and that the names – Nicholas Street, Fishamble, Bridge and Winetavern – reeked of history and worried that perhaps he might be on his way to becoming part of it.

They marched him between them, pinning his arms. He watched the sky darkening into night, clouds coalescing, the damp reddish tint of autumn twilight compressed by the narrow ways. He heard his heels echo on broken pavements, the *skiff-skiff-skliff* of the detectives' shoes. Then they pushed him into a doorway.

He saw another door, solid as the Rock of Cashel. It swung open. He was bundled into a building, a tall clean building that rose up like a pencil-box in the midst of the stinking tenements. And when the door thudded shut behind him he was engulfed by a great black wave of despair.

'It is not incumbent upon me to declare charges at this stage in the proceedings,' Vaizey said. 'Under the new emergency powers act, however, I may detain you for a period of three days if, in my judgement, you represent a threat to security. Do you understand that, Mr McCulloch?'

'I do,' Gowry said.

'Do you know why you have been brought here?'

'No, I do not.'

'I suppose you'll be telling me next you don't know what happened at Woodenbridge this afternoon,' the inspector said.

'I only know I was jumped on by a dozen policemen at the Nugget Hotel.'

'You still stand by your story then?'

'Story?' Gowry said. 'What story?'

'The story you told to my man.'

'I didn't tell him any sort of story,' Gowry said. 'I was given no opportunity to tell him anything before he—'

'Something about a funeral, I believe.'

'That's no story; that's the plain fact of the matter,' Gowry said. 'If you're not willing to take my word for it, check my logbook. I was hired to drive two men from Dublin to the Nugget Hotel at Woodenbridge yesterday afternoon and collect them again at three o'clock today.'

'Who were these men? What were their names?'

'I've no idea,' said Gowry. 'I was told they were brothers going to a funeral.'

'You have a brother, don't you, Mr McCulloch?' Vaizey said.

'Several,' Gowry said.

So it was Charlie, was it? Charlie had finally dropped him into the mire. Anger frizzled within him. He straightened on the stool that Ames had placed before the desk. There was no window, only a grating high on the wall with an oblong of smoked glass behind it, the room shorn of all furniture except for a table, a chair and the stool. Ames leaned against the wall under a gas bracket that hissed and flamed erratically. Vaizey was seated at the table.

'Name them,' Vaizey said.

'Peter, Charlie and Forbes.'

'Forbes?'

'He lives in Glasgow. He's been there for years.'

'What does he do in Glasgow?'

'He's in shipping,' Gowry said.

'Ah!' said Vaizey. 'Yes, married to one of the Franklins. I have him now.'

Mention of his older brother's name only added to Gowry's apprehension.

He wondered if Forbes was involved somehow, if the surly pair he'd conveyed to Woodenbridge were emissaries from Forbes. He wouldn't put it past Forbes to be mixed up in shady dealings.

'Charlie,' Vaizey said. 'Tell me more about Charlie.'

'There's nothing to tell. Him an' me don't rub along.'

'He drinks at your house.'

'It isn't my house. It's my wife's house.'

'He drinks there with known criminals.'

'Charlie isn't a criminal,' Gowry said. 'He's a brewer.'

'Was it not Charlie who asked you to drive those thugs to Woodenbridge?'

'Of course it wasn't Charlie. Mr Flanagan assigned me. If you don't believe me, ask Mr Flanagan.'

'We have,' Vaizey said.

'Well, there you are,' said Gowry.

'Mr Flanagan denies all knowledge . . .'

Gowry shot to his feet and would have lunged across the table if Ames hadn't grabbed him and flung him to the floor. He landed on his elbows and tailbone. His anger did not abate. He had been betrayed, betrayed by Flanagan, made Flanagan's scapegoat. He struggled to his knees.

'Bad boy,' Ames said, shaking his head. 'Bad, bad boy.'

Gowry sat back, propped on his hands. The detective towered above him like a part of the masonry. All he could see of the inspector was shoes, stockings, trouser legs and, separated by the plane of the table, a bland, almost uninterested face peering down at him.

Vaizey gave his moustache a little wipe with his forefinger. 'It's not going to profit any of us if you go all redheaded. What did they look like, these men? Had you seen either of them before?'

'No,' Gowry said. 'They were strangers to me. One had a beard.'

'Aw now, there's a tellin' detail, sir, is it not?' said Ames.

'They were well dressed,' Gowry said. 'They were about my age.'

'What did they say to you?' Vaizey, still leaning over the table, asked.

'Hardly a word,' said Gowry. 'Told me to collect them at three o'clock at the gate of the Nugget Hotel where — where you — your boys were waiting for me.'

'Were they staying at that hotel?'

'I thought they were. I dropped them at the gate.'

'When did you drop them?'

'Yesterday afternoon, about three or half past.'

'And then,' said Vaizey, 'you returned to Dublin?'

Gowry hesitated. It was the first question he could not answer truthfully.

He said, 'I did not come back to Dublin.'

'Did not come back to Dublin?' Vaizey said. 'Why not?'

'I lodged out.'

'How far is it from Woodenbridge to Dublin? About forty miles?'

'Nearer fifty,' Gowry said, dry-mouthed.

'In that machine, the German machine, how long would it take you to—'

'I was told to lodge out,' Gowry said.

'Told? By whom?'

'Mr Roddeny.'

'Not Mr Flanagan?'

'Yes, by Mr Flanagan.'

'Which is it?' the inspector said.

'I was offered a bonus for——'

'A bonus,' Vaizey put in, 'for a forty – pardon – a fifty-mile drive? He's surely a very generous employer, your Mr Flanagan.'

'It was Saturday.'

'Do you not usually work on Saturday?'

'I do, but . . .' Gowry paused once more. 'I didn't want to do it.'

'Do what?' said Vaizey.

'Go to Woodenbridge. Make the run.'

'Why not?'

'I'd been on the road all week, up and down to the Tip – to Tipperary running recruits to the training camp.'

'Tipperary,' Vaizey said. 'Now that is a fair way to travel.'

'It is.'

'But Woodenbridge is not.'

'I was told to stay over.'

'Where,' Vaizey said, 'did you lodge last night?'

'In a boarding-house.'

The lie was out before he could stop it.

He suspected that the inspector might know where he had stayed but he would not be drawn into betraying Maggie Leonard no matter what they did to him. If they found the guns in the loft of the cottage in the Galtees then Maggie, and Maurice too, would be arrested. He could not allow that to happen.

'In Woodenbridge?' Vaizey said.

'No, in Arklow,' Gowry said.

He was gone now, patently gone. He had stepped into the pitfall he'd dug for himself all those weeks ago when he'd appropriated Charlie's guns and hidden them out of harm's way. He had done it with the best of intentions, but Vaizey would never swallow that tale. He was still on the floor, legs stuck out. He leaned back, swaying away from Ames, and cocked his head. He was no longer angry and his fear had lessened, leaving wiliness, a sensation of cleverness that might prove to be his undoing. He would have to play Vaizey's game now, however.

'Do you recall the name of the guest-house?' Vaizey said.

'No, sir, I do not.'

'Oh, really! Were you drunk?'

'All right,' Gowry said. 'I'll tell you the truth: I slept in the back of the limousine.'

'Slept in the limousine?' said Vaizey. 'Do you often sleep in your vehicle?'

'Not in the bus,' said Gowry. 'The limousine's different.'

'Why did you sleep—'

'To save money,' Gowry interrupted. 'The limousine's warm and comfortable and sleeping in it saved me one and sixpence. You want to know what I did last night; I'll tell you then. I drove back to Arklow and went into a pub and had a drink, then I ate fish and chips from a newspaper and walked on the strand for a bit and then I went back to the motor-car and fell asleep in the passenger compartment.'

'You were drunk?'

'I wasn't drunk,' Gowry said, 'I was tired.'

'I see,' said Vaizey. 'Boris, will you help Mr McCulloch to his feet, please.'

Reluctantly the burly detective extended a hand.

Gowry ignored it. He lifted himself up with an agility that surprised him. He dusted his trousers with the flat of his hand and seated himself again on the little three-legged stool. He wasn't daft enough to suppose that the interrogation was over or that his tale of sleeping out in the Benz had cut any ice with the policeman. He had bought himself breathing space, though, and decided there and then to stick with the lie and brazen it out.

In a half-hour it would be dark. The bell of St Olave's sounded across the water, one sonorous note repeated again and again, as if to summon down the night. In the hallway of the Shamrock the grandmother clock *tocked*. In the bar the moon-faced clock seemed to whirr like mad as Sylvie dashed in and out of the kitchen, in and out of the bar, torn by a desire to keep Fran with her as long as possible and to be rid of him before Gowry came home.

Fran was settled in the bar reading the latest issue of *Irish Freedom*, drinking a glass of stout and showing no sign of wishing to leave.

They had made love in the night and billed and cooed throughout the morning whenever they could steal a moment. He had accompanied Maeve and she to church and was waiting for them when they came out. She had walked with him down Sperryhead Road without a shred of guilt, let the neighbours think what they like. Francis Hagarty was just as entitled to stay at the Shamrock as anyone else.

Maeve did not seem to mind. She skipped and chattered and strove to draw Fran's attention to herself, for which she could hardly be blamed. They ate lunch in the kitchen, walked again in the afternoon when Maeve had gone to Bible Class, then came back to drink tea in the parlour and, so Sylvie thought, say farewell. But Fran had idled away the hour between five and six when the guests were beginning to drift in – only three of them – and Gowry was presumably whizzing back up the road from Woodenbridge.

'Is he not for goin' yet?' Jansis hissed.

'I don't know,' Sylvie whispered.

'He shouldn't be here at all at this hour.'

'I know.'

'The fur'll fly if—'

'For God's sake, Jansis, that's enough!'

'I'll tell him, if ye like. I'll even be polite about it.'

'No.' Sylvie hesitated, biting her thumb. 'No, I can't ask him to leave.'

'Does he not know Mr McCulloch's due back? Does he not understand?'

'Oh, yes, he understands,' said Sylvie, and it was Fran's understanding that worried her most of all.

'Now, McCulloch,' the inspector said, 'you may as well come clean. You didn't sleep in the motor-car at all, did you?'

'Aye, I did.'

Ames was behind him now and he waited tensely for a blow to the back of his head. Surely it was only a matter of time before Vaizey gave the signal for the beatings to begin. He clenched his fists, poked them down between his knees, and tucked his chin to his breastbone.

'Perhaps I did have too much to drink,' Gowry conceded.

'Where did you have breakfast?'

'I ate some bread.'

'Where did you buy the bread?'

'I had it with me.'

'What did you do today?'

'What d'you mean?'

'How did you spend the morning? Did you walk on the strand again? Fish from the rocks? Ride a donkey?'

'I walked on the strand.'

'Where was the Benz?'

'Where I left it.'

'And where was that?' said Vaizey.

'On a road by the shore.'

'Good,' Vaizey said. 'Someone's bound to have noticed it. In fact, unless I miss my guess, the presence of a German motor-car in Arklow will have drawn quite a crowd. It shouldn't be difficult to corroborate your story, if it's the truth.'

'It isn't the truth,' said Ames. 'He's lyin' in his face.'

'Really, Boris?' said Vaizey. 'What makes you so sure?'

'The clocking device attached to the wheel o' the motor-car showed it had been driven a lot further than fifty miles,' Ames said. 'One hundred an' seventy-one miles for to be exact.'

'Perhaps,' said Vaizey, 'the clocking device wasn't set properly when Mr McCulloch left Flanagan's garage?'

'The clocking mechanism's always set at zero before a journey,' Ames said. 'I checked that fact wi' Mr Flanagan.'

'When?' Gowry heard himself say.

'None o' your bloody business when,' Ames told him.

There was no point in arguing. He had been betrayed by Flanagan, set up by Flanagan. Someone had told the officers to check the clock – which meant someone knew about Maggie. He still had no notion of the nature of the crime of which he stood accused and could only assume that it had to do with the smuggled guns.

'You're not a nationalist, Mr McCulloch, are you?' Vaizey asked.

'I certainly am not.'

'Not a member of the Brotherhood of Erin, say?'

'No.'

'Not associated with any subversive group?'

'No, I'm not,' said Gowry.

'So you had no reason to take part in a plot to murder John Redmond?'

Gowry opened his mouth but no sound came out. He gaped at Vaizey. Redmond at Woodenbridge, the parade this afternoon; his conversation with Maurice Leonard came rushing back. Shooting; an assassination. He could be hanged just for being involved. Was that what they thought he was doing in Woodenbridge at three o'clock this afternoon? Picking up the assassins? He closed his mouth and sat silent for four or five seconds while Vaizey gently stroked his moustache and waited patiently for an answer.

'Do you expect me to believe that you didn't know Johnny Redmond would be inspecting the ranks at Woodenbridge this afternoon?' Vaizey said, at length.

'I – I heard about it only this morning.'

'This morning? From whom?'

'Someone. I don't know.'

'Where did you really spend the night?' Vaizey said.

'In Tipperary,' Gowry said.

'Is that where you've been keeping the guns?'

'Guns? What guns? I don't know what you're talking about.'

'Was it Charlie who asked you to hide the guns?' Vaizey said, picking up the pace of his questioning. 'Was it Charlie or your father who persuaded you to hide the German Mausers safe out of Dublin? Was it Charlie or your father or Eamon Trotter you were supposed to pick up today at the gate of the Nugget Hotel right after the shots were fired?'

'Was Redmond killed?' Gowry asked.

'Answer my question, please.'

'There's nothing to answer,' Gowry said. 'I know nothing about guns and I had no idea Redmond was even going to be in Woodenbridge until this morning.'

'What were you doing in Tipperary?'

'I was with a woman,' Gowry said.

'Ah!' said Vaizey. 'I see. A married woman?'

'Yes.'

'Whose reputation you intend to protect at all costs?' Vaizey said.

'I won't tell you her name, if that's what you mean,' Gowry said.

'Aye well, you might swing for the sake of this woman,' said Ames. 'I think he's lyin', boss, don't you?'

'I'm not so sure,' Vaizey said. 'Frankly, I'm not so sure at all.'

*　　*　　*

'I wonder,' Sylvie said, as casually as possible, 'where your daddy is right now?'

'If he was picking the clients up at three he should be back any minute,' Maeve said, 'unless they sent him on somewhere.'

'Sent him on?' said Sylvie. 'On a Sunday night?'

'You never know what Mr Flanagan will do,' said Maeve. 'Do you know Mr Flanagan, Fran?'

'We've met once or twice,' Fran said.

'Where would that be now?' said Maeve.

'Here and there.'

'No, I mean,' Maeve insisted, 'where?'

'Don't be impertinent,' said Sylvie. 'Let Fran enjoy his supper.'

Maeve lifted her pork chop and gnawed at it, snipping away the meat that adhered to the bone. Sylvie watched, too nervous and preoccupied to chide her daughter for her manners. From the tub room behind the larder came the sound of crockery being thrown about, for Jansis had said that she would eat her supper later and had begun washing up. Mr Dolan had gone to bed, Mr Pettu to chapel and Mr Rice – she wasn't sure where Mr Rice had got to.

'What time *is* it?' Sylvie heard herself say.

Fran wiped his fingers on his handkerchief and extracted a watch from his pocket, a watch she had never seen before, not cheap nickel, but heavy silver. He flipped open the case. 'Twenty minutes to eight o'clock.'

'That's a nice thing,' said Maeve. 'Did it cost a lot of money?'

'Maeve . . .'

Sylvie's reprimand tailed off. She could not look at him now, or at Maeve, the pair of them so cosy, so casual, as if they were hell-bent on stretching her nerves to breaking point. She should tell him to leave. Should insist. Should make it clear that while she loved him she didn't want to see her husband hurt.

She watched Fran swing the watch on its chain in front of Maeve, like one of the Mesmerists she'd seen on the stage of the Tivoli. She heard his voice, languid and creamy, telling Maeve that the watch had been a gift, a token of appreciation from friends in America. Heard Maeve say she longed to visit America. Heard Fran promise that he would take her there one day.

She got to her feet, pushing back her chair. 'For God's sake,' she snapped, 'where is he? What's happened to my husband?'

Fran continued to hold the watch in front Maeve's eyes, spinning, spinning, pausing and reversing, spinning again, but neither he nor the girl were looking at it now. Sylvie felt his hand upon her wrist. His fingers, slight and slippery, slid around her wrist and pulled her back down beside him.

'Believe me, he'll be fine,' Fran said. 'I promise you, Sylvie, he'll be fine.'

'How do *you* know?' Sylvie said.

'I just do,' Fran Hagarty said.

There were no more questions about the female in Tipperary or the men he had dropped off at the Nugget, and not one word about Charlie or his father.

'How well do you know Francis Hagarty?' said Vaizey.

'I've never met the man,' Gowry answered.

'But you do know who he is?'

'He's a journalist of sorts, I think.'

'He spends a lot of time at your house?'

'He's acquainted with my brother, I believe.'

'Do you know that he's at your house right now?' Vaizey said.

'I – I would be surprised at that.'

'Do you know he spent last night in your house?'

'Well,' said Gowry, carefully, 'it is a boarding-house, after all.'

'Are you blind, man,' Ames said, 'or just stupid?'

'That's enough, Boris,' Vaizey said. 'Have the guns turned up yet?'

'Wally has them next door.'

Vaizey stood up. He was shorter than Gowry had imagined, less intimidating.

'Come with me, Mr McCulloch,' he said.

Gowry followed the inspector out of the bleak office and along a tiled corridor to another bleak office next door.

The building seemed extraordinarily quiet, even for a Sunday evening. There were three coppers in the room, however, including the cohort, Rogers. Only one of the officers wore uniform. In the centre of the room was a long trestle table and on the table were two rifles, identical to those he had stored in Maggie's loft. In a porcelain pie dish beside the rifles were twenty or thirty empty cartridge cases.

Ames steered him to the table. The officers, especially the one in uniform, seemed embarrassed to be there and did not meet his eye. Vaizey came up behind him and stood by his side.

He said, 'Have you ever seen these guns before?'

'No.'

'Have you ever seen guns like them?'

'No.'

'Are they not identical to the guns you had in your possession at the end of the month of July, Mr McCulloch?'

'I've never had guns in my possession.'

'Where are the guns you hid away?'

'I don't know what you mean,' Gowry said.

He expected more, much more: to be forced to his knees in front of the table, to have one of the Mausers thrust into his face. But there was none of that, no bullying. His denial seemed to be exactly what the detective expected.

'Did you convey these weapons from Dublin to Woodenbridge?'

'No, I did not.'

'Very well, Mr McCulloch. Thank you. You are free to go.'

'What?'

'We need detain you no longer,' Vaizey said.

'Am I not to be charged?' Gowry said.

'What would we charge you with?' Vaizey said. 'Sleeping with a woman who isn't your wife? Your morals aren't my concern. We've nothing against you, Mr McCulloch. You may go home now. In fact, I am going that way myself and I'll accompany you for a bit – if you've no objection.'

'I – I . . .' Gowry was at a loss. 'No, I've no objection.'

Five minutes later he was out in the lanes under a cloudy night sky, walking towards College Green with Vaizey at his side. He felt as if he had been away for months, as if he were coming back from a long voyage. Gradually he began to breathe more easily.

'You'll be glad to be out of there, I expect,' Vaizey said.

'I am,' said Gowry. 'Of course I am. Are you really not goin' to charge me?'

'No,' Vaizey said. 'I believe your story – or most of it.'

'In that case,' Gowry said, 'I'd be obliged if you'd tell me what happened at Woodenbridge. Was Redmond murdered?'

'No, no,' Vaizey said. 'He made himself an easy target, however, and I imagine our parliamentary representative will have learned a valuable lesson

161

from today's little incident. Nobody was hurt. It was a fireworks display, a show of force. Whoever fired the shots – there were two gunmen, by the way – they only intended to draw attention to the fact that they disapprove of Redmond's deal with the government. They fired over the heads of the crowd.'

'A warning, in other words?' said Gowry.

'That's it.'

'How did you find out?'

'We had advance notice,' said Vaizey.

'Why didn't you stop it?'

'Didn't have time,' said Vaizey.

'You had time to pick me up at the Nugget,' Gowry said.

'You were our best lead.'

'You thought I was the gunman?'

'Oh, no,' Vaizey said. 'But we thought you might be the getaway.'

'I see.' Night air had unfogged his brain. He was thinking clearly again. 'Someone told you where I'd be, the place and the time?'

'Yes,' Vaizey said. 'Someone needed you to provide a distraction.'

'And I suppose I did, didn't I?'

'Not entirely,' Vaizey said.

'Can't you tell me who has it in for me?'

'Why? So you can take your revenge?'

'I wouldn't know how to take revenge,' Gowry said.

'You could tell us what you know about the brotherhoods.'

'I suspect you know more about the brotherhoods than I do, Inspector.'

'It isn't your father or your brother we'd like to lay by the heels.'

'Who is it then?' said Gowry.

'The man, Hagarty. Oliver Francis Hagarty.'

They had followed the tramcar lines down to the O'Connell Bridge. Gowry could smell the salty tang of the river on the swell of the tide. He could see the bridge lights scrolled on the surface of the water and thought how small the river looked tonight, how insignificant.

'How far are you going with me, Inspector?' Gowry asked.

'To the Shamrock.'

'Why?'

'To talk with your wife.'

'My wife?' Gowry said. 'Is she involved in this affair?'

'I'm afraid she is,' said Vaizey.

'With Hagarty, do you mean?'

'Yes, with Hagarty,' the officer told him.

'He's not just a scribbler, is he?'

'Oh, no. He's a whole lot more than that.'

'What? Chieftain? Arms dealer? I know: he's a paymaster. Am I right?'

Vaizey smiled, took Gowry's arm and led him on across the bridge.

'Why do you suppose the guns were left behind?' he said.

'To incriminate me?'

'That's part of the reason.'

'To draw attention away from themselves?'

'That too,' said Vaizey. 'And to provide Hagarty with an alibi.'

'An alibi? How could I give him an alibi when I've never even met him?'

'Not you,' Vaizey said. 'Your wife.'

'Is that,' Gowry said, 'why you're going home with me now?'

'It is,' Vaizey told him. 'Alas, Mr McCulloch, it is.'

Chapter Eight

By eight o'clock, she could contain herself no longer. She opened the front door and peered out into the darkness. She looked towards O'Connell Street, hidden behind buildings, and along Sperryhead Road. They were visible beneath the gas lamps, walking side by side and chatting like old friends. She stepped back, back again, back into the hall, then, swivelling on her heel, rushed into the bar.

'It's Vaizey,' she shouted. 'The peelers are coming down the road, bringing Gowry home. Out the back way, Fran, before it's too late.'

His lids were heavy, his eyes amused. He sipped from the pint glass and licked the froth from his lip with the tip of his tongue. 'Too late for what?' He sat back and stretched out his legs and when Sylvie tugged his arm, pushed her away, then, changing tack, snared her waist and dragged her on to his lap.

She struggled, wriggling, beating at him with her fists.

Fran held her tightly, though, locking her knees with his thighs and, as casually as you like, lifted the glass to his lips and sipped again.

Sylvie heard Maeve cry out, 'Daddy, Daddy.'

And Gowry, with Vaizey behind him, came marching into the bar.

'Go to your room, Maeve,' her mother told her but Jansis put a hand on her shoulder and held her steady. Her heart was beating hard like it did when she was late for class of a morning and Mr Whiteside made the late-comers line up and came down the line and smacked each of them on the hand with the pandy-bat, one stroke for girls, two for boys; that same hard pumping sensation filled her chest when Daddy and the policeman strode into the bar and found Mam seated on Fran's knee, an arm about her waist.

'Here I am, Inspector,' Fran said. 'Here I am and here I have been all weekend long, never out of sight of this darlin' lady for more than one hour. Church that was, the church at the corner. I would have accompanied her into the service if I hadn't feared that the roof would fall on my unholy head.'

He used the same tone of voice he used when he spoke to her. Fran's voice was always soft, never loud like Daddy's voice when he was piddling on about something he wanted you to understand. She always understood what Fran was talking about, for he could lull you into believing him without a slap or a kiss or a stroke from the pandy-bat or a sixpence or a length of red silk ribbon for a bribe. The policeman seemed smaller without the big men behind him. He looked the way her grandfather did when he was smarming up to Daddy.

'Is this true, Mrs McCulloch?' the policeman said.

Mam's eyes filled with tears. They clung to her lashes like raindrops to a leaf. Maeve could not remember having seen her mam shed tears before. She could not understand why Mam was crying or why she didn't answer the policeman's question. Surely there was nothing wrong in Mr Hagarty spending the night. A lot of men spent the night in the Shamrock. Unless – unless it had to do with the hugging? Yes, Maeve thought, it might have to do with the hugging. She had been told never to let Mr Pettu hug her and remembered how odd it made her feel when Turk hugged her. Certain dark little mysteries that lurked on the edges of her experience and certain furtive conversations from the schoolyard came suddenly to mind and if it hadn't been for Jansis's hand on her shoulder she would have turned and fled from them right then and there.

'Is it true, Sylvie?' Daddy said. 'Tell the man the truth, damn you.'

Mam stiffened and gave a little shake of the head

to cast off tears. Her eyes weren't blue now but colourless, like glass in a window.

'Yes, it's true.'

'All,' Daddy said, 'all night?'

'Never out of my sight,' Mam said.

The policeman laid a hand on Daddy's arm.

'I'm sorry it had to come to this, McCulloch.'

'Ah well, Inspector,' Fran said, 'now you see what happens when you arrest an innocent man. If I wasn't a charitable fellow I'd be tempted to rub your nose in it and make you eat the dirt.'

'I didn't arrest you the last time, Hagarty,' the policeman said. 'I'd nothing to do with your unfortunate experience. I wasn't even serving in Dublin.'

'Your kind,' Fran said, 'your dirty, shite-eating kind cost me my wife and sons. And for what? For nothing. On the strength of a hint from some bloody informer, you ruined my marriage and cost me my college career.'

'Blame yourself, Hagarty, not the law. You may have got off with your neck the last time but don't pretend you're not guilty of treasonable offences. I know you, man, I know what harm you've done and what harm you're capable of doing.' The policeman's skin was whiter than bleached cotton and he spoke through clenched teeth, like a dog that would bite you if you got too close. 'You're a damned duplicitous blackguard and what you've done tonight is unforgivable.'

'In the eyes of the law, Vaizey, I'm guilty of no

crime. And this time I can *prove* my innocence. This time I have a witness who'll swear under oath I was with her last night, all night, and all day today. Sylvie, is that not so?'

Mam clasped one of Fran's hands, the one without the glass in it. At that moment her mam looked like a doll, like a speaking doll she'd seen on the stage of the Empire three or four Christmases back. She'd thought that the doll was alive and had cried against Daddy's shoulder when he'd told her it was just a trick performed by the man with the doll on his knee. Oh, how she had loved that speaking doll and had hated her father for spoiling the illusion.

'Will you, Sylvie?' Daddy said. 'Will you swear you spent the night with this man?'

Mam closed her eyes and opened them again. 'Bring me a Bible and I'll swear with my hand on it.' She leaned forward against Fran's arm. 'There, Gowry! Are you happy now?'

Jansis let out a little groan, like a door creaking in the wind. Mr Vaizey raised his fist as if he were about to punch Fran, then let his hand fall again. Fran smiled and shook his head and said, 'Now, what can I be doing for you, since you went to all this trouble to find me?'

'You bastard!' Mr Vaizey said. 'I know you orchestrated the whole thing. But your henchmen bungled it. Redmond survived.'

'Redmond? Our dear, deplorable Johnny? What's he been up to now?'

'Did you really suppose I'd fall for your tricks and arrest McCulloch?' the policeman said. 'You and Flanagan set it up, didn't you? Now you'll sit back and bask in the glory and let others take the blame. At least the volunteers have guts enough to challenge us openly and not hide away behind a woman's skirts. And I expected more from you, Mrs McCulloch. I'm disgusted. Frankly disgusted.'

'I don't know what you're talking about, sir,' Fran said.

'Gun-running, for one thing. German weapons, purchased with money you skimmed from the Clan.'

'Ask *him*,' Fran said, nodding towards Daddy, 'about the guns.'

'He knows nothing about guns,' Vaizey said. 'You're the one with the guns.'

'If only that were true,' Fran said. 'Tell him where you hid the guns, McCulloch. Go on, be decent, give the poor inspector something to show for his night's work.'

'I know nothing about guns,' Daddy said.

Maeve knew that her father was lying. She might even have blurted it out if Jansis hadn't crushed her elbows into her ribs, holding her so tightly that it hurt to breathe. If that was a lie, then Daddy might have told more lies; everything Fran said might be the truth and everything Daddy said might be lies. Suddenly she didn't know who to believe, who to turn to – Mam or Fran or Daddy, her gruff, growling Daddy, who had never been one with the rest of them and did not believe in the Irish cause. Then Mam leaped from Fran's knees and shouted at Daddy. Daddy lifted his hand as if to strike Mam. Fran was on his feet, spilling stout from the dregs in the glass in his hand, and Daddy and Fran were wrestling like bears.

Maeve's confusion curdled into revulsion. She thrust back against Jansis, broke away, ran blindly into the corridor, into the kitchen and plunged out into the yard. She threw herself on to the coal box where, knees to chin and arms wrapped around her shins, she sobbed and sobbed in fear and confusion and waited for someone to come and fetch her and tell her what was true and what was not.

But this time no one came to fetch her, not even her dear old dad.

Sylvie dropped a slice of bread into sizzling fat. Gowry was at the table, wolfing down ham and eggs. Her first lover, Forbes, had been a finicky eater. She had never liked that about Forbes. She preferred heartiness in a man. For an instant she wanted to put out her hand and ruffle her husband's hair, but the gesture would have been tactless under the circumstances. She had slept with another man and boasted of it; not even Gowry could be expected to forgive her that.

'Is Maeve asleep?' he said.

'I don't know. She put herself to bed.'

'Shouldn't you go up?'

'Jansis is with her.'

'I'll go up when I've finished.'

'Best not,' Sylvie said. 'Leave her. She's had a shock.'

'She isn't the only one,' Gowry said.

Sylvie placed the pan on the cold end of the stove.

'What are you going to do now?' she said.

'Sleep in one of the empty rooms.'

'You don't have to, Gowry.'

'Oh, but I do.' He lifted the bread in both hands and bit into it, wiped grease delicately from the corner of his lips with his knuckle. 'Will he be back?'

'Not tonight, no,' Sylvie said.

'Tomorrow?'

'Probably.'

He went on chewing. 'Is it Hagarty you want, Sylvie?'

'I think it is.'

'Aren't you sure?'

'It's a bit late to change my mind now, isn't it?'

'Why did you do it?'

'He – he persuaded me.'

'To lie for him?' Gowry asked. 'To furnish him with an alibi?'

'It wasn't a lie,' Sylvie said. 'He *was* with me all weekend.'

'And before that?'

'Yes,' she said. 'Before that.'

Gowry chewed for a while in silence, then said, 'He's better placed to take care of you than I am, I suppose.'

'Better placed? What do you mean?'

'Well off. Rich.'

'Fran's not rich. He's hardly got a penny to his name.'

'Is that what he told you?'

'He didn't have to tell me. It's as plain as the nose on your face.'

'Sylvie, I think you've been duped.'

'If you saw his place, his room . . .'

'You have, I take it?'

'Yes.'

'Often?'

'Often enough.'

'Where is it?'

'Endicott Street,' said Sylvie.

'Which side?'

'The far side, up towards the Mountjoy.'

'There are worse places to live,' Gowry said.

She wondered why he was so calm, if he hoped to draw her into a full confession, into telling him what Fran and she had actually done in Endicott Street. Her foster-father had always been curious about what Forbes and she did together in the bedroom and she had been free with the intimate details, mischievously leading her foster-father on. She would not do that to Gowry, though, not now she had all but traded him away.

He handed her his empty plate.

She put it on the stove.

'Hagarty isn't what you think he is, Sylvie,' Gowry said. 'He isn't just a scribbler for the trash press. He's a paymaster for the brotherhoods.'

'A paymaster?'

'He brings money from America, a great deal of money.'

'He told me all about it.'

'All about it? That,' Gowry said, 'I doubt.'

She leaned against the cold end of the stove, arms folded. Her guilt was diminishing rapidly. She had anticipated – and deserved – recriminations, but this sly whittling away at Fran's character was not what she had expected.

She said, 'How do you know so much about Fran Hagarty all of a sudden?'

'Vaizey told me.'

'Vaizey's a peeler. Surely you don't believe what a peeler tells you?'

'Vaizey believed me, did he not?'

'Fran didn't send you down to Woodenbridge. It was Mr Flanagan.'

'Flanagan and Hagarty are obviously in cahoots. It's logical to suppose that if Hagarty is bringing large sums of money into the country then he needs someone who has a legitimate business to provide cover for him. Flanagan is a powerful man and a known sympathiser. Men like Flanagan, and your friend Hagarty too I imagine, are in it for what they can get, for a place in an Irish parliament and all the power and influence that money can buy.'

'What does this have to do with trying to murder John Redmond?'

'They didn't try to murder Redmond. If it had been a serious assassination attempt then Hagarty would have made sure it achieved its aim. From what I hear you could have shot Redmond with a popgun. No, it was just a bit of a show to excite and impress the moneymen.' Gowry shook his head. 'Damn me, but I should have turned those guns straight over to the authorities.'

'Why didn't you?'

'I didn't want to get Charlie and my father into trouble.'

'Where are the guns now?' Sylvie said.

'I'll see to it that they are destroyed.'

'Will you?' she said. 'Or will you hand them over to your friend Vaizey?'

'I'll hand them over to nobody,' Gowry said. 'Especially not Vaizey.'

'Fran will pay you for them, you know.'

'Christ!'

'If he has money behind him, as you say, he'll pay you.'

'Stop it, Sylvie, for God's sake,' Gowry told her. 'I've had more than enough for one day.' He got to his feet. 'What's vacant? Room four?'

'Yes.'

'Is the bed made?'

'Yes, but it may need aired.'

'I reckon I can sleep in an unaired bed for one night,' he said and, plucking his tunic from the chair, made towards the door.

'Gowry,' she said again, 'what are you going to do?'

'That depends on Flanagan.'

'I mean about us?'

When he looked at her blankly, almost without interest, she experienced a sudden pang of regret, for she knew that she had lost him and, curiously, wanted him back.

He gave her the ghost of a smile, fleeting and faint.

'I'll have to think about that one,' he said.

Maeve felt the touch of his hand on her brow, his fingers stroking her hair. She was not alarmed. She knew it was Daddy. She turned sleepily on the pillow. Her cheeks were hot and the events of last night were still in her mind like the eerie floaty feelings of the winter before last, when she'd been sick.

It was still pitch dark outside. Rain hissed in the street. The room smelled damp but she was warm and safe with Daddy by the bed, brushing her hair from her brow. 'Sweetheart,' he whispered, his voice thick and soothing, like cocoa in a cup. 'Sweetheart, I love you. I want you to remember that.'

She was not alarmed, though perhaps she should have been.

'Aye,' she murmured, sleepily. 'I'll remember.'

He put an arm behind her and lifted her from the pillow, held her to him for a moment, then laid her down again and tucked the blankets up to her chin.

'Goodbye, dearest girl,' he said.

And was gone.

It was shortly after seven o'clock when John James Flanagan arrived at the garage. He wore no collar to his shirt and his ulster cape and colonial hat had both seen better days. They were the first items that had come to hand when the boy mechanic had arrived at the servants' entrance to the house on Merrion Square bearing an urgent message from Mr Roddeny.

The urgency of the message was apparent to John James before the boy had uttered a word, for the boy had been despatched not on foot or by tramcar but in a hired hackney, horse-drawn at that, which had been the first conveyance Mr Roddeny had been able to lay hands on at that ungodly hour of the morning.

The message was terse, but John James had managed to overcome the boy's awe and elicit from him the nature of the emergency, and such was the alacrity of John James's response that, rain notwithstanding, the limousine was still burning when he arrived on the lot.

Mechanics and drivers huddled by the wall of the

maintenance shed, too wary to approach the crackling hulk in its pool of water and spilled fuel. Even Mr Roddeny hadn't dared tackle the blaze and when he had ordered the mechanics to run out with buckets and dowse the flames he had been greeted with such derision that he had prudently retreated to the kiosk to wait for the fire to burn itself out.

Smoke palled away over the line of charabancs and the stench of burned leather and melted rubber was strong enough to make you gag. It was the river of spilled fuel that really worried the boys, though, and they puffed carefully on their cigarettes, dropped the butt-ends at their feet and stamped on them quick to avoid igniting the petrol lake. When the hack came clipping into the lot they scattered and when Mr Flanagan came lolloping across the yard to the kiosk where Mr Roddeny had taken shelter, they stood well back.

Burned down to a shell, the Benz hissed and spluttered in the falling rain, then, as if to greet the boss's arrival, found within itself an unconsumed pocket of something combustible and released a small explosive roar and a gout of acrid smoke that billowed across the yard and had all the lads – John James too – covering their noses with their sleeves.

Mr Flanagan went into the kiosk and closed the door.

There was hardly room for two in the little wooden building.

Roddeny pressed himself back against the window

and stammered, 'There was n–nothin' I could do, s–sir, n–nothin' at all.'

'Probably not,' John James said.

'I was here when it started, just arrived,' said Roddeny. 'I was down under the counter fetchin' out the books when it went up with a bang, just burst into flames, like. Is this the work o' the peelers? Is this some o' their doin'?'

'I doubt it,' John James said. 'In fact, no. If you glance behind you you'll find a solution to the mystery hanging on the hook in the corner.'

Roddeny spun round and, reaching out, snatched down the cap and driver's tunic that he had failed to remark before the explosion.

'What?' he said, frowning and shaking the gar-ment. 'McCulloch?'

'Who, if I am not mistaken, will be halfway to Holyhead by now.'

'We can still catch him, can't we?'

'No, no,' said Mr Flanagan. 'Let him go.'

'Let him go, sir? Let him go?'

'Perhaps it's for the best,' Mr Flanagan said.

'But he blew up your limousine.'

'Did he? I think it was an accident, don't you, Mr Roddeny?'

'An accident? That's what I've to tell the boys, sir, is it?'

'Spontaneous combustion,' John James said and, with Gowry's tunic draped over his arm, went off to find a hack to take him home.

* * *

The recruiting station was all but deserted at that hour of the morning. Perhaps, Gowry thought, the keen ones had gone up to the barracks at Portobello where you could sign on for the Fusiliers. He didn't care what regiment he joined. He wanted only to be sucked off the streets and given shelter, to become anonymous, a little man without worries or responsibilities who would do his duty for king and country and be drilled into mindless indifference in exchange.

The officer was in full dress uniform. Brilliant shamrock-green facings and a scarlet flask cord made him look like the villain in an operetta. He peered out from behind the wire mesh screen that separated the army clerks from civilians in the funeral parlour that the battalion had requisitioned and, wagging a gloved hand, signalled a sergeant to hasten to the door and nab Gowry before he could change his mind and escape.

The sergeant wore service dress, puttees waxed, boots and buttons shining. The only drops of colour were the badges on his cap and arm, shamrocks and crossed rifles, gleaming like gold. He had a great heavy jaw and shoulders like an ox and bore no resemblance to Maurice Leonard.

'Come along, lad,' the sergeant said. 'Come along. Don't be fright. It's what you're here for now, ain't it?'

'It is,' said Gowry, humbly. 'Aye, it is. What regiment is this?'

'The 2nd Battalion of the Sperryhead Rifles,' the sergeant said and for some reason that Gowry couldn't fathom gave him a discreet salute. 'Best of the little 'uns, I can tell you, just waitin' to write a new page in history.'

'Whose history?' Gowry asked.

'*Our* history, lad, *our* history,' the sergeant answered and, laying a massive hand on Gowry's shoulder, steered him gently towards the wire.

PART TWO

Rebecca

Chapter Nine

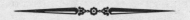

The winter stand was over and the fighting had begun in earnest once again. The hospital had been moved from sixty miles behind the lines to a position close to the railhead in expectation of a big spring push.

The line, so Rebecca had heard, was ninety miles in length and stretched from Langemarck on the Yser to Dompierre on the Somme, but she had only a vague notion where these places were, for over the months one unit, one tent, one clearing station had become very much like another. Over by Christmas, they'd said, back at the beginning! There's a laugh! It was 1916 now and no end in sight. There were a million men in France and Flanders, half a million more would arrive by mid-summer and many of those would wind up here in the Ecole de Saint-Emile or some other hospital where, according to the will of God and the skill of the surgeons, they would either live or die.

As operating theatres went the Saint-Emile's was rather nice, a dazzlingly white room, not very large, with a door in one wall and two high windows through which, when the night lamps were extinguished, the clear light of day shone down. Until recently it had been the school cloakroom and lavatories faced you and the sinks where the surgeons scrubbed up. The operating tables were covered with oilcloth and in one corner a polished copper tank steamed on an oil-fired stove. It wasn't Becky's job to fish the sterilised instruments from the tank. She left that menial chore to an orderly or one of the half-baked probationers, for she, Rebecca Tarrant, was a staff nurse.

Seasoned by fourteen months in the field, she could lay out a supply table without having to think about it and do everything the surgeons required of her without one slip or stumble, even at the end of a fifteen-hour shift. Her mother considered her stubborn, of course, but her refusal to admit defeat kept her going and would keep her going until the flood of wounded dried up and the tables were wiped down and packed away and the circus of suffering moved on.

Two of the three operating tables were occupied. While Becky opened the parcel that contained a freshly sterilised gown, the orderlies brought in another stretcher. The table had been wiped with a damp cloth but there were traces of blood along the edge of the mat and Mr Sanderson – he insisted on being addressed as 'Mister' – nodded wearily to a probationer to swab it down again.

Becky shook out the gown by the neckband and let Mr Sanderson step into it. She tied the strings behind and held out a bowl of alcohol for the surgeon to rinse his hands. That done, she gave him a pair of rubber gloves with long turned-back wrists. He pulled them on with a little snap. The orderlies lifted the soldier from the stretcher to the table. On the surgeon's instruction they folded down the blanket and exposed the injured thigh. They tucked the blanket around his feet, buckled on two stout canvas straps, one around his knees and the other across his chest and cut away the pack that had been applied at the dressing station.

Becky studied the damage. Shrapnel; simple enough. She had seen a hundred injuries just like it, a thousand much worse. She transferred scalpels, sponges, and haemostats from the supply table to the surgeon's tray while the orderlies shaved the patient's thigh. Shrapnel wounds might be commonplace to the medical staff, Becky thought, but the soldier had suffered a strange and terrifying insult to his body. The soldier had uttered not one word since he had been brought in but when she pushed the trolley-tray up to the table she could see fear in his eyes. She was tempted to say something, give him a word of reassurance or make a stilted little joke as Mr Sanderson did sometimes but she made it a rule to keep patients at a safe distance, for sentiment had no part in professional relationships as far as Nurse Tarrant was concerned.

The padre was busy at the top of the operating table. The Ecole had been requisitioned only eleven days ago and staffing was not up to strength yet. The padre, Father Coyle, had been sent back from the lines with a painful crop of boils that had become so infected that they needed lancing. Boils on the backside were considered comical and the poor middle-aged priest had had to endure quite a ribbing. Her mother would have liked Father Coyle, for her mother, a Catholic convert, was pious without being stuffy.

The father laid out his cans of ether, gauze, Vaseline and the clips for pulling forward the patient's tongue. Becky could sense his apprehension; he was afraid that he'd bungle the job and kill the poor patient. He leaned forward, tilting the stool, and rested his elbows on each side of the soldier's head.

'Don't be frightened, son,' he said. 'This stuff will soon knock you out and you won't be feeling a thing. It'll all be over in a minute.'

'Will I be dead, sir?'

'No, no, sure and you won't be dead. You'll be patched up and back with your chums before you can say "knife".'

The soldier's eyes widened. 'Knife?'

The padre blushed. 'You'll be all right, I promise you. Try not to think about the knife.'

The boy shook his head and chuckled, painfully.

'It's not the holy oil you have in that can then, Father?'

'It's Vaseline, just Vaseline,' Father Coyle said. 'What regiment?'

'The Dublin Fusiliers.'

'Ah, at Hulluch?'

'Aye, sir, Hulluch. Fritz came over in force at dusk.'

'You held them off, I take it?'

'We did, Father, that we did.'

'Brave boys,' the padre said, humbly. 'You are all brave boys.'

Becky tapped the priest on the shoulder. He nodded and smeared a little Vaseline around the soldier's eyes and, holding the mask a few inches above the young man's face, began to drip ether on to it.

'Breathe deeply,' he said. 'Don't fight it.'

He had long bony fingers, the priest, his fingernails bitten to the quick. He lowered the mask and wrapped a piece of gauze around the edges to retain the fumes. He poured the ether quickly, while the fusilier moaned and struggled against the straps. Then the moaning became faint and died away.

Alarmed, the padre glanced up. 'Is he all right?'

'He's fine, Father Coyle,' Mr Sanderson said, reassuringly.

Without further ado the surgeon painted the soldier's thigh with iodine and placed around the wound the four sterilised towels that Becky handed him.

Mr Sanderson's assistant, Captain-Surgeon Bracknell, took his place at the table. Becky positioned herself by the trolley, the orderlies at the patient's feet, and, with the team complete, the commonplace little operation began.

Nine years of nursing had developed Becky's stamina to the point where she could stand upright all day – all night too if necessary – without a tremor. She came from hardy stock, of course, daughter of a shepherd, granddaughter of a fisherman, and the fatigue that had taken possession of her recently was, she felt sure, not a weakness of the body but a weakness of the will.

She had been all right until January. In January, at the temporary camp at Mallefort, she had come down with a feverish infection and at Sister Congreve's insistence had been pulled off all duties for the best part of a week. The CMO had offered to send her home, give her leave. Outraged at the suggestion, she had lain for five days in a cot in a bell tent, dizzy and sore and dried out, willing herself well again.

Since then she had not been herself, though. Backache and urinary problems were the least of it: it was the dreams that really undermined her.

She dreamed almost every night, grim, sweating dreams in which she saw her cousin Robbie lying naked on an operating table, sweet and smiling as a cherub but with his manhood exposed and erect. She would waken abruptly, shivering, a swooning cry in her throat, the smell of sodden canvas and horse-dung in her nostrils. The smell reminded her of her grandmother's turf-roofed cottage on Mull and brought longing and regret rolling over her like waves from the Atlantic. In other dreams she found herself wandering again through her Aunt Biddy's great gloomy house on the Fetternish peninsula where she had worked as a servant when young Robbie, not much more than a schoolboy, had seemed so innocent, so angelic and asexual that just the sight of him coming down the staircase in the hall had made her want to laugh. In her dreams, however, Robbie was changed, so changed, not innocent at all but manly and provocative in his nakedness, now that he was safely dead.

The ache in her back radiated down into her hips and spread into her belly and thighs. She tried to put it out of mind, to discard it like a wad of cotton wool. She suspected that the pains were simply phantoms that her brain had conjured up to keep her from thinking about Robbie, about Mull.

Three years since she had last visited the island, three years since she had last seen her mother and almost as long since her sister Rachel and she had had a real good chinwag. What she wanted, what she needed was to talk to Rachel, to confide in Rachel, to weep on Rachel's shoulder.

Only Rachel could possibly understand that stoicism and efficiency were no protection in time of war and that all the pain and suffering that she, Becky, had seen had left indelible marks. But Rachel was married now and living in Portsmouth, of all places. She had her sailor husband and two babies to take care of and no time to spare to reply to Becky's letters or pay heed to Becky's complaints about the war in France.

'Nurse Tarrant, are you quite well?'

'Sir?'

'I realise it's been a very long night for all of us but I would be obliged if you would try to stay awake just a little longer.'

'Sir.'

'The tubes, please,' Captain Bracknell said. 'Give me the tubes.'

What had been a small jagged wound in the soldier's thigh was now a gaping hole that smiled up at her like a red mouth. She lifted a handful of thin rubber tubes from the tray, spread them across her palms and offered them to the captain who took them one at a time and held them at waist height for Mr Sanderson to pluck away and push down into the wound.

Becky watched the chief fill the cavity with chlorine-soaked gauze, lay gauze strips plastered with yellow Vaseline around the edges of the wound, then, his work done, step aside to allow the captain to close. She stared at the patient's thigh out of which the drainage tubes crawled like worms.

'The pad, the pad, Miss Tarrant,' the captain snapped.

She gave him the absorbent pad.

The pain in her back gnawed deep into her vertebrae and sank its teeth into her hip joints. The shaking in her legs was in danger of becoming uncontrollable. Then the door in the wall crashed open and an officer stood in the aperture, light streaming behind him. He was nothing, a creature without authority, a mere subaltern, a dishevelled snotty with a piece of sacking over his mouth and another flung like a scarf about his neck, his tunic smeared with green as if he had been rolling about on wet grass.

'Oh, God! Oh, my God!' the padre said.

The officer swayed in the doorway while two orderlies hovered behind him, trying vainly to persuade him to leave. When he lifted his head Becky saw that his eyes were swollen shut and guessed that all he could see of the operating room was bleary white light.

'Gassed,' the officer shouted. 'We've all been bloody gassed.' Then ripping away the sacking from his mouth, he roared out hoarsely, 'Christ Jesus, will no one listen? Christ Jesus, is no one there?'

Becky ran along the brown corridors to the French doors in the dining-hall and out on to the broad stone steps that overlooked the lawn. Seven or eight trucks were drawn up on the grass. There were no orderlies with the men who crawled out from under the canvases, men who had probably been hoisted out of the sector and shipped to Saint-Emile just to get rid of them; somewhere back at base a scarlet major would be patting himself on the back for solving that little problem in logistics and morale.

Becky smoothed her apron and stepped on to the grass.

The soldiers who toppled from the trucks had indeed been gassed. They stumbled about the grounds, blind, terrified and choking. Becky looked for someone in authority to tell her where to begin. Cooks had emerged from the kitchen and on the steps of the main building a couple of surgeons, one clad in a blue silk dressing-gown, had appeared, together with nurses and walking wounded from the wards. Beds, Becky thought. Beds in the cloisters outside the old gymnasium – the gymnasium itself was being used as a temporary morgue – cots, blankets and wet dressings, oxygen tanks and masks. She had never dealt with gas cases before and her classes in the subject seemed so distant that she could hardly remember them.

She flinched when a soldier grabbed her arm. His mouth was wide open and green saliva coated his tongue. He shouted at her then burrowed his chin into her cheek and in a low, rasping voice begged for help.

Becky pushed him away. Chlorine or phosgene? He wouldn't be able to tell her. He was unintelligible, incomprehensible. Chlorine or phosgene or something worse? Lung irritants. Oedema, pulmonary lesions, asphyxia, death by drowning when fluid filled the lungs. How many dead already? Oh, God, why hadn't she been at Ypres last December when the Boche had first used gas? She spun like a skittle as one soldier after another blundered past her, weeping in the blind white darkness.

'Nurse Tarrant, Nurse Tarrant?'

Captain Bracknell, still in his bloodstained surgical gown, was furious, his face as livid as the faces of the victims. 'What is this? What the *hell* is this?'

'I – I don't know, sir.'

The captain had specialised in treating female disorders in a hospital in Buckinghamshire. He was a surgeon and there was nothing here to put a knife to. 'Where did they *come* from? Why have they just *appeared*?' he ranted. 'Who *sent* them here? *We're* not equipped for gas. My God, are they *all* blind?'

Soldiers tottered on worn swards and paved pathways, pawing at the air and wailing or, falling, crawled about in miserable confusion. Becky put a hand to her brow and covered her eyes. She could not bear to see men so pitifully reduced.

'Find out precisely what we're dealing with,' the captain told her. 'Is it airborne gas or was the damned stuff delivered in shells?'

'Beds . . .'

'We don't *have* beds, woman. We must do what we can for them where they stand. Thank God it isn't raining.' He turned on his heel and stalked away.

Becky was no longer alone. Doctor Caufield, Mr Sanderson, Sister Congreve and four or five white-faced probationers were assembling oxygen tanks by the front steps. Ammonia sprays: fumes of ammonia, yes, that would help relieve milder cases of congestion. Trying hard to think straight, Becky walked through the rabble in search of someone sensible enough to answer the captain's question.

The sun had come out, a hazy wintry sun. The sky overhead had a strange blue tinge to it but no clouds, no depth. She headed for the trucks in the hope of finding a driver but the drivers had dispersed into the crowd.

Soldiers lay writhing and gasping on the grass; a corporal had toppled into a flowerbed and lay motionless, face down, as if the earth itself had soothing properties. And then she spotted a quiet, sensible-looking fellow seated against the wheel of the truck in the shade of a tarpaulin. His battledress was so caked with mud that she could not make out his regiment. He sat very still, legs stuck out, hands flat on the ground, breathing high in his chest, mouth open and head cocked as if he were listening to the beating of his heart.

She knelt by his side. 'Can you speak?'

He nodded.

'Are you in pain?'

He nodded again.

'Can you see me?'

'Not much of you.'

He was Irish, like most of the troops in the sector. She wondered where the priest was and glanced round for Father Coyle. The soldier touched her on the knee, lightly. He had lost his helmet and his hair was matted with the residue of the gas. On his forehead was a thin wound over which mud had congealed. His eyes were not shut, not completely, but they were horribly wet. Becky fished in the pocket of her apron, found a small embroidered handkerchief, her own, and carefully wiped his sticky lashes.

He flinched, and she said, 'I'm sorry.'

He gave a wheezy little grunt. 'Are you Scottish?'

'I am,' Becky said. 'Do you know where you are?'

'France,' he said, wheezing. 'Somewhere in France – I think.'

It was chilly in the shadow of the tarpaulin. She could feel the cold seeping through the ground. She should be elsewhere, should be up and doing. Sister Congreve would be hunting for her.

She wiped the soldier's eyes with the embroidered rag and listened to his congested laughter. She wondered if laughter was a sign of delirium, if she had picked the wrong man.

'Tell me,' she said, 'how was the gas delivered?'

'Shells first, then a greenish mist. Smelled musty, like hay.'

'Where did the attack take place?'

'Fire-trenches. Our lines in the chalk-pits. Loos to Hulluch. Easterly breeze. Stiff. No chance to sack up.' He coughed. The fluid in his lungs seethed and bubbled. She held the handkerchief to his lips and caught a glimpse of brown eyes under the sticky lashes. 'Inniskillings. Dublin Fusiliers. Us,' he said, panting again, 'the Sperryhead Rifles.'

'Can you walk?'

He nodded.

She tucked the little handkerchief into her pocket and clasped his hand. 'Come along,' she said. 'I'll see to it that something's done for you. It seems worse than perhaps it is.'

'Sure,' the soldier said, 'an' that's a comfort.' He allowed her to haul him to his feet. 'What's your name, Sister?'

'Tarrant. I'm only a staff nurse, by the way.'

'An' I'm – I'm . . .'

She gave his hand an urgent tug. 'Who? Who are you? Tell me.'

'Gowry.'

'Gowry?'

'McCulloch. Gowry McCulloch.'

'Well, Gowry McCulloch,' Becky said, 'you'll soon be as right as rain.'

'Sure an' I will,' he said cynically and let her lead him out of the shadow into the light of the wintry sun.

Chapter Ten

Gowry's first eight months of training in the barracks at Fermoy had been taken up with physical conditioning and rudimentary drills, for few of the officers were capable of teaching more sophisticated martial skills. He had not been unhappy there, though he missed Maeve and tried not to think of her too much. He had written five or six letters home but received no replies from either his wife or daughter and, bowing to their wishes, did not write to them again.

He chose not to go to Dublin on leaves and weekend passes. Instead he stayed in billets or jogged out on the train to Tipperary where Maggie picked him up in a pony-trap and took him back to her cottage. He had told Maggie most of what had taken place in Dublin, and Maurice and he had dug a great deep pit by the side of the manure heap in the paddock and buried the guns in it. It galled Maurice to have to bury thirty new rifles when the instructors on the Kilworth ranges were crying out for training weapons.

The company commanders were retired officers from the Irish militia or veterans from the Afghan wars and the majority of the recruits were nationalists. Gowry kept his mouth shut about his nationalist associations. He was afraid that Flanagan might seek compensation for the burning of the Benz or that Vaizey would pull him out of the army on a trumped-up charge but as weeks piled into months and spring followed winter, his anxiety and resentment faded.

After almost a year in training at Fermoy, the Rifles were shipped across to England and put into barracks near Aldershot to learn about the weird and cunning engines of war and become more proficient in musketry. In November the battalion was inspected by the Archbishop of Westminster, in December by Queen Mary, then, just before Christmas, each man was issued with an identity disc, field dressings and a Bible and they all entrained for France.

On Christmas Day a second lieutenant was shot dead by a stray bullet. He was the battalion's first fatality. The following morning, Boxing Day, the men of the 2nd Battalion were sent up to join a forward unit north-east of Melville to have their first taste of trench warfare.

At first Gowry was filled with a strange sense of elation. Finally shot of his old life in Dublin, he felt as if he had been born anew. Of course he hated the rats, the body lice, the cold and wet, the garbage stench of the dugouts and the carnage caused by shrapnel shelling but, even so, he remained confident, absolutely confident, that he would somehow survive the war.

In January the Rifles were transferred to a cushy bit of trench in the Hulluch sector where the enemy lines were held by Bavarian troops, an easy-going lot. When Prussians replaced them, however, the pace hotted up and the Boche, rehearsing for a large-scale attack, released a 'whiff' of cylinder gas on the tail of the dawn shelling. The Rifles, dug in to windward, bore the brunt of it.

'And here you are,' Rebecca said.

'Here I am,' said Gowry. 'Is that you?'

'Who else would it be at this hour of the morning? Did I wake you?'

'I wasn't asleep.'

'Can't you sleep sitting up?'

'I see things,' Gowry said. 'Flashes, like lightning. Are we near the front? I can't hear the guns.'

'We aren't near the front. Do you really not know where you are?'

'Saint-Emile,' said Gowry. 'Wherever that is.'

'We're about ten miles from Heuvert.'

'Heuvert?' Gowry said. 'I've been there.'

'A well-travelled man, I see,' Becky said. 'When did they last change your dressings?'

'Last night, I think.'

'Will I change them for you now?'

'No,' Gowry said.

'Why not? Don't you trust me to do it properly?'

'I'm sure you've better things to do than fuss with me. What time is it?'

'About five,' Becky told him.

'A fine morning, is it?'

'It promises to be,' Becky said. 'There isn't a cloud in the sky.'

'I can smell grass,' Gowry said.

'You're in a bed in the cloisters,' Becky said. 'If you listen you'll hear birds singing. The playing fields are just outside.'

'Playing fields?'

'The Ecole de Saint-Emile was a school, quite posh, I think.'

Gowry heard the clink of porcelain and knew that she had brought the ice-cold fluid with her. They had washed his hair, washed his whole body in the icy liquid. It had burned like fire for hours.

Afterwards he had explored his face with his fingertips and found a ribbon wound on his brow that had been laved with a greasy substance but not stitched. His head ached and there was pain in his chest and he could not lie down properly. When he leaned over and coughed, he retched up great wads of stuff and the pain in his chest increased. Now he knew he wasn't going to die he had become afraid of the white darkness, sure that he'd be packed off home to grope and shuffle about the Shamrock while Hagarty laughed at his infirmity and made love to Sylvie behind his back.

The Scottish nurse sat on the bed beside him. He could feel her weight on the mattress. He wanted to hold her hand, but didn't dare.

'What are you doing?'

'Nothing,' she said. 'Resting.'

'Have you been on night duty?'

'Longer than that, much longer.'

'How are they, the boys?' Gowry said.

'Oh, they're fine.'

'Don't lie to me,' he said.

She hesitated, then said, 'We lost eleven. Nothing we could do to save them. They were too far gone. Our padre is very upset. Three died on the operating table and he blames himself for giving them too much ether.'

'He should be blamin' the Boche, not himself,' Gowry said, and coughed.

'You shouldn't be talking so much.'

'What – what about the others?'

'Those who are badly wounded we keep here,' Becky said, 'until they have recovered enough to survive the journey.'

'Home to Blighty?'

'Yes.'

'What about me?' said Gowry.

He felt her weight shift and her hand on his brow above the dressing. Her hand had rough little calluses across the palm. He wondered what sort of nursing put calluses on a woman's hands. She wore no wedding ring.

'Let me change your dressing.' Her voice was soft, even softer than Sylvie's. 'Come on, Private McCulloch, big, brave chap like you. What would your wife think of you, scared of having your bandages changed?'

He did not deny that he had a wife, but he did not confirm it either.

To appease her, he said, 'All right.'

'You don't want one of the youngsters doing it, I assure you. They wouldn't do it like this.' Deftly she unpicked the knot at the side of the dressing. 'They're good girls but they can be clumsy.'

'An' — an' are you never rough, Nurse?'

The dressing came away from his face in one piece. Cold morning air pressed against his lids. His eyes were a mess. He knew they were a mess. He kept them shut. He could see threads of colour, though, and the darkness was no longer white but black. He felt the icy solution dribble down his cheeks.

'Oh dear,' Becky said, 'you've forgotten my name already.'

'I'm sorry, I . . .'

'Open your eyes.'

He opened his eyes and saw natural light and in the light the nurse's face, solemn and sallow and drawn with concern.

'Can you see me?' she asked.

Beautiful, he thought, she's quite beautiful.

But all he said was, 'Yes.'

*   *   *

Becky shared a tiny room on the third floor of the Ecole with Angela Harrison. Angela had been in her second year of training when the war had broken out. She was young, barely twenty. Becky and she had billeted together in bell tents at Mallefort and Angela had been kind to Becky when she had been ill and Becky, in turn, put up with Angela's vanity and perpetual chatter about boyfriends; boyfriends in the plural, that is, for Angela's correspondence with men was prodigious.

Wherever she travelled Angela was accompanied by an astonishing array of clothes, skimpy little garments that had no thermal value whatsoever but that packed neatly into a small suitcase. Even in damp and draughty bell tents her dresses were hung tenderly on hooks and strings and she would repair and clean and cold iron them hour upon hour.

Angela was popular in the wards, though, for she carried her gentle touch with clothes into the handling of splints, fomentations and catheters, and managed to make every man feel that what she was obliged to do was not embarrassing or indelicate but part of a shared intimacy.

Becky wakened, rolled out of her cot and stumbled down the corridor to the lavatory. When she returned, she sat on the end of the cot for a moment to gather herself for the effort of washing and dressing.

Angela was brushing her hair. In spite of the

chill, she wore only a silk peignoir with elaborate sleeves that slithered up and down her plump arms. She sang to herself while she contemplated her image in the mirror on the desk that served as a dressing-table.

'Feeling better, are we?'

'Not much,' Becky answered.

'I wonder if we'll be able to have dances here?'

'A what?'

'Dances, parties.' Angela sighed. 'It's been so long since old Congreve allowed us to have any fun at all.'

'I don't know if I have the energy to dance,' Becky said.

'If your little pet asked you, you would.'

'My what?' said Becky.

'Your Irish pet. What's his name?' Angela swung round, hair spilling across her ample shoulders, and gave Becky a toothy smile. 'I've seen how you lavish attention on him. Is he going to die?'

'Of course not,' Becky said, then, too late, added, 'I don't know who you're talking about.'

'How do you know he ain't a-going to die then?'

Angela put her elbows on the table and stared at a postcard of Virgin and Child that had been sent to her by a devilishly handsome young lieutenant who had undergone a religious conversion during the storming of a German gun emplacement and thought it only decent to inform her. Angela hadn't written him off quite yet, apparently.

'Those who are, have,' Becky said. 'We won't lose any more now.'

'That's not what Bobby says. According to Bobby Bracknell, delayed onset is not uncommon in phosgene poisoning,' Angela said in the same tone she used when recalling her last visit to Swan & Edgar's. 'Sudden death can occur up to forty-eight hours after inhalation. Wasn't it odd that Jerry used lachrymal shells to soften up the line? One would have supposed that phosgene would have done the job perfectly well. It does occur to one that perhaps Jerry don't know what he's doing either. What is the chappie's name, your Irishman?'

'They're all Irish – almost.'

'I mean the one you've been cuddling up to.'

Becky pressed her fists to her hipbones and stretched her spine. She was hungry, ravenous; a jolly good sign, for her appetite had been poor of late. Unless the ambulances brought in fresh wounded she would be on general ward duties tonight. Bed-rest and careful monitoring would bring most of the soldiers round and in a week or ten days they would be sent back to their units.

Angela said, 'You're thinking about him now, ain't you?'

'I'm doing nothing of the kind.'

'Oh, look. She's blushing. Never seen you blush before, Becky.'

'I wish' – Becky got her feet – 'you'd put something on, Angela. It isn't right to sit about in that – that scanty thing.'

'Changing the subject, are we?' Angela said, cheerfully. 'I do believe you've already got a teeny-weeny crush on this Irish chappie.'

'Ridiculous!' Becky exclaimed. 'He's just another patient as far as I'm concerned.'

'Hoh!' said Angela. 'You've never cuddled up to patients before. What's wrong? Don't you believe in love at first sight? I certainly do.'

'I'm well aware of *that*,' said Becky, testily.

She put on her drawers and vest and the stiff waist petticoat that gave the uniform its severe, unfeminine line. She grabbed a towel from the rail of the cot and her toiletry bag from the locker and headed, barefoot, for the washroom at the end of the corridor. She needed time away from Angela, time to think.

It was still daylight outside. The doctors, Mr Sanderson and Captain Bracknell among them, were messing in the administrator's office on the second floor and the gathering would probably become bibulous, for Captain Bracknell's wife had sent him down a case of wine.

Becky had received no mail. Only her mother wrote to her regularly and, now and then, her cousin Donnie but it had been months since she had heard from Aunt Biddy, not since Robbie had been killed, in fact.

She brushed her teeth in the washroom and tried

not to stare at her haggard face in the flyblown mirror above the sink. She wondered if there was any truth in what Angela had said about love at first sight and if any man, even an Irishman, could possibly find her attractive in her present sorry state.

For the first time in months, quite softly, Becky began to cry.

'Sure and you don't have to feed me,' Gowry said. 'At least you've got rid of that teapot thing. What's on the menu tonight?'

'Soup. Can you sit up a little more, please?' Becky said.

'I can't do much else but sit up.'

'If you don't eat you'll never regain your strength.'

'I'm sorry.' Gowry coughed. 'I'm just feelin' a bit down tonight.' Becky held the spoon to his lips. He craned his neck and looked down his nose at the contents. 'I'm really not very hungry.'

The day nurse had told Becky that Private McCulloch had been panting all afternoon and that he had discharged a small quantity of albuminous sputum but, so far, no blood. His skin was clammy but there was no fever to speak of and in Major Caufield's opinion the inflammatory complications were minor and Gowry would be up and about in three or four days and back with his unit by the end of the week.

She bumped the spoon against his stubborn lips.

'Eat something,' she said. 'For me.'

He raised a hand laboriously from the covers and coughed politely into his fist. 'For – for you?'

'Just eat the blessed stuff, will you,' Staff Nurse Tarrant told him.

'Why?'

'Because I want you to get well again.'

'So I can go back up the line and get shot?'

'Oh, what an awful thing to say.'

She whipped the spoon away from his mouth and dropped it with a little *splosh* into the bowl. She made to get up, but he caught her arm. For a sick man, she thought, he was both strong and quick.

'I shouldn't have said that,' Gowry said. 'It was a bad thing to say and I apologise.' He craned forward and opened his mouth wide. ''Eed me, 'leese,' he said. ''Leese, 'ursie.'

She hesitated, the bowl cupped in her hands.

The night wind had got up now and the big, patched tarpaulins that the orderlies had roped in the arches of the cloisters flapped noisily. In the next bed was another Irishman, hardly more than a boy. He watched the little pantomime without expression. Further down the ward a gunner from the Leinsters was moaning and thrashing and flinging his blankets all about, but Angela – bless her – was trotting up from the station to calm him down.

'Can't you feed yourself?' Becky heard herself ask.

'Aye,' Gowry answered, 'but if I do, you won't stay.'

'Do you want me to stay?'

'For as long as you can.'

'Are you afraid?'

'No, I just want you to . . .' He lifted his shoulders helplessly.

She seated herself on the bed again and presented him with the soup bowl. He took it in one hand and carefully picked out the spoon. She leaned over him, holding her hand under the spoon to catch the greasy little drips before they fell upon his chest. He dipped the spoon into the soup and put it into his mouth, sucked on it and said, 'French onion, eh?'

'Don't you like it?'

'Hmm,' he said. 'Lovely!'

She wiped his lips with her handkerchief.

'Then have some more,' said Becky.

During the long watches of the night Gowry could not help but think of Maeve. He wondered if she was lying in bed thinking of him, wondered if she was taller than her mother yet and had undergone that curious transformation from child into woman. With the wind buffeting the piebald tarpaulins above his bed, he even imagined he could hear her calling out to him in her shrill Dublin twang, '*Dad, Daddy? Daddy, Dad?*'

He watched the nurses come and go. Pretty girls, plain girls, young and not so young. Heard their voices in the shadows, the squeak of trolley wheels, the apologetic clatter of oxygen cylinders rolling on the paving. Imagined Maeve, his little daughter, back in Dublin just as he had left her, innocent and unchanged. Thought too of Sylvie – a little. He wished that she would come to him, swaying down the cloistered corridor, her stiff skirts hissing, the odd sad little smile on her mouth that indicated that she cared more for him than for any of the other soldiers in the here and now of Saint-Emile.

He knew he wasn't going to die and wasn't going to stumble through the rest of his life unsighted. His first excuse for going home had turned out to be a dud. Propped up on a bolster, he listened to the sounds in the cloister ward. There was something almost offensive about soldiers in clean nightshirts, pinioned by clean sheets. In the lines, blood and mud and corruption seemed so much of a piece that he had learned, almost, to ignore it. Here in Saint-Emile, however, indifference proved impossible; sturdy young athletes with stumps instead of legs, poets reduced to voiceless wrecks, observers with their eyes gouged out, a hand gone here, an arm there, organs pulped and blood, blood everywhere, bloodstained dressings, blood dripping through red rubber tubes into white enamel basins, filling them up like soup.

'Are you Gowry McCulloch?'

The voice was very light, very Irish. The speaker was a small man with a small, round head set on a neck like a celery stalk and a stiff, unyielding collar two sizes too large for him. Gowry wondered if the priest had shrunk and if when the war was finally over he would swell out to fill his vestments once again. The padre held a steaming tea mug in each hand and nodded a greeting.

'Nurse Tarrant sent me along. She said you wouldn't be asleep. Is it the pain keeping you awake?'

'No, sir, not pain exactly.'

'Are you – ah, disturbed?'

'I'm thirsty, Padre, thirsty rather than disturbed.'

The priest grinned and handed over the mug. Gowry took it in both hands and, clearing his throat first, sipped the hot sweet tea. There had been nights on the line when he would have sold his soul for a mug of hot tea. Now here it was, conjured up when he needed it. He felt grateful to Becky, and spoiled, and glad of the man's company to lift his mind from impossible longings.

'May I sit with you?' the priest said.

He was courteous and self-effacing, unlike several priests who had lodged at the Shamrock. Gowry shifted his legs beneath the blanket.

'Please do, Padre.'

'Are you well? I mean, are you feeling stronger?'

'I am, thank you.'

'Your eyes?'

'Not so bad, sir.'

'And the breathing?'

'Easier than it was yesterday.'

The priest seated himself on the bed. He seemed

almost weightless and made no indentation on the edge of the mattress. He took a great gulp of tea and sighed. 'By George, I needed that.'

'What time is it, Padre?' Gowry asked.

'Three, or close after. I say, do you mind if I smoke?'

'Not in the least,' Gowry said.

'I'd offer you one but in your condition . . .'

'Bad for me, I know.' Enviously, he watched the padre light a cigarette. 'Do you do rounds every night, sir?'

'Only when someone needs me – which, come to think of it, is pretty well every night,' the padre said. 'I gather you're not a Catholic.'

'I'm afraid not, Padre. It must be easier when you are.'

'Easier?'

'Dying, I mean.'

'Oh, I doubt that,' said the priest.

'Don't you comfort them at the last?'

'God comforts them. I'm only a representative of God's forgiveness and redemption. Are you from Belfast?'

'If I were an Ulsterman, Father, would I be letting you sit on my bed?'

The priest laughed. 'No, I doubt if you would.'

'Did Nurse Tarrant send you to find out if I'm Catholic?'

'Why would she be doing that?'

'Is she one – a Catholic, I mean?'

'She is,' said the padre. 'Her mother converted some years ago and Becky was confirmed in the faith.'

'Does she – I mean, is Nurse Tarrant devout?'

'No, no,' said the priest. 'Not devout at all, alas.'

Gowry watched smoke from the priest's cigarette spiral upwards and disperse in the vault above.

'Father,' he said, 'I'm a married man.'

'I know you are,' said the priest.

'Do you now?' said Gowry, faintly annoyed. 'How do you know that, sir?'

'It's in your records, your pay book.'

'Is Nurse Tarrant aware that I have a wife?'

'No – and it's not up to me to tell her.'

'Nurse Tarrant is an attractive young woman but I'm not after – you know what I mean?'

'I do,' said the padre.

Gowry handed back the empty tea mug and the padre put it on the floor.

Gowry said, 'I hardly know the lady. After I leave here in three or four days I doubt if we'll ever meet again.'

'Ships that pass,' the padre said, nodding.

'Besides, I'm in no fit state to take advantage of any lady and even if I was, I wouldn't.'

'Be easy,' said the padre. 'I didn't come to deliver a sermon on morals. Nurse Tarrant is a friend of mine, that's all. I think she's become quite fond of you.'

'What, in three days? Surely you're mistaken, sir.'

'It would do no harm to write to her when you go back to your unit. Becky would welcome a letter or two, I'm sure. Anything to offer a bit of comfort in these unfortunate times,' the priest said. 'Will you do it, Gowry McCulloch? Will you write her? She could do with a friend.'

'If you think it's proper?' said Gowry, guardedly.

'I think it's perfectly proper,' the priest said. 'Just don't tell her I suggested it, if you know what I mean.'

'I know what you mean, sir,' Gowry said.

His battledress had been cleaned and lay in a bundle under the bed. Underwear too. Stockings without holes in them. His own boots with a yellow label attached to the laces. All that was missing was his gas mask, his water bottle and his rifle. He had no idea where his rifle had got to after the gas shells splattered about him. He had a vague notion that he might be court-martialled for losing his rifle or have the cost of a replacement deducted from his pay.

The gunner from the Leinsters assured him, however, that that was a load of bollocks and he would be issued with everything he'd lost in the attack as soon as he got back to the depot. The gunner from the Leinsters was reluctant to leave Saint-Emile. He had developed a crush on Angela, an acute condition for which there was no hope of a cure.

The gunner had a wife back home and a regular

understanding with a girl in Heuvert, though Gowry doubted if the gunner and the French girl defined 'understanding' in quite the same way. He was making hay, the gunner said, while the sun shone, for when the war ended it would be back to shovelling coal on Dublin dock and that would be the end of his malarkey.

The kits were wheeled into the cloisters in the middle of the afternoon. Soon thereafter a surgeon and a physician ambled down the line of beds with Sister and a staff nurse trailing behind them. The officers pointed to a man here and a man there and in twelve or fourteen hours those men would be back in reserve at Heuvert, awaiting orders to move up to the front again.

After breakfast Gowry had been helped out of bed, given floppy sandshoes and a scratchy dressing-gown and told to test his legs by walking round the lawn. It was a fine, quiet morning with a pale sun visible behind cloud. Many patients had been moved out into the sun. There were beds on the terrace, chairs on the paved walks and a strange, unreal air of tranquillity over the place. Gowry walked around the threadbare grass on the lookout for Becky.

Ever since the padre had told him that the nurse had taken a shine to him he had felt boyishly excited. Last night, before Becky had gone on duty, they had talked for a long time and, screwing up his courage, he had told her that he was married, had told her quite a lot about Sylvie, Maeve and the Shamrock in fact.

Becky had been quiet for a little while but not unduly dismayed. But still, he was anxious to see her again, to test the strength of their friendship in, as it were, the cold light of day.

He circled the lawn, peering at every starched apron. Teacups and soup basins began to appear on the terrace. Orderlies were serving the midday meal outdoors. Behind the trees two doctors, still in white coats, were playing tennis, and a dozen walking wounded, including one subaltern, had found a set of French boules and were betting on the toss.

'Gowry. Gowry. Here, I'm up here.'

He looked up. She leaned from a tiny window on the third floor. Her blouse was open at the neck and a towel was wrapped about her head. She looked so fresh and cheerful in the sunlight that he uttered a little sigh, a little *ay-hay* of pleasure at the sight of her.

'Wait there. I'll be down in a second.'

Gowry stayed right where he was, legs shaking, sure now that the padre had not lied and that, married or not, he was in danger of falling in love.

The Germans had dragged six field guns into position behind a knoll four miles south of Mallefort and were shelling a section of the branch line close to Saint-Emile. The bombardment started without warning and two railway coaches suffered direct hits before anyone in headquarters twigged what was happening. Sappers were sent to haul away the wreckage and repair the damaged track, but the German gunners had the range and all night long shells came whistling over. The track remained closed until the third day when a concerted assault by the Royal Irish managed to breach the defences around the knoll and, with sporadic artillery support, drove Jerry back some three or four hundred yards. The cost to the Irish was high and the respite for the staff at Saint-Emile over all too soon. By midnight the worst of the wounded were pouring in and the operating theatre was in full swing.

Becky could spare only a few moments to say goodbye.

She came running down the length of the cloister. Sister Congreve opened her mouth to reprimand the girl then thought better of it.

Becky had taken off her bloody gown and gloves but she looked scared and her eyes were big and starcy in the flickering light of the cloister lamps.

Fourteen soldiers in battledress, Gowry among them, were seated among their packs by the blank stone wall. They were waiting to be marched to the railhead to board a train back to Heuvert. The war seemed much closer now. The incessant pummelling of the guns and the flicker of star shells in the sky intimated that there had been movement somewhere along the line, that some great plan or strategy had been put into operation without their knowledge or participation. Clad and kitted like fighting men, the soldiers were restless. Even the gunner from the Leinsters was keen to get back to the fray.

When Gowry saw Rebecca running down the cloister, he scrambled to his feet and went to meet her. He took her in his arms and held her tightly, pressed against the rough grain of his tunic, against buckles, buttons and straps. Held her and let her cry. He could think of a million things to say but none of them seemed appropriate. He held her in his arms and let her weep. When he kissed her he could feel her tears on his mouth.

'I can't stay,' Becky said. 'I'm sorry. I'm sorry. I can't stay.'

'I know,' Gowry said. 'I know, dearest.'

'Hold me, please, just for one more minute.'

'Yes,' he said, stupid and formal. 'Yes, of course I will.'

He kissed her again.

One of the soldiers jeered and another gruffly told him to shut up.

'Will you write to me?' Becky whispered.

'Yes, as soon as I can.'

'Where will you be? Where will I find you?'

'I don't know. It's all gone to hell out there by the sound of it,' Gowry said. 'I'll write you and tell you where I am.'

'And then I'll write back.'

'Yes.'

'I have to go, Gowry. Oh, I have to go now.'

'I know,' he said. 'I know.'

He took her hand and walked with her up the length of the cloister. He tried not to look at the men in the beds, at tubes and splints and great bloody wads of lint, tried not to hear the sounds of their distress. He looked down at Rebecca and held her hand. He could not remember when anyone had last cried over him and felt strong again, stronger than before.

'You'll forget me,' she said. 'Won't you?'

He shook his head. 'No. I'll write. I'll write tomorrow.'

'I will see you again, won't I?'

'Yes.'

'Tell me, please tell me I'll see you again.'

'You will, you will,' said Gowry. 'I'll make sure of it.'

'Dearest,' Becky said, 'take care.'

She stretched on toe-tip and kissed his mouth and, pushing herself away, ran into the main building out of sight. Gowry stared at the emptiness for a moment or two, then, wiping a hand over his face, turned and rejoined the men.

He sat on the stone floor and leaned against his pack.

The gunner poked him gently in the ribs.

'You've found a right corker there, old son,' he muttered. 'You lucky beggar, McCulloch, you bloody lucky old beggar.'

Then a transport sergeant appeared out of the darkness and shouted, '*Hup!*' and a few minutes later Gowry was en route back to the front.

Chapter Eleven

Angela had known for some time that Venus had once been a lover of Mars and that war and sexuality were inextricably linked. Long before she had donned a uniform she had been an outrageous flirt. She had gone into nursing only to escape her tyrannical father and suffocating village-green existence.

During training she had frequently been in trouble with men and two young residents had even fought over her favours in the cloakroom of the urological department. She counted herself fortunate not to have been dismissed. The moment war was declared she enlisted for active service and during a tour in a military hospital in Devon had made the ultimate sacrifice to a young second lieutenant in the Ox & Bucks who had sustained a dreadful wound in the abdomen in the retreat from Mons. The great, half-healed scar across Clive's belly had made not the slightest difference to his performance which had been brisk and efficient and as down-to-earth as an inexperienced girl could wish for. He had taken her again, less briskly, in a London hotel room just before he had gone off to the front to get himself killed.

Angela had wept buckets, of course, but was consoled by the attentions of the lieutenant-surgeon who had brought her the news about Clive. Nine days later, in another hotel room in London, she had discovered that poor Clive had not been quite so adept at love-making as all that.

Captain Bobby Bracknell was adept, very adept and although she knew perfectly well that he had a wife and three children back home she gave herself to him almost at first asking.

'I really don't know what you see in that chap,' Rebecca said.

'Ah, but you don't know him as well as I do.'

'Thank God for it,' said Becky. 'He's such an imperious swine.'

'Imperious? What's that mean?'

'Cocky.'

Angela smiled and brushed her hair.

She was well aware of Becky's inexperience in matters of – um, the heart. It had been typical of Becky to strike up a friendship with a priest, for instance, and to fall like a ton of bricks for an Irishman who, in Angela's opinion, Rebecca would be unlikely ever to see again.

'You're in love with Captain Bracknell, are you?' Becky asked.

'Lord no!' said Angela. 'I'm not that much of a fool.'

Becky was lying on the bed, propped up by two hard pillows. She had received a letter that forenoon and had run off into the lavatory to read it while Bobby Bracknell was entertaining Angela.

'He's only using you, you know,' Becky said.

'How do you know I'm not using him?'

'Angela! Really!'

Chin propped on hand, Becky leaned across the cot. She looked even more serious than usual, Angela thought. Becky was a socialist, of course, and socialists were always serious, same as Scotsmen were always dour and the Irish short on common sense. Her father was forever telling jokes about Irishmen called Paddy or Mick and, though she never found them especially amusing, they did not offend her.

Becky said, '*Are* you using him?'

'Who? Bobby Bracknell? Why, of course I am.'

'For what?'

'My pleasure,' Angela said. '*Un petit divertissement*.'

Becky edged closer, as if the subject of sex were so seditious that they might be sent home just for discussing it.

'How can it be pleasurable when you don't love him?'

'Oh, don't be utterly . . .'

Angela set down her hairbrush and got to her feet. She felt slightly dizzy for an instant, for Captain

Bracknell had been very thorough in his ministrations that afternoon. She lay across the cot, tummy down.

'Becky,' she said, 'have you really never been with a man?'

Becky shook her head.

'Never?' Angela said.

Becky shook her head again. 'No. Never.'

Reaching across the beds, Angela took Becky's hand and patted it sympathetically. 'Oh, I'm sorry,' she said. 'I'm so very, very sorry.'

'For what? It's not your fault,' said Becky.

'Have you never been asked?'

'Asked? What do you mean by asked?'

'Has no one, no man ever tried to . . .'

'Oh, that! Yes, of course they have.'

'But you didn't . . .'

'I most certainly did not,' said Becky.

'Weren't they attractive enough? Was that it?'

'No, that wasn't it,' said Becky. 'They were nice, some of them.'

'Well?'

'I wasn't in love with any of them.'

'But you don't have to be in love to – you know.'

'I believe you do,' said Becky. 'That's where you and I differ, Angela. It's none of my business if you choose to make a fool of yourself with a married man but I couldn't possibly do that sort of thing with someone I didn't care for very much.'

'Are you telling me,' said Angela, 'that you've never been in love?'

'Not to my knowledge, no.'

'Now that,' said Angela, 'is sad.'

Becky lay back on the bed, forearm across her eyes.

'I thought I was in love once,' she said, 'a long time ago.'

'With whom?' said Angela, not pressing.

'My cousin.'

'No harm in that,' said Angela. 'Cousins may kiss, you know.'

'Robbie hardly knew I existed,' Becky said. 'He went off to school in Edinburgh while I worked in the kitchens in his mother's house. I might have been his cousin but I was still a servant, you see.'

'So you loved him from afar?'

'He didn't treat me badly. He just didn't seem to – I mean, I thought perhaps when we were older, when he'd grown up, but . . .' She sighed. 'Robbie was killed seven months ago. In Picardy.'

Angela moved to her friend's bed and lay beside her, one foot on the floor.

'Who was he with?' she asked. 'What regiment?'

'The Gordon Highlanders.'

'In those wonderful kilts he must have looked very dashing.'

'I never saw Robbie in uniform,' Becky said.

'You dream about him, though, don't you?' Angela said.

Becky took her forearm from her eyes. 'How did you know that?'

'A guess, just a guess,' said Angela. 'Did he know you were over here?'

'Probably,' Becky said. 'Yes, he did. I'm sure he did.'

'Perhaps,' Angela said, 'he dreamed of you.'

'Well, it's a lovely thought.' Becky lay back and stretched her arms above her head. 'A lovely thought, even if it is nonsense.'

She had a sturdy little figure, Angela realised, not dainty but robust. She could well imagine Becky on a farm somewhere, scattering seed from a basket, like one of the illustrations in *Country Life*. Becky Tarrant was no farmhand, however. She was a highly trained surgical nurse and, Angela reminded herself, not so young as all that.

'Don't you dream about your Irishman?' Angela said.

'I pray for him,' Becky said, 'but I don't dream about him.'

'Why ever not?' said Angela.

'Because he isn't dead,' said Becky.

The trench was a stinker. Paddy Morgan, Burke and he had been detailed to locate the source of the smell and remove it. The source of the smell remained elusive, however, and no amount of sniffing at sandbags, peering into dugouts or probing in pools of slime brought it, as it were, to light.

The shelling was unrelenting and indicated that

Johnny Hun was up to something in the enemy trenches just a few hundred yards away across the flat, waterlogged terrain. Gowry heard from the boys who brought up the water buckets that Jerry was shifting men out of the quiet sector to reinforce the armies that were gathering along the Somme and was covering the withdrawal with heavy bombardment and a lot of vicious sniping.

It was around mid-morning when Sergeant Rafferty came round and asked what the hell they thought they were doing. Paddy Morgan told the sergeant they were looking for a smell and the sergeant went into one of his tight-lipped fits and said that if that soddin' Nervous Nellie, Lieutenant Quinn, wanted every soddin' stink tracked down then he'd better soddin' come and do it himself. Still muttering, the sergeant went off along the trench to the accompaniment of several *spangs* and *snits* from sniper bullets.

Paddy Morgan sat down and lit a Woodbine. Private Burke went off to find a corner in which to ease his stomach cramps, and Gowry McCulloch took a pad of greenish-grey notepaper and a chewed pencil stub from his pocket and began another letter to Becky.

Gowry's life these days was not exciting: trenches, billets, training fields, movement up and down the lines, in and out, back and forth, stand-to every morning, muster late in the afternoon, night attacks designed to keep Jerry jittery and the lads who wore the shamrock from becoming too complacent.

Soon it would be Easter, however, and the battalion would be pulled back for the Catholics to take a special mass.

Gowry wondered what it would be like to have a priest like Father Coyle hand you the wafer and the wine and if the wafer and the wine really did transform themselves into something powerful inside you and if you felt better afterwards. He was tempted to ask Becky if she would be taking mass but the question seemed too intimate for paper lovers. Paper lovers were all they were so far but, squatting on the firing step in a trench in the Hulluch sector, he felt quite optimistic about their future prospects.

'McCulloch, what do you think you're doing?'

He had been half asleep, the notepad flopping on his lap. He blinked and looked up. Lieutenant Quinn, hands on hips, glowered down at him.

He was young, was Quinn, and spoke a quaint brand of English, all clipped and nasal. He had schooled in England and served in the regiment there, and though his father was only a muckrake landowner in Sligo the lieutenant fancied himself as good as any Englishman. He certainly had the bearing and the right sort of moustache and, so Gowry had heard, had turned up in the officers' mess one night wearing a monocle and got laughed at for his pretensions.

The men regarded Lieutenant Quinn as dangerous, a Nervous Nellie so agitated and rash that he'd lead the platoon over the top with a whistle in his mouth and a revolver in hand, egging them on like that damned king at Agincourt. More to the point, he wouldn't let them back again, wouldn't retire. Miraculously unscathed, he would perch on a hummock and yell out in a voice as shrill and nasal as a whistling shell, 'Stand to me, damn you. Stand to me,' while the lads dropped around him like flies.

'I'm writing a letter, sir,' said Gowry.

'Did I tell you you could write letters?' Quinn said.

'No, sir,' said Gowry.

'Have you found the source of that appalling stench yet?'

'No, sir,' Gowry said. 'We have not.'

'Where's Burke?'

'Gone to relieve himself, I think.'

The lieutenant swung round and round and with his hands still on his hips, looked as if he were about to break into an Irish jig. He bent forward and peered at Paddy Morgan. Old Paddy was dead away, sleeping sound as an infant, the Woodbine smouldering in his fingers. The lieutenant knocked him with the toe of his boot until with a snort and a start Paddy awoke.

'Napping on duty, Morgan, are we?'

'Not me, sir. I ain't on duty.'

'Did I not give you an order?'

'Didn't think it was a order, sir, exactly,' Paddy said.

'Then what, pray tell me, do you suppose it was?'

Stirling

Paddy shook the remnants of the cigarette from his fingers and got reluctantly to his feet. Gowry eased himself from the firing step, tucked the writing pad into his jacket and tried to appear attentive. The lieutenant had looped the loop, of course, everyone knew that, but he was still an officer and officers had to be obeyed.

'You are a working party,' Lieutenant Quinn said. 'I have detailed you as a working party. For your information, Morgan, the condition of our section of the defences has not gone unremarked by the divisional commanders. We are fast becoming a laughing-stock for the state of our trenches. Look around you. Aren't they disgusting, man? Are they not disgusting?'

'They are, sir, aye, they are,' Paddy agreed.

'Then do something about it,' Quinn snapped. 'Find the body.'

'Pardon?' Paddy said.

'Find the body. There's a body buried here. I can smell it. Can't you smell it, McCulloch? Surely you can smell it?'

'I believe I can, sir, now you mention it,' Gowry said.

'Then find the blessed object and do the decent thing with it.'

'An' what would that be now?' Paddy said.

'Christian burial. Give the chap a good Christian burial.'

'What if he's a Hindu, sir?' said Paddy.

'Do not be insolent, Morgan. I know he's a Christian and deserves a Christian burial.' The lieutenant took his hands from his hips and, just as Burke came tottering round the corner, leaped up on to the firing step. 'How do I know he's a Christian? By the smell, man, by the smell.'

'Catholic, sir, or Protestant?' said Paddy.

'Catholic, of course,' the lieutenant said. 'So once you find him you had better fetch the priest. Do the decent thing. Do the . . .'

The object on the top of the trench was sufficiently hard to deflect the sniper's bullet and reduce its velocity and the lump of metal tore a huge hole in Lieutenant Quinn's throat. He let out a gurgling cry, lifted his hands to his face, pitched from the firing step and landed in a heap at Paddy Morgan's feet.

'Jaysus!' Paddy said, wide-eyed.

'He dead?' said Burke, coming forward.

'Aye, he's dead,' said Paddy. 'Poor bastard.'

'Now what do we do?' said Burke.

'Send for a priest?' Gowry suggested.

'Nah, wait for the sergeant,' Paddy said and, seated cross-legged at the officer's feet, lit another cigarette while Gowry, shaking just a little, fished out his notepad and resumed his letter to Becky.

The sky shone like polished plate and a warm breeze from the river bore the fragrances of spring. On the lawns of the Ecole the grass had returned, bulbs burst out in neglected flowerbeds and the budding leaves of the oak trees fluttered valiantly as a party of off-duty nurses set out for town.

Saint-Emile had suffered some loose shelling, a German aeroplane had crashed behind the tiny twelfth-century church, and a row of cottages at the bottom of the hill had been smashed. In spite of the damage cafés, taverns, cheese shops and fruit-sellers did good business and, hidden behind the wagon-lairs, the brothel where queues formed from dusk until dawn.

The nurses walked in twos and threes, arm-in-arm, light-hearted because they had an afternoon off and a holiday spirit was abroad. Becky and Angela, a shade more dignified than the others, brought up the rear.

Men were everywhere, not just elderly French shop-keepers but hordes of soldiers hopping on sticks or resting their bandaged heads while they bathed their throats with good strong beer. They cheered and whistled at the nurses, for hospital discipline did not extend beyond the school gates and here, in April sunshine in a battered little French town, Mars and Venus met on equal terms.

'Bong-joyer, Madam-yo-zell.'

'Bong-joyer yourself, Raymond.'

'*Parl-lez vouz l'amour?*'

'*Ah, Monsieur Soldat, si je le parlais vous ne me comprendriez pas.*'

'Par-dong?' The soldier shrugged his thin shoulders and glanced helplessly around. 'What'd she say? What'd she say?'

'Told you to bugger off, sonny.'

'She what?'

'Told you to bugger off or she'd stick another horse pill up your arse.'

'Yay, I've had enough o' those t' last a bleedin' lifetime.'

The nurse, a probationer, fashioned an unladylike gesture with forefinger and thumb then, chuckling, followed her friends on down to the chocolate shop, while the soldiers outside the tavern continued to rib the young Casanova.

Two or three minutes later Angela and Becky passed by.

'What about 'er then, Raymond? You not 'ave a fancy for 'er?'

'Not me! She'd eat me for breakfast. 'Sides, she's Bracknell's bint.'

'What about 'er chum then? She looks like she could use some fun.'

'She's a staffie.'

'Maybe she is, but sure an' she's got a nice little bum.'

Becky and Angela were well aware of the soldiers' intentions and glanced at each other and smiled. For a moment Becky even fancied that Gowry might be seated among the wounded – but Gowry was at the front, of course. She'd had a letter from him yesterday and would have another tomorrow, perhaps. She would open it carefully, slitting the censor's seal, and sit on the bed and read it over and over and tell herself that she couldn't possibly mean as much to Gowry McCulloch as he meant to her, that he had a wife, a daughter, a life in Dublin and that she was no more to him than a pleasant little diversion.

'Oh, look,' Angela said. 'It's Bobby.'

'Where?'

'There in the courtyard. See.'

'Did you know he'd be here?'

'Oh, don't be silly.' Angela gripped her elbow and drew her towards the courtyard café where the officers were seated. 'Come along. We're just as entitled to be here as they are.'

'Angela!'

'Well, we are, ain't we?'

If the officers were displeased to have women intrude on their leisure they gave no sign. With almost Teutonic formality Captain Bracknell rose from his chair at the rickety iron table, clicked his heels and bowed.

'Ladies,' he said, 'good afternoon.'

'Good afternoon, Captain Bracknell,' Angela said. 'May we join you?'

Becky was dismayed to see that Bobby Bracknell's companion was none other than Surgeon-Major Sanderson. She flushed and began to apologise but Mr Sanderson smiled and told her to sit by him. He looked different in the broad light of day, older, wearier, less rather than more relaxed. His cap and gloves were upon the table next to a plate of greasy black sausages and a basket of bread rolls. Becky felt dreadful about interrupting his lunch.

'What will you have, Nurse Harrison?' Bobby Bracknell enquired.

'What's that you're drinking?'

'Plonk,' the captain told her. 'It's palatable, though.'

'A glass of that would be perfect.'

Angela had the enviable confidence of good breeding and was quite at ease in male company. She sat back and looked around.

'What about you, Rebecca?' Mr Sanderson said.

'I've no head for wine,' Becky said. 'Is there tea to be had, sir?'

'The tea's undrinkable but the coffee's not bad.'

'Coffee then, if you please.'

The surgeon signalled and a young girl in a floral apron came scurrying out from under the awning. She had pinched, sallow features and looked fevered. From the cavernous shadow behind her came the hiss of a steam urn and a waft of beer fumes. Mr Sanderson spoke quietly to the girl in French. He was gentle with her, almost tender, for he, like Becky, knew that she was ill. He touched her skinny forearm as if taking her pulse, and made sure she understood what was required before she hurried back indoors.

'Tubercular?' Becky said.

'Probably,' Mr Sanderson said.

Jessica Stirling

'Should she be serving food and drink?'

'Probably not,' said Mr Sanderson. 'But what else is she to do?'

The café had been a gatehouse at one time. The windows were boarded over now and the doors had been removed. Becky could see little of what lay within, only a figure in an apron, the glint of a hot-water urn and the flicker of a stove. Beyond that, nothing. She wondered if the Germans had ever held Saint-Emile, if German nurses had sat where she was sitting now.

'Ah.' Captain Bracknell broke off his conversation with Angela. 'Now here's a little lady who might be able to shed some light on the mystery.'

Becky looked up. 'What mystery's that, sir?'

'Why the Irish are here,' Bobby Bracknell said.

'I'm Scottish,' Becky said, 'not Irish.'

'Ah, but you consort with the Irish, don't you?'

'We all consort with the Irish,' said Becky.

'I think, Robert,' Mr Sanderson said, 'that we might let our argument lapse now ladies are present.'

'Why shouldn't we be friends with the Irish?' Becky asked.

'Because they are lazy, insolent and interested only in drink,' Captain Bracknell said. 'Look at the fiasco with the gas masks.'

'Robert, Robert, please,' Mr Sanderson said.

'They're so ill-trained and ignorant they don't even know where to find the hole to stick their

238

heads in,' Captain Bracknell said. 'Then they come crying to us to help them out of a jam entirely of their own making. Typical!'

Becky bridled. 'Typical of what, sir?'

'They don't want to be here. The vast majority would be much happier rampaging through the streets of Dublin. They're trouble-makers, born trouble-makers. What sticks in my craw is that they aren't awfully good at it.'

'At what?' said Angela.

'Making trouble.'

Mr Sanderson sighed. 'Would you include the Ulsters?'

'Certainly not. The Ulsters are loyal to the crown.'

'Robert, you're a bigot,' Mr Sanderson said. 'Change the subject, please.'

'I'm no bigot,' Bobby Bracknell said. 'I'm a realist, if anything.'

Becky heard herself say, 'There aren't any conscripts in the Irish brigades, Captain Bracknell. They are all volunteers. If they volunteered to fight for king and country surely they deserve to be treated with more respect.'

'I know how I'd treat them,' the captain said. 'I'd shoot the damned lot.'

'What do you have against the Irish, Bo— Captain?' said Angela. 'The regiments are full of them. Surely there are some decent soldiers among them.'

'Those from the north, yes,' said the captain. 'It's all this nationalist twaddle I can't stand. Baying for freedom, freedom, as if we didn't look after them properly.'

'You are in a mood today,' said Angela.

Mr Sanderson examined a sausage, prodding it cautiously with a fork. His gaunt cheeks had a dusky tinge and Becky knew that he did not share the captain's prejudices. She watched the thin, black sausage slither on the plate while the serving girl brought coffee, a cup not a pot, and a tiny glass jug of boiled milk. Captain Bracknell crossed one leg over the other and shifted his chair on the cobbles. Angela propped her plump elbows on the tabletop, not in the least embarrassed by her lover's remarks.

'Aren't you Irish, Captain Bracknell?' Becky heard herself say.

'What if I am?' the captain said. 'Surely that gives me the right to criticise, don't you think?'

'Kerry,' said Mr Sanderson, 'is a far cry from Belfast, Robert.'

'Am I to be held responsible for where I happened to be born?'

'Are they?' said Becky, quickly. 'The Irish volunteers, I mean?'

'What do you know about it? You're a Scot, for God's sake.'

Mr Sanderson put the sausage out of its misery by cutting it in half. He transferred a portion to his mouth, slipped it into his cheek and let it stay there.

'Robert,' he said, 'I do believe you're worried.'

'Worried? What do I have to worry about?'

Captain Bracknell said. 'I'm having the absolute time of my life.' He glanced at Angela, then quickly away. 'When the show's over I'll go back to Buckingham to cut and stitch those dear ladies who are in need of repair, but if the Sinn Feiners have their way I won't be able to go home to Ireland ever again. Damn it all, I'll be an outcast in my native land and the war – *this* war will count for nothing.'

'Robert, that's nonsense,' Mr Sanderson said.

Becky recalled Gowry's accounts of mountains and plains and remote whitewashed cottages and wondered if his view of Ireland was a total illusion. There was something desperate and despairing in Captain Bracknell. She studied him from the corner of her eye and noticed that Angela was doing the same.

'Oh, I know what you're thinking,' the captain said. 'You're wondering if poor Bobby Bracknell has lost the place entirely. Not so. There is trouble brewing in Ireland, serious trouble.'

'When is there not?' said Angela.

'I believe,' the captain said, 'that the nationalists are trying to make a pact with the Germans.'

'Surely not?' said Mr Sanderson.

'If there is an armed insurrection and the Germans support it then every last Irishman will come under suspicion.'

'They wouldn't shoot *you*, Bobby, would they?' Angela said.

'Of course not,' Captain Bracknell said. 'But I would be stigmatised along with the rest. All of us.'

'Except the unionists?' Mr Sanderson put in.

'That's true,' said the captain. 'The unionists would be heroes, a situation that would suit the British government very well.'

Becky listened as the argument opened up again. She knew no more than anyone else what it really meant to be Irish. She had always thought of Ireland as a larger version of Mull. Now she realised how naïve she'd been, that Captain Bracknell – Gowry too perhaps – were men divided against themselves and that the captain's anger was justified.

She sipped coffee and said nothing while Mr Sanderson wearily tried to calm his deputy. Soon they would be sweating over the damaged souls that the stretcher-bearers brought out of the darkness, working together as a team, anonymous in sterilised gowns and masks. Would it matter then what views they held, what prejudices?

There had been no division in her dear cousin Robbie. He had gone willingly to fight and die for a cause in which he believed. Were the Irish so very different? she wondered. And listening to Captain Bracknell, that stiff, surrogate Englishman, she realised to her dismay that they were.

Chapter Twelve

The theory that Kaiser Bill had organised a Sinn Fein uprising in Dublin gave the boys in the line a laugh, if nothing else.

The newspapers were full of German machinations and the big war had been wiped from the headlines. Among the Irish in the line there was much speculation about the timing of the rebellion and its eventual outcome. They were still sore and disgruntled when, on a fine April morning just after Easter, Fritz launched another gas attack.

Gowry counted himself fortunate to have been out of the sector on that particular morning. He had had enough gas to last a lifetime. He had in fact been sent to the west of Heuvert with a small detachment from the Rifles to join a Rangers' raiding party. Raiding was the latest bright idea to come down from GHQ, the first tweak of a policy of aggression, and the Connaughts had been training behind the lines for several weeks and imagined they knew how stunting worked.

Led by Lieutenant Soames, the little detachment from the Rifles arrived in the Rangers' support trench about two in the afternoon. They were fed, given time to rest, briefed on their role in the raid, then guided through a series of communications trenches to the front line. It was a fine evening, the sky streaked with skimpy cloud. Dipping below the wasteland the sun shot long bars of radiant light into the trench and, dazzled by the glow, Gowry didn't notice Maurice at first.

'You, soldier, smarten up. Look at those buttons. Look at that badge. Disgraceful. I don't know what me owd mother would be thinking of you now.'

'Maurice,' Gowry said, grinning.

'You, what's your name?' a Connaught officer barked.

'Private McCulloch, sir.'

'Do you know this man, Sergeant Leonard?'

'I do, sir, I do.'

'Good man, is he?'

'One of the best,' said Maurice.

'Not another bloody Boy Scout then?'

'Been in khaki since the beginning, sir.'

'Thank God for that,' said the lieutenant. 'One never knows what will come piddling up from the reserve these days. Be bloody Girl Guides next.' He peered at Gowry for a moment longer then turned to greet Lieutenant Soames.

'I didn't know you were in the neighbourhood, Maurice,' Gowry said.

'Been out since February. Have you heard from me mam lately?'

'I had a letter last month.'

Maurice nodded. 'You've no fresh news from Dublin then?'

'Only what the officers tell us. You?'

'Nothing definite. I hear they've caught that bastard Roger Casement, though. Soddin' traitor. Hangin's too good for him.'

'Who told you Casement had been caught?'

'Our lieutenant.'

'What's he like, your lieutenant?'

Maurice shrugged. 'Steady enough, I suppose.'

'He's not a regular then?'

'Straight out o' college in 1914.'

'He'll take us in, will he?' Gowry said.

'Aye, an' bring us out again,' said Maurice. 'Some of us at any rate.'

'When's the muster?'

'Midnight,' Sergeant Leonard said.

At a quarter past the hour the wire-cutters slipped stealthily over the parapet into no-man's-land. Gowry waited in the trench, listening for the *tric-trac* of machine-gun fire that would indicate they'd been spotted, but no sound came from the German lines ninety yards away.

Maurice was somewhere to his left, along with Lieutenant Soames. He had been allotted a flank position and would go out with the second wave. He didn't know the man beside him and all he could see was a shape grafted on to the wall of earth below the breastwork. He could hear the man breathing, though, panting. He wanted to make conversation, to crack a joke, share a blessing, but knew he'd be punished if he uttered a sound. Spoken commands had been replaced by hand signals and he had been told that he must count to fifty before he went over the top. He rested the rim of his helmet on the earth and tried to concentrate. He found himself thinking of Becky, though, and wondered what it would be like to lie with her, to feel her body against his. If I'm killed tonight, he thought, what a waste it will be, what a shameful waste.

Shapes stirred beside him. Someone punched his arm. Clink and clatter of equipment. Muffled scrabble of boots on the steps. Shapes above him silhouetted against a dark blue sky. Bad night for a stunt. Far too clear, the moon well up over the horizon. He wondered where Maurice was. He moved left, shuffling along a duckboard strewn with straw. Things moved in the straw. Living things. He was afraid of the darkness below, and looked up at the sky. He began counting. Twenty-eight. Twenty-nine. He ran his hands over his webbing. Bayonet, water bottle, field-dressing kit, butt of his rifle, smooth and stiff. Thirty-nine. Forty. Forty-one. He was wheezing again. Forty-five, six, seven. He thought of Father Coyle and crossed himself like a Catholic and for an instant was one with Becky.

Then he gripped the ladder, found the step, and slithered over the top.

At first it appeared like a simple gunshot wound, the path of the bullet obvious. In Captain Bracknell's opinion a flaccid abdominal wall indicated no gut lesion but Mr Sanderson preferred to err on the side of caution and the patient, a sandy-haired private, was immediately prepared for surgery.

The ache had returned to Becky's spine but she was steady enough on her feet and clear in the head as she arranged the instruments required for the laparotomy, a procedure that called for both speed and delicacy and that carried a high risk of infection. Sister Congreve was acting anaesthetist and Angela and another theatre nurse made up the team.

As soon as the patient had been rendered drowsy, Captain Bracknell prepared the skin surface for the first incision while Becky counted swabs and packs and laid them on a sterilised tray. Counting took her mind off the rivet in her spine. She brought out saline bags and a drip blood stand and positioned them, then she gowned and gloved Mr Sanderson.

It was crowded in the operating room. All three tables were in use. She could hear the cries of the wounded in the examination room and one huge, unintelligible shout, like someone cheering at a football match. Outside, though, the night was quiet. The distant bombardment had ceased. She wondered if the deadlock had been broken at last, wondered where Gowry was right now and prayed that he was safe out of harm's way.

Sister Congreve administered gas and oxygen and the soldier went out like a light. Mr Sanderson gripped his scalpel firmly, made a skin incision three inches above the umbilicus and drew the blade down around the belly button. Becky handed him towels. He ligated the bleeding points, completed the incision through the abdominal wall and peeled back the wound edges.

Captain Bracknell swiftly mopped up the viscous fluids within the peritoneum and the blood that had accumulated in the cavity.

'I see the Germans have invaded Ireland,' he said.

'Not now, Robert,' Mr Sanderson murmured.

'Is that true, sir?' Becky asked.

'Of course it isn't true,' said Mr Sanderson.

'The English are shooting our dear wives and children,' said the captain.

'That's just dirty German propaganda,' Sister Congreve chimed in. 'Our boys won't be duped by Fritz's nonsense.'

'In case anyone's interested,' Mr Sanderson said, 'this young fellow has a perforation in the small intestine. We'll pack it before we continue.'

Becky unwrapped a pad of warm, moist gauze and passed it to Captain Bracknell. Leaning carefully across the chief's forearms, he wrapped it around the intestinal tear before Mr Sanderson teased out a further ten or twelve inches of the soldier's small bowel.

'How's his breathing, Sister?' Mr Sanderson asked.

'Steady,' Sister Congreve answered. 'He's a strong boy.'

'Oh, look, there's another hole,' Captain Bracknell said. 'Bit of a mess, ain't it? Any damage to the mesentery, sir?'

'There doesn't appear to be.'

'We won't be doing a resection then?'

'No, we'll suture,' said Sanderson. 'The perforations are obvious and not too extensive. Robert, what do you say?'

'I couldn't agree more. Give the poor devil a fighting chance. I'm glad we opened him, though. Nurse Harrison, the artery forceps, if you please.'

The operation proceeded without drama or mishap and in due course Mr Sanderson handed over stitching to Captain Bracknell whose long, blunt fingers passed confidently in and out of the lips of the incision while the chief adjusted the tension of the clamps and snipped away little tabs of ragged tissue with the beak of his forceps.

'I must confess,' the captain said, 'that Irish though I am, the nation and what it stands for remain a complete mystery to me. Lord knows, I was brought up breathing an air of suffering and injustice, but to have our Tommies being shot in the streets of Dublin while I'm here in France stitching the beggars up strikes me as a ridiculous irony.'

'Why don't you talk to them, Robert?'

'Talk to whom?'

'The rank and file?' Mr Sanderson said.

Becky could see the captain's hard, dark eyes slotted between his mask and the tight, damp band of his sterile cap. Even with most of his face obscured he looked decidedly Irish. He was a good surgeon, though, and according to Angela a tireless lover, but something about the captain, something hybrid, disturbed her.

'What can I possibly learn from the rank and file?'

'Humility,' Sister Congreve told him.

The captain was far too professional to let anger interfere with his craft. Without lifting his head he darted a glance at the woman at the top of the table.

'Humility, Captain Bracknell,' the sister went on, 'is not the same as servitude, you know.'

The rivet in the small of Becky's back tightened. Pain bored up her spinal cord. She let out a little '*uh!*' of shock and surprise.

'What it is, Rebecca?' Sister Congreve enquired. 'Are you sick again?'

'No, I – I . . .'

'Nurse Tarrant, do you wish to be relieved?'

'No, Sister, I – I'm – my back hurts a bit, that's all. It's just a twinge.'

'Too much exercise,' said Sister Congreve.

'Or not enough of the right sort,' said Captain Bracknell.

'What do you mean by that, sir?' said Becky, snappishly.

She felt Angela's hand on her arm, a warning squeeze. She had almost forgotten where she was. It wouldn't do to cheek an officer and risk being sent back to England, not to be here when Gowry came back for her.

'Dreaming of thee, dreaming of thee,' the captain crooned. 'Oh, how I long to be dreaming of thee.'

'Robert, have you been at the bottle?'

'Not I, sir. Not I.'

'Please concentrate on your sutures and never mind the serenade.'

'Of course,' said Bobby Bracknell.

He was satisfied now that he had exacted revenge, not on Sister Congreve but on the pathetic little Scots woman who, so Angela told him, had never had a man inside her. He knew precisely what Becky Tarrant needed to get rid of her back pain. If it weren't for clingy Angela he wouldn't be entirely averse to administering the treatment himself.

'Are you all right, Rebecca?' Mr Sanderson asked.

'Absolutely fine, sir.'

'Are you sure?'

'I'm sure, sir,' Becky said.

'Good, then let's close this fellow up and move on?'

*　　*　　*

From the moment he stepped into no-man's-land Gowry was lost. He scuttled along behind the Rangers and prayed that he wouldn't be left behind. He was afraid less of being shot than of failing to keep up. He longed to make Becky proud of him, to be her Irish hero. He stumbled and fell to his knees while the Rangers vanished into the darkness. Ninety yards to the German line. Ninety yards? How far was that in kilometres? Maurice would know. Maurice was good at measuring things. Where the heck *was* Maurice? Why wasn't Maurice here to look out for him?

The rifle tangled in his legs when he tried to rise. He hadn't trained hard enough, hadn't trained at all. The flash of an exploding grenade was astonishingly violent and in the same split second he saw the livid little tongue of a Maxim gun spitting out bullets at six hundred rounds per minute. He flattened himself on the ground and heard the lieutenant – he assumed it was Soames – screaming, '*Down, down, down. Get down, damn you.*'

All fear went out of him. He was a fighting man after all, a fighting Irishman. He got up and ran through the rain of bullets towards the silhouettes on the edge of the German trench. He groped. Found his bayonet. Cinched it to the flanges. Came up hard behind the backs of the Rangers lying against the sap. He flopped down beside them, slapped one of the Rangers on the buttocks and shouted into his ear, 'Where's the gun? Where is that soddin' Maxim?'

The Ranger gave no answer. His helmet was tilted at a funny angle, cocked like a straw boater on a hot race day. Faceless. Sightless. All blood. Gowry rolled away. Another man, flung back like a crucified ram. A sergeant – not Maurice – on his belly, retching blood, the vivid little tongue of the Maxim spitting lead around him. Gowry rolled again, holding the rifle close to his body. Rolled under the springy ends of the wire and tumbled into a clamshell crater close to the rim of the enemy trench. Four soldiers were already cowering there, pinned down by machine-gun fire.

'*Christ, ah Christ, ah Christ!*'

'What's wrong with you?' Gowry shouted.

'Who'll take us back. Who'll take us back?'

'Back?' The possibility hadn't occurred to Gowry. 'Back where?'

The Maxim was off to the left, thirty or forty yards away. He couldn't see it but he could hear its insatiable chatter.

'It's all gone wrong,' one of the soldiers told him, shouting. 'There's wire in the trench. The bastards've laid wire in the trench.'

'How many went over?' Gowry shouted.

'Both officers an' fifteen or twenty men.'

'Are you sure?'

'Sure an' I'm bloody sure.'

'We'd better go back then?'

'We can't go back, not till we're told.'

Gowry leaned against the side of the crater, turned on his hip, pulled himself up to the lip and peered back at the British lines just as the shelling commenced and trench mortars pummelled German positions. The high screaming note of the shells and the pulsations of the mortar bombs landing on the trenches engulfed him. He could see the wire twisting away like a thorn hedge to the site of the machine-gun emplacement. He could see nothing in the trench in front of him, though, no sign of forward movement or retaliatory fire. The attack had been smothered. The raiders were lying dead or wounded or doggo or, if the soldier was right, had been swallowed up in a German trap. There was nothing to aim at, nothing to be seen, only the Jerry machine-gunners' incessant strafing and a sky bright with the glare of star shells.

Gowry was thinking what to do next, how to get out of it, when nine or ten Tommies swarmed over the rim of the depression. They came from all sides at once and Gowry would have stuck the bayonet in if he'd had room to swing.

'*Wey, wey, wey, wey, z'us, z'us, z'us.*'

'Reilly, that you?'

'*Aye, aye, z' me.*'

The support unit, his mob. Seemed he'd got here first after all. He was surprised that any of them had made it. Several had to be bundled over the edge, wounded, mortally or otherwise. None of them, he realised, could tell him what to do. He wondered again where Maurice was. God, but wouldn't Maggie be mad if Maurice left him out here to die?

Here we go again, Gowry thought, a choice that's no choice at all.

Take it or leave it: Flanagan's law.

'*McCulloch? McCulloch, what the bloody 'ell do you think you're doin'?*'

'Gettin' out of here,' Gowry said, and, clambering over legs, buttocks and thighs, hauled himself out of the clamshell crater and crawled up the pock-marked slope towards the German trench.

She was dewed with perspiration and her undergarments clung uncomfortably to her hips and thighs. The night air was cool, though, and above the oaks the moon hung in a haze of starlight. She was not alone on the terrace. An ambulance crew was drinking tea by the kitchen doors and one of the regular chaplains was strolling up and down the terrace with his arm about the shoulder of a weeping soldier.

The sandy-haired Tommy had been stitched up and wheeled away to a recovery ward. In a few minutes she would be obliged to return to the theatre where another soldier would be hoisted on to the table and the whole process would begin again. Meanwhile, she sipped tea, let her body cool and wondered when the ache in her loins would ease.

He came up on her, stealthy as a ghost. He had peeled off his gown and unbuttoned his shirt. She could see his under-vest and the curly dark brown hair on the upper part of his chest. Angela had told her that he was hairy all over, a revelation that Becky found disgusting.

The captain flipped open a worn silver case. 'Cigarette?'

Becky shook her head. 'No, thank you.'

He stood close to her, looking out across the lawn, cigarette held between finger and thumb. He inhaled deeply and released smoke from his mouth.

'I'm sorry if I upset you,' the captain said.

'You didn't upset me, sir.'

'You don't have to call me "sir". Angela doesn't call me "sir" when we're alone.' He tugged on the cigarette. 'How bad is that back of yours?'

'It's just a sprain,' Becky said.

'Someone should take a look at it.'

'You?'

'I was thinking, rather, of Major Caufield. On the other hand if you'd like me to examine you, I'm sure that can be arranged.'

'Don't you ever think of your wife?' Becky said.

'Pardon?'

'When you're with Angela, don't you ever think of your wife?'

He dropped the cigarette to the paving and trod on it. 'My wife is in England. Angela is here. And never the twain shall meet, thank God. In any case, I doubt if Eleanor would grudge me some of the comforts of home.'

'Angela isn't the first, is she?'

'How curious you are, Rebecca. No, Angela isn't the first.' He paused. 'Nor can I guarantee that she will be the last. Men do have needs, you know.'

'I'm well aware of that,' said Becky.

'Don't women have needs too?' Bobby Bracknell said. 'I'm certain they do. Much the same sort of needs as men, in fact. Don't pretend you don't know what I'm talking about.'

'I know perfectly well what you're talking about,' Becky said.

'Don't you agree with me?'

'It's not a subject to which I've given much thought.'

'Really! Even with your new Irish sweetheart panting in the wings.'

'What do you know about my—'

'I know he has a wife,' Bobby Bracknell said.

'What has Angela been telling you?'

'No need to fly off the handle,' the captain said. 'We only have your welfare at heart, Rebecca.'

She wanted back to the tiled white room, out of range of the rich Anglicised voice of the Irish surgeon. She had given much thought to what she would do if Gowry returned to Saint-Emile or if by some marvellous chance they were able to meet away from the fighting. She had made no decision, however. She preferred to dwell on a kiss and a fond embrace and close the door on how far affection – love – might take her.

'He isn't a Catholic, you know,' the captain said, 'your Irishman.'

'So he told me.'

'He isn't even a nationalist.'

'He told me that too.'

'Good God! Is that all you two did – talk politics?'

'We – we didn't do anything else, anything wrong,' Becky said.

Why did this man, this hybrid, have to make chastity sound like a vice? He thought her naïve; that was it! He thought her naïve because she had never yielded to a man. Oh, what a grand excuse the war had become for Bobby Bracknell and his ilk.

'What regiment is he with?'

'The Sperryhead Rifles,' Becky said.

'Well, they'll be in the thick of it soon.'

'What do you mean? What have you heard?'

'The Germans have been targeting the Irish divisions,' the captain said. 'I reckon the Irish will be pushed forward, partly to test their loyalty, partly to keep them from brooding on what's happening in Dublin.'

'What does that have to do with Gowry, with Private McCulloch? He isn't a nationalist. You said so yourself.'

'Oh, we're all nationalists at heart,' the captain said. 'If you make a deep enough incision in any Irishman you'll find a pocket of nationalism somewhere inside him.'

'Even you?'

The captain sighed. 'Even me.'

'Why are you telling me this?'

'If anything should happen to your sweetheart, Rebecca, and you feel the need of a shoulder to cry on . . .' He had the decency to pause. 'I'm always available. After all, we're much the same, you and I.'

'Are we?'

'Strangers in a strange land.'

'Oh, for God's sake!' Becky said.

'No, really! Really, we are.'

'Is that the story you spun to get into Angela's bed?'

He shrugged. 'I didn't have to spin Angela any sort of story. She got what she wanted, all that I have to give.'

'And what is that?' said Becky. 'And don't tell me it's love.'

He laughed, a furry sound in the back of his throat, and leaned closer.

In the night air she could hear restless sounds from the wards and the plaintive drone of the chaplain's voice praying over the soldier at the terrace's end. The captain whispered in her ear. His suggestions brought Gowry vividly to mind. She realised then that she wanted him, wanted to have him within her. There was no vagueness, no wavering in her resolution. Suddenly she felt as light as smoke in the air of the night.

'What do you say, Rebecca?' Captain Bracknell murmured.

She sluiced away the dregs of the tea with a twist of the wrist and thrust herself boldly against him, pressing her breasts against his chest. He seemed, she thought, alarmed by her response and looked down his long autocratic nose at her while he awaited an answer.

'Sod off, Captain Bracknell,' she told him, then, with a little skip, went off down the terrace to refill her tea mug and stuff down a bun before she returned, refreshed, to the next order of business that the war brought in.

Gowry lay on his belly and peered into the trench. Sure enough it was a dummy, a false arm of the main trench, wired and sandbagged to deceive observers. There were no signs of Rangers trapped there, only three or four dead Germans, and one Irish corporal – Soames's batman – who was trying vainly to extricate himself from the tangle with a pair of wire cutters.

From the waist down his body was encased in the wire and he snipped away at the strands with astonishing patience and even when Gowry's head appeared above him seemed disinterested in the possibility of rescue.

'Are you stuck?' Gowry said.

'Sure an' I'm stuck. I'm bleedin' to bloody death down here.'

'Is that you, Donnaghy?'

'Aye, Gowry. It's me.'

'Where's your man? Where's Soames?'

'Gone chargin' off with the others.'

'An' the Jerries?'

'We shot a few, the rest scarpered.'

'Anythin' I can do for you?' Gowry asked.

'Could do with some water, you got any spare.'

Gowry unstrapped his water bottle, dangled it into the trench and released it. There wasn't much by way of light but the oily blue mud on the bottom of the trench gave off a faint sheen and he could see that it was all pretty hopeless as far as Donnaghy was concerned.

The batman's sleeves were torn to shreds, his hands and arms bleeding. If Soames had abandoned him there was nothing to be done. If they took the Jerry emplacements and held them Soames would send a party to bring Donnaghy in but that, Gowry knew, was a long shot and he suspected that the batman would be dead before then.

'There's more behind me,' Gowry said. 'They'll get you out.'

'Aye, sure an' they will,' Donnaghy said.

'I'd better push along.'

'You'd better,' Donnaghy said; then, 'Gowry?'

'What?'

'Good luck.'

Perhaps he should have stayed to look out for Donnaghy or have gone back to the clamshell and told the others that it was safe to advance, but instead he pressed on. He was on a parallel extension to the Maxim's position and so far the gunners hadn't spotted him. He wondered where Soames's party had got to and how he could link up with them. Crouched low, he picked his way along the top of the trench towards the machine-gun.

There was one almighty racket coming from the line now, the party in full swing. He couldn't see the moon any more. He kept inside the wire, glancing down now and then into the main trench in case he ran on to Jerry. He had made about thirty yards when the second phase of the bombardment began. Field guns, heavy stuff pounding away, the British gunners seeking the range. What the artillery thought they were doing targeting a salient occupied by a raiding party he couldn't imagine. Breakdown in communications, most like. Hardly mattered. One gun was much the same as another. When the shells came whistling over Gowry dropped his rifle and threw himself down on the dirt.

The explosion deafened him and the blast ripped over him with such force that he thought it would strip him bare. He opened his mouth and gasped as air was forced out of his lungs. The air around him turned searingly hot and a rain of debris came down around him, great chunks of earth, metal fragments, rocks, pebbles and wire thudding and pattering around him, striking his body like firm little blows from a boxer's fists. Then dust, acrid, choking dust. A viscous hissing filled his ears and the ground seemed to be flowing away from under him – then stillness, everything dimmed and reticent, just the distant chirrup–chirrup–chirrup of the Maxim, faint and far away.

Gowry had no idea whether he was out for seconds or minutes. Couldn't have been much longer than a minute or two, though, for the machine-gun was still singing and the sound had grown loud again. He lifted his head and spat out dirt. His mouth was bleeding. He explored with his tongue, found a gash on the inside of his cheek and a big, mousy bruise on his lip. When he tried to get up his legs failed him and he promptly fell down again.

He lay motionless, willing his head to clear.

Clouds of dust settled over the crater where the raiders had been. There was nothing much left of them: no raiders, no heroes or cowards, no batman, only bits of cloth attached to an arm or a leg, and a pair of boots, curiously upright, with wet ragged red tops in lieu of stockings. Gowry got up, groped for his rifle and pushed on towards the emplacement.

At least the bombardment had ceased. Stopped as suddenly as it had begun. Perhaps someone had got a message through to the gunners. Maurice was out there somewhere. Soames too. They couldn't be far away. Smoke and darkness, blinding flashes of light along the skyline. Something had gone badly wrong in the planning and the Jerry strongholds were still intact.

When the German soldier bellowed at him Gowry fired without thinking. The man vanished. Another

German appeared. Gowry fired again, saw this one vanish too. It was becoming awfully interesting all of a sudden, Gowry thought. He felt bright and alert, almost sprightly as he stepped to the rim of the trench and peered into it.

Someone fired a shot, one shot.

Gowry started firing into the trench, not caring. Then they were swarming up at him, surging out of a dugout.

Gowry stepped back, dropped on one knee and rammed the bayonet upward. He felt resistance and rammed the bayonet in again. The German fell against him, a ton weight hanging on the blade. He had only used the bayonet on sandbags until now and the German didn't feel like a sandbag. He dangled on the end of the bayonet, shrieking, young, big-jawed, like Trotter, remarkably like Turk Trotter. Gowry dragged out the bayonet and let the German fall and when a second Jerry came at him swung and struck again, twisting and pulling out the blade. Simple stuff this killing, he thought, then there were six, eight, ten Germans fighting each other for the ladders and a grenade went off and Gowry knew it was time to go.

He turned and ran for home.

19th April 1916

My Own Dearest Son,
   I know you have not heard from her for I have been telling her she should do the decent thing and

tell you herself from her own lips what has happened here. It was none of my doing and I have not written before because it was not for me to interfere between a husband and his wife. She has told Charlie it is nobody's business but hers and the man's because you left her in the lurch.

If I had not been staying with Forbes I would have seen what was going on and would have tried to put a stop to it before it got too far but it is difficult for me because I have been in Glasgow and none of them thought to drop me a line with the news. It is all the German Menace here and I have been well out of it at Forbes insistance and did not see the true state of affairs until I came back when Your Father was ill in the New Year. He is better now. It was nothing but stones the doctor said but to hear him talk you thought he was at death's door. She has had a child. She will not be giving it up although she knows it is not yours. She will not be giving it up although I told her to. The man is staying in the house with her but he is not there when I am and will not come to discuss it with me although I have written him several times. They say they do not want you to know because you are fighting for England and left her to fight for England. It is left for Your Mother to write you with the news. I am sorry.

Your Loving Mother
Kay McCulloch (Mrs)

When the sun came up the rats fell asleep. They

had been in the shell hole when Gowry had arrived around half past two in the morning, sharing it with Tom Ring, a lance corporal with the Rifles whom Gowry had known since training days in Fermoy. Ring had been smashed up pretty badly and it wasn't until daylight that Gowry had been able to identify him. By that time the rats were all over him. Gowry had tried to chase them off by pelting them with stones but the creatures would not abandon the shell hole. When sunlight crept into the crater they scratched out shallow burrows and, with their paws curled over their noses and whiskers twitching, fell asleep.

Gowry shovelled dirt over Tom Ring's body. When that wouldn't do he took off his jacket, spread it over the lance corporal's face and weighted it down with earth. The rats watched him warily but when he sat down they settled again too. At least it wasn't raining, Gowry thought, and the shrapnel wound in his upper arm wasn't serious. He had attended to it immediately, of course, for the soil itself was polluted and he had no desire to pick up an infection. He had cleaned the gash with spit and disinfectant powder from his field dressing pack and had bandaged it tightly. He was pleased when it began to throb. He took that as a sign of healing.

The little crater smelled as if it had been disinfected. The reek of lyddite from high-explosive shells was heavy in the air and there was no water, not so much as a patch of dampness in the chalky base. He wouldn't drink puddle water anyway, no matter how bad his thirst. Drinking puddle water could kill you as surely as a Jerry bullet. He searched round Tom Ring's body for a water bottle but didn't find one. He wondered what had happened to Donnaghy. Now, now, now, he told himself sternly, I *know* what happened to Donnaghy. The poor beggar was buried alive. I know what happened to the others as well. Blown sky-high. Direct hit probably. Nothing much left of any of them, just bits and pieces of skin and bone.

Missing in action: what would it be like, he wondered, to have your hubby, your son or your sweetheart reported missing in action? Do you continue to wait for the rap on the door, the whistle in the letterbox long after the war ends, after the kiddies have grown up, after you have taken another man or borne another son to another man? He couldn't imagine what that would be like. Come to think of it, he couldn't imagine a time when the war would be no more. And when it was over – if ever it was – what would he do then? Go back to Maeve and Sylvie and the Shamrock? Drift down to Maggie's cottage in the Galtees and look for farm work? Set off in search of the nurse who had been nice to him, who wrote him letters every day and who, now, right now, lying in a shell hole in no-man's-land, he wanted so badly it made his groin ache worse than his arm.

Hell's bells, he thought as he sprawled in sweltering spring sunshine waiting for nightfall, the war really has changed your perspectives. Thirty yards from the German line with a swelling corpse at your feet and blood drying on the point of your bayonet and all you can think of is what a wee Scots lassie will feel like under her clothes.

What's become of you, McCulloch? What *has* become of you?

Soon after, still dreaming of Becky, he joined the rats in sleep.

'Good God, McCulloch, is that you?' Lieutenant Soames enquired.

'It is, sir, it is,' Gowry answered.

'Are you all in one piece?'

'Aye, sir, more or less.'

'Did you see anything of Davy out there?'

'Davy?'

'Donnaghy, my batman?'

'I'm afraid I did, sir,' Gowry said. 'I think you can take it he's dead.'

'Damn, damn and blast! Where did you run into him? In the trench, was it, snared in the wire?'

'Yes, sir. He took a direct hit.'

Soames was seated on an ammo box a few yards from the lantern that marked the steps of the field dressing station. Drawn up next to the station was a tea-stall with eight or ten men hanging round it. Gowry was too groggy to make out what unit they belonged to or to wonder why they were taking refreshment in the midst of so much activity. The raid had obviously been a disaster but at least the Germans hadn't counter-attacked and no-man's-land had remained deserted until after sundown.

A stretcher-bearer had discovered him and had guided him back as far as the British line and packed him off down the trench to the rear. He had cadged tea and a couple of mouthfuls of stew from a cook-up but had encountered no one he recognised and no one who recognised him. In due course he had emerged on a narrow road crammed with troops heading up to the front. Horses, horse-sleds and motor-ambulances were stuck in a mass of infantry with just two or three mounted officers to keep the column moving. Gowry reckoned that divisional headquarters had decided that the salient must be taken at all costs and a general attack was imminent.

More by luck than intention, he stumbled on the dressing station and found his commanding officer, Lieutenant Soames, seated by the steps.

'Well, you're the first to come out of it, McCulloch,' Soames said, 'and I expect you'll be the last.'

'What?' Gowry said, wearily. 'Have they all gone down?'

'Like ninepins,' the officer said. 'My fault, my responsibility.'

Gowry seated himself cross-legged on the grass at the lieutenant's feet. He still had his rifle but every-thing else, including his jacket, had been left behind. 'I saw Ring too, sir. He won't be coming back either.'

Soames was sleek, round-cheeked and bull-necked. He had been a solicitor in London before the war and had returned to Dublin to join the Rifles only because his father had insisted on it.

'How many of the Connaughts made it back?' Gowry said.

'None, none that I'm aware of.'

'Not even Sergeant Leonard?'

'I don't know Sergeant Leonard. Is he a friend of yours?'

'Used to be, sir,' Gowry said.

There were lights within the dressing station, doctors and medical orderlies moving about. Someone cried out, not moaning but yelling.

Gowry felt like a fraud. He had spent the whole day asleep under Fritz's nose and had been rescued by a stretcher-bearer who had risked his neck under murderous bursts of machine-gun fire to fetch him in. The stretcher-bearer was a true hero. He was nothing but a sham, even if he had killed a couple of Jerries hand-to-hand. The fact was, he had sniffed at glory and rejected it. Becky would not be proud of him or Maurice either for that matter.

'How many did we lose all told, sir?'

'One hundred and forty,' Soames said. 'The majority on the first assault. Fritz was on to us from the first. Spotted us straight away and hung fire, sly bastards, hung fire until we were all caught in the open. Jerry knew the emplacements were impregnable.' He shook his head. 'It wasn't so much an emplacement as a stronghold, fortified like a damned Crusader castle. Dear God, we couldn't have taken it with half a battalion let alone a raiding party.'

'How did you get back, sir?'

'On my belly.' Soames suddenly began to sob and shake. 'I crawled away on my belly, on my damned, blasted belly. Oh, God! Oh, God forgive me.'

Gowry shouted, 'Officer needs attention. Officer needs attention.'

An orderly came hastening down the steps from the dressing station and led the lieutenant away and Gowry, exhausted, slumped back on the grass.

At the end of the Easter month the staff in the Hulluch sector had more to worry them than clerical inaccuracies. The confusion over Private McCulloch's death was never officially explained and, after a brief exchange of letters, was dismissed as just another error in battalion administration.

When Gowry arrived back at his unit he found the division intent on counting its dead and evacuating its wounded. It was early afternoon before he was directed to the brewery on the south side of town where a field headquarters had been set up. He was relieved to see a familiar face. Major Keating was seated at a long deal table on the sward outside the brewery and several pay-clerks were packing up the money-boxes to return to Divisional HQ, for, it seemed, the rituals of army life continued unabated even while the dead were rotting in the fields.

The afternoon sun was hot and the stink of unburied corpses strong. Major Keating had a briar pipe in his mouth and a cloud of blue smoke around him and, even with that protection, held a khaki handkerchief sprinkled with peppermint oil to his nostrils. Behind the table, in the shade of the broken wall, a couple of signalmen in shirt-sleeves were contemplating a skein of wires from which they were expected to assemble a telephone system. As Gowry approached the major stirred, looked up and scowled.

Gowry could hardly blame the major for scowling at him, for he looked more like a scarecrow than a fighting soldier. He had been patched up at the dressing station and handed over to an NCO who had dug him out a battledress from a pile behind the tent and allocated him a billet in a barn along with a dozen other lost souls. In the morning he had been fed from a mobile cookhouse, given a pack, a full water bottle and a pencil map and sent back to join his unit twelve miles away. He had tarried long enough to ask if he might be permitted to see the handful of battered corpses that the stretcher-bearers had retrieved during the night but was told in no uncertain terms that his presence was unwelcome and that he had better make himself scarce. Thus, well fed and well rested, he had set out from the salient around the crater leaving his old friend Maurice, or what remained of him, behind.

'Name?' Major Keating said.

Gowry reeled off his service number. 'Private Gowry McCulloch, sir.'

'You're too late, McCulloch. We've finished paying out.'

'I'm reporting in, sir.'

'Pay book.'

'Lost, sir.'

'Lost?'

'Been on detachment, sir.'

'Detachment? Oh, with Soames's lot.'

'Yes, sir.'

'Fortunate for you, what?' The major puffed on his pipe and released a cloud of dense smelly blue smoke. 'Been all rather nasty round here, what?'

'Yes, sir. So I've heard, sir.'

'Flat broke, are you? Been wasting your portion with those wild men from Connaught, have you?'

'Not exactly, sir,' said Gowry.

'Seen anything of Lieutenant Soames?'

'The lieutenant was wounded, I think.'

Keating took the pipe from his mouth and spat on to the grass. He dabbed his lips with the handkerchief and riffled the papers on the table.

'Badly?'

'Sir?' said Gowry.

'Soames?'

'I – I don't know, sir.'

'Ah!' Keating tapped a forefinger against the paper. 'There you are: McCulloch, Gowry. Got you now. Where are the others from your detachment?'

'I'm the only one, sir, the only survivor.'

The major looked up quickly and then, too wily to show his feelings, sighed. 'So you've lost your pay book, have you, McCulloch? Deuced careless, what? Have to get you another one, won't we? Can't pay you without a pay book. Where is the pay book, incidentally? Fallen into enemy hands, has it?'

'I'm afraid it has, sir,' said Gowry.

'Hmmm, pity! Still, you look fit enough to me. Are you fit?'

'I am, sir.'

'Tell you what, you toddle off to base. Do you know where it is?'

'Not exactly, sir,' said Gowry again.

'Down to the end of the high street and cross the highway to the river. You'll see the tents and some of your chums. Not sure who's currently OC but you'll be in bags of time for supper and I expect someone will take care of you.'

Gowry licked his dry lips. 'What about my pay book, sir?'

'I'll stamp one up and get it down to you, never fear.'

Keating eased his chair back from the table and got to his feet. He was very tall, enormously tall. He stared down at Gowry from an imposing height.

'Well, what are you waiting for?'

'Sorry, sir. I just wondered if I had any mail lyin' here.'

'Good God, man!' Keating said, with a little snap of temper. 'Mail! Is that all you chaps ever think about, apart from beer and women? All right, all right. Murphy,' he shouted. A corporal came running from within the brewery. 'Fetch this man his mail. McCulloch, Gowry, 2nd Battalion, Sperryhead Rifles.'

'Sah!' Murphy saluted and vanished indoors.

He returned a few minutes later and handed Gowry three letters, two from Saint-Emile, from Becky, the other from Dublin.

'Happy now, McCulloch?' the major asked.

'Yes, sir. Thank you, sir,' Gowry answered. 'Very happy now.'

PART THREE

Maeve

Chapter Thirteen

'Look at him, the darlin',' Maeve said. 'Isn't he lovely?'

She held the baby out in both hands but Gran McCulloch barely glanced at him, though he looked, Maeve thought, irresistible in his lace-fringed skirts and angora-wool shawl. She had put on the little bonnet Jansis had knitted and the tiny wool bootees Fran had brought in three weeks before her brother's birth. She had been puzzled by the size of the bootees for, given how big her mother was, sticking out in front like the sail on a yawl, she couldn't believe that the baby would be small enough to fit them.

He was nine weeks old now, little Sean, heavier in weight and squallier than he'd been when he was brand-new. He didn't appreciate being held out like a rugby football and flailed his tiny legs under the skirts and grizzled at his granny as if he couldn't stand the sight of her, which, Maeve thought, showed

remarkable perception in one so young. She drew
him back, cradled him in the crook of her arm and
gave his nose a dab with the tip of her pinkie to get
rid of the bubble that blemished perfection.

Gran McCulloch watched, unimpressed.

'Where is he? Isn't he here?'

'Who do you wish to speak with?' said Maeve.

'The man. Hagarty. I thought he'd be here. I
wrote him a letter.'

'Did you? Fran never said anythin' about a letter.'

'He isn't here then?'

'No, he's not,' said Maeve.

She felt ready for anything with Sean in her arms
and wasn't afraid of her grandmother who'd had so
little to do with her over the years that she seemed
like a stranger.

'Would you not like to hold him?' Maeve said.

'Why would I want to hold him?'

'Well, he's your grand—'

'He's not,' Kay McCulloch said curtly.

Maeve thought about it. 'I suppose he isn't,
not really.'

'Where is Hagarty?'

'He's awfully busy.'

'Too busy to hear what I have to say?'

'He left a message,' Maeve lied. 'He told me to
tell you he was sorry he had to go out. He'll talk to
you another time.' Gran obviously didn't believe her
but Maeve brazened it out. 'What do you want to talk
to Fran about anyway?'

'Nothing that concerns you.'

'Why not?' said Maeve.

'Because you're only a child.'

'I am not.'

'What age are you?'

'Twelve,' Maeve said. 'Near enough.'

'Where's your mother?'

'Upstairs in her bed. She's not to be disturbed.'

'Is she sick?'

'Feedin' Sean takes a lot out o' her,' said Maeve. 'Besides, she doesn't want to see you.'

'Fetch her down here this minute.'

'She won't come.'

'Then I'll go up.'

'*No*,' Maeve said.

'Is the man in bed with her, is that it?'

'Fran's out an' Mam's restin',' Maeve said. 'If you need a cup of tea before you start back I'll make one.'

'Tea, I'm not here for your tea,' Gran said.

'Why are you here then?' Maeve said.

Gran was seated in a corner of what had been the bar. It was a bar no longer, for the Shamrock's liquor licence had been revoked within a month of her father's enlistment in the British army. Mr Dolan had died of pneumonia in that winter's cold snap and Mr Pettu, full of apologies, had moved out soon after. The only guests who came in now were odd characters, friends of Fran's. They would stay for a night and move on. The old crowd, the convivial commercials, had been scared away by the peelers, for everyone knew that Mr Vaizey had the Shamrock under observation. Changed circumstances had raised Maeve's stock in school, however. Mr Whiteside treated her like a princess and was forever asking her what Fran was up to now. The minute her dad had gone off to fight for England his name had been mud and nobody who counted seemed to mind that Mam had taken up with Fran instead.

'I'm looking after your father's interests,' Kay McCulloch said, 'since nobody else seems to care enough to do it for him.'

'Dad's in the army, fightin' for England.'

'Does he write to you?'

Maeve pursed her lips. 'No.'

'He sends money, though, part of his pay, doesn't he?'

'That's none o' your business.'

At first Maeve had cried because there had been no letters from Daddy. Every morning she would come running downstairs and ask Mam or Fran, 'Is there a letter for me?' and Mam and Fran would shake their heads and Mam would give her a little hug to make up for the disappointment. She was hurt by his silence then she became angry and when Mam became pregnant more or less forgot about her father who, after all, had never given her a baby brother.

'By God!' Kay McCulloch said. 'You've a right snippy tongue for a twelve-year-old. I know where you got that from, and it wasn't our side of the family.'

'I think you should go, Gran,' Maeve said. 'If you want to know what's happenin' ask Uncle Charlie or Granddad. They know what side the bread's buttered on and that Mr Hagarty's a good man even if you don't think so.'

'Hagarty's one of the brotherhood and that'd make him a saint in their eyes even if he grew horns and a tail,' the old woman said. 'She'll rue the day she took up with that man, believe me.'

Her grandmother was not as old as all that, not nearly as old as Mr Dolan had been when he'd died. She was smart-dressed too, like the ladies who ate their lunch at the Hibernian or took tea at Fuller's. Her money came not from Granddad or the profits of the brewery but from her son, Forbes, whom Maeve had never met. He was a rich businessman and, according to Charlie, more Scottish than Irish. She had asked her mother about Uncle Forbes but her mother would not speak of him and just said that the past was the past and better left buried.

'What has she told you?' Gran McCulloch went on. 'Has she told you your dada might not come back? Aye, well, she might have something there for the slaughter in France is terrible. Has she taken up with Hagarty in case your father doesn't come back?'

Maeve snuggled her brother close to her chest. 'What do you mean – not come back?'

'You're not so clever as you think you are, Maeve McCulloch. Don't you read the newspapers?'

'I read the newspapers.'

'Aye, rebel trash, most like.'

'I'm goin' upstairs now,' Maeve said stiffly. 'Sean's needin' his feed. You can let yourself out the front door.'

'You're just like your mother: head in the clouds,' Kay McCulloch said. 'An intelligent girl like you shouldn't be livin' under the same roof with a fool like Francis Hagarty. Read the right newspapers, girl. Thousands are being killed every day, Irish lads among them, all out there dyin' for us while we rest easy in our beds.'

'Daddy'll come back.'

'And what if he doesn't?'

'Fran will look after us.'

'And what if he does?' the woman said.

'What do you mean?'

'There's no place for your father here, is there?' Gran said, meanly. 'Who'll welcome him home? Your mother? Your precious mother and her precious Hagarty?'

'Me,' Maeve said, in a trembling voice. 'I'll welcome him home.'

'You,' the old woman said, 'and your wee bastard of a brother?'

She moved out of the corner and touched a gloved hand to the shawl. The infant let out a cry, uncertain and frail but a cry none the less. Maeve pushed her grandmother away.

'Leave us alone, just leave us alone.'

'I've heard that said before,' the old woman said.

'I've been hearing that said ever since I first came to this country.'

'Get out. Get out and leave us alone.'

'Oh, I will,' Kay McCulloch said. 'I'm sorry she won't talk to me, for I won't be calling again. I'll not be here when you need me.'

'We don't need you. We've never needed you an' never will.'

'I wouldn't be too sure of that, Maeve,' Kay McCulloch said.

Dublin appeared peaceful in the run-up to Easter and the officers of the garrison were looking forward to the holiday. In the building off Winetavern Street, however, Inspector Vaizey had just received an order for the wholesale arrest of leading nationalists and a leaked copy of the document was already in possession of the nationalist executive council.

Provocative action by Dublin Castle was nothing new but the latest move was disturbing, for a large shipment of German guns was en route to Tralee Bay to arm the Easter Sunday parades prior to a full-scale uprising. The nationalist leaders held a secret meeting to discuss the situation but the meeting was acrimonious and broke down in confusion.

There was no confusion in Mr Vaizey's office in spite of the quantity of paperwork that had to be squared away before the navy pounced on the captain and crew of the German vessel and provided enough evidence of 'hostile associations' to bring about the arrest of prominent members of the brotherhoods including – Vaizey rubbed his hands in glee – that scruffy little moneychanger, Oliver Francis Hagarty.

Fran Hagarty was no Roger Casement and certainly no Patrick Pearse. He was a moneyman, a purchaser and distributor of arms, very skilled at manipulating ordinary men and women to whom the cause of Irish freedom was bred in the bone. Vaizey could not forgive the heartless manner in which Hagarty had used the attractive little Scottish woman who owned the Shamrock and made her not only his accomplice but also his dupe. Her name topped the list attached to the arrest order for he, Inspector Vaizey of the Crime Special Branch, could be just as heartless and unscrupulous as Hagarty when it came to the bit. He would have brought in the girl too, for she was a strong-willed, long-legged child who could pass for fifteen or sixteen under the red lamps of the Monto, but he drew the line at intimidating children.

When the time came and the balloon finally went up, then, Inspector Vaizey promised himself, he would have them all at his mercy, including Sylvie McCulloch.

'Vaizey?' Fran said. 'I don't for the life of me see why you worry about that arrogant bugger. He's not a law unto himself, you know.'

'He frightens me,' Sylvie said. 'Look what he did to Gowry, how he chased Gowry away. Now we have this.' She slapped her hand on the newspaper spread beside her on the bed. 'Are you telling me this is nonsense too?'

'I'm not saying it's nonsense,' Fran answered. 'I'm just saying it shouldn't be taken at face value.'

'Would Alderman Kelly read it out at a public meeting and allow it to be printed in the newspapers if it wasn't true? How did it fall into the hands of the council in the first place?'

'Copied piecemeal from files in the castle by someone in the know.'

'Who did the copying?'

Fran spread his hands. 'Sylvie, I've no idea.'

He had come home in the hope of finding respite from quarrelling. There had been enough of that at the meeting of the revolutionary council. He had been admitted on Charlie's say-so, for Charlie had a little bit of power now that the brotherhood had been reorganised. He had sat at the back of the hall by the pillars and said not a word, for his work in Dublin was almost done. The arms that would be unloaded from the German ship *Aud* were none of his purchasing and the weapons bought with Clan money were already stored in the city. Only he knew where all the dumps were and which organisations would be armed. More importantly he still had the password to the account set up by John James Flanagan in the North Mercantile Bank, an account intended to fund the establishment of a revolutionary government as soon as the city was secure.

He watched the infant suck.

He was proud of the boy but no more so than he was of his other sons. He was also rather annoyed that Sylvie would not put all else aside and devote herself to motherhood. He had only himself to blame, he supposed. He couldn't switch this woman off as he had done with his other women, for Sylvie had fallen in love with what he purported to stand for. In a way he regretted that he'd have to leave her behind when he sailed for America but once he reached Philadelphia he would be a free man again, all his wives, all his women and children put behind him, Sylvie McCulloch included.

Sylvie kept her dress closed and allowed him no glimpse of her breast while the baby was on her. Even at night she wrapped herself up in thick winter nightgowns and padded drawers to keep him off.

'What are you staring at?' Sylvie said.

'Nothing,' Fran said.

'Aren't you going to tell me who did the copying?'

'For God's sake . . .'

'You really don't know, do you?'

'No, I don't. Rory O'Connor at a guess.'

'Has he been here? Has he stayed at the Shamrock?'

'Of course he hasn't,' Fran said.

It was late and he needed sleep. God, how he

288

needed sleep. He would have to store sleep the way a camel stores water if he were to get through the weekend.

He was familiar with the plans, of course, for he was still trusted by the men in high places and would do what he had to do before he departed but, unlike Charlie and Peter McCulloch, Turk, Kevin and the rest of the brotherhood, he had not signed on for a blood sacrifice.

Sylvie was not hidden under the covers. She lay like an odalisque, with the baby supported on her arm. She didn't much resemble the woman he had felt so passionate about back at the beginning. Pregnancy and motherhood had robbed her of her attraction.

'Aren't you going to tell me what's going on?' Sylvie said.

'It's just the usual talk,' Fran said.

He was tired and hungry. Jansis had promised to cook him ham and eggs. Maeve was lurking downstairs, eager to hear all the news. The girl had the finely tuned sensitivity of a true fanatic and reminded him, just a little bit, of Countess Connie Markievicz. She knew what the sanctioning of precautionary measures meant, even if her mother did not, for Colin Whiteside was a captain in the Citizen Army as well as a schoolteacher and for weeks now had been telling his little charges that the day of atonement was at hand.

'It's *not* just the usual talk,' Sylvie said. 'What have

you been up to, Fran, while I've been stuck here with him? I've hardly seen you all week.'

Pregnancy and labour had been hard on her, much harder than she'd anticipated. He'd given her as much time as he could afford but he was busy salting away arms and trimming cash from the Mercantile account. He had removed his share, a fair share given what he had done for them. Sylvie would not go short. At least he would make sure of that.

'Would it not be the thing for you to go off to Malahide for a day or two and show the child to Daniel and his wife?' he said.

'Malahide? A fine welcome I'd have in Malahide.'

'It's the holiday time, dearest. The city will be packed.'

'I am not going to Malahide or anywhere. Besides,' Sylvie said, 'Sean isn't Daniel McCulloch's grandson – or hers either.'

'Has she been back here, bothering Maeve?'

'Who? Kay McCulloch? No, she won't show her face here again.'

'Is Maeve still upset by what the old woman told her?'

'Maeve's young and forgets things quickly.' Sylvie turned her back on him, fumbled with her dress and transferred the baby to the other breast. 'Unlike me.'

What could he tell her, that the plans the council had laid had been dictated more by daring rather than sound military strategy; that the commandants in Limerick and Kerry were already distributing ammunition in anticipation of a massive shipment of German arms; that on Sunday the Citizen Army would entrench in St Stephen's Green, and key points in the city defences would be seized by the Dublin brigades; that the road to Kingstown would be blocked, railway termini brought under control until the military council occupied the General Post Office and proclaimed the founding of an Irish republic? How could he possibly tell her that the Brotherhood of Erin had been ordered to take and fortify Watton's warehouse just behind the Shamrock and that she and her children would be in grave danger if they stayed here?

'Why do you want rid of me, Fran? Is there another woman?'

'Oh, for God's sake, Sylvie, of course there isn't another woman. Where would I find time let alone the energy to pleasure myself with another woman?' He threw his hands in the air in exasperation. 'Don't be so damned stupid.' He closed on the bed and looked down at her and the child. 'All right, all right! I'll tell you the truth – but you mustn't tell anyone, not even Jansis.'

'It's the rising, isn't it?' Sylvie said.

'Yes,' he said. 'It is.'

'How bad will it be and how long will it last?'

'I honestly don't know.'

He brushed a finger over the infant's silky black hair. There was a little dew of perspiration on the child's brow and he was enveloped in baby smell, the warm corporeal odour of milk and pee.

When Sylvie looked up he saw the determination in her eyes.

'And you expect me to leave?' she said. 'Now? When you need me most? Oh, no, Fran Hagarty, even if I did have somewhere to go – which I haven't – I wouldn't leave you now for all the tea in China. This is my house and you are my man and I'll stick by you whether you like it or not.'

'Sylvie, it isn't necessary.'

Even as he spoke, though, he knew that she was right. It *was* necessary, was, in fact, inevitable. He had persuaded her to fall in love and now she must pay the price. She would risk everything for him and he would risk nothing for her. His work came first, the cause, the surge of allegiance to a resurgent nation that would surely follow, whether the uprising succeeded or failed.

'I love you, Fran. I'm not going to leave you now.'

'No,' he said. 'But you don't have to die for me, Sylvie.'

'I'm not going to die – and neither are you.'

She shifted the baby in her arms and, stretching up, offered Fran her lips. He was taken aback, almost undermined by her courage. He knew for sure that if he stayed with her long enough she would weaken and possess him – and he would let no woman, not even Sylvie McCulloch, do that.

Reluctantly, he kissed her.

'Now tell me,' she whispered, 'when will the rising begin?'

'Sunday,' he said, whispering too. 'Sunday at twelve o'clock.'

'Are we ready for it?' Sylvie asked.

'As ready as we'll ever be,' said Fran.

Chapter Fourteen

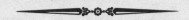

Early on Saturday morning Inspector Vaizey received news that the *Aud* had been scuttled off Queenstown, that the German captain and crew had been taken prisoner and, more by luck than design, Roger Casement had been captured while trying to land from a small boat on the Kerry coast. He welcomed the tidings from the south, for the loss of the arms shipment would surely put paid to the brotherhoods' plans for an uprising.

Across town the rebel military council met and elected to call off the mobilisation that had been scheduled for Easter Sunday, a decision that the rank and file viewed as cowardly, for, in their view, any gesture was better than no gesture at all. The rebel council met once more and this time, bowing to the wishes of the majority, voted to strike at noon on Monday.

'Here it is,' Turk Trotter shouted. 'Here it is in black and white.'

'What does it say, Turk?' Maeve begged. 'Tell me what it says.'

'Four city battalions will parade for inspection at ten a.m. today.'

'The signature, man, the signature?' Kevin demanded.

'Thomas MacDonagh signed it.'

'The brigade commandant wouldn't let you down,' said Maeve.

'No he would not,' said Turk. 'So more of that bacon, me buttercup. More eggs, more tea, more of every damned thing, for we are needin' to be fed like fightin' cocks for *this* ten o'clock parade.'

'Does Charlie know about the order?' Peter McCulloch asked.

'Charlie it was who gave me the copy,' Turk answered.

'Where is he then?'

'Marshalling the troops.'

'An' where's Fran?' Peter said. 'Is he upstairs knockin' his fancy-wife?'

'Enough o' that now,' said Turk while Jansis, in the passing, gave Peter a rap on the ear to remind him there were ladies present.

'We haven't seen Fran since yesterday afternoon,' Maeve said. 'But he'll be here to go over the wall with you, I'm sure.'

'I hope he brings gelignite,' said Kevin, 'so we can blow the road if it comes to a retreat.'

'A retreat?' said Turk. 'There'll be no retreat.

We'll hold Watton's warehouse till they raise the flag o' the republic over City Hall.'

'Aye,' said Peter, 'or until we're all kilt.'

Her uncle was ugly, Maeve thought, with gargoyle features and a wispy straw-coloured beard.

'I've no intention o' getting killed,' said Turk. 'I want to be alive an' free as a bird, an Irish bird flying round the Irish flag.'

'An' shittin' on Bedford Tower,' Peter said, grinning.

'I'll do that dirty thing on you, sonny, if you don't shut your gob.' Turk reached and pulled Maeve to him. 'What about you, my sweetheart, will you go flyin' round the Irish flag with me?'

'Sure an' I will, Turk,' said Maeve.

Jansis and she had cooked supper for them last night and breakfast this morning, for Mam was busy with Sean. The men had spent the night in the Shamrock and when they had appeared this morning they wore the uniform, Erin's pride, and looked grand and manly in light green with bandoliers criss-crossed over their chests. Turk wore a sombrero and a holstered revolver that he let her hold when she asked him, the weapon big and heavy in her small hands. There was no sign of her grandfather, for he was ill again, though not so ill he couldn't attend the races, it seemed. Charlie had taken over from her grandfather. The brewery at Towers had been shut down, for Charlie had been promised a seat in the new parliament by the president, Patrick Pearse.

Lovely it was, at dawn in the smoke-filled kitchen with the men in uniform. Her breath caught in her throat when Turk put his big hand across her stomach and told her what a fine time they would have fighting the British, how the spirit would prevail and Ireland would belong to the Irish again for the first time in four hundred years. The stove was roaring and through the open door she could see the hens, the few that were left, sleepily pecking at the gravel. She would feed the hens soon, feed everyone and anything, then she would go out to watch her friends marching, only this time the march wouldn't end back in the drill hall or in the pub but on the barricades.

She leaned against Turk, resting on his stomach and thigh. The boys were laughing, even Peter. She wished Daddy could have been here with them, not fighting for the English a thousand miles away. She despised him and yet she loved him too in spite of all Mr Whiteside had told her about the nature of betrayal and that the Germans were their allies against the English and that no decent Irishman should bear arms against an ally.

Turk pulled a watch from his breast pocket and consulted it.

'Eat up, lads,' he said, soberly. 'It's time to push along.'

Kevin got to his feet. 'Death or glory, chaps, what, what?' he said in a mock English accent. 'Up and at 'em.'

'Up an' at 'em is it.' Slipping Maeve from his knee,

Turk got to his feet too. 'Sure this is one parade we don't want to miss.'

'That we do not,' said Peter.

The uprising took everyone by surprise and the ease with which the warehouse fell to twenty-two men from the brotherhood struck Maeve as an anticlimax. They did not clamber over the wall from the back yard of the Shamrock but marched unchallenged down Sutter Street to the warehouse gates.

'Now what's all this, son?' the gateman said. 'Don't you know we're closed for the bank holiday?'

'Aye, we know,' Kevin said, rather sheepishly. 'We are here to claim the property for the Brother-hood of Erin in the name of the new republic.'

'An' what the devil are they goin' to be doin' wit' it?' the gateman said.

He was a fat fellow, round as a cannonball, with thick white hair and a white moustache. He had on a uniform of sorts, not military, and a big key-chain dangled from his belt.

'Occupy it,' Kevin said, 'in the name of a free Ireland.'

'Home rulers!' The gateman shook his head. 'Well, well, well!'

'It's the revolution, man,' said Kevin. 'It's the uprising.'

The gateman remained unmoved behind the pad-locked gate.

At this hour of a Monday morning heavy lorries would normally have been rolling in and out, for Watton's stored a vast assortment of piping for the gas and water companies as well as steel plate and corrugated iron, bales of raw cotton and jute and gigantic slabs of granite that the cranes slung about as if they weighed no more than communion wafers. Over a hundred people, including women and girls, were employed by the company but today only a few storemen were visible in the yard.

Turk had told Maeve that it wasn't safe for a girl on her own, for there might be shooting and he didn't want to have to carry her home to her mamma with a bullet in her head. She had followed them down from the parade ground at the Green none the less, down and across the bridge again, back to dreary cobbled Sutter Street that seemed to have nothing in it but dusty sunshine and flocks of pigeons. Turk knew she was behind them, but he was intent on playing the soldier and ignored her.

He squared his shoulders, stuck his thumbs in his belt and eyed the gateman with ferocious patience. Charlie, dapper as a dandy in his uniform, seemed content to let Kevin do the talking.

Kevin said, 'Joseph, for God's sake, will ye not be lettin' us in?'

'I'm thinkin' about it.' Joseph, the gateman, was alone at his post, the wooden hut behind him empty. 'Tell me, son, what it is you want with a warehouse? There are no English soldiers here.'

'It's a strategic position,' Kevin hissed.

'Is it now?' Joseph stroked his moustache, jangled his key-chain, looked nonchalantly up and down Sutter Street. 'What's strateeejeeeck about it?'

'Jaysus!' Turk burst out. 'Why are we arguin' with this idiot?'

Hauling the revolver from its holster, he stepped to the gate, took aim at the big iron padlock and pulled the trigger. The clang of metal striking metal echoed sullenly over the rooftops. Pigeons rose in unison and flew off while the boys of the brotherhood dived to the ground, ducking the fragments of metal that ricocheted from the gate and the gateposts.

The remains of the padlock dangled on the chain for a moment then fell off with a tinny sound, and the big gate swung open.

Joseph shook his head again. 'Sure an' there was no call for that.'

'Aye, but there was,' said Kevin.

'Forward,' Turk cried.

The boys of the brotherhood scrambled to their feet and fell in behind him as he swaggered into the yard to occupy the warehouse in the name of the new republic.

'I saw a man get shot tonight,' Maeve said.

Sylvie glanced up, astonished not so much at the nature of the information as the casual manner in which her daughter delivered it.

'Where?'

'Up by St Stephen's Green, near the Shelbourne.'

'What were you doing there? I told you not to cross the Liffey,' Sylvie said. 'Did you take the tram?'

'There are no trams,' Maeve said. 'Have you not been out at all?'

'We've been a-waitin' for Mr Hagarty,' Jansis said. 'Tell us about this fellow you saw shot; an English soldier, was he?'

'Nup,' Maeve said, 'just an ordinary bloke.'

'One of us then?' said Jansis.

'One of nobody by the look of him,' said Maeve.

All the excitement had been squeezed out of her. When Turk wouldn't let her into the warehouse with them she had gone up town again and had spent most of the day wandering from one barricade to another. She sat at the kitchen table now, elbows spread out and if she hadn't been so famished Sylvie reckoned she would have put her head down and would have fallen asleep.

The back door was open and there was still light, though not much of it. Sylvie could see the chicken coop and the wall of the yard and part of the warehouse roof outlined against a dark blue sky so calm and bland that she could hardly believe that her brothers-in-law were crouched inside, making ready for a shooting match. Even in the snug kitchen, though, you could make out the little whip-snaps of rifle fire floating down from the town.

Head propped on one hand, Maeve scooped up peas with her fork.

'Funny,' she said, 'you couldn't see a soul in the park, though you knew they were there. But I hardly saw a policeman all day long.'

'The Metropolitans aren't armed,' Jansis stated. 'You won't see much of them when there's real trouble in the streets.'

'Did you see any British soldiers?' Sylvie asked.

'No, but I heard a lot had been killed in the Portobello Road.'

'Is that where the man was shot?' Jansis said.

'Nup, at the barricade at the Green. Motor-cars an' beds an' barrows an' all sorts of stuff was piled on to it. They'd taken the man's trade cart, I think,' Maeve went on. 'There wasn't a volunteer in sight until the man – a big chap – came stridin' out o' Bellevue Street an' headed straight for the barricade. He wanted his cart back and he'd come to fetch it. The volunteers – Citizen Army – appeared behind the palings, come out of hiding in the bushes.'

'Where were you while this was happening?'

'Standin' in among the crowd.'

'Crowd? What crowd?' said Sylvie.

'Some folk had just got back from the seaside. There were no trains an' no trams so they'd had to walk all the way an', by Gad, were they bad-tempered,' Maeve said. 'The cart man was near as old as Granddad and up he went to the palings with his finger waggin' and told them he wanted his cart back. They told him to leave it right where it was if he didn't want shot, but the chap said he needed the cart to earn a livin' and ran back to the barricade and started to haul it out of the pile. That's when they shot him. Blew a hole in the top o' his head, I think.' Maeve sighed. 'Then a woman ran out into the road, screamin' like a banshee. I thought they'd shoot her too, but they never did. She got down on her knees in the road and shrieked at them and they vanished away into the bushes again. Some folk from the crowd lifted the man an' carried him to the hospital next door to the Arts Club. Do you know where that is, Mam?'

'No,' Sylvie said.

'Was he dead?' said Jansis.

With finger and thumb, Maeve removed a piece of gristle from her teeth and laid it on the side of the plate. She was drowsy with fresh air and exercise, the long day behind her. She had no fear in her, no anxiety, no horror. The shooting of a man, an ordinary citizen, had not affected her; Sylvie was dismayed by her daughter's apparent callousness.

'Did Fran not come back?' Maeve asked.

'No, he did not.' Jansis had never taken to Fran Hagarty and still regarded him as a cuckoo in the nest. 'What else have you heard? Is there no word of the Germans landin' in Kerry yet?'

'I heard all sorts o' things, but nothin' about Germans. We've taken the Custom House and the Post Office but not the castle. Mr Pearse declared the republican government in power from the steps o' the Post Office and the tricolour is flyin' from all the flagpoles.' Maeve paused, mouth open, meat visible on her tongue. 'Listen to the guns,' she said. 'Don't you hear the guns?'

'I do,' said Jansis, crossing herself. 'God help the boys behind them.'

The garrison had been taken completely by surprise and if he had been the commandant he would have stormed the castle regardless of the cost in lives. On the whole, though, the brigadiers had done a fine job and by Tuesday morning the city centre was as secure as it would ever be. Kaygan assured him that most of the strategic points south of the Liffey were well defended and that if the Brits wanted to prevent the rebels extending the lines they would have to bring in cannon.

Fran had been in Kaygan's company for two solid days. Kaygan was a blather and a bit of a show-off but he possessed a press card that allowed him to cross the lines without impediment and together they had spent the latter part of Sunday night in the Hudson guiding the brewer's dray, one that Charlie had supplied, around the town.

The drayman was utterly trustworthy, of course, and they had worked hard to clear all seven dumps of guns and ammunition. The two Clydesdale stallions in the shafts of the dray had strained against the loads that nestled under the tarpaulins, movement about the streets had been slow and the tour hadn't finished until the sun was up and the first platoons were beginning to assemble. Fran had handed over the arms to the deputy commandant of the Citizen Army and had headed back in the motor-car to Endicott Street to clear up his personal business and snatch a couple of hours' sleep.

The cash, in English banknotes, was housed in a scuffed black leather portmanteau. He would have left it in the account until last thing if Monday hadn't been a bank holiday.

In the flat high up in the Endicott Street tenement he had extracted thirty pounds from the twenty-eight hundred in the bag and had wrapped them in newspaper, and at ten thirty on Monday morning had left his eyrie for the last time, carrying nothing but the portmanteau and the packet of cash.

At the foot of the iron staircase, he had turned to the left and let himself into the room where Pauline and her babies slept. He had stepped over the sleepers on the floor and found Pauline on a mattress in the corner by the window, a baby in her arms – his baby, as it happened, not a cast-off. He had looked down into her blue eyes and touched her lips with his fingertips because he didn't want her to say anything. He had placed the package by her head and had kissed her, then, clutching the bag, had left Endicott Street for the last time.

It would be Tuesday afternoon or even Wednesday before Flanagan discovered that the Mercantile account had been cleaned out and was as empty as the priest-holes where he had stored the arms for the uprising. And by then he would be safe aboard the *Empress of India*, sixty or eighty miles out into the Atlantic, beyond even John James's reach.

On Monday the portmanteau full of cash had never left his sight. He kept it on his knee while Kaygan drove him round, leaned his notebook on it while he recorded the words and deeds of the men who mattered, slept with it for a pillow in the motor-car in the warm evening after the Post Office had been taken and Pearse had declared the republic. He even ate with it clenched between his knees in Rossiter's public house before he joined Kaygan in the newspaper office across the street from the castle, from which vantage point rebel snipers were making things hot for the British.

Fran was not stimulated by gunfire or the rumours of Citizen gains. He was excited by the words that formed in his head, for words would shape the events in which he was involved, words would separate him from all he had done and disengage him from all the women and the girls he had known in Ireland, Pauline and Sylvie among them. He had become so preoccupied with the voices in his head that he was almost indifferent to the outcome of the rebellion and suspected that something so spacious and sublime in concept would be reduced at the last to murderous pettiness.

Kaygan passed him the bottle.

Fran wiped the neck and drank. Whiskey had always helped sharpen his sense of reality. He drank again. Seated on a desk in the editor's room, away from the snipers at the front of the building, Kaygan chewed on a dead cigar and watched him anxiously. Kaygan was married with three daughters and a little garden villa on the Dormanside Road. He was a reliable political journalist and a stringer for several English newspapers. He had smooth cheeks and an aquiline nose and if he had been taller might have cut a handsome figure, Fran supposed.

Kaygan chewed on the cigar. 'Don't go drinking it all now, Francis, since it is the last bottle we have, unless you're for raiding the Vinery or Patsy Dene's to top up the supply, and I've a fancy that half the citizens of our fair city will have got there before us.'

Fran took a final mouthful. 'You're right, Kaygan. Besides, time I was on my way before my head splits with this noise. I can hardly hear myself think.'

'Are we for the south side, for the canals?' Kaygan said. 'I reckon that's where we'll find most activity.'

'I'm headed for Watton's.'

'Sperryhead?' Kaygan retrieved the bottle, corked it and put it inside his coat. 'What's doing at Sperryhead that might be worthy of a line or two?'

'If the British want a back door to the quays – I'm certain they will – they'll have to close off Sutter Street and the Sperryhead Road and isolate our positions this side of the river.'

'Is that not clever now?' said Kaygan. 'Would it

be some Whitehall pundit who would be dreaming that up, or some general fresh from Flanders?'

'What would you say, Kaygan?' Fran asked him.

'I would say it was shrewd on somebody's part to occupy Watton's, that's what I would say. How many men are there, Francis? Have you any idea?'

'Charlie expected fifty to turn out this morning.'

'Citizen Army?'

'Brotherhood of Erin.'

'Ah, young McCulloch's stout brigade. How did they shake off damned old Daniel then? Did they screw him into a barrel?'

'I think he went to the races,' Fran said.

There was a lull in the firing at the front of the building.

Kaygan raised an eyebrow enquiringly. 'Tea-break?'

'I doubt it,' Fran said. 'Perhaps they've run out of ammo.'

'Already?' Kaygan said. 'I thought we delivered enough to storm Ypres, let alone the castle.'

As if to answer the journalist's question the lull was broken by a furious burst of rifle fire. The sound of shattering glass was followed by the boom of a shell exploding nearby. Kaygan clutched a hand to his heart, to the whiskey bottle in effect, and pulled a long face.

'What the devil was that?' he said. 'Surely the British can't have gunboats in the river already?'

'Field gun,' Fran said.

Another bark and boom prompted the men to step hastily away from the window. 'Holy Mother of God!' Kaygan said. 'Should I wave my *carte blanche* at them, do you think?'

'Wave your ding-dong at them if you like,' Fran said, 'but I doubt if it'll serve much purpose.'

Kaygan did not smile. 'So they've moved in artillery, have they?' he said. 'Don't they care about Dublin?'

'Did they ever care about Dublin?' Fran said. 'Say farewell to the boys out front and let's get out of here. Are you coming to Sperryhead, or have you other fish to fry?'

'Don't you have a wife down that way?'

'Don't I have wives everywhere?' Fran said.

'Will she conjure us up a bite of breakfast, do you think?'

'I imagine she might,' Fran said and, pressing the portmanteau firmly to his chest, ducked out of the doorway and scuttled down the steep back staircase with Kaygan hard on his heels.

Schools were closed, no bread was to be had and there were no deliveries of milk or mail. Maeve cared not a fig about such inconveniences.

She struck out for Sutter Street at eight o'clock with the sack of potatoes that Jansis had lugged up from the cellar. She carried the sack on her shoulder and was forced to rest now and then which gave the neighbours an opportunity to question her.

'What have you heard from that man o' your mother's?'

'If you mean Mr Hagarty,' Maeve replied, 'I have heard nothin' but the best of news.'

'Is it true the volunteers have took the whole town?'

'Aye, that's true,' Maeve said.

'An' thousands o' Germanians have landed at Kingstown?'

'True an' all, every word.'

She re-gripped the sack, slung it up. It thumped against her spine, almost knocking the breath out of her. It had been careless of Charlie not to take food into the warehouse. At least there were no snipers in Sperryhead Road yet, though Jansis said – and Jansis had been out very early – that down beyond the laneway a handful of British soldiers were marching up and down with rifles on their shoulders waiting for an officer to arrive.

'I hear the cavalry's lined up for a charge at the Post Office?'

'The lancers, aye,' Maeve said. 'They've been told to spike everything that moves, startin' with the women and children.'

'Have they really now?'

'Aye, they really have,' Maeve lied, 'really.'

She went on around the corner into Sutter Street where half a hundred angry warehouse employees had gathered outside the gates. They were arguing with her Uncle Charlie. To give himself stature and a view of the crowd Charlie had climbed up on one of the bales that formed part of the defences. Turk and a handful of other men in uniform, all armed to the teeth, stood outside the warehouse's sliding doors.

'You can't keep us out, McCulloch. We work here.'

'Aye, no work, no pay.'

'You've a damned, blasted cheek raidin' Mr Watton's warehouse.'

'We're not raidin' anywhere,' Charlie shouted. 'Calm down.'

'Calm down! Calm down, he says!'

'Where's Mr Watton anyway?'

The crowd stirred and a few among them squinted suspiciously at Maeve as if they thought she might have Mr Watton hidden in her sack. She put the sack down, folded her arms and listened to the shouted questions.

'Where's Mr Giles, where's Mr Ottway?'

'Where's Mikey Lamb too?'

'They'll be hidin' away from the trouble.'

'Or fighting,' Charlie shouted. 'Perhaps they've got more sense than you have an' they're out with the brigades fightin' for our cause.'

'Our cause? By God, it's not our cause. I'm not for your daft rebellion.'

'Nah, nor me.'

'Don't you want to be rid of English oppression?'

Charlie shouted. 'Don't you want to rule your own destiny?'

'I just want t' get paid.'

'Me too, me too.'

Charlie made a gesture of disgust and spat on to the cobbles. 'You sicken me, so you do. Call yourselves Irishmen. You're just toadies to the wage packet.'

'It's all very well for you, McCulloch, you an' your bottled stout. You can afford for to play at soldiers wi'out your family starvin'.'

Her uncle was close to losing his temper. 'You've no idea what sacrifices I've had to make to stand here before you.'

'Bugger your sacrifices. Let us in, let us in.'

'I'll let you in,' Charlie yelled, 'only if you want to join us in the fight.'

A large woman, a year or two younger than Gran McCulloch, threw herself against the ironwork and screamed abuse at Charlie while the men around her shook and rattled the gates.

When the crowd surged forward Maeve was left behind. Lifting herself on tiptoe she heard the sound of gunfire in the sultry air. She tried to catch Charlie's eye, to signal that she had brought food and ask what she should do with it. But her uncle was preoccupied. He was howling at the mob now and dancing up and down like a little monkey on top of the bale, then he tripped, flailed his arms to regain his balance and toppled head-over-tail to the cobbles, the sombrero tipped over his eyes.

The big woman brayed with laughter and everyone brayed with laughter at her uncle's misfortune.
Maeve couldn't stand to see Charlie being treated like
a clown. She elbowed a path through the crowd.

'What's wrong with you?' she cried. 'Are you all
bloody deaf?'

She slapped down the potato sack and plastered
herself against the gates.

Charlie struggled to his feet, the sombrero hanging
round his neck. Turk unholstered his big revolver and
held it up like the starter of a foot race, the lanyard
making a heavy elegant loop in the air. He looked
grim, grim and heroic, Maeve thought, and she would
not have wanted to cross him at that moment.

Maeve shouted, 'Listen, listen. Can't you hear
it?'

And, miraculously, the warehousemen, carters,
cleaners and even the skittish young girls who did the
invoicing listened because she, Maeve McCulloch,
had told them to. Rifle fire had crackled throughout
the night, of course, but they were listening now,
all of them, to the boom of the big guns shelling
the city.

Maeve shouted, 'Do you know what that is?
That's British soldiers blowin' up our town. Try
tellin' them you just want to earn your pay.'

'Who the hell is that girl?'

'One o' the McCullochs.'

'Is she right, though? Sure an' she is right?'

'It is artillery. Is it comin' this way?'

'I think maybe it might be.'

'Where's Mr Watton? He should be here t' talk
to them.'

'He'll have run off to his big house in the country.'

'Is that a fact?'

''Course it's a bloody fact. If you had a big house
in the country, wouldn't you be runnin' off to it?'

'The dirty coward!'

They dispersed quickly, breaking away from the
railings until only a handful remained, stubborn and
scowling. The big angry woman put a hand on
Maeve's shoulder and pushed her back against the
gate. Turk stuck the barrel of the revolver through
the railings and in a quiet, Wexford voice said, 'Lay
a hand on her, missus, and you're dead.'

The big woman lifted her hand from Maeve's
shoulder and held it up placatingly. 'Sure an' you
wouldn't shoot me, would you?'

'By Gad I would,' Turk said, 'if you come between
me an' my breakfast.'

'Is it food she's got in the sack?'

'It is,' Turk said. 'Now go home, missus, go back
home an' look to your children. It'll be over soon
enough.'

'I need the work,' the woman said. 'That's all it
is – the work.'

Turk withdrew the revolver, holstered it, and
unlocked the gate. He opened it a little, drawing
it inward. Maeve pushed her shoulder against the
ironwork but Turk refused to let her enter. He took

the sack from her and passed it back to Kevin who carried it into the building.

Maeve said, 'Let me stay, Turk. Please let me stay.'

'That I cannot do,' said Turk.

'Please.'

He was already linking the gates, dropping the vertical bolt, reaching for the shiny new padlock. Maeve put her hand on his wrist. He glanced down at her. He did not seem hard now or military. He looked like a big soft Wexford farmer even with a sombrero on his head and bandoliers crossed over his chest. He stopped fiddling with the padlock and reached through the ironwork and caught a strand of her hair between his finger and thumb. He tugged gently until her brow was pressed against the cold iron then he kissed her brow and said, 'Don't forget to bring us our dinner, now.'

'I won't, Turk,' Maeve said, meek at last.

'Off you go then, my sweetheart, off you go.'

She left the gates of the warehouse and went away, drifting up Sutter Street in the wake of the crowd, drifting towards the sound of the guns.

Up in the vicinity of Sackville Street a candy shop had been broken into and the pavements were littered with barley sticks, peppermints and liquorice straps. On the steps in Magellan Lane the young citizens of Dublin were gorging themselves on midget gems and

316

red jelly eels, comfits and Empire creams or fought over chocolate bars and boxes or scratched in the carpet of broken glass for a toffee or a marzipan that had somehow escaped.

In Brower Street shoes, hats, stockings and ribbons trailed sadly away from looted shops, and a woman told her that the volunteers had shot twenty looters and Patrick Pearse himself had signed an order saying that all looters were to be shot. Maeve had seen a man shot yesterday and had not been much affected but at the tail end of Brower Street she saw a dead horse, a fine handsome stallion with its legs sticking up in the air and a huge reddish-blue pool of blood around it, and before she knew what she was doing she was running for the shelter of the Sperryhead Road.

She slipped down the lane and in by the kitchen door and, tugged by a familiar voice, went along the corridor into the dining-room.

Two men were seated at the table. The polished surface was protected by oilcloth and a vase of flowers, withered now, had been pushed to one side to make way for plates, cups, a teapot, and a bottle of Powers and two glasses. The men were hunched over the table, laughing tipsily. One of them was Fran. She had seen his back often enough to recognise the tight old suit he wore. The other man was a stranger to her, a round jolly fellow sucking on the short end of a cigar and sipping whiskey from a glass. Mam sat with the baby on her lap as if she were just another wife entertaining her husband and his friend and there was no rumble of gunfire loud in the air outside.

'Now here's a young lass who's just been up town by the look of her,' the stranger said. 'She'll give us all the news, won't you, chicken?'

'Ah, Kaygan, let the girl alone.' Fran glanced over his shoulder and winked at Maeve. 'Come here, darlin', come and give old Fran a kiss.'

Fran had never asked her for a kiss before. She had kissed him only when she felt like it. She had sat on his knee once or twice but it was not the same as sitting on Turk's knee or, as far as she could recall, on Daddy's knee. She was relieved to see Fran, however, and went to him and kissed him on the lips because she knew he was showing off to his friend Kaygan how good a father he could be when he tried.

Mr Kaygan said, 'Would it be unpardonably forward of me to ask the young lady for a kiss too, even though we are of but slight acquaintance and I'm not inclined to class myself as a relative, blood or otherwise?'

Maeve ignored the stranger's request and leaned against Fran. She could smell strong whiskey off him and knew that he had been a while at the bottle.

'Have you been at the fighting, sir?' she said.

'I have been fighting with your father – Francis, I mean – to ensure that news of this great adventure of ours reaches the enemy's ears and the ears of the world at large. And' – Mr Kaygan held up the cigar and waved it about – '*and* to make sure that our brave volunteers are armed, not with sword and buckler, not with hayfork and hoe but with the best weapons that dollar money can buy. We have, in a word, been distributing arms.'

'Aren't you going to the warehouse?' Maeve asked.

'Fran's exhausted,' her mother said. 'He needs sleep.'

'Oh!' Maeve said. 'What's in the case?'

'Case?' Fran said.

'In the case between your knees?'

'Oh that!' Fran said. 'Nothing for Nosey Parkers.'

'Is it a revolver?'

'What a girl!' Mr Kaygan said. 'By gum, Francis, what a girl! Tell me, lass, would you like a revolver? Would you like to go shoot a few British soldiers, is that why you put the question with such fervour?'

'It's not, is it?' Maeve said.

'No,' Fran said. 'It's not.'

Sean looked like a little papoose all wrapped up in wool and lace, Maeve thought, but a bubble of milk clung to his lips and she left Fran's side, went around the table and daintily wiped it away with a corner of her sleeve. She kissed her tiny brother on the brow.

'Ah well.' Mr Kaygan put the cigar back into his mouth. 'I see that kisses in this household are reserved for those and such as those. I'll just have wait until I get home to claim my rightful dues.'

Maeve drew out a chair and seated herself close to her mother.

She felt that she had earned the right to sit with the adults now. She had seen a man shot and a dead horse, had been close to the fighting and had not been afraid. Thanks to her uncles and granddad, to Turk and Fran, she had been in this thing from the beginning and would be in at the end, even with the British moving through the streets with all the cunning of wolves. Who had said that about wolves? Mr Whiteside. Mr Whiteside was up at the Green with the Citizen Army. She wished she could be at her teacher's side right now, the whole class lined up at the gates of the Green, chewing on their looted toffees or sucking their liquorice straps and chanting like the twelve times table, '*Shoot us. Shoot us if you dare.*'

She said, 'I promised Turk I'd take more food.'

'Is it safe?' Mam said. 'Are there no troops in Sutter Street?'

'If there aren't,' said Mr Kaygan, 'there soon will be. Martial law will prevail tonight or if not tonight by tomorrow, and that will surely wipe the smile from the face of the populace.'

'What's martial law?' Maeve said.

'The law of the gun,' said Fran, wearily.

'Our law?' said Maeve.

'Military law, the right to do wicked things with government approval.'

'Mr Pearse won't stand for that,' Maeve said; then added, 'Will he?'

'Mr Pearse, little lady, can only hold out so long.'

'What about the reinforcements?'

Mr Kaygan and Fran exchanged a glance that she could not interpret. They had been laughing together when she had entered the room but they were not laughing now. They were not so much sober as resigned. The abrupt change in mood troubled her.

Her mother said, 'Jansis has bread, cheese and boiled eggs ready in the kitchen but you've not to go round to Sutter Street, Maeve. You can toss it over the wall. Charlie will know where to look for it.'

'I'm not afraid. I'll take it right round to the gate.'

'No,' Fran said. 'It isn't safe.' He dribbled whiskey into his glass and into Mr Kaygan's. 'Drink up, Kay,' he said, 'then you'd better be on your way.'

'I better had, yes,' Mr Kaygan said. 'Will I take the Hudson, and if so, when will I call back for you?'

'Leave the car behind the house,' Fran said. 'You can walk, can't you?'

'I suppose I can,' said Mr Kaygan. 'Are you endeavouring to indicate that you no longer require my assistance?'

Fran pushed himself back from the table. He seemed weary and rather sad. Maeve could not fathom why. He had planned for this day of triumph but now it had finally arrived he seemed to have lost all interest. She felt a vague sense of unease, a suspicion that many of the things Fran had told her had not been exactly the truth.

He offered Mr Kaygan his hand. It stuck out pale

and bony from a threadbare sleeve. 'My thanks for all you've done.'

'It was nothing, Francis, nothing at all. The likes of you and I will really come into our own in the glorious years ahead, will we not?'

'We will,' Fran said. 'I'm sure we will.'

Mr Kaygan let himself out by the front door, and Fran sat down again. He looked across the table at Mam and at the baby and gave a little jerk of the head, almost, Maeve thought, a twitch.

'He's been fed and changed,' Mam said. 'Will you take him, Maeve, and put him in his crib in the parlour.'

'Where are you going?'

'Upstairs to make up the beds.'

'I have to catch some sleep,' Fran said. 'A couple of hours will do.'

Maeve lifted her half-brother, snuggled him against her shoulder and stroked his back to help him bring up wind. She rocked one side to the other while Fran, bottle and glass in one hand, reached between his feet and fished out the strange black leather bag. He hoisted it up and tucked it under his arm, and carried it along the corridor to the stairs.

'Are you goin' to take a rest too, Mam?' Maeve said.

'Yes, I think I am,' Sylvie answered and, leaving the baby in Maeve's care, followed Fran upstairs.

*   *   *

Jansis was not in the kitchen. A big wicker basket packed with tea, sugar and bottled milk, bread loaves, boiled eggs and slabs of cheese stood on the table. The provisions had been bought with Fran's money. Since the Shamrock had closed its doors they were dependent on Fran to pay the bills, though a postal order for half her father's army pay arrived through the mail every other Thursday.

Hardship had many faces, Mr Whiteside had told her but she hadn't known what he'd meant at the time.

Now, as she stood in the kitchen of the deserted hotel with the baby against her shoulder, it dawned on Maeve that people who thought feeding their children more worth while than fighting for freedom might have a point.

She had never gone hungry. She had always had a warm coat to wear in winter and boots for her feet and had never been obliged to sleep with five or six others in the bed, like some of her schoolmates. There had always been money in the family. Gran McCulloch's relatives in Glasgow lived in big houses and had lots of servants and owned motor-cars, but she had never had ambition foisted upon her and had come to believe that oppression and poverty were all the fault of the Westminster government.

Cuddling her half-brother, she contemplated the basket of food, the length of rope, and the shamrock flag that was tied to a broom handle. The basket reminded her of an illustration in her Old Testament, and she knew what the rope and flag were for: she had overheard Fran tell Charlie that the Shamrock was the back door to the warehouse.

She moved to the stairs that led to the basement. 'Jansis, are you there?'

'Here I am.'

Jansis appeared in the kitchen doorway. She had thrown off her mobcap and apron and put on her Sunday-best overcoat, the dark green one with the buttons on the breast. The coat went well with the dark green beret that Charlie had left in the bar and never reclaimed.

She wore gloves too, gauntlet-style gloves borrowed from Mam's bottom drawer. They were tight on Jansis's big muscular hands and the stitching stood out like veins. Her face was white as flour, her eyes dark-circled. She held a rifle in one hand and a box of cartridges in the other.

'I have to go now, dear,' she said.

'Where did you get the rifle?'

'Stole it.'

'From the lot that Fran brought here and Daddy took away?'

'Aye, I hid it where the peelers couldn't find it.' Jansis gave a little grunt of satisfaction. 'The bullets too.'

'But why?'

'Just in case this day ever came.'

'Where are you going?'

'Over the wall.'

'Jansis!'

'There are soldiers down the road, more at the end of Sutter Street.'

'Does Turk know they're there?'

'I'll tell him when I get over there.'

'What are they doing, the soldiers?'

'Waitin' for artillery.'

'Do they know the warehouse is occupied?'

'Sure an' they do,' Jansis said, 'but they'll not know how many men are inside. Well, there'll be one more in a minute.' She smiled. 'Me.'

'Oh, Jansis!' Maeve said. 'Oh, Jansis!'

'No tears, dearest. You're my big girl. Look after the wee fellah. Come on now, put him in his basket in the parlour an' help me over the wall. Turk will be dyin' for his dinner.'

Maeve went into the parlour, put the baby into the crib on the carpet and placed a cushion top and bottom to hold the cradle steady. Sean lay on his back, eyes closed, lips pursed, a little frown creasing his brow. His tiny pink fists were raised like a man enraged but when Maeve kissed him he gave a snuffle and a sigh and did not wake up. It was quiet in the house, uncannily quiet, but far away in the distance she could hear the chatter of a machine-gun. She returned to the kitchen and Jansis opened the back door and went out on to the worn step with the cartridge box in her pocket and the rifle across both shoulders.

'On to the top of the motor-car,' she said, 'then on

325

to the top of the chicken coop. We'll show them the flag so they'll know we're friends. After I'm over, tie the rope to the basket handle an' lower it down to me. Bring the rope up after, in case you need it again.'

'Does Fran know what you're doing?' Maeve said.

'Fran! Fran doesn't care.'

'What a thing to say!'

'Ah well, think what you like about Fran,' Jansis said, 'just don't think badly o' me, Maeve, that's all I ask.'

'I wish I was comin' with you.'

'Turk would skin me alive if I brought you over.'

They moved across the yard, scattering the hens, scrambled on to the roof of the motor-car and on to the roof of the chicken coop. The tarpaper roof creaked and sagged beneath their weight and Maeve lifted up the little green flag on the broom handle and waved it. There was no response from the warehouse.

'That's enough,' Jansis told her and elbowed herself on to the top of the wall and straddled it, the rifle across her back. She edged around, lowered herself on her hands and dropped out of sight.

Maeve heard a thud and a little shout as Jansis struck the ground.

'Are you all right?'

'Aye, I landed on my fat bum. I'm fine. Give me the basket, Maeve.'

Maeve tied the rope around the basket and lowered it over the wall.

She paid out the rope until she heard Jansis call out.

'Got it. Pull up the rope now.'

'Is Turk there?'

'He's seen me. He's wavin' from a window. He's blowin' kisses.'

'Tell him . . .' The rope snaked suddenly over the brickwork and tumbled about her. 'Tell him . . .' She could not think of a thing to say; then she heard a cheer go up and a couple of celebratory shots echo over the rooftops.

Maeve coiled the rope about her hand and elbow.

Only when she turned to step from the roof of the chicken coop on to the top of the Hudson did she realise that she was no longer alone.

The man wore a sombre black overcoat and a trilby hat and had his hands in his pockets. He looked up at her and smiled.

'Hello, girlie,' Mr Vaizey said. 'Remember me?'

Chapter Fifteen

'For God's sake!' Fran shouted. 'You've no right to haul me off without a charge. I haven't done anything.'

'Under the new special powers act, Hagarty, I have every right.'

'All right, take me if you want to, but for God's sake leave the woman in peace. She's done nothing wrong.'

'She's harboured criminals,' Vaizey said.

Ames held Fran in an arm lock, forcing him almost to his knees. He wore nothing but trousers and a vest.

The front door was wide open and there were armed men outside in the road. Mam had already been taken away. She had been allowed to throw on an old grey skirt and blouse for decency's sake but her stockings were draped around her neck and one of the detectives carried her boots as if they were valuable pieces of evidence. Mam did not look back even when Maeve tried to run after her into the road. Vaizey restrained her with an arm about the waist, smothering her frantic thrusts. As soon as Mam had vanished, though, the inspector released her.

Fran was bent almost double and there was spit coming out of his mouth.

Maeve didn't feel sorry for Fran. It was as if she had dreamed it all before and the dream was simply fulfilling itself. What frightened her most of all was the thought of Sean lying helpless in his crib in the parlour. She wondered if she should try to make a dash for the parlour or if they would shoot her for trying to escape.

'Christ, Vaizey,' Fran groaned, 'there's a child in the house, a baby.'

'Your baby?'

'What does that – yes, yes, my baby.'

'Aren't there enough bastards in Dublin without you fathering more?'

Vaizey looked up into the gloom of the stairs and snapped his fingers. Someone dropped the portman-teau over the rail. Vaizey caught it neatly and held it inches from Fran's face.

'Well now, Hagarty,' he said, 'I thought *this* was your baby.'

'You bloody evil bastard!' Fran said.

'Take him away,' Vaizey said.

Ames yanked Fran up and ran him out of the house.

Vaizey turned to Maeve. 'Where's the infant?'

'In the parlour.'

'How old is it?'

'Ten weeks.'

'Is your mother feeding it?'

'Aye.'

He came closer, blotting out the light from the doorway.

Maeve glanced down the corridor to the kitchen. A big man in a tweed jacket guarded the back door. Between his legs she could see the hens dipping and strutting unconcernedly.

'Is it a boy?' Vaizey said.

'Aye.'

He was so close to her now that she could smell him. He smelled of tobacco and a musty odour that reminded her of old books from a market stall. The smell and his neatness did not seem to go together. He tucked the heavy black bag under one arm, spread his hand on the panelling beside her head and said softly, 'I've half a mind to take you in too, girlie, young as you are. I'll bet you know a great deal more than a girl your age should, and a great deal more than is good for you.' He pushed himself back. 'You've five minutes to gather up the infant and whatever else you can carry and get out of the house.'

'Out?' Maeve said. 'We live here.'

'Look,' Vaizey said, 'the moment we're finished here the soldiers will occupy the building. You know what's happening in Sutter Street, don't you? Of course you do. Why, you could probably tell me how many men are in the warehouse and how well they're armed.'

'Hundreds,' Maeve said. 'An' they've plenty of ammo.'

'Was it Colin Whiteside who taught you to lie?' Vaizey said. 'Well, Colin Whiteside won't be teaching you any more bad habits.'

'What do you mean?'

'Your Mr Colin Whiteside was shot early this morning in St Stephen's Green park. Fine piece of marksmanship, so I'm told, clean through the heart.'

Maeve bit her lip and clenched her fists. She refused to let this man intimidate her even if what he said about Mr Whiteside was true.

'What are you going to do to my mother?'

'I don't know,' Mr Vaizey said. 'It depends.'

'You'll get nothing from her. My mam won't squawk.'

'She might,' the inspector said, 'if she wants to see her baby again.'

'You wouldn't harm my brother, would you?'

'I'll do what I have to do,' Vaizey said, then, relenting, 'No, I won't harm your brother, but it's up to you to get him out of here before the shooting starts. Is there somewhere you can go? Someone who'll give you shelter?'

'Yes.'

He took his hand from the panelling, fished in his overcoat pocket, brought out a shilling and offered it to her. 'The trams are off, but you might find a train going to Towers. You'll be safe enough there.'

'Have you not arrested my grandfather then?'

'He isn't worth arresting,' Vaizey said. 'Here, take the money.'

'I'm not takin' money from the likes o' you.'

'Suit yourself,' Vaizey said. 'You're not my responsibility, thank God.'

He stepped away and changed his grip on the leather bag, dropping it into his hand. Fran hadn't told her what the bag contained, but she reckoned it would be plans, plans or gelignite or something equally important. She was clear about one thing: this was what a rebellion was really all about. Mr Whiteside had prepared her for it. Had told her all about famine and strikes, the horrors of injustice and the beauty of sacrifice. If Mr Whiteside had made his sacrifice there was nothing to be gained from bursting into tears. He would be in the hands of God now and, like all good martyrs, at peace.

She hastened across the corridor into the parlour.

Sean was awake but not crying. When she lifted him from the crib he uttered not a sound. Carrying the baby, she went back into the kitchen.

The man at the back door turned, smiled and gave her a wink as if they were allies, not enemies.

The motor-car had gone. Four soldiers were setting up a machine-gun on the roof of the chicken coop. She took Jansis's shawl from the hook and the three shillings that Mam kept for emergencies from a jar on the dresser. Soldiers were already piling in through the front door and thudding upstairs. She put a bottle of milk into her school satchel, wrapped the big shawl about her shoulders and brought the ends up around her head the way Jansis did when it rained.

'Hurry,' Mr Vaizey said.

She moved faster, not out of obedience but lest her nerve fail.

He ushered her out of the house, out into the road past the soldiers. At that moment Maeve had a feeling that she would never live in the Shamrock again, that before this day was over the slate would be wiped clean. Sean would be her passport through the cordon, though she had no idea what she would do until her mother was released.

A crowd had gathered to watch the arrests. Maeve recognised one man in particular because he was very distinctive and because he should not have been there. Mr Flanagan walked briskly towards the inspector, shoulders thrown back under his swanky alpaca overcoat.

He planted himself before the inspector and held out a hand.

'You have my property, I believe.'

'Do I now?' Mr Vaizey said. 'Do I really?'

'Of course you do,' Mr Flanagan said. 'You know damned well you do.'

Maeve watched in bewilderment as the inspector handed over the portmanteau to Mr Flanagan who, saying nothing, swung round and carried it off into the crowd. The bag could not have contained plans or gelignite after all. Mr Vaizey glanced at her, seemed about to say something and then changed his mind. He tapped her shoulder and gave her a little push towards the crowd.

Down beyond the lane the soldiers were spread across the width of the road. Maeve turned on her heel and headed towards them, Sean held against her breast, snug under the shawl.

Amused not alarmed, the soldiers watched her approach.

'One o' your mistakes then, 'arry?'

'Nay, not one o'mine.'

''ow about you then, Bill?'

''ow about yerself, Cocker?'

'You lookin' for the daddy then, love?'

'My daddy,' Maeve said, 'is fightin' in France.'

'Lucky 'im,' one of the soldiers said, and allowed her to pass through.

Sylvie assumed they would take her to the castle, hold her for an hour or two and release her. She asked one of the men in the van where they were taking her but received no reply. The pair sat on a wooden bench attached by chains to the wall of the van and stared down at their hands. She was tempted to go and sit by them just to see what they would do, but she was afraid they would hit her.

She sat still and submissive until the van drew to a halt.

The door was opened from the outside and a little wooden ladder lowered from its holding. One of the men got out and helped her down. She was still barefoot, her stockings around her neck. She hadn't dared lift her skirts and show them her bare legs in case it gave them ideas.

When she stepped on to the cobbles in a tiny square yard with tenements all around, she knew that they hadn't brought her to the castle. Fear rose up in her throat. Ames was holding open an iron door in the wall of a building that soared up into the grey sky. One of the men gave her a nudge and she hurried across the cold cobbles as if she were anxious to be out of the rain. Ames caught her arm, drew her into a narrow stone–floored passageway and, leaving the guards outside, closed the heavy iron door and bolted it.

'Where's Fran? Where have you taken him?'

'Hush now,' Ames said, 'just hush.'

'What sort of place is this?'

'I told you to hush,' Ames said.

She could have turned on the waterworks but she would not give him the satisfaction. He steered her along the flagged passageway, up a flight of worn stone steps into another passageway. He stopped in front of a wooden door with a grille set into it. He opened the door to reveal a cell, empty save for a bucket on the floor and a big sink with a dripping brass tap. There

was a glazed window high on the wall facing her but no chair or table, no cot or mattress. Ames pushed her inside and closed the door.

She stood quite still, staring up at the grille, waiting for she knew not what; then the door opened again and Ames tossed in her boots. They fell noisily on to the stone floor and she stepped back from them as if she expected them to explode. She peered down at the boots and saw that the long laces had been removed from the eyelets. She sighed, sat down on the floor and pulled on her stockings and boots. Without laces the boots didn't grip her calves and flopped when she walked.

She went to the sink, climbed up on it and tried in vain to see out of the window. She climbed down from the sink and leaned on it, resting, then she twisted the squeaky cock on the brass tap until the drip became a flow, the flow a gush. She stepped back quickly, worked the tap, and thrust her face into the water, wetting her skirt and blouse. She filled her mouth with the ice-cold, metal-tasting water and drank, for she had read somewhere that drinking quantities of cold water thinned a mother's milk. She worried about her milk and what would happen if it clotted in her breasts, worried too about Sean, though she was sure that Maeve would keep him safe from harm.

She leaned against the sink, waiting. Certain sounds from within the building increased her fear: wailing, thuds, laughter, then footsteps loud and fast as if a gigantic animal were being pursued through

the passageways. Noises from outside too, though faint: machine-gun fire, the crackle of artillery. She didn't really know what artillery was, or what damage it could do. She had seen photographs of captured German howitzers in the *Mirror*, massive devices shrouded in netting, horses pulling guns on carriages through a sea of mud but could not imagine such fearsome weapons on the streets of Dublin.

So far she had taken scant interest in the war. It should have been her war, for her father in Glasgow was helping build ships to destroy the German navy, and Forbes – she didn't know what Forbes was up to, though she was sure he wouldn't put himself in danger and would emerge from the conflict richer than he went into it. It had been a long time since she had thought of her father. To her surprise, her embarrassment, she wanted him now and, thinking of him, found hot tears welling in her eyes.

Then, abruptly, the door flew open.

Sylvie stepped away from the sink and stood up straight.

Ames carried a table and chair into the cell, a square wooden table with its legs in the air, the chair, a cane thing, balanced on top.

'You're for it now, missus,' Ames said, cheerfully. 'By God, you are.'

He was strong and agile, like a circus performer. He righted the table with one hand and swung the chair down with the other, sweeping them into position in the centre of the room. She watched him, her

posture defiant, her eyes angry, but with a strange, sick lurching in her stomach at what was about to take place. Ames went away again, leaving the door open. A moment later Inspector Vaizey entered the cell. He was eating a ham sandwich and carrying a mug of tea. He placed the mug on the table and signalled. Ames closed the door from outside. Vaizey put the last big bite of sandwich to his mouth and pushed it in with his forefinger. He wiped his fingers delicately on the side of his trousers and looked appraisingly at Sylvie.

'Well, Mrs McCulloch,' he said, smiling, 'alone at last, it seems.'

There were soldiers on the Strand, several army trucks whizzed past, heading towards the city, and artillery fire grumbled in the distance, but by the time Maeve reached the bridge near the end of the North Strand she had left the fighting behind.

It had been her intention to walk to Towers but she had covered barely a couple of miles before her arms began to ache and Sean, now wide awake, cried hard and unremittingly. She tried loosening the shawl to make a cradle but that didn't work and he continued to cry and cry until his little face was as red as a beetroot and Maeve feared that he would do himself an injury.

She seated herself on the pavement at the side of the road, laid the baby across her knees, lifted up his skirts and felt the towel, which was soaked and smelly. She thought of removing the nappy but she had nothing with which to replace it. She soothed him as best she could and looked forlornly in the direction of Malahide which now seemed impossibly far away.

Surprising amounts of traffic were rolling into the city, carts and trade vans, even an omnibus heading off, she assumed, to Howth to let the trippers see the ships that lay in the bay and the gunboats moored off the mouth of the Liffey. Odd to think that for half a crown you could stand on Howth Head and watch Ireland shake herself free of oppression.

She wondered if Sean were hungry, though it was still an hour short of his feeding time. She wondered if she should try him at her breast and then, blowing out her cheeks, realised how stupid an idea that was. Her breasts were dry bumps and sucking on them would do the poor wee soul no good. She really needed someone to tell her what to do. Perhaps she should go back to the Shamrock and hope that the soldiers had gone away and her mam had returned; but that would mean that the warehouse had fallen and Charlie and Peter, Jansis and Turk, her lovely Turk, were prisoners or, like poor Mr Whiteside, dead. She felt small now, shrunken by anxiety and responsibility.

The hack appeared on the Fairview corner. It was one of the old-fashioned kind with a sleek horse trotting between the shafts and a black hood, the driver, in a tall hat, riding above the cab.

Maeve wrapped the shawl over Sean and, lifting

the satchel, got to her feet, stepped out into the road and waved.

To her vast relief, the hack drew to a halt by the kerb.

The driver had a face like a weasel and didn't appear friendly.

'How much would it be costin' for a ride to Towers?' Maeve asked.

He leaned down and squinted at her. Sean howled.

'I'm not goin' to Towers. I just been t' Portmarnock.'

'Have you not got a licence?' Maeve heard herself say.

'What sort o' question is that?'

'How much to Towers?' Maeve said again.

He peered at her without pity. 'Ten shillin'.'

'Hah!'

'Five then.'

'Three.'

'Show me the three.'

She dug into her pocket, fished out the coins and held them out in the palm of her hand. 'There you are. See.'

'Get in,' the driver told her.

'Are you hungry?' Inspector Vaizey asked.

'No.'

'Would you care to share my tea?'

'No,' Sylvie said. 'Thank you all the same.'

'Take off your skirt?'

'Pardon?'

'It's wet, isn't it? Why don't you take it off and let it dry.'

'I'll do nothing of the kind,' Sylvie said.

'I wouldn't want you catching your death.' Vaizey stroked his moustache for a moment, his head on one side. 'Your blouse is wet too. Is that milk?'

'Water, from the tap at the sink,' Sylvie said. 'Where's Fran, where's Mr Hagarty? What have you done with him?'

Vaizey lifted the chair and put it down again. 'Please be seated.'

'I'll stand.'

'No you won't. You'll sit.'

She hesitated, bridling and afraid, then seated herself on the edge of the chair facing him, her knees pressed tightly together. She glanced down at the dark water stain on her skirt and wondered if she would be obliged to give him what he wanted before he would set her free.

'Well, that's better.' Vaizey leaned against the table. 'Are you more comfortable now?'

'No,' Sylvie said. 'I won't be more comfortable until you let me go.'

'Is Francis Hagarty your lover?'

'What business is that of . . . Yes, he is.'

'Is the child his?'

Sylvie nodded.

'And your husband is fighting at the front with the Rifles?'

Sylvie nodded again. There was no moral justifi-
cation for what she had done. She had betrayed her
husband's trust to satisfy her desire and had climbed
into bed with Fran of her own free will.

'Does Hagarty reside at the Shamrock Hotel?'

'Yes, sometimes.'

'Does he come and go as he pleases?'

'Of course – but I think you know that already.'

'Where does he go when he's not with you?'

'I have no idea.'

'Don't you ask him?'

'No.'

'Why not?'

'I'm not his keeper.'

'You're really just his whore, Mrs McCulloch.
Isn't that the long and short of it?'

'Say what you like about me, Mr Vaizey, I'm not
giving you any information.'

'Is that because you won't tell or because you
don't know?'

'What difference does it make?'

'It makes a great deal of difference,' Vaizey said.
'You see, if you know something about Francis
Hagarty's dealings with, say, the Germans and elect
to keep it to yourself then I'm entitled to wring it from
you. On the other hand, if you know nothing . . .'

'The Germans? Fran wouldn't do business with
the Germans.'

Vaizey pushed himself away from the table.

'Why did you close the Shamrock?'

343

'I didn't close the Shamrock. You cancelled my licence to serve drink and that did for the commercial trade.'

'And the meetings of the brotherhood, did they also cease?'

'You seem to know everything, don't you? If you've questions to ask, ask and let me be on my way.'

He walked behind the chair and leaned over it. 'Look, I could have left you and your infant in the house in Sperryhead Road and let you take your chances with the soldiers.'

'The soldiers are under orders not to harm women and children.'

'Do you think I'm not under orders?' Vaizey said. 'My orders are to apprehend everyone connected with this idiotic revolt and you, Mrs McCulloch, are sleeping with one of the leaders.'

'Fran isn't a leader. He's just a journalist.'

'Fran Hagarty is a lot more than just a journalist. He's an arms buyer, a gunrunner and a dealer in foreign currency,' Vaizey said. 'He couldn't care less about independence. Hagarty is as much a threat to the integrity of the Irish brotherhoods as he is to the British government.'

He moved from behind the chair. Sylvie twisted round, not daring to let him out of her sight. He came around the chair and crouched before her as if he were about to lace up her boots. She drew in her feet and pressed her knees tightly together. He laid no hand on her, however, but squatted on his heels and spoke softly.

'Before nightfall, by dawn tomorrow at the very latest,' he said, 'your husband's brothers will be either dead or in prison and the Shamrock, your house, will be rubble. My task is to scatter the ashes of this outrageous uprising so that nothing of the sort can flare up again. The brotherhoods, the Citizen Army, most of the volunteers will be spared or given prison sentences; the real traitors will be charged with treason, found guilty and hanged. They are not my concern. My concern is with the half men, the grey men, opportunists like Francis Hagarty. Hagarty's part of a self-perpetuating myth, and if I don't do my job properly he'll fan that myth and more innocent people will suffer.'

'What do you expect me to do about it? I'm not part of your myth.'

Vaizey sighed, got up and returned to the table.

'I feel sorry for you, Mrs McCulloch,' he said. 'You say you love this man, and perhaps you do – let's say you do – but loving a man is not the same as loving one's country and supporting a man is not the same as supporting a cause. It's not even your country, or your cause.'

'What *do* you want from me?'

'I need you to be my witness.'

Sylvie shot to her feet. 'I'll never give court evidence against Fran.'

'That,' Vaizey said, 'isn't what I mean.'

345

'What do you mean then?'

'You'll see,' said Vaizey.

He rapped on the door and when it opened, stepped into the passageway. He nodded to Ames who closed and bolted the door, and Sylvie was left alone once more. Table, chair and tea mug had been left behind, however. Clearly the inspector wasn't finished with her yet.

She was baffled by what had taken place. She would have been less anxious if Vaizey had tried to pump her for information about Fran, Charlie and the brotherhood – but Vaizey probably knew more about the workings of the brotherhood than she did. The building was uncannily quiet for a time, and then, filtering up from deep within the building, came a sound, a soft sound, like a whisper of the wind. Her first thought was that Vaizey was coming back, that she would be punished for defying him, but as the noise in the passageway became louder she realised that someone – Fran – was calling her name.

'*Syl-vay. Syl-vay.*'

She ran to the door and tried to reach the little grille, to pull herself up.

'*Syl-vay, Syl-vay, Syl-vay*': closer now, louder now.

Scuffle of feet in the passageway, Ames guffawing and another voice, not one she recognised, yapping, 'Move 'im along. Move 'im along.'

She hammered on the door and shouted Fran's name.

Fran cried out, '*Sylvie, is that you?*'

She snatched up the chair, flung it against the door and climbed upon it. She peered through the grille. She could see nothing but a fragment of empty passageway, nothing of Fran. A door slammed. Cold air breathed against her face. She jumped from the chair, carried it to the sink, hoisted it into the sink and clambered after it.

Balanced on the chair, fingernails digging into the window ledge, she peered through the dirty glass into the courtyard. The window was at ground level and she could not see the sky. Initially the courtyard was deserted, then, suddenly, Fran came running out across the cobbles. He ran like a man whose legs had been broken, lurching one way and then another. He wore nothing but trousers and a vest and he was still barefoot. She shouted his name. He turned and saw her or saw at least the arc of the window. He stumbled towards her, legs bent, arms held out as if he thought she might be able to pull him to safety through the glass. His mouth was open and he was shouting. Sylvie heard not a word, only the muffled crack of a revolver. Fran fell forward, his chin tilted up, blood trickling from his lips.

Sylvie shouted and slapped her hands to the glass, slapped her hands to the glass to pull him in. He crawled towards her, his lips redder than cherries. She could not make out whether it was the stranger or Ames or Vaizey himself who fired the second shot. Fran jerked, rolled on to his side on the sloping cobbles and squeezed his cheek against the window. Nothing separated them now but the thickness of the glass and the dirt on the glass, his mouth and cheek plastered against the glass, blood smearing the glass.

She called his name, saw his lips move, knew that he was saying her name, repeating her name over and over again. She saw the toe of a shoe, a trouser leg, and a fist holding a revolver. The third shot vibrated against the glass and there was blood all over the glass.

The chair swayed and tilted and Sylvie toppled backwards. She fell to the floor and lay there for a moment, winded. Then she scrambled to her feet, clambered back on to the sink and stared up at the glass. The glass was stained all red, and Fran was gone.

She climbed down out of the sink and righted the chair.

Something told her that she should weep, that Vaizey would expect to find her weeping and hysterical. She seated herself on the chair, facing the door, and waited for Vaizey to return. Ames came instead.

He escorted her out of the cell and along the passageway and down the steps to the iron door. He said nothing and she said nothing. He unbolted the door and opened it, releasing her into the world at large, to tell the world at large what she had witnessed and to assure all those concerned – including John James Flanagan, of course – that Mr Francis Hagarty would trouble them no more.

Chapter Sixteen

'And why, may I ask, did you come here?' her grandmother said.

'I'd nowhere else to go,' Maeve answered.

'Well, you'll have somewhere to go in a minute, m' girl, once you've finished that pancake.'

'You're not turnin' us away, are you?'

'I'm sending you to Malahide to buy a jar of Mamnhu.'

'Mamnhu?'

'Infant food,' the woman said, 'unless you want your brother weaned on pancakes. Can you drive a trap?'

'No.'

'Ride a horse?'

Maeve shook her head. 'Sorry.'

Her grandmother tutted. 'Blessed if I know what girls are coming to these days. Where have they taken your mother?'

'I don't know,' Maeve said.

'Who took her, the soldiers or the police?'

'The police,' said Maeve. 'Mr Vaizey came for Fran . . .'

'Aye, I thought Hagarty would be involved somehow.'

They were in the kitchen at the back of the brewery cottage. The kitchen was not like the kitchen in the Shamrock. It was big and airy with windows on two walls and you could look out at the trees and fields and, with the door open, smell both the brewery and the sea.

Gran laid Sean on the kitchen table as if she were going to dust him with flour and pop him into the oven. She worked a yellow sponge over his bottom, squeezed the sponge into a bowl of warm water and dried his parts with a towel.

Sean whimpered quietly. If he appreciated being released from the wet nappy and damp petticoats he wasn't going to admit it. He focused on his grandmother's stern features – she wasn't his grandmother, of course, but Sean didn't know that – and gave her a crooked little grimace.

'He's got wind,' Gran said. 'He needs something in his stomach.'

'They're fighting all over Dublin,' Maeve said through a mouthful of sweet pancake. 'Has Granddad gone to help Turk?'

'Don't be so daft.' Gran snorted. 'He's upstairs, sleeping off a skinful.'

Maeve sipped from a glass of milk and glanced at the ceiling.

'Doesn't he know the uprising has started?'

'The only uprising he cares about these days is stomach heaves.'

'But the brotherhood—'

'Finish that milk and get on down to the shops.'

'Will we be needin' a bottle?'

'I've bottles somewhere,' her grandmother said, 'but we'll need a card of rubber teats. The only teats I've got are for goats.'

'I don't have any money, Gran. I spent it all on the cab fare.'

'I'll give you the money.'

'We'll pay you back,' said Maeve. 'Mam'll pay you back.'

Gran wrapped the towel loosely around the baby and lifted him. She held him lightly, one hand under his bottom. It seemed to Maeve that Sean was supporting himself and all that her grandmother was doing was keeping him in balance.

'Did she tell you to come here?'

'No,' Maeve said. 'I came off my own bat.'

'Is there much shooting in town?'

'Aye, a lot. Mr Whiteside, my teacher, got killed.'

'Did you leave your mother a note telling her where you'd be?'

Maeve shook her head. 'There wasn't time to leave notes.'

'No, I don't suppose there was,' her grandmother

conceded. 'All right, I'll keep you here, you an' the child, but when she's released and comes for you then it's straight back off to Dublin. Is that understood?'

'Why don't you like my mam?'

'It's a long story,' the woman said, 'and it doesn't concern you.'

'It does concern me,' Maeve said.

'Hasn't your mother told you anything?'

'Not much.'

'Well, Gowry wouldn't – your father wouldn't.'

'Why wouldn't he?' said Maeve.

'This poor baby is starving and all you can do is ask questions. Get away down to the town and buy two large jars of infant food and a card of teats.' Gran carried the baby to the Welsh dresser, pulled open a drawer, took out a big brown purse and shook out two half-crowns. 'Seiffert's, the chemists, will have what we need. It's the first big shop off the Towers road and has a sign sticking out over the pavement.'

'I'll find it.'

'And don't dawdle.'

'No, Gran,' Maeve promised. 'I won't.'

Numb with the horror of what she had just witnessed Sylvie had no idea where she was or what she was doing. Fran was gone. Fran was dead. Vaizey had forced her to witness his murder. She felt drained and empty and could barely put one foot in front of the other. Her boots slapped at her ankles and she twisted over on the heels and had to right herself and take her bearings just to keep going on at all.

The castle welled up before her through a haze of smoke. She heard shooting, the whip-snap of snipers' bullets. She stopped in the mouth of a lane and looked up at the rooftops, saw a man, not a soldier, scuttle and slide behind a chimney head. She had a vague notion that she was inside the British cordons and a long way from the Sperryhead Road.

Sudden blazing anger possessed her, not just that Vaizey had murdered Fran and made her a party to the killing but that she had been tossed out unprotected now that she had served her purpose.

A vehicle thundered past, an iron-clad thing with a silly-looking gun jutting from its turret. She was so angry now that she did not feel threatened. She had to get back to Sperryhead Road, had to get back home to Maeve and Sean; with Fran dead and Gowry at the front, Sean and Maeve were all she had left. She closed her eyes: Oh, Christ, oh, God, please God have mercy on me and lead me home. A bomb exploded high above. Debris rained down into the lane. She covered her head with her arms as an avalanche of slates crashed on to the cobbles behind her.

'Mrs McCulloch, is that you?'

Little Mr Pettu politely lifted his bowler, grabbed her hand and swung her into the shelter of a doorway just as another bomb went off and another shower of splintered black tiles clattered about them. Mr Pettu put her behind him, his legs spread and elbows cocked in a posture most unbecoming to a broker of communion wine. When the dust began to clear he leaned from the doorway and peered up and down the lane.

'I thought it was you, Mrs McCulloch, though you're a fair way from the Shamrock and should not, I fear, be lingering in this neighbourhood.' He glanced round. 'Are you in good health?'

'No, Mr Pettu, I'm not,' Sylvie said and, to the little man's astonishment, threw herself into his arms and burst into a flood of tears.

Maeve ran all the way to Malahide and most of the way back and, almost before she got her breath back, had Sean on her knee and a feeding bottle in her hand and was watching her half-brother suck on the teat without any persuasion at all. The stuff in the bottle was rich and thick and Gran had widened the hole in the teat with a sewing needle so that Sean, a strenuous feeder, could get all the nourishment he needed without too much effort.

It was raining quite hard outside now. Maeve could hear the hiss of the rain in the trees, for Gran had opened the kitchen door to let out the cooking smells. It was peaceful in the brewery cottage and sea air and the jog down to Malahide had made her sleepy. It was all she could do to keep awake while Sean guzzled on his bottle. Then her grandfather got up and she could hear him lumbering about overhead like a pachyderm

– poor Mr Whiteside's word – which, Maeve knew, meant a thick-skinned quadruped. It occurred to her that her daddy had been born in this house and had lived here as a boy. She tried to imagine her daddy as a boy, tried to imagine the house filled with children – Charlie, Peter, her Scottish Uncle Forbes and the girls she had never met – tried to imagine what sort of quarrels had driven them away.

Sean paused in his sucking. His eyes were closed, his brow damp with perspiration. Maeve let him rest for a moment before she squeezed out a globule of the milky substance and dropped it on to his lip.

Sean fastened on the teat again, sucking even more greedily than before.

Her grandfather came clumping downstairs.

'Where's my breakfast, Kay?' he enquired, then, spotting Maeve and the baby and showing no surprise, said, 'Sure an' what's the news from Dublin?'

'The police have arrested Mr Hagarty,' Maeve told him.

Her grandfather's trousers were unbuttoned and his suspenders dangled over his buttocks. In daylight he looked older than his years.

He peered blearily at Sean. 'What's that? Is that yours?'

'His name's Sean. He's my brother.'

'Got him now. Fran's boy, right?'

'Granddad, didn't you hear me? The police have taken Fran away.'

'How old is he now?'

'Ten weeks.'

'He's a big wee chap for ten weeks.'

'Granddad, Fran an' Mam have been arrested,' Maeve persisted. 'An' Turk an' Charlie are occupying Watton's to stop the British bringing in reinforcements to blockade the quays.'

'The quays? Have they taken the quays, do you tell me?'

Her grandmother leaned against the door of the pantry, arms folded.

'That was the word last night,' Maeve said.

'Last night? What night was that? Sunday, was it Sunday?'

Maeve opened her mouth to correct him but Gran said, 'It's no use talking to him, Maeve. His brain's gone soft. He's good for nothing now.'

'I am,' her grandfather said petulantly. 'I am too.'

He seated himself on a chair and stared sulkily out at the rain.

'That's why the brotherhood got rid of him,' Gran went on, 'why Charlie took over. Is Peter with them at the warehouse?'

'Yes.'

'I could be doin' with a drop right now,' her grandfather said. 'The strain o' the struggle is very sore on an old man like me.'

'Is Trotter with them too?' Gran asked.

Maeve nodded.

'So it'll be a fight to the death, will it?'

'Aye, Gran,' Maeve said, 'a fight to the death it'll be.'

Mr Pettu's method of breaching the British lines was odd, but effective. First of all he led Sylvie to Dominic Sloan's, one of the small Catholic retailers in that part of town. Leaving Sylvie outside he entered the shop and conversed with the proprietor then both men came out and Mr Sloan shook Sylvie's hand, locked the door of the shop and guided Sylvie and Mr Pettu to St Theresa's convent school in Lebrun Street. They slipped into the school by a door in the wall of the garden at the rear. The garden was tiny. There was a statue in the middle, the saint herself perhaps, half life size. Dominic and Mr Pettu gave the statue a respectful little bow and went on into the school building, leaving Sylvie outside once more. It was raining gently and steadily and the rain deadened the sound of gunfire. She felt strange now, as if she were caught in a dream.

After a few minutes Mr Pettu returned, accompanied by two nuns. There was no sign of Mr Sloan. The nuns were middle-aged, muscular women, one of whom wore eyeglasses. They gave Sylvie the once-over. They clearly did not approve of her, perhaps because she was a Protestant, more likely because she was a nationalist: the Catholic hierarchy did not approve of nationalists. One of the nuns brandished a white sheet tied to a window-pole.

The other carried a large wooden crucifix. They seemed to know Mr Pettu well and addressed him as Vincent. To Sylvie they said nothing at all.

She followed the nuns out into the laneway and along it to Lebrun Street. The women walked briskly and chatted to Mr Pettu while Sylvie, her boots flopping, trailed along behind. When they reached Lebrun Street she saw why Mr Pettu had enlisted the aid of the nuns: the centre of the city was under siege. When she looked down from the crown of the road to the bridges she was shocked at the damage that had been done to the fine buildings and how many troops and artillery pieces were visible, focused, Mr Pettu told her, on the General Post Office, which was the rebels' stronghold and headquarters.

There was no shooting going on in Lebrun Street but at the street's end, where it dipped down towards the Liffey, government troops had erected a barricade of beer barrels bristling with rifles and machine-guns. Between the crown of Lebrun Street and the troops the cobbles were strewn with debris including two dead carthorses, the body of a dog and an upturned float that had flooded the gutters with milk. The nuns were not deterred. The flag and the crucifix were raised before them and Mr Pettu, ever the gentleman, took Sylvie by the arm.

'Are you fit, Mrs McCulloch?'

'I am,' said Sylvie.

She was less afraid of the government troops than of Vaizey's plainclothed ruffians. There was order and discipline among the soldiers, the threat of reprimand if they should forget themselves. Holding tightly to little Mr Pettu's arm, Sylvie followed the nuns as they advanced on the barricade.

A head came up, and another, then another. One of the soldiers crossed himself but whether in mockery or respect Sylvie could not be sure. The nuns were confident, almost arrogant with the cross and the flag held out before them. The moist wind off the river blew their garments against them so that they looked even more robust than they were. Sylvie felt again the quirky, unsought-for sense of pride that she had first experienced when she'd marched by Maeve's side at Bodenstown all those months ago, before she had met Fran Hagarty, when Gowry had been driving the charabanc.

The nuns stopped short of the barricade and looked up at the officers on the rickety little platform. They said nothing, just stared up at the British officers, their cheeks glowing and their eyes as hard as hob-nails, but there was something so admirable in their stance that one officer saluted them and, without being asked, signalled the little procession to pass through.

'Sister Veronica?' The soldier was young, his moustache still feathery. 'Sister Agnes? Don't you know me?'

'Oh, I know you, William Kelly,' the nun with the flag said out of the side of her mouth. 'How's your dear mother these days?'

'Still ailing, Sister. Will you be rememberin' her in your prayers?'

'That we will, that we will.'

They were through the barricade and beyond the troop line and walking down towards the bridge and Sylvie saw more devastation and folk poking among the rubble and then the river reaching out to the docks and to the sea. She did not trail behind now. She walked upright, head up, with Mr Pettu at her side. Fran would have been proud of her fortitude, she thought, as they passed through another cordon and followed the nuns up Jagger Street to the end of the Sperryhead Road.

'Do you know where you are now?' Mr Pettu said.

'I do,' said Sylvie.

'There's no word of street fighting here,' Mr Pettu told her, 'but I'd keep out of Sutter Street if I were you, just in case.' He offered his hand and Sylvie shook it. 'I'm sorry to hear about Mr Hagarty. He'll not be the last we'll lose, I fear, but it must be a sore trial for you with a little one, and your husband still at the war. Will you manage on your own from here, Mrs McCulloch?'

'Yes, Mr Pettu,' Sylvie assured him. 'My thanks to you and your friends.'

'The sisters are pleased to be of help,' Mr Pettu said, then he left her to join the nuns for the march back to Lebrun Street, and Sylvie set off down Sperryhead Road in search of her daughter and son.

*　　*　　*

Within an hour of occupying the warehouse Charlie sensed that their position was hopeless. The news that Jansis had brought over the wall was discouraging: the Shamrock, their supply line and escape route, had been closed off.

'What do you think, Turk? There's still time to get out before a shot is fired or a drop of blood spilled.'

'Don't be bloody stupid, man,' Turk said. 'We're here to fight.'

'That's what I thought you'd say.'

The empty sprawl of Watton's warehouse might have been held by sixty men but a mere twenty could not hope to hold off a government attack for long. Charlie placed guards by the gates and snipers in the windows then Turk and he climbed up to the cabin of one of the cranes to take a dekko at Sutter Street.

'I thought we'd have reinforcements by this time,' Charlie said. 'Weren't we told they'd come flocking in to town as soon as the thing got started?'

'Never mind the boys from the south, Charlie. Where are our lads? Put off by cancelled orders, by confusion and disorganisation, that's where,' said Turk. 'Now I'm asking myself what I'm doing sitting in a wooden box a hundred feet above Sperryhead watching the British assemble enough firepower to blow half Dublin to smithereens.'

'I'll ask you again; do you want to surrender?'

'No.'

'Well,' Charlie said, 'if we put three men front and back and a pair in each of the cranes at least we can take out a fair share of soldiers before we go down. It'll be like shooting ducks in a barrel.'

'Fish,' said Turk. 'Fish in a barrel.'

'Do you believe Sylvie's woman?'

'Jansis has no reason to lie to us. I just hope Maeve is well out of it.'

'She would be with us if you'd given her half a chance.'

Turk grinned. 'Aye, she's a spunky wee thing, is Maeve.'

'She's far too young for you.'

Turk gazed through the greasy glass in the side of the cabin at the green hills beyond the city, at the spires, steeples and tenements that climbed into the rain-washed sky.

'In four or five years she'll not be too young for me,' he said wistfully. 'I ask you, what would be so wrong in a fine fellah of twenty-eight marrying a girl of seventeen?'

'Marriage is it, now?'

'Aye, of course it's marriage. What do you take me for, Charlie?'

'I take you for an idiot,' Charlie said, patting Turk on the shoulder. 'Who'd have thought there was a big soft lump inside you. Will we show the white flag an' go out peaceful so you can marry my niece when she's old enough an' have a multitude of hairy-faced sons to fight the fight we ran away from?'

'No,' Turk said. 'I'm thinking we had better do it ourselves.'

'Then,' said Charlie, 'we'd better do it quick.'

'Why's that?'

'Because they're bringin' up a field gun to shoot us out of the sky.'

The soldiers were well organised. They had formed four ranks, two facing down Sperryhead Road towards the docks, and two facing back towards the bridges. The troops in the front rows knelt each on one knee, rifles trained on the crowd. The troops in the rear rows had fixed bayonets. Three sergeants and an officer patrolled the ranks to keep order but there was no sniper fire to distract the men who appeared to be enjoying their confrontation with the citizens of Dublin now that the onlookers at the broad end of Sperryhead Road were no longer hurling insults at them.

'Have you seen my children?' Sylvie's voice sounded as if it came through a hollow tube. 'My daughter and my baby, has anyone seen them?'

The folk in the crowd paid her scant attention. They were waiting to see what would happen next. If they needed a scapegoat, however, Sylvie McCulloch with her airs and graces, her money and her fancy man would surely fill the bill.

'Won't they let me in to look for my children?' Sylvie said.

'They won't let anyone cross the line,' a woman told her. 'Have you a house down there?'

'Aye, sure an' she has a house down there, her an' her rebel friends. It's because o' her we're all out in the street here.'

'I thought it was because the Citizens had took the warehouse?'

'Bloody Citizens. Bloody brotherhood,' an elderly man snarled. 'The only thing they're good for is makin' trouble for the rest o' us.'

'Please,' Sylvie said, 'tell me what's happening?'

'I'll tell you what's happenin',' the fierce old gentleman said. 'They've cleared all the houses and tooken their troops out. They'll not be for stormin' the warehouse after all. Change o' plans. They'll be for usin' the big guns to blast the poor beggars before they send in the soldiers for to mop up.'

'I've lost my children,' Sylvie said.

'You should've thought o' that before,' a woman, a neighbour, told her; then, relenting a little, added, 'If it's Maeve you're lookin' for, she went off down the road three or four hours ago, carryin' the baby with her.'

'Went where? What road?'

'Down through the lines. She'll be safe enough down there.'

Sylvie wriggled through the crowd and peered at the long length of Sperryhead Road.

It was empty as far as her eye could see, a great blank damp space, no sentries at the gates of the cottage rows, no guards on the doors of the house, her house. The Shamrock stood bland and shallow in the post-noon light, like something cut out of cardboard. She saw a cat, two cats, skulking down the pavement's edge, and heard a dog bark, and realised that what the old man said must be true and that the troops intended to raze Sperryhead Road to the ground. She experienced a moment of overwhelming terror at the thought that Maeve and Sean might still be in the vicinity. She let out a cry as a harsh, whirling whistle sounded overhead and a shell struck the front of the Shamrock. The brickwork round the window of Mr Dolan's room imploded, spewing debris and blowing the lace curtains into the air like frozen breath.

'Dear Christ, will they be leavin' us nothing?' the woman asked.

Shaking his head, the old man answered, 'Nothing.'

The shells came looping over from behind the dockside warehouses. The gunners' accuracy was uncanny. The Shamrock was the target and the Shamrock was struck again and again, five, six, seven shells pounding into the front of the building until nothing could be seen but a huge cloud of dust billowing across the cobbles. The crowd was silent now, cowed at last, as the dust drifted and settled and revealed the extent of the damage.

The Shamrock had been torn wide open, bedding exposed, bedding and torn curtains and carpets, the gap of the staircase, the stairs crushed under a mass of panelling and brickwork, then the roof collapsed, plunging down in another roar of dust, and fire bloomed from a fractured gas pipe.

'Aye, you'll have no more rebel tea-parties in there, I'm thinkin',' Sylvie's neighbour said as a government platoon, moving at the double, entered the courtyard from the alley and, a moment later, began peppering Watton's warehouse with grenades.

A hand to her mouth and tears in her eyes, Sylvie turned away.

As soon as they were forced to take to the rooftops Turk knew the game was up. He had hoped they might survive until nightfall and that some of them might manage to escape into Sutter Street to fight another day. When the Shamrock was shelled, however, and government troops swarmed around the warehouse all chance of holding out until sunset vanished.

The brothers, those who were still alive, were scattered throughout the building. He had no idea where Charlie was, or Kevin. He had Peter with him, hauling the lad by the collar, while Peter shrieked with the pain of the hole in his side. Jansis was wounded too and he pushed her ahead of him up the narrow staircase towards the door that opened to the air and the sky.

They had two rifles, a revolver and a pocketful of ammunition to hold off the final onslaught. He wished he didn't have to do this, to decide what was right and what was wrong, what was sensible and what was not, and what would haunt him for the rest of his life, if any life was left to him – or if it would be better to become one with the angels before the sun slipped down behind the rain-cloud behind the Dublin hills.

'Come on, lad,' Turk said. 'Come on, Patie.'

Peter screeched and clung to the steps, dragging his heels on the stone.

Big rump bulging under her Sunday overcoat and still with the beret on her head, Jansis held the Mauser in both hands and would not let go. She fell through the little door on to the roof. There was a ledge around the door, not much of one, eight or ten inches, leaded, then the roof pitched down and dropped into the loading bay at the front of the warehouse.

He grabbed Jansis by the belt and pulled her against the upright. He pulled Peter from the stairs and laid him belly down across the ledge. The boy was hollowed out by pain, the first real pain he had ever felt in his life, Turk reckoned. Well, Turk thought, never mind, it'll all be over soon enough and there'll be no pain where we're going.

Away to the west, beyond the hills, the cloud was breaking up a little as it often did this time of an evening. Below, the soldiers were running from the shelter of the gatehouse into the warehouse. More soldiers crouched behind the jute bales and three troopers were scaling the iron ladder that led up to the cabin of the jib-crane. The brothers who had been sniping from the crane were probably dead. In the window of the crane Turk noticed a glint of sunlight, very pale and watery. There were motor-cars in the street now, for Mr Watton had returned from the country and had assembled other partners and managers to negotiate with the army commanders. There had been no heavy shelling of the warehouse. Only the Shamrock had been destroyed. Turk wondered why they'd done that, why they'd blasted a hole in the Sperryhead Road: to cut off the possibility of retreat, of course, and save British lives.

Jansis said, 'I think I'm shot.'

'I think you are,' Turk said.

He took cartridges from his pocket and fed them into the Mauser.

Jansis leaned back against the little door and looked down the slope of the roof to the loading bay below. The troops were firing into the building but not at the rooftop. Jansis's arms hung slack by her sides and the front of her coat was wet with blood.

'Does it hurt?' Turk said.

'By God, does it not,' said Jansis.

He snapped the Mauser and gave it back to her.

She lifted her arms as if they were made of lead and took the rifle, cradled it against her breast and fumbled for the trigger.

'Not now, not yet,' said Turk. 'Wait, if you can.'

She looked secure enough with her boots propped on the ledge and her legs braced. He knelt down by

Peter and lifted him. There was blood on the boy's tunic, but not much, just a thin dark red tassel looped across his thigh. He was sheet-white, though, and terrified.

Turk groped in the boy's pockets, found five cartridges, and transferred them into his own pocket, then he eased the boy back until he was more inside than out, kneeling on the little bit of landing, head protruding from the doorway. He had stopped screeching now and as Turk made to step out on to the ledge, he grabbed the skirt of Turk's tunic and said, 'Give me a shooter, man, for God's sake give me a shooter.'

Turk took the revolver from its holster and fitted it into Peter's hand. He unclipped the lanyard and wrapped it round the boy's wrist. Sunlight came slanting over the rooftops and for an instant Peter's eyes were filled with sunlight and Turk could see sunlight pink through the boy's big ears.

'Take the stairs,' Turk said. 'See we don't get back shot.'

'Right,' said Peter.

Easing round, he propped his elbows on the doorstep and gripped the revolver in both hands. He was grinning, or grimacing, as he peered down into the dark of the stairs, and the waiting, Turk thought, would keep him going.

Turk held the Mauser in the crook of his arm and put his other arm around the woman's waist. She was far gone, weakened by blood loss. He doubted if she would last through it. She leaned shyly against him, as if she thought he might be courting her. She put her head against his shoulder and he could feel her hair against his cheek, her lank hair stirring in the breeze that came in off the sea.

'I think I hear them coming,' Jansis whispered.

'I do too,' said Turk.

Chapter Seventeen

It was not yet dark when Gran McCulloch put her to bed. Sean was tucked up fast asleep in a drawer from the tallboy in the big bedroom upstairs. Gran had padded the drawer with blankets before she put Sean down and though he seemed snug enough, the drawer had looked too much like a coffin for Maeve's liking and she had begun to cry.

Granddad had followed them upstairs. He had taken drink with supper and was more sensible because of it. He had put an arm about her shoulder and had let her weep into his big protuberant belly.

She wasn't crying for Sean. She was crying for Mr Whiteside, for Fran and her mam, because the novelty of being in her grandmother's house in Towers had worn off and she wanted to be back in the Shamrock with Mam and her daddy, to be eight or nine again, not coming up for twelve. But when she caught herself wishing that none of it had ever happened, she felt as if she were betraying Turk and Charlie and Jansis, and that made her feel even worse. She had wept so sore that Gran had left the baby and scurried downstairs and had come back with milk in a glass, milk that tasted sweet and sharp because, Granddad had told her, it had a spoonful of brandy in it and wasn't she the lucky girl to be having brandy for a nightcap at her age.

'You, look out for the baby,' Gran had told Granddad. 'Don't sing to him.' Then she had detached Maeve from her grandfather's stomach and had led her to a bedroom at the back where the bed had been freshly made up, a stone pig put in to warm it and the sheet turned down in a vee, the way Mam did for guests when they weren't too busy.

The room was plain with a slope to the ceiling and a window with floral curtains, tied back. She had looked out on fields, clouds and a blink of sun on the horizon, all watery with rain. The bed was broad and soft. Gran had put the glass on a whatnot by the bedside and had gone away again. Maeve had sat on the bed, too sleepy to feel sorry for herself, but when she'd closed her eyes she'd seen the soldiers again, lots of soldiers in khaki uniforms dragging her mother away, and Fran, crouched like a hunchback, shouting and spitting at the peelers. She had seen the dead horse, its legs jutting into the air, and the winding road to Malahide and the weaselly man with the whip, and she was suddenly chasing the hack down the empty road while it clipped away into the distance with Sean inside, growing smaller and smaller and smaller.

'Wash your face and put this on,' Gran told her.

Water in a basin, a face-rag, soap, and a clean, patched shift that her grandmother laid across the bed; Maeve blinked and rubbed her eyes.

'Go on,' Gran said. 'You're not going to bed with a dirty face.'

'She hasn't come for us, an' it's nearly dark.'

'If she isn't here in the morning,' Gran said, 'I'll send his lordship up to town to find out what's going on.'

Maeve nodded, too weary to sustain fear for long. She took off her dress, washed her face at the basin and dried it on a towel. Veils of rain had obliterated the blink of sunlight and it was near night now, near dark. Gran struck a match and lit an oil lamp. The room became warm.

'Do they say you're like her?'

Maeve glanced up. 'Like who?'

'Sylvie – your mother.'

'Aye, some folk do.'

'You're not,' Gran said. 'You're more like he was at your age.'

'Daddy, you mean?'

The wrinkle down each side of Gran's mouth deepened.

'Aye, your daddy. Do you write to him at the front?'

'He never writes to me,' Maeve said.

'He's angry with you.'

'I know,' Maeve said. 'I didn't try to make him

373

angry, though.' She lifted the patched shift from the bed. 'Was this his room?'

'He slept down below with the boys,' Gran said. 'This was the girls' room. Winn and Blossom shared it first of all, then Rena and Roberta.'

'I've never met any of them, have I?'

'No,' Gran said.

Maeve took off her stockings and underthings and slipped on the long shift. It fell about her loosely, covering her feet. She put her hands across her chest and sat down on the edge of the bed.

'I had a sister once who was fiery, like you.'

'What happened to her?'

'She died young.'

'Before you married Granddad?'

'Just before.'

'In Glasgow?'

'Aye, in Glasgow.'

Maeve felt no connection to the family that lived across the sea in Scotland. Her mother refused to talk about them and Daddy had never said much about his time in Glasgow. If she hadn't been so sleepy she would have asked Gran to tell her about them. She climbed into bed, put her head on the soft pillow and looked up at her grandmother.

'Sleep tight, wee lassie,' Gran McCulloch said and, to Maeve's surprise, kissed her quite fondly on both cheeks.

★　　★　　★

By the time Sylvie reached Endicott Street there were no soldiers to be seen and the sounds of gunfire had faded. Though she was leg-weary her head was absolutely clear and she knew precisely where she was going and what she intended to do when she got there.

There was nothing to be gained from denying that Fran was dead and the Shamrock in ruins. It could only be a matter of time before the rebellion was crushed and life got back to normal. Her life had not been 'normal' since the day Fran Hagarty had stepped into it, of course, but she didn't grieve for him just yet; time enough for grieving after she had found Maeve and Sean.

Maeve was sufficiently level-headed to head for Towers. Home rule was all very well but when it came to the bit there was no tie like the tie of blood and even Kay McCulloch would hardly turn away her grandchild in a time of crisis.

Sylvie was tired and hungry. If she'd had any money at all she would have gone into one of the public houses and bought a penny pie or a pickled egg to keep her going. At this moment, though, she was as poor as any woman in the mansions and crumbling tenements.

It was still raining, though the sky had cleared a little to the west, but when she crossed the lane she found that Endicott Street was no longer dim and furtive and empty. Looters had been out in force across town and had trailed back to the tenements carrying shawls stuffed with stolen goods. Women

375

and children had gathered outside McKinstry's public house to display their trophies, and the men, the loungers, were pawing through the litter of rugs, shoes, golf clubs, boxed toys and rolls of linoleum that were scattered on the pavement.

Out of habit she glanced up at Fran's window as she approached.

She half expected to see his pinched face watching out for her from behind the unwashed glass. There was no Fran, of course, only blank glass and the gloom of his cheap, inelegant eyrie.

She entered the hallway at the foot of the iron stairs.

The boy was clothed in a pair of chequered plus-fours two sizes too large for him. The trousers were held up by a scarlet sash that covered his belly and chest and his new, startlingly white gentleman's dress shirt. A silk top hat perched on his head and he had traded the bent whistle for a euphonium, brand-new and shiny. He pumped at the keys, blew out his cheeks and huffed and rasped mightily to despatch echoes into all corners of the building.

Holding on to the banister, Sylvie started upstairs.

She had hardly taken a step before a skinny blonde girl with a child in her arms appeared in the doorway on the left of the hall.

'He's gone,' the girl called out. 'Mr Hagarty ain't here.'

'I know,' Sylvie said.

'He ain't comin' back.'

Sylvie leaned against the rail. The light was sour but she could see the girl clearly enough, her upturned face, the silent infant in her arms wrapped not in newspaper but in a new striped bath towel. From the doorway peeped four or five small faces, pale and round as oatmeal puddings. The boy took his lips from the mouthpiece and gaped up at Sylvie, saliva glistening on his chin.

'Who told you Fran isn't coming back?' Sylvie asked.

'I know he ain't,' the girl said. 'He never took you with him neither. He left you behind too.'

'Where do you suppose he went?'

''Merica,' the girl said. 'Fran's gone to 'Merica.'

'What makes you think that?'

'Told me.'

'What exactly did he say?'

'Gave me money for the babies.'

'Yes, but what did he say?'

'He allers gives me money when he goes to 'Merica.'

'How much money did he give you?' Sylvie asked.

'A lot.'

'Five shillings, ten shillings?'

'Lots o' pound notes.'

'Why does Fran give you money?'

''Cause he's kind.'

'Did he say he was going to America?'

377

'He allers goes to 'Merica when he gives me money.'

'But how do you know he isn't coming back?'

The girl shrugged. 'Just do.'

It was on the tip of Sylvie's tongue to ask more questions but she was not at all sure she could cope with the answers right now. She nodded and went on up the spiral iron staircase to Fran's room on the top floor.

The door was locked, of course. She should have known it would be locked. She leaned over the railing and looked down into the hallway. The boy was seated cross-legged on the stairs, hugging the euphonium. She opened her mouth to call out to him then saw that the girl, still clutching the child, was toiling up the stairs to join her.

The girl wasn't so young as all that. She was child-like and childish but well into her twenties. She wore a high-waisted skirt with a torn pocket, and a plain blouse. She pulled herself, one-handed, on to the narrow landing. The baby, somewhat older than his size suggested, gripped his mother's arm like a little monkey. He had a splash of jet-black hair and large dark brown eyes that roved curiously over everything that came within range. His silence, however, was unnatural and unnerving.

The girl tugged a key from her pocket and offered it to Sylvie.

'You'll be needin' this, I'm thinkin'.'

Sylvie took the key and cupped it in her palm.

'Who are you?' she said. 'Tell me your name.'

'Pauline.'

'Pauline what?'

'Pauline, sure an' I'm just Pauline.'

'You live downstairs, don't you?' Sylvie said.

'Aye, we all live downstairs, me an' the babies.'

'How long have you known Fran?'

'Years – years an' years.'

Again the question hung on Sylvie's lips. She wanted the girl to go away, to let her enter Fran's room alone. She hoped that seeing the bed, the little table, the typewriting machine, even the whiskey bottle, all intact would erase the image of Fran lying dead in the cobbled yard. She knew she couldn't alter reality but hoped she might be able to tamper with it, distort it just enough to get herself through this long and awful day. There was no being rid of the girl, though.

Sylvie unlocked the door and pushed it open.

The room smelled musty. The bed had been stripped to the mattress, sheets and blankets, even the quilted spread, stowed away. The typewriting machine had been covered with an oilcloth shroud and all Fran's papers were gone. She scraped open the drawers of the dressing-table and found them empty.

The girl had told the truth. Fran *had* intended to leave Dublin. She remembered the leather portmanteau and how he had refused to be parted from it, how it had stood close by the bed in the Shamrock while he and she made love.

Without turning, Sylvie said, 'Is he Fran's baby?'

'My baby.'

'Is Fran the father of your child?'

'All my babies.'

Sylvie swung round. 'All? How many?'

'He lookit after all my babies.'

'Were they all his?'

'All mine.'

'Stop it,' Sylvie said. 'You know what I'm asking? Are you Fran Hagarty's wife?'

'I am, I am.'

'Did he take you before a magistrate? I mean, do you have a certificate, a paper that says you're his legal wife?'

'Fran says we're as good as married.'

'Do you know he has another wife, a wife in England?'

Unabashed, the girl held the child in the crook of her arm with a casualness that Sylvie had never mastered. 'Aye, he told me all about her.'

'Did he tell you about his three sons?'

'I gave him a son.'

'You mean that boy downstairs?'

'Algie? Nah, not Algie.'

'Who is Algie then? Is Algie your brother?'

Puzzled by the question, the girl shrugged once more.

Sylvie didn't have the heart to tell her that Fran was dead. She wondered, though, what complications would arise from the manner of Fran's death, who would lay claim to his legacies and possessions. It occurred to her then that Vaizey did not intend Fran's body to be found and that the scribbler's estate might be tied up for years to come.

'How many babies do you have?' she asked.

'Nine,' the girl said.

'You can't possibly have given birth to nine children.'

'He brought them.'

'Who brought them?'

'Fran brought them.'

'Are they his children?'

'Mine, they're mine.'

'To look after?'

'Aye, to look after.'

'Where did he get them? Where did they come from?'

'The streets,' the girl told her. 'He bringed them in from the streets.'

'You mean they're orphans.'

'Lost,' the girl said. 'Lost till Fran found them.'

Sylvie swallowed. Had she misjudged Fran Hagarty? Had she seen only his selfishness and conceit, not the muddled humanity of the man? She seated herself on the end of the mattress and put her hands in her lap. She looked up at the girl who had begun to sway her slender body from side to side.

'Did – does Mr Hagarty pay the rent for you?'

'He don't have to,' the girl said.

'What do you mean?'

'It's his house.'

'Are you telling me Fran owns the building?'

'Aye, his house.'

'But the other rooms . . .'

'Let out.'

'Let out to whom?'

'Some men.'

'Do they pay rent?'

'Aye.'

Sylvie said, 'Who collects the rent?'

'I do.'

'What if they won't pay – or can't?'

'Fran sees to it.'

Sylvie let out her breath. She felt better now, much better. Fran hadn't gone at all. He was still here in Endicott Street and would be with her for years to come, for all eternity perhaps. No, she told herself, not for all eternity. Fran was dead, missing, gone to America. Something. What he'd left behind were the mysteries that remained in the aftermath of a life cut short, elements and issues left unsettled to which she, like the girl and the children and the Irish cause, were somehow all attached.

She put her hands flat on the mattress upon which Fran and she had first made love and pushed herself to her feet.

Pauline stopped swaying, drew the child up from his precarious position in the slack of her arm and hugged him tightly to her bosom.

'I'm going now,' Sylvie said. 'I'll be back soon.'

'Back here?'

'Yes,' Sylvie said. 'In the meantime, Pauline, I'd be terribly obliged if you'd lend me half a crown.'

'What for?'

'A pork pie, a glass of stout, and a ticket to Malahide.'

Sylvie didn't begin to panic until she reached the seaside town and set off down the country road into the darkness. Up to that point she had put so much faith in her daughter that it hadn't occurred to her that Maeve might not be at Towers at all, but once doubt entered her mind it spread like wildfire and with her boots flapping painfully about her chafed calves, she broke into a run.

The rain had ceased and the night was mild and almost windless but the country road was darker than anything she was used to and she fell and tore her hands and elbows, and rose up and ran on again, sobbing in fear and desperation and calling out Maeve's name long before the square, whitewashed shape of the brewery came into view and the lights of the McCullochs' cottage.

She reached the cottage at last and bleeding, dishevelled and wild with grief she threw herself against the front door. Daniel opened it warily.

'Are they here? Are they here?'

'Aye, lass,' he told her. 'They're here, all safe and sound.'

And Sylvie, swamped by relief, blacked out.

In the early hours of the morning she dragged herself from Maeve's side and went downstairs to feed Sean by the kitchen stove. She couldn't get warm, couldn't stop shivering. It was not until she'd bared her breast and felt her son's lips close upon her nipple that she came back into herself, and the shivering ceased. She was still filled with a strange accusatory aggression, as if everything that had taken place had been Daniel McCulloch's fault, as if he were to blame for her falling in love with Fran and driving Gowry away, for Fran's murder and the destruction of the Shamrock.

Her mind was a great ungainly jumble of guilt and anger and the sleep that had come upon her after her swoon had been more feverish than restful. When she'd heard Sean whimpering in the room next door she had wakened and had gone to him at once. The old woman had been sitting up in bed, the nightgown falling from her shoulders, a nightcap tied over her grey hair, her eyes bleary in the light of the lamp that she had lit only a moment previously. Daniel had lain lumped beside her and had stirred and rolled over but hadn't wakened, as if the infant's cry had been but a memory.

Sylvie had lifted Sean from the drawer and had carried him downstairs to the patch of light that fell from the grate in the stove. Seating herself on one of the kitchen chairs, she had exposed her breast

SHAMROCK GREEN

and had let him suckle. A moment later she heard the creak of the stairs and lamplight brightened the kitchen.

'You should have slept,' Gran McCulloch said. 'I'd have given him his bottle.'

'He's my son. I'll feed him.'

Gran put the lamp on the table and stationed herself behind Sylvie. For fully a minute there was no sound in the kitchen save the baby's little grunts.

'Is it true what you told Daniel?' Gran said. 'Is Hagarty dead?'

'Yes.'

'Are you sure?'

'I saw him shot in cold blood. I witnessed it with my own eyes.'

'What of my boys, Charlie and Peter? Have you any word on them?'

She had no cause to resent the woman's question. Perhaps what she really resented was the fact that Gran McCulloch hadn't lived up to the low opinion she, Sylvie, had of her. The conspiratorial bond between Forbes and Kay McCulloch had always troubled her. She thought back to the sight of the Shamrock blown to pieces, thought too of the soldiers crowding into the yard and what slaughter would be wreaked in Watton's warehouse if there was any resistance. In her concern for herself she had all but forgotten that Charlie and Peter were fighting for their lives. She glanced round at the woman's drawn features and realised how selfish she'd been, that Kay McCulloch

385

must be just as worried about her sons as she had been about Maeve and Sean.

'I'm sorry,' she said.

'Is it bad with them?' Gran McCulloch said.

'Yes, it's bad,' Sylvie said and proceeded to tell the woman what she had witnessed in Sperryhead Road. 'They won't surrender.'

'No, I don't think they will,' said Sylvie.

Gran McCulloch put her hand to her cheek and sighed. 'Then they'll all be gone, all my fine boys.'

It was out before she could prevent it: 'Except Forbes.' There was nothing sharp in the tilt of the old woman's chin. The motion was too small to be significant, yet Sylvie bridled at it. 'Is it because of Forbes you don't like me?'

'I don't want you going back to Glasgow, throwing yourself on his mercy and starting it all up again.'

'I wouldn't go back to Glasgow for all the tea in China,' Sylvie said. 'I shouldn't have taken up with Fran Hagarty, I admit, but I'm not the only one to blame for Gowry joining the army. You must bear some responsibility for that. How is your dear son Forbes, by the way? I take it *he's* not in uniform.'

'He has ships to build.'

'Navy contracts?'

'Yes.'

'How profitable that must be,' said Sylvie.

'This is hardly the time to be talking about Forbes.'

'You're right,' Sylvie said, without sympathy now, 'not when you've three other sons fighting for their lives.'

'On opposite sides,' said Kay McCulloch. 'I think that's what galls me most of all. You Irish, you and your causes.'

'I'm not Irish.'

'No, but your son is, and your daughter.'

'Well, we both made the same mistake, didn't we?' Sylvie said. 'We were both daft enough to marry Irishmen.'

'Was Gowry not good enough for you?'

'Oh, Gowry was – Gowry is a good man, a very good man.'

'Then why did you betray him?'

'He didn't love me,' Sylvie said.

'Did Forbes love you?'

'Forbes would have married me if you hadn't pushed him into marrying his rich cousin instead.'

'Forbes never had any intention of marrying you. I knew what you were from the first: a conniving wee trollop who thought she could get herself out of the gutter by marrying my son.'

'But I did,' said Sylvie. 'I did marry your son. I married Gowry.'

Brain-weary, soggy with grief, anger and anxiety, she had hoped that she might hold out the olive branch and that Kay McCulloch might snatch at it. But it was not to be. Just as she blamed Daniel and the brotherhood for all the bad things that had happened so her mother-in-law blamed her for the tragedies that shadowed her life.

Sylvie drew Sean from her breast to let him rest.

She looked down into the grate and seemed to see there the flames that had poured out of the Shamrock, the great soft, devouring flames from the gas pipe that would consume all that was left of her lovely Dublin house. It hadn't crossed her mind that Forbes might still think fondly of their days together, that she still might have a pull on him.

Glasgow, Forbes, her father, home and redemption; she wondered.

Kay McCulloch said, 'What are you going to do, Sylvie?'

'Take care of my children until Gowry comes back.'

'If, as you say, your house is in ruins, where will you stay?'

'Is that an invitation?'

'No,' the woman said, not forcefully. 'You can stay here until matters in Dublin are settled but after that . . .'

'Have no fear, Kay, you won't have to put up with us for long.'

'Do you have insurance for the Shamrock?'

'Of course not. Even if I had, do you think the insurance company would pay me what the building's worth? I doubt it. Some folk might try to wring compensation from the government but it'll cost more in lawyer's fees than I can afford. No, I'll find work and a place to stay and try to keep body and soul together until my husband returns.'

'And finds you nursing another man's child?'

'Gowry's a good man. He'll forgive me.'

The woman seemed about to speak again, then changed her mind.

She went into the pantry and came out with a batch of freshly laundered towels. She placed them on the end of the stove and, kneeling, rattled up the coals in the grate and shifted the kettle on to the aperture to make it boil faster.

'He'll need changed,' she said. 'Will I do it?'

'I'll do it myself. Thank you all the same,' said Sylvie.

The woman leaned against the iron and folded her arms. 'You're very sure of yourself, Sylvie. Did Hagarty give you money?'

'He did not. Fran never had any money.'

'That's not what Daniel says.'

'Daniel can say what he likes.'

'What if Gowry doesn't come back?' Gran McCulloch asked.

'He will,' said Sylvie. 'I know he will.'

'What makes you so sure?'

'He has nowhere else to go,' Sylvie said.

PART FOUR

Gowry

Chapter Eighteen

Once affairs at Hulluch had been settled the Rifles' 2nd Battalion was pulled out of the line and promised leave. Naturally, there was no question of being allowed to return to Ireland and the lads were under no illusions that they would soon be part of the big push that everyone knew was coming. Even so a certain party spirit reigned over the training grounds and the drills they were required to undertake to earn their five-day passes did not seem too arduous.

Gowry had received his new pay book, duly signed and stamped, and had no inkling that he'd been reported missing. It would have astonished him to learn that his family was grieving for him and that his friend, Maggie Leonard, had mourned his passing along with that of her lovely son, Maurice, and, defeated at last, had sold her ponies, abandoned the cottage in the emerald hills and had gone to stay with her daughters in Boston.

He had written to Maggie, a most difficult letter. He had informed her that he had been with Maurice at the end, that Maurice had died bravely and that she should be proud of him.

In fact, he had no idea how Maurice had died. He assumed that the sergeant had simply been mown down by that damned machine-gun, like so many of the Connaughts. He could reveal nothing about the raid to Maggie, however, and fell back on platitudes and clichés, pathetic in their inadequacy to convey sympathy. He wrote her again from the temporary billet at Mallefort before the battalion moved on. But if she replied to his letters her answers failed to reach him and it was almost as if the woman had died with her son in the darkness west of Heuvert.

In the late May month, under a warm sun, sweating at the tasks that mean-mouthed sergeants allotted him, Gowry spared little thought for Maggie Leonard or the rest of the folks back home. His mother's letter had angered him, but once he'd calmed down he found some satisfaction in imagining Sylvie big with child and in the punishment nature had inflicted on that insidious seducer, Fran Hagarty, who would be stuck now with all the responsibilities of fatherhood. The news that Sylvie was pregnant also freed him from the constraints of conscience and gave him hope that his relationship with Becky might blossom into something more enduring than a paper romance. With that thought in mind he booked two rooms in a hotel near the great cathedral in Amiens that one of the quartermaster sergeants had told him about, and wrote to Becky inviting her to join him there for a few days' leave.

He waited anxiously for Becky's reply and lay huddled in his scratchy blankets counting all the impediments that circumstances could throw at him and all the military folderol and fatuous objections that might prevent Becky taking leave from Saint-Emile.

Amiens was a refuge for high brass, war correspondents and enlisted men alike. The city had not been beaten into the ground and offered many of the comforts of home to weary soldiers. There he would have a bath, a shampoo and a haircut and get his uniform properly cleaned. Then he would eat good home-cooked food, drink a few beers and stroll with Becky through the cathedral or go out to look at the market gardens and the boats on the canals and perhaps the poppy fields that flanked the road to Albert. The war would not be far away, however. Gowry guessed that they would be able to hear the rumble of the guns and that the night sky would glow brighter than moonlight; but he didn't care. He would be with his nurse, he would kiss her, hug her, feel her breasts pressing against his chest and if the gods were on his side, and Becky willing, would make love to her in a bed with clean sheets.

Becky's letter arrived just two days before leave passes were due to be distributed. She would, she said, be delighted to join him in Amiens on 22nd May and had successfully completed all arrangements at her end.

She was, she said, greatly looking forward to renewing their acquaintance and was sure they would find many interesting things to do in the cathedral town.

Gowry read the letter five or six times before he folded it into his pay book, then, grinning, went off to his tent to count the money he had saved from his meagre pay and plan how he would blow it all on impressing Becky in Amiens in three days' time.

'Are you sure you know what you're doing?' Angela said. 'After all you've only met the chappie under sterile conditions, one might say, and for all you know he could turn out to be a cad.'

'A cad?' said Becky. 'In what way?'

'Well – demanding.'

'Gowry isn't demanding.'

'How do you know?' said Angela. 'He could be one of those dreadful rebels we've all been reading about.'

'If he were a rebel he'd hardly be fighting on our side, would he?'

'Bobby says—'

'I've no interest in Bobby Bracknell's twisted opinions,' said Becky. 'Sometimes I think Captain Bracknell would like to see us all shot. Scots, Irish, English – all those of us who lie below the salt.'

'Rubbish!' said Angela. 'In any case, we're not discussing Bobby. I do hope you won't let this Gowry chap land you in trouble.'

'If you mean what I think you mean . . .'

'However meek and mild your Irishman may seem to be, he isn't going to treat you to five days in Amiens without expecting something in return.'

'We're just going to get to know each other a little better.'

'Now where have I heard *that* song before?'

'Certainly not from me,' said Becky.

'Would you like me to give you some advice?'

'What sort of advice?'

'Concerning what to do while you're getting to know each other.'

How typical of Angela to assume that she had only one thing on her mind. The truth was that she *did* have only one thing on her mind. And Angela did have a point; Gowry's letters revealed little of his character. She wondered if he would turn out to be shallow and duplicitous, if the blandness of his letters had been designed to deceive.

Angela shrugged her plump shoulders. 'Oh, what does it matter? He's a married man; I expect he'll know what to do. However, at least take this.'

'What?'

Angela held out a diaphanous garment that Becky had never seen before.

'What is it?'

'A nightdress.'

'I have a nightdress, thank you.'

'But not one like this?'

'I should hope not,' said Becky.

Becky could see the flesh of Angela's arm quite

clearly through the transparent material. Embarrassed, she looked away.

'Take it,' said Angela.

'I couldn't possibly . . .'

'It's perfectly clean.'

'It isn't that. I'd just feel such a fraud wearing it, especially if . . .'

'Really, my dear, you *must* learn to finish your sentences. Even the Irish know how to finish their sentences.' Angela shook out the nightdress once more and raised an enquiring eyebrow. 'Now, do you want it, or don't you? It takes up very little space in one's luggage.'

'It – it isn't my size.'

'Let it drape loosely about you,' said Angela. 'I always do.'

The evening was warm and from the window Becky could see the tennis court and two officers in shirt-sleeves thrashing a ball about.

She had been slightly put out when Mr Sanderson had signed her request for leave and the CO had endorsed it, for a little part of her resisted meeting Gowry in Amiens and she had hoped that the decision would be taken out of her hands. She had been dreaming again, not dreams of death, of Robbie naked on a table, but dreams involving Gowry. She wakened from these dreams in a sweet, moist sweat, smiling and relaxed and filled with astonishment that this thing could be happening to her in the midst of so much bloodshed.

'All right.' Reaching out, she took the nightgown and folded it carefully, ready for packing. 'Thank you, Angela. I'll make sure it comes to no harm.'

'Harm?' said Angela. 'Dear God, Becky, it's only a nightgown.'

'You know what I mean.'

'Yes,' said Angela, gently. 'Of course I know what you mean.'

Paris was eighty miles away, Boulogne seventy. Trains on the Nord railway carried troops and ordnance towards the front, though where the front would finally be established not even the know-all corporal in the crowded compartment would hazard a guess. The corporal was a notorious pain in the arse and Gowry was relieved to stumble out of the carriage and watch the corporal vanish, still yapping, into the crowd.

Paris, though: he could picture himself in Paris with Becky. Could picture himself in Boulogne too, looking out over the sands at the Channel, with London just three hours away. That, Gowry thought, was something for another day. Right now he was in Amiens, a stone's throw from the Somme with the faint grumble of guns in the distance and, much closer, a French military band playing a sprightly tune.

French soldiers were everywhere. They mingled with the British in well-cemented friendship; what did they call it — an *entente cordiale*? He lingered on the steps of the railway station for a moment, watched the band pass the mouth of the street and inhaled the rich, pervasive aroma of coffee and the muffled odours of the fustian factories, and thought how pleasant it was to be in a place that hadn't been pulverised by shelling.

Twenty-one months ago the Iron Guard had goose-stepped through these same streets, singing songs of victory. They had forced the ancient capital to surrender and had torn down the tricolour from the town hall before marching on to take Paris. But the Jerries hadn't taken Paris and would never take Paris and the Iron Guard weren't singing songs of victory any more. How did he know such things? How did any soldier know anything? By rumour and gossip, tales told over cooking stoves and in the dark watches of the night. As he loitered on the step under the station arch, Gowry wished that he could have been here when Froggie fought back, when the Jocks and the Lancers joined the fray and Paris was saved and this town, Amiens, relieved.

Slapping him on the back and yelling, 'Buck up, McCulloch. Don't keep the lady waiting,' Burke brought Gowry to earth again.

Shaking his head and laughing as Burke and Paddy Morgan brushed past, Gowry stepped down on to the cobbles and set off to find the Cathedral Hotel where, with luck, Becky was waiting to welcome him.

*   *   *

At that hour in the afternoon the foyer was deserted. It smelled of aniseed and wax polish, was shabby but clean. Above the staircase a huge electrical fan softly paddled the stale air.

Becky was seated on the staircase, anxiously watching the door and looking, Gowry thought, like a little Dublin flower-seller. He felt a pang of remorse at all the lustful thoughts he had harboured towards her and was glad that they were alone. Becky rose timidly. She wore a navy sports coat with a shawl collar and a round, stiff-brimmed hat. She had applied some face powder and a touch of rouge that made her cheeks glow brightly. Her eyes glistened and he wondered if she'd been crying and if so what she had been crying about. Then, putting the question behind him, Gowry slipped off his pack and took her in his arms and let her lean on him, as if weeks of parting had wearied her and she needed rest. He held her without pressure and only when she leaned back to look up at him did he kiss her.

She thrust her face up, eyes closed, and drew him to her so tightly that for a moment he could hardly breathe.

He smelled of sweat and tobacco smoke, of packed railway carriages, trench latrines and the dust of the training grounds, the stink of war that no amount of yellow soap and lukewarm water could remove. He had shaved carefully, though, and his cheek was fairly smooth, and Becky didn't seem to mind what he smelled like, and she was so flowery and fresh that Gowry, the bold, brave soldier, suddenly found himself crying.

'Oh, Gowry, dearest darling,' Becky whispered, 'what's wrong?'

With the same embroidered little handkerchief with which she had wiped his eyes on the lawn at Saint-Emile, she dried his tears once more.

The wife of the hotelier appeared behind the upright desk.

She was a large woman in her fifties, sallow-skinned and hollow-eyed.

'*Monsieur, êtes-vous malade?*'

Becky answered, '*Non, madame. Il a simplement le mal de guerre.*'

'*Le pauvre. Tu sauras le guérir, alors?*'

'*Oui, Madame Gaubert. Je ferai de mon mieux.*'

'What did she say?' Gowry asked.

'She asked if we were lovers.'

'What did you tell her?'

'I told her we were,' said Becky and, lifting Gowry's pack, led him to the room upstairs.

'Are you feeling better now?' Becky asked

'I am,' Gowry answered. 'Sorry I made such an exhibition of myself. I don't know what came over me.'

'I didn't think I was *that* ugly,' said Becky.

'It wasn't you who reduced me to tears.' Gowry rested his cheek on his hand, an elbow propped on the chequered tablecloth. 'Well, perhaps it was. You looked so – I don't know – so lovely, I just couldn't help myself.'

'That's an awfully nice thing to say to a girl,' Becky told him. 'Are you buttering me up by any chance?'

'Why would I want to butter you up?' said Gowry.

'Because I'm here with you. Because we're here together.'

'I meant it,' Gowry said. 'I'd never lie to you.'

Becky adjusted the dessert fork and spoon for the umpteenth time since they had seated themselves at the corner table in Madame Theo's, a back-street restaurant off the Boulevard Baraban.

There were too many red-hatted staff officers present for Gowry's liking but several of his cronies from the Rifles were unconcernedly scoffing oysters at a table by the window, for Madame Theo's was an open house and anyone was welcome here, provided they could pay the bill. Brusque, statuesque Madame Theo and three young serving girls apart, Becky was the only woman there and Gowry was well aware that half the men in the room were giving her the eye.

They had eaten lentil soup, stew and sweet potatoes and had mopped up the gravy with pinches of bread from a long soft oatmeal loaf. Gowry had drunk two glasses of beer and Becky a glass of wine and now they were waiting for a cream cheese pudding and a jug of real coffee to finish off with. He felt much better now, better than he'd done a couple of hours ago when he had lain chastely with Rebecca on the quilt of the bed in the room in the Cathedral Hotel and Becky had soothed his distress with funny little Scottish endearments.

'You needed something in your stomach, that's all,' Becky said.

'Is that a medical judgement?'

She laughed, though she was still rather tense.

She had been anything but tense on the bed in the room, though there had been no hanky-panky. He wondered what her friend had told her, the buxom blonde nurse. He blew out cigarette smoke and watched Becky manoeuvre the fork into a new position on the chequered cloth.

'I just didn't expect you to – to react the way you did.'

'Believe me,' Gowry said, 'I didn't expect it either.'

'I thought when we were upstairs together you'd . . .'

'What?'

'I thought you'd want to . . .'

Becky's sidelong glance reminded him of a love long since lost. He had been young then and bubbling with sexual need and had stolen Sylvie from his brother to prove himself the better man. He couldn't explain why the Scots nurse had captured his heart or why, in a smoke-filled restaurant in a French town only twenty miles from the front, he was suddenly reminded of Sylvie.

'I do,' he said. 'I do want to, but I don't want you to run away with the idea that's all there is to it.'

'To what?'

'Us, to our meeting again.'

'I'm not a wee girl, Gowry. And there aren't any rules, are there?'

'Damned few,' Gowry admitted. He paused, then said, 'What'll you do when the war's over? Go home to Scotland, or stay in nursing?'

'I've no idea,' Becky said. 'What about you? Back to Dublin?'

'There isn't much for me in Dublin any more.'

'Your daughter, your wife?'

'My wife's taken up with another man.'

She covered his hand with hers. 'Oh, Gowry, I'm sorry. I had no idea.'

'She's had a child by him.'

Again, 'Oh, Gowry.'

'It started before I enlisted.'

'Did she tell you,' Becky said, 'about the child?'

'My mother wrote me. It's the only letter I've had from anyone back home. Even my daughter cut me off when I joined the army. I reckon my dear old darlin' mother wrote me more out of spite than pity. Sorry if I sound bitter, Becky, but I thought I should tell you before we become too fond of each other.'

'I didn't mean to pry.'

'You're not prying. You're entitled to know how it is with me.'

'Am I?'

She had her hand in his now, fingers entwined.

'I've no wish to deceive you into thinking I'm

better than I am. I've only myself to blame for what happened to my marriage,' Gowry said.

'*You* didn't have a lover, though, did you?'

'No, I did not.'

'You drove an omnibus,' Becky said.

Gowry tried to laugh, to make light of his confusion.

He said, 'Aye, that's vice enough for any man.'

'Were you involved in the troubles?'

'My father and brothers were. I don't even know what's happened to them and, callous as it may sound, I don't much care. I'd like to know about my daughter, but I'm blowed if I'll go beggin' for news.'

'Is there no one back home you can write to?'

'Not in Dublin, no.'

'Not even your mother?'

'Especially not my mother.'

'How sad.'

'Well, I made my own bed and I'll have to lie on it,' Gowry said. 'But it's different now; some things have changed.'

'Have they?' She squeezed his hand. 'Yes, they have.'

'You know I'm not a Catholic, don't you?'

'Yes.'

'But you are.'

'Nominally,' Becky said.

'Nominally? What does that mean?' Gowry asked. 'When you're confirmed in the Roman faith don't you sign on for life?'

'I suppose you could say I've lapsed.'

'Does that make a difference?'

'To what?'

'If – I mean, after the war – if we . . .'

'If we both live through it,' Becky said, 'we'll worry about it then.'

'Do you know what I'm talking about?' said Gowry with a trace of annoyance. 'I'm serious about this, Becky.'

'I know you are,' Becky said.

'I – I'd like to know where we stand.'

'After the war,' she said, 'after the war we'll make plans.'

He nodded. 'So we don't tempt fate?'

'No,' Becky said, 'it would never do to tempt fate.'

One of the serving girls brought a great blue bowl to the table and placed it between them. Gowry looked down at the light brown crust on the dish in the bowl and then, raising his eyebrows, said, 'What on earth is that?'

'Picardy pudding,' Becky answered and, smiling, handed him her spoon.

There was thunder in the air, though you could hardly distinguish it from the grumble of the guns along the winding course of the Somme. You could smell the heat, and the thunder, presaging rain, seemed frail and distant over the poppy fields. Becky could see nothing of the poppy fields from the window of the hotel. She looked down on a cobbled side street with soldiers spilling out of bars and cafés: Frenchmen, Irishmen, English, even the odd Jock reeling and prancing and holding up his kilt like a washerwoman. Music added another dimension: an accordion, a Victrola playing dance tunes, soldiers chanting about Piccadilly and Leicester Square and, like a descant, the whistle of a locomotive hauling ordnance to the front. She shivered when Gowry touched her. He caressed her so lightly that the material of the borrowed nightdress tickled her spine.

Gowry drew back. 'I'm sorry,' he said. 'I thought you were . . .'

She reached behind her, took his hand and put it to her waist.

'It's all right,' she said. 'It's just this dashed nightdress.'

'It's beautiful.'

'It's Angela's — and it tickles.'

'Take it off then,' Gowry said.

He was wearing a nightshirt. She was glad it wasn't pyjamas; she had seen too many sick men in pyjamas. Her cousin Robbie had worn a nightshirt, a pretty little garment of pure Irish lawn that she had washed and ironed a dozen times without it becoming worn. She remembered how he'd looked in the nightshirt when he was only half grown, how he would come out into the kitchen yard behind her aunt's house of a morning, bare-legged and barefoot and throw himself against her as if she were his rock, his mainstay.

What age had she been then? Twelve or thirteen.

Gowry was rough by comparison. His palms were flinty from digging trenches and snagged on the night-dress when he closed them about her hips. Big, rough soldier's hands, clumsy and broken-nailed; he spread his fingers over the bones of her hips and put his thumbs on the knob of bone at the back of her pelvis. She shuffled her feet, spread her legs, and leaned back. The strap of Angela's nightgown slid from her shoulder. Gowry's lips were on the crown of her shoulder and his belly pressing against her back, the cotton nightshirt stretched. She was moved by his tenderness and not at all afraid when he stroked her and made her wet.

He kissed her shoulder and neck.

She turned her head and kissed him on the lips. He pressed into her, his hand on her belly, and she was filled with sensations that bore no relation to what she had heard about the act of love-making, sensations so deep and insistent that she felt something going off within her like the soft, white light of a flare.

She turned in his arms and let him rub himself against her.

Another rush, another explosion, and she was gasping, gasping as if the air in the room had been robbed of oxygen. She felt dizzy, dizzy but not dopey. Everything was so vivid, so unexpectedly clear that she seemed to be standing apart from herself. He danced with her, shuffling, her legs wide apart, his hips snug between her thighs, danced with her, shuffling, until her calves struck the edge of the bed and she tumbled back on to the quilt.

'Wait,' Gowry said. 'Wait, please.'

He looked massive above her, the nightshirt billowing about him as he pulled it over his head. It hooked on his nose and ears and she saw him headless for an instant. His torso was lean and energetic, unlike those of the men she'd nursed at Saint-Emile or the corpses she'd washed or the diagrams she'd learned from long ago. If he had been impatient she would have cowered before him, but Gowry – her good friend Gowry – held the nightshirt down by his side and gave her time to look at him, not arrogantly but cautiously.

She reached between her knees, took a fistful of Angela's nightdress and pulled it up to her waist. She was possessed by a desperate need to show herself to him. He settled over her, hands on either side of her head. He braced himself and lowered his hips and she felt the touch of his flesh upon her, just that part of him touching her. He lowered his mouth to her mouth and she let his tongue enter her mouth, and the thing beneath, the thing between them entered her too. Again she experienced the explosive shock and the trembling that came after it. She was wet now, wetter than she had ever dreamed possible and when he entered her properly it was smooth not hesitant and it was she, not he, who tilted up her hips and brought him down and into her.

One solitary flash of pain, one stab of pain, then she was filled with him, filled with love, love and no fear, pleasure and no fear.

And he asked, 'Yes?'

And she answered, 'Yes, Gowry. Yes, my love. Yes.'

Chapter Nineteen

Mass on Sunday was well attended by French and Irish soldiers. Gowry needed no persuasion to accompany Rebecca to a mid-morning service. They had already ventured inside the cathedral and marvelled at its space and Gothic splendour, and at the astonishing number of sandbags that had been stacked against the walls. In fact, it struck Gowry that the cathedral of Our Lady in Amiens must be the best-built bunker in the whole of France.

The mass was conducted in Latin. Becky did not understand it any more than did Gowry but she followed the form with a piety that Gowry envied. He wished he could pray so devoutly, preferably in Latin, for the souls of the glorious dead, for Maurice, Donnaghy and Tom Ring, even for poor old Lieutenant Quinn; pray too for his own salvation and negotiate with Rebecca's version of God to bring them both safely out of the valley of the shadow. But

Jessica Stirling

somehow he felt that the uncompromising potency
of Catholicism might be mocked by prayers from a
milk-and-water Protestant and, for the sake of what
was left of his soul, he'd better not indulge in such
hypocrisy.

The priests were very old and seemed bowed by
the weight of their vestments. In contrast, the altar
boys were very young, too young, Gowry reckoned,
for the tasks they were expected to perform. When
he leaned out into the aisle he saw that several of the
boys were barefoot under their angel gowns, their
heels browned by seepage from the sandbags.

Gowry did not offer himself for the sacrament
but he was impressed and a little bit amused by the
speed with which the priests dispensed the wafers
and the wine; God's army, it seemed, was more
efficient than most regiments. His amusement faded,
however, when Becky returned to her seat and knelt
to pray. When she rose from her knees she gave him
a smile, a little, wistful, glistening smile that almost
broke his heart.

He was still thinking of that smile when the mass
ended and they moved with the crowd towards
the door.

By the doors were iron racks of candles, dumpy
little stumps that burned with yellow light. Beside the
racks were a long trough filled with candles and a big
worn wooden box to hold the coins. Smoke seeped
up into the arch and many women and some men,
soldiers, knelt on the stone. High above the racks

was an effigy of Christ flecked with paint and grey with age. The Mother, Mary, flanked Him. She was serene and beautiful, unwithered by the prayers that floated around her.

Gowry watched Becky select a candle, light it from a taper, kiss the air over the flame and stick it down quite forcefully into the dripping wax. She bent her knee and crossed herself; lapsed or not, Becky Tarrant hadn't abandoned her beliefs entirely. She returned to him, took his arm and they went out together into the warm, moist air of the morning, into streets wet with overnight rain.

The band was playing once more, drums beating out march time while behind the musicians in column of route came the gallant French Lancers and behind them a column of infantry, whiskered and moustached, each man with a shako and a rifle and a pack. They were heading across the canal to the Bois Bonvallet where, Gowry guessed, transportation awaited to carry them to relieve the forces that were defending Paris.

Hastily, he drew Becky into a side street.

'Who did you light the candle for?' he asked.

'My cousin.'

'Where did he die?'

'Not too far from here, I think.'

'Nowhere is far from anywhere in this country,' Gowry said. 'Who was he with, what regiment?'

'The Gordons.'

'An officer?'

'Subaltern.'

'Be Loos, I expect,' said Gowry. 'It was bad for the Jocks at Loos.'

'Yes,' Becky said. 'Loos – or somewhere like it.'

She walked stiffly, hobbling a little. He wondered if he had hurt her that early morning when playfulness had given way to sudden fierce passion. There had been no tenderness in either of them and she had twisted under him with wild urgency. Her willingness to yield had surprised him but her voracity surprised him even more. He ached a little in his parts and felt so relaxed that it was almost like fatigue. He wondered if Becky felt the same way but, being a gentleman, didn't dare ask in case she thought he was bragging.

He stopped to let her rest, an arm on her shoulder.

She was smaller than he was, not much taller than Sylvie. Her hat brim was level with his chin and when he tapped it with his forefinger, she obediently lifted her head and let him kiss her.

She smiled and they strolled on again, going nowhere.

'Do you want to go home?' Gowry said.

'Back to the hotel?'

'No,' he said. 'I meant home to Scotland, to your island?'

'I'd like to see my mother and my aunt,' Becky said. 'But I wouldn't ever go back to Mull to live. There's nothing there for me now.'

'Is it not peaceful?'

'The life is hard,' she said, frowning, 'not peaceful.

Besides, most of my relatives are in Glasgow and – my sister – in Portsmouth. I couldn't find a nursing post on Mull. It's too remote.'

'Is that what you want to do – nurse?'

'I don't know what I want to do,' said Becky.

'I know what I want to do,' said Gowry.

She sensed what was coming and glanced up at him. They were in a narrow street, old buildings on either side of them, picturesque old houses set above shops, pretty but somehow depressing. The shops were shuttered and some were sandbagged and the windows of the houses impenetrable.

Becky said, 'Oh, and what *do* you want to do, Mr Irishman?'

'Marry you.'

'Can't,' she said.

'Because I have a wife?'

'Yes.'

'If I divorced Sylvie . . .'

'Are you sure you want to?'

'I certainly have good reason,' said Gowry.

'But do you want to? Are you *sure* you want to?'

He hesitated, then said, 'I'm as sure as I'll ever be.'

'The Church – my Church – won't let me marry someone who's divorced.'

'I see.'

'Especially a Protestant.'

'I see,' said Gowry again.

'If you asked me to live with you, though . . .'

'What?' he said. 'In sin?'

'Sin! My God, after what we've been through how do you define what's sinful and what's not?' Becky said. 'Isn't hell what we've been through, dearest? Isn't it hell we're suffering now? I love you. I'll love you until my dying day. I'll live with you, darling, because I don't think I can live without you. There! I've said it. I expect I've scared you away for ever.'

'Don't be so bloody daft,' Gowry said, pleased.

'How long will it last?'

'The war?'

'Us,' she said. 'Us, how long will we last, Gowry?'

'There's nothing to take me back to Dublin,' Gowry said.

'Your daughter?'

'Yes, well, perhaps my daughter.'

'You see?' Becky said.

'If the war lasts another year — and I'm damned sure it will — then Maeve'll be grown up, or nearly so, and she'll have made her life without me.'

'With another man for a father?'

'She likes him well enough.' Gowry grunted. 'She admires him. He stands for things Maeve believes in. I don't know where I am, Becky, to tell you the truth.'

'You're in Amiens,' Becky said, 'with me.'

'Aye, sure and that's good enough.'

'Gowry, take me back now, please.'

'Back?' he said. 'Where?'

'Home,' Becky said.

'Home?'

'To the hotel,' she said. 'Home to our hotel.'

'What, now?'

'Yes,' said Becky. 'Now.'

At that hour of the morning, lying passive and half dressed on the bed in the Cathedral Hotel, his pack ready and the franc notes for the bill laid out on the dressing-table, Gowry was afraid that he would break down and weep again and that Becky would return to Saint-Emile thinking him unmanly. Anything he said now was bound to sound like twaddle, for there were no words that hadn't been used before, that hadn't been worn thin by a hundred thousand partings and a hundred thousand promises. He kept her at a distance, a safe little distance, and when she tried to kiss him refused to open his mouth.

There had been enough love-making and in their last minutes together he had no desire for more, only for love itself.

'How long do we have?' Becky whispered.

'Five minutes.'

He would leave first. He would go, as soldiers tend to do, just as the sun came up over the spires of the cathedral. She wouldn't accompany him to the railway station. They had agreed on that. He didn't want to show her off to Paddy Morgan or to Burke or to any of the other Rifles who might be on the platform, to have her with him at the assembly where he was obliged to slide out of one skin into another.

He would leave her here where they had been happy together. He would write to her, of course, just as soon as he found space to open the tattered pad. He would write and tell her what she had come to mean to him and how, once the war was over, they would never be parted again. He would tell her that home wasn't Dublin, home wasn't Ireland or Scotland, but that home would be any place where they could be together and that their next meeting would be their beginning and that there would be no more partings, no more goodbyes.

She took his wrist and held it up to the light. He had his pocket watch in his hand, cupped to hide it from her. She prised his fingers open and looked at the face of the watch, at the black second hand whisking round the dial.

'Won't you let me come to the railway station?'

'No,' he said.

She was lying against him, holding him tightly. She had washed the nightdress, Angela's nightdress, and had hung it on a chair to dry. It would be dry now, all clean and dry. He knew that he would have to live with this moment, and prayed that he would come through it just to be with her again, not to have her hurt, not to leave her mourning and marred by grief. There was no romance in a soldier's parting, no romance in dying too early, only a terrible, spurious finality that was better to contemplate than to endure.

'I won't make a scene,' she said. 'I promise I won't make a scene.'

'No,' Gowry said, 'but I might.'

He felt her laugh, or try to laugh, the little thump of her breast against his back. He rolled over, holding the watch high above them. There was light in the window now, too much light.

He said, 'Sweetheart, I will have to go.'

'I know,' she said.

'Will you be all right?'

'I'll be fine.'

'I mean, your train and everythin'.'

'Yes.'

'Are you on duty tonight?'

'Yes.'

'Try to get some sleep on the train.'

'It's only an hour. It's hardly worth closing my eyes.'

'Forty winks will do you good.'

'Yes, I'll try.'

He didn't want to look at her in case there were tears in her eyes. He turned towards her and put his arm over her. He put his face close to her cheek and felt her hair brush against his cheek.

'Get something to eat too, some fruit or cheese.'

She nodded and nuzzled into him, hiding her face. She looked like a child lying there, a sturdy little child. Gowry drew in breath and rolled from the bed. He went to the chair, seated himself, put on his stockings and boots and wrapped his puttees around his ankles. Becky lay on the bed, her hand to her mouth, watching everything he did. He looked up at her and managed to wink.

'Won't be long,' he said.

He got up from the chair and slipped into his tunic, buckled and buttoned it and patted it down. He had his pay book, his pass, his few remaining francs all tucked away in his pocket. He buffed the shamrock on his hat with the heel of his hand, put the hat on, and squared it. He turned again to the bed. He stepped to the side of the bed and stooped over her. She stared up at him, eyes huge, her lips pursed as if she were pouting, as if it were his fault that he must leave her now, like this.

He slipped a hand under her waist, lifted her up and held her against him. She was helpless in his arms, so helpless that it was all he could do to bring his lips to her lips and brush her hair with his hand.

'Soon, love, we'll be together soon.'

'Yes,' she said. 'I know we will.'

Then he let her go, hoisted up his pack and went out and down the narrow staircase and through the empty foyer, out into the streets of Amiens.

He did not dare look back.

In case he tempted fate.

PART FIVE

Sylvie

Chapter Twenty

When Sylvie brought Sean downstairs at six o'clock on Thursday morning she found Kay McCulloch packed and ready to leave. Dazed and dopey and not at all sure what was expected of him, Daniel was crouched at the table wolfing into a great plate of bacon and eggs.

'We're going to Glasgow to stay with Forbes for a while,' Gran said, as soon as Sylvie appeared in the kitchen. 'Pat Emmett's bringing the cart round at half past six to take us north to catch the boat. You're welcome to come with us.'

'What about the boys? Are you just going to abandon them?'

'I can do nothing for the boys now,' Kay McCulloch said. 'I didn't push them into this fight and I'll not stay to see them shot. I have to get Daniel away before the police arrive to arrest him. Jail would kill him. Come with us, Sylvie. Forbes will find a place for you and the children and look after you until you get on your feet again.'

'No,' said Sylvie. 'I'm staying to see it through.'

'Then you're a bigger fool than I took you for. Think about Maeve, think about the child. Your house is in ruins and you've no money. We'll pay your fare to Glasgow. You'll be safe there.'

'I thought you didn't want me to go back to Glasgow?'

'I've changed my mind.'

'What'll happen to the brewery?'

'The brewery's closed. It's mortgaged to the hilt anyway. One of my girls – Blossom – will come down and see everything squared away. Look, in half an hour we're going out of that door and either you come with us or you go your own way. You can't stay here.'

'Why not?'

'Because it isn't safe. For all you know you're still on the peelers' list of suspects and you'll be picked up and thrown in jail.'

Sylvie looked out of the window at the crows winging silently down from the trees and the mist beginning to rise up off the fields. Ireland was her home. She had shared in its troubles and become part of them. She thought of Fran dying shamefully with a bullet in the head, of the girl, Pauline, and the daft lump of a boy, Algie, whom Fran sheltered in the tenement house in Endicott Street. She thought of the lives that Fran had lived that she knew nothing of, her challenge, her point of entry into a fortress of intrigue.

'Thank you,' Sylvie said. 'I prefer to stay put.'

'You've another man waiting in the wings, haven't you?'

'Yes. His name's Gowry,' Sylvie said. 'What'll I tell Charlie?'

'Tell him I took his father to Scotland. Charlie'll understand.' She took a pace towards Sylvie. 'At least let me take Maeve. She'll be well looked after, I promise.'

'There's nothing for Maeve in Glasgow. She stays here with me.'

The old man pushed away his plate, lifted a mug of strong tea and drank it down as if it were a pint of stout. He put a hand to his chest, burped and then, wide-eyed and wide-awake, looked round.

'Where is it we're going again, my sweetheart?' he asked.

'To the races,' his wife told him.

'I've things to do here, you know, things to be taken care of.'

'You can take care of them later, Daniel.'

'Aye,' he said, rising and buttoning his overcoat. 'Aye, later will do.'

And a half-hour later they were gone.

'Gone?' Maeve said. 'You mean she just shot off an' abandoned us?'

'She's gone to visit your Uncle Forbes in Glasgow. She offered to take you with her but I told her you wouldn't want to leave Dublin. Was I right?'

425

'Aye, you were.' It was after eight o'clock and Maeve had slept through her grandparents' departure. 'What about Charlie and Peter?'

'A man came last night after you were asleep and brought us news.'

'What sort of news? Is it bad?'

'Bad enough. Peter's in hospital, wounded, and Charlie's in jail.'

'What about Turk?'

'He's in jail too.'

'An' Jansis?'

'We've no word on Jansis.'

'Oh, she'll be all right,' said Maeve. 'Turk wouldn't let anythin' happen to Jansis. Is the fightin' over?'

'No, we're still holding out in some places.'

'It can't last much longer, Mam, can it?'

Sylvie had washed Maeve's blouse, drawers and stockings and had hung them out in the misty sunshine. The girl was clad in an old overcoat, like a gypsy. She would iron the blouse as soon as it was dry, Sylvie promised herself, then she would go through the house and search for any small items that could be converted into cash. Under the circumstances she had no scruples about stealing from her in-laws, for she doubted if she'd find anything worth retrieving in the ruins of the Shamrock.

She had some money in the bank and three postal orders from the War Office were stuck somewhere in the system.

'Are we staying on here then?' Maeve said.

'We can't.'

'Why not?'

'Because we haven't any money.'

'Did Gran not leave us some?'

'No, she didn't,' Sylvie said.

'Mean old bitch!'

'Maeve, that's enough.'

'Well, she is. Why has she abandoned us and the boys?'

'She didn't want Granddad to go to prison.'

'What'll they do to Turk and Charlie?'

'I don't know.'

'They won't shoot them, will they?'

'I don't know,' Sylvie said again.

'They're prisoners of war.'

'The British might not see it that way,' said Sylvie.

'They wouldn't shoot Turk,' Maeve muttered. 'Nah, nah, they'd never shoot a brave man like Turk.' She looked up, frowning. 'They shot Mr Whiteside, though. Did Turk surrender? I wonder why he surrendered?'

'Perhaps he was overwhelmed,' said Sylvie, tactfully.

How could she possibly explain to her daughter that there were no cowards in this war, that they were all just victims of history, whether you wrote history in large letters or small?

Maeve said, 'You're not goin' to cry, are you?'

'No,' said Sylvie. 'I'm not going to cry.'

'What are we goin' to do?'

'Go back to Dublin.'
'An' do what, Mam?'
'Look after ourselves,' said Sylvie.

As soon as Patrick Pearse surrendered his sword and the remaining rebels threw down their weapons at the foot of the Parnell statue in O'Connell Street, the gloves were off and summary executions began. According to Pauline they were dragging prisoners into the square at Portobello Barracks and shooting them in cold blood. There was no firm news concerning Turk or Peter and Charlie McCulloch, however, and with so many killed and wounded it was hardly surprising that Jansis, a last-minute volunteer, was missing in the confusion.

For five days and nights Sylvie hid in Fran's room in Fran's tenement in Endicott Street waiting for Vaizey to come and drag her away. She would have hidden in another part of Dublin if she'd had money to pay for lodgings but Gran's trinkets had brought little, for the pawnbrokers were awash with items that had not so mysteriously appeared in the hands of the street people.

On Sunday morning she left Maeve to look after Sean and slipped down to Sperryhead Road to see what was left of the Shamrock.

There was nothing much left of the Shamrock, only a blackened shell. She picked her way over the rubble in the alley and stared up numbly at the remains of piping and panelling, at a twisted iron bedstead hanging in space, curtains burned like battle-flags and the corpse of one of her poor chooks that had been blown too high for scavengers to reach. The site had been picked clean of every scrap that might fetch a ha'penny on a market cart.

Watton's warehouse was almost undamaged and no other house in the Sperryhead Road had been hit. It was almost as if the hand of God had popped out of the clouds and crushed her house and no other. It was pointless to rake through the bricks and mortar in the hope of finding a dress or a pair of shoes or even some small thing to serve as a memento of the years of peace and prosperity when she had been a happy, modest, married lady.

As she stood amid the rubble of her home it was all too obvious that wilfulness had brought her here. She had pushed the limits of selfishness too far by assuming that she could have everything she wanted without paying for it. No point in crying about it now, Sylvie decided, and walked swiftly away from the debris, back to Endicott Street where all she had left in the world, all that mattered, was waiting for her.

Maeve was standing on the pavement, with Sean in her arms. The baby was clean – Sylvie made sure of that – but Maeve had already become almost indistinguishable from Pauline's brood. She was taller than the children who gathered around her, though, and emanated such an air of superiority that she was already on the way to becoming a leader of the little gang. When Sylvie came upon her she was engaged in telling some fanciful tale about Mr Whiteside. Deprived of his euphonium – it had already been sold – Algie stood proudly beside his new-found friend, arms folded as if to indicate that he would thump the first little heretic who showed signs of inattention.

'What's going on here?' Sylvie said.

'Nothin',' Maeve said. 'Did you find my summer blouse?'

It was on the tip of Sylvie's tongue to order her daughter upstairs but she hadn't the heart. She admired Maeve's adaptability. She too would have to adapt if she were to have any hope of holding the family together until Gowry returned. She must write to Gowry, she reminded herself, send him something useful like a pair of woollen stockings or a tin of cigarettes.

Sylvie shook her head. 'Sorry, dearest, no.'

'Didn't you find any of my clothes?'

'Everything was burned to cinders.'

'You should have tooken me with you,' Maeve said, irritably. 'I'd have found somethin' we could use. Heard any news about Turk?'

'No, nothing.'

'He'll be in Richmond Barracks with the others. What about Jansis?'

'I spoke to no one,' Sylvie said.

'Not much use, are you?' Maeve said and, rotating

430

the baby on to her shoulder, turned and stalked into the tenement, with Algie trotting at her heels.

Glasnevin Cemetery was just across the canal from the bottom of Endicott Street but the route taken by most funerals was along the Phibsborough Road under the shadow of the Mountjoy.

For the best part of a week cortèges trundled up the Phibsborough Road, plumed horses pulling carts draped with laurel and crape, men walking in great long winding snakes behind them. Motor-cars too, shiny limousines from posh funeral homes where someone of importance had been laid out. Priests by the score, widows and orphans, those brothers who remained at liberty all trudging behind the coffins until it seemed to be just one interminable funeral with the sound of the bagpipe – salvos were banned – like the voice of a nation that has wakened to find itself mourning a whole new crop of martyrs.

Four hundred and fifteen souls were laid to rest close to Parnell's tomb and the grave of that wild old Fenian rebel, Jeremiah O'Donovan Rossa, whose body had been brought home from Staten Island less than a year ago. There was no air of celebration now, however, only grief and anger.

Sylvie was still lying low in Endicott Street, but there was no holding Maeve who, with Algie as her guide, roved the lanes and alleyways and attached herself to every funeral party that rolled past and walked with them for a piece.

It was Maeve who found the newspapers that had been thrown out of the back door of a doctor's consulting room, who discovered among the listings the name of Miss Jansis Kennedy, late of Ardee, a civilian victim of the fighting. As soon as she saw the name, she rushed home, rushed up the iron stairs, screaming at the pitch of her voice, '*Jansis is dead, Jansis is dead.*'

Sylvie was peeling potatoes into a bucket but the instant she heard Maeve's cry she threw open the door and let Maeve fling herself into her arms.

Poor Jansis had been 'lost' for a week. Her body had been brought to the city hospital on an army truck and stuck in the morgue until Peter had told the authorities who she was and her parents had been notified and, accompanied by her three brothers and two small sisters, had hastened to Dublin to fetch her home to Ardee. She had been buried in the graveyard near the river with the wake in the cottage in which she'd been born, and those who had loved her best had not been there to bid their friend farewell.

It was a bad time for Maeve, the worst time; Sylvie feared that her daughter would injure herself with weeping. Sensing his half-sister's distress, the baby wailed too and turned so red-faced and breathless that Sylvie had to shout for Pauline to come up and take him away for a spell.

She was glad to be in Fran's bed that night, far from the Sperryhead Road and Sutter Street where Jansis had met her end.

She held Maeve in her arms, for she understood what grief meant to the girl, that raw, peeled feeling around the heart when waves of recollection and regret rippled over you. She was too self-centred to suffer that sort of pain and did not suffer it now, not for Jansis and not for Fran. Lying in bed listening to Maeve's sobs, she wondered if she would ever be possessed by grief of that magnitude and if Gowry died would her heart break?

Gowry would not die, though. Gowry would live through the war and come back and forgive her. That was Gowry's way, his role.

Fed and changed, the baby was asleep in an old creel that Pauline had found in the cellar. Sylvie, worn out, was almost asleep too when Maeve stirred.

'I need to see Turk,' Maeve declared.

'How can you? He's in prison.'

'Take me to see Turk.'

'I wish I could.'

'If you won't take me, I'll go by myself.'

'No,' Sylvie said, sharply. 'Don't you even think of it.'

'I want to see Turk. I want to see Turk. I want to see—'

'Hush, you'll wake baby.'

'I don't *care* about baby. I don't care about *you*.' Maeve sat bolt upright, her face white in the darkened room. 'If you hadn't lain down with Fran none of this would've happened. Jansis wouldn't be dead an' Turk wouldn't be in jail.'

'Maeve, that just isn't right.'

'I know what you did with Fran. It was more than the huggin'. You did the thing that makes babies, the thing that made Sean. I know what it is, an' don't you think I don't.' Sylvie reached out but Maeve did not want consolation. She waved her arms and kicked against the bedcovers. 'If you hadn't let him put his – his thing in you we wouldn't be here. We'd be at home with Daddy.'

Sylvie caught Maeve's arms and pushed her back against the bolster.

'Stop it this instant. Do you want the whole building to hear?'

'*I don't care.*' Fresh tears spurted from Maeve's eyes. '*I want my daddy.*'

Sean was awake too now, and girning.

Lying in the darkness with her daughter and son crying, it dawned on Sylvie that what Maeve said might be true, that it was her recklessness that had brought disaster in its wake, that she *was* responsible. She had thought of it only as a love affair, something written in the stars, but it had been nothing of the sort: she had loved not the man but the love-making. The rest had only been play-acting, her own little drama, too personal and absorbing to include the larger issues that had driven Gowry away and caused Fran to be murdered.

'You can't have your daddy,' Sylvie said. 'You're stuck with me. All right, all right, if you stop crying I'll take you to see Turk.'

'When?'

'Tomorrow.'

'What if the peelers are waitin' for you?' Maeve said. 'What if Mr Vaizey's got scouts at the barracks?'

'I thought you didn't care what happens to me?'

'No,' Maeve said, soberly. 'What if they are?'

'Too bloody bad,' said Sylvie.

For the military authorities Richmond Barracks was merely a clearing house for rebels but for the police it was their last chance to settle old scores. Sylvie was taken aback by the ease with which she and the children were admitted. Escorted by armed soldiers, they were led past the guardhouse to an earthen square sectioned by barbed-wire fences. The surrounding buildings were three storeys tall and in the windows of the second- and third-storey rooms Sylvie could make out prisoners crammed against the glass. Soldiers were everywhere and sullen little groups of peelers in dark green uniforms eyed her suspiciously. She had no Sunday-best dress but she'd borrowed a bonnet from Pauline and had washed her hair and screwed in curl papers and, all in all, presented a picture respectable enough to impress the men in khaki, if not the men in green.

It was a cold, grey morning. Spring seemed to have retreated from the proximity of the barracks and the air was heavy with the smell of cooking and smoke from the coke braziers around which soldiers on stand-down huddled for warmth. Behind the wire were rows of washstands and two standpipes with great dribbling puddles of water around them. There were two doors in the front of the building, each guarded by a sentry with a rifle. Maeve and she were told to wait by the fence

435

while the prisoner was brought down. Two soldiers positioned themselves about ten paces behind them. Sylvie held Sean to her shoulder so that he could look at the soldiers, which, goggle-eyed, he did.

Maeve was less sanguine than her brother, though, and shot daggers at any soldier who had the temerity to glance in her direction.

'Don't,' Sylvie said.

'Don't what?'

'Make faces at them.'

'I'm not makin' faces.'

'Behave yourself, please.'

Sylvie placed the brown-paper parcel on the ground at her feet. Maeve was looking towards the building, waiting for Turk to emerge, when an officer came striding up behind them. 'Is that parcel for prisoner Trotter?' he enquired. 'Please stand to one side while the contents are examined.'

'Sure an' what d'you think's in it?' said Maeve. 'Gelignite?'

The officer, who was handsome in a boyish way, looked down at her and, not without amusement, said, 'One never knows, does one?'

'One might find out when one cuts the bloody string then,' said Maeve.

'You people, you never will learn, will you?'

'I'm not people,' Maeve said. 'I'm Maeve Mc-Culloch.'

On the officer's signal a corporal came trotting over, knelt beside the parcel, untied the string and spread the wrappings. The parcel contained four mutton chops, a string of sausages, two tins of kidney soup and an oval loaf, split and buttered.

'All clear, sor,' the corporal announced.

'What about the tins?'

'Will you be wantin' me to open the tins, sor?'

'Just give them a good shake.'

This the soldier did.

'Also all clear?' said the lieutenant.

'Aye, sor, clean as whistles. Will I be wrappin' the stuff up again?'

'Leave it as it is.' He glanced at Maeve. 'Is it in the sausages?'

'What?' Maeve said.

'The gelignite.'

'Hah–hah!' Maeve said, then, turning, lit up with joy as the love of her life, Turk Trotter, emerged from the barrack-room door.

'Well now,' Turk said, 'if it isn't a treat to be seein' you again. Seems like a lifetime since we were all together singin' songs in the Shamrock. Why, my sweetheart, I reckon you've grown even prettier since I saw you last.'

Maeve blushed and offered him the sausages coiled on a sheet of wrapping paper. 'We brought you something to eat.'

Turk eased the gift through the wire, lifted the sausages to his nose, and sniffed their bouquet.

'Manna from heaven,' he said.

'How bad is it inside?' Sylvie asked.

'Not so bad,' Turk said, 'but there's twenty of us in every room so it does get a bit stinky.'

'Are there beds for everyone?'

'No beds at all. We sleep heads to the wall, feet in the middle. Aren't enough blankets to go round, so it's cold in the night. I don't mind the hard floor so much now my hipbones are gettin' used to it.'

'Do they beat you?' Maeve said.

'Nah, nah. They get us up at six. We go out for a wash, one room at a time, and then they feed us. Mostly it's slop. Aren't enough spoons or knives so you have to be makin' do as best you can. I bought this old jack-knife from an English soldier and it does me well enough, except for the porridge.'

'How do you eat the porridge?' said Maeve.

'Like this,' said Turk, scooping a cupped hand to his mouth.

'Do you have money?' Sylvie asked.

'I'd two quid in my pouch when I was captured.'

'Didn't they steal your money?' Maeve said.

Turk shook his head. 'They bargain for favours, but they're not thieves.'

Sylvie passed Sean to Maeve, lifted the chops, bread and tins and passed them through the wire. Turk held out the gifts for the guards to see, then wrapped them in the paper and laid the package on the ground. He still wore the uniform of the brotherhood, though the emblems had been torn from the sleeves and shoulder. He seemed well enough, Sylvie thought, but he'd shaved cold that morning and pinpricks of blood peppered his jaw-line.

'How were you captured?' Sylvie asked.

'I gave up,' Turk replied. 'Surrendered.'

'You said you'd never surrender,' Maeve told him.

'I done it for Peter. If you'd been there you'd have seen how pointless it was to go on after the warehouse had fallen.'

'Pointless!' Maeve shrilled. 'The cause – pointless?'

'Where is Peter?' Sylvie put in.

'Upstairs in the room with Charlie and me.'

'Is he all right?'

'He's wounded but he ain't goin' to die. He took a bullet in the side. They done him proud in the hospital, I'll give the bastards that much. He would still be there recuperatin' but he told them he was a soldier an' if they were goin' to be shootin' the rest of us he wanted to be lined up against the wall too. They handed him over to the military who brought him here.'

'Are they goin' to shoot *you*, Turk?' Maeve said.

'I doubt it. I think most of the shootin's been done.'

'They shot Fran,' Sylvie said.

'Jaysus!'

'Vaizey ordered it. I saw it.'

'Jaysus, Jaysus!'

Turk scratched his brow, a hand over his eyes.

'Where did Jansis die?' Sylvie asked.

Turk sighed again. 'She was trapped on the roof

with me an' Peter, sore wounded. She fought to the last but she was dyin' before they reached us.'

'Reached you?' said Maeve.

'Before I showed the white flag,' said Turk.

'Hopeless, was it?' Sylvie said.

'Aye, hopeless,' said Turk. 'Totally outnumbered, we were.'

Maeve grimaced. 'The white flag, though, the bloody white flag.'

Turk closed his eyes, scratched his brow again. He was close to tears, Sylvie realised. She would not for all the world push him to that limit, not with Maeve watching. She reached out, eased Sean from her daughter's arms and cradled him in the crook of her elbow. The baby wriggled, struggling to sit up. Now that he had his sight he found everything fascinating. He stared at the hulking figure behind the wire and stretched out his little pink fists.

'I think he likes you, Turk,' Sylvie said.

'Aye, he's a sweet wee fellah,' said Turk. 'Keep him safe till I get out an' I'll bathe his head in whiskey.'

'When will you get out?' said Sylvie.

'We'll be deported to England, I'm thinkin',' Turk said. 'They don't know what to be doin' with us since so many are bein' brought in every day. The court martials will start soon. We reckon the peelers'll have the last word on who goes down for penal servitude, an' who doesn't. I fear Charlie, for one, won't see Irish daylight for a long time to come.'

'An' you, Turk,' Maeve said, 'what about you?'

'I don't know,' Turk said. 'I only done what I had to do.'

'Would you do it again?' said Sylvie.

'In a flash,' Turk said. 'Anyway, I'll soon be stuck with a formal charge then I'll know whether I'm goin' to be classed as a criminal or a prisoner o' war.' He paused, then said, 'Maeve?'

'What?'

'Will you not look at me? Why won't you look at me?'

'It's you, you haven't been lookin' at me.'

'I'm lookin' at you now, my sweetheart,' Turk said, softly.

And Maeve began to cry.

'Stupid bitch, my sister-in-law, bringin' us raw meat. Does she think this is home from home an' we've got gas in every room? How are we supposed t' cook the stuff? Never mind,' said Peter, 'me mam'll bring us somethin' decent soon.'

'Your mam won't be bringin' you anythin',' Turk said. 'Your mam's chased off to Scotland an' took your da with her.'

'What!' Peter sat up, winced and clapped a hand to his ribs. 'Who told you that? Sylvie? That lyin' bitch.'

'It's the truth, most like,' said Charlie. 'If the peelers are hauling in everybody who even spoke to a republican they'll have the old man's name high on their list. He'd never last ten minutes in here, let alone on Dartmoor.'

'Is that where they'll send us?' Peter said.

'I don't know where they'll send us,' said Charlie. 'Could be China for all I know. Dartmoor's an English prison, though, and since we're prisoners of the English it seems logical . . .'

'Sod your logic,' Peter chipped in. 'Who's goin' to look after things at Towers if Mam's skipped an' we're banged up?'

'Bloss an' the girls, I suppose.' Charlie glanced at Turk who was seated cross-legged in a corner with the parcel of food in his lap. 'Bloss an' the girls will take care o' the house. The brewery's sealed up and the vats are empty.'

'Uh!' Turk said, almost to himself. 'The old Shamrock went up in smoke. I was right about that. I thought it'd taken a direct hit. Everythin' was blowed-up or burned. Even the piano. I'll miss that old piano, so I will.'

'Are you goin' to be sharin' that bread, Trotter?' another man asked.

Charlie hunkered by Turk's knees. Peter was propped against the wall, legs stretched out. A medico had changed his dressing that morning and the wound was smarting.

Charlie said, 'We can bribe one o' the soldiers to let us cook on the braziers at the out-break. I could do with some grease in my belly.' He tapped Turk's knee. 'What other news did Sylvie bring?'

'Fran's a goner. Vaizey had him executed.'

'What's this you're tellin' me?'

'Took him to the headquarters an' had him shot outside in the yard.'

'Are you certain?'

'Sylvie was a witness.'

'How could that bitch be a witness?' Peter said.

'Vaizey arrested her too. She saw it from a cell window.'

'If that's the bloody case how come she's still runnin' loose?'

'I reckon Vaizey couldn't fiddle a charge to hold her,' said Charlie. 'If the Shamrock's gone where are she an' the kiddies stayin'?'

'Fran's place in Endicott Street.'

'If Vaizey wants her, he'll find her there quick enough,' said Charlie.

'Maybe she already gave Vaizey what he wanted,' said Peter. 'Maybe she gave them all a good feel an' that's why she walked.'

'Shut your dirty mouth, Peter,' Turk said.

'Does she know who else is dead?' said Charlie.

'Kevin – I told her about Kevin.'

'And Jansis?'

'Aye, I told her about Jansis.'

'She'll be upset,' said Charlie.

'Her? Nothin' upsets her,' said Peter. 'She'll have another man up her drawers before the month's out.'

'If you don't shut your dirty mouth . . .'

'Did she cry?' said Charlie, hastily.

443

'The girl did. Maeve did. I made her cry. Oh, Christ!' Turk said with a shuddering sigh. 'Look at this, will you?'

He let the brown paper fall open to display the drawing of a heart rendered in indigo ink with an indelible pencil.

The paper was butter-stained and the drawing blurred but it was still possible to read the words that Maeve had traced within the arrow-pierced heart:

Maeve & Turk.
One True Love.

'Haw,' Peter sneered. 'She loves him. The stupid wee bitch loves him.'

'It's just as well someone does,' said Turk.

Schools had reopened. Algie had been shooed off along with the others, a satchel on his shoulder, a fish-paste sandwich in his pocket, tin whistle sticking out of the back of his shirt like the key of a clockwork toy. Tomorrow, come what may, Sylvie would register Maeve at Endicott Street School for the summer term. Now that she had talked with Turk, Maeve was more settled and relaxed. She seemed almost cheerful as they rode the tramcar down to College Green.

It was the first sight Sylvie had had of that part of town since the uprising had been quashed. She was dismayed to see that many fine buildings had been damaged or destroyed. The streets were busy, though, and carts, tramcars and vans packed the roads around the bridges.

The day was still cold and grey, more like March than May. Sylvie hardly noticed the weather. She was already planning what she would say to the manager of the North Mercantile, how she would explain the loss of her bank book. Several tellers knew her by sight and would vouch for her and she didn't think there would be a problem in emptying the Shamrock account.

After that was done and she had cash in her purse, she would walk to the sorting office to pick up her letters and postal orders and notify the authorities of her change of address. She had already decided to stay in the tenement in Endicott Street until Gowry returned.

The North Mercantile bank was undamaged. The commissionaire, with his huge white moustaches and spotless white gloves, still presided over the doors, the tellers were all in place and Mr Grover, the manager, was still behind his desk in the office at the rear. He listened sympathetically to Sylvie's tale of woe, had her sign her name three times on a typed document, then, consulting a ledger, informed her that she had twenty-six pounds and thirteen shillings in her account and that, if she wished, she may draw all or part of it.

She withdrew twenty-six pounds, filled in another slip of paper with her new address, then, with her purse tucked securely into the pocket of her skirt, she collected Maeve and Sean and set off on the long walk to the sorting office.

'How much?' Maeve asked, as soon as they had left the bank.

'Twenty-six pounds.'

'Well, well!' Maeve said. 'That should see us right. Ten bob a week for exactly a year to add to the money Daddy sends us. We can muddle through on that, can't we?'

'Of course we can,' said Sylvie.

'What'll we get for the Shamrock?'

'Nothing.'

'I thought the Shamrock was ours.'

'It wasn't insured.'

'Won't we get com – com . . .'

'Compensation?' Sylvie said. 'I doubt it.'

'So they can just blow up our house – an' that's it?'

Sylvie nodded. 'I'm afraid so.'

She lacked the energy to explain that she was reluctant to pursue a claim against the government because the lease had been purchased with money that Forbes McCulloch had provided.

In addition, she had taken out a small mortgage with a Union Society and was afraid that if she sued for compensation and lost the judgement then the Union Society would come down on her to clear the mortgage immediately. The situation was further complicated by the fact that she had been harbouring men who were classed as criminals and if she made a fuss about compensation Vaizey would appear before her and make more trouble. Maeve's calculations were accurate, however. Ten shillings a week added to the

sum received from the War Department would do very
nicely, especially as she'd be living rent-free in Fran's
tenement – at least until Gowry came home.

Sperryhead Road sorting office wasn't in Sperryhead
Road. It occupied the wide corner at the city end of
Sutter Street, a quarter-mile or so from the Shamrock.
It was a busy little office and the shop attached to it sold
newspapers and magazines and tobacco as well as stamps
and postal orders. The woman who served behind the
counter was named McFee. She knew Sylvie well
enough by sight, though she didn't approve of Sylvie's
choice of company or her goings-on.

Leaving Maeve outside with Sean, Sylvie went into
the shop alone.

Three or four folk were queuing at the counter but
she could see Mrs McFee's grey bun bobbing about
under the racks of magazines and smell the reek of the
stove that burned away, winter and summer, at the old
woman's back; all so familiar, so comforting.

At length she reached the worn wooden counter,
and leaned upon it. 'I think you might have some
letters for me, Mrs McFee,' she said, giving the sour
old woman a pleasant smile. 'The Shamrock . . .'

'I heard about the Shamrock,' the woman said.

'Well,' Sylvie said, 'I'll thank you for my letters
then.'

The woman said nothing. She shuffled through the
open doorway into the sorting office. It was unusually
bright in the big room, for skylights bathed the long
tables with an excess of daylight. Sylvie watched Mrs

McFee move down the line of the tables, saw her pause at one small table, turn and come back carrying a little bundle of letters fastened by a rubber band. She emerged from the office and placed the bundle on the counter in front of Sylvie.

'You'll not be thanking me for these, I'm thinking,' she said.

Sylvie stared at the bundle. Three oblong enve-lopes, grey-green, with War Department stamps. One other, square-shaped, biscuit brown. She stripped off the rubber band, picked open the seal of the biscuit-brown envelope. Her throat burned and her legs were trembling even before she unfolded the single sheet of buff-coloured paper and glanced down at it.

'Yes,' she said. 'Yes, I see.'

'Are you all right?' the old woman asked.

'Yes, I'm fine,' said Sylvie, 'thank you.'

She lifted the envelopes, crushed in one hand, and went out to the cold, grey pavement where Maeve waited with Sean in her arms.

'Mam, what is it?' Maeve said, alarmed.

'It's Gowry. Your father,' Sylvie said. 'He's missing.'

'Missing?' said Maeve. 'What does that mean?'

'Missing,' Sylvie told her. 'Believed killed.'

Chapter Twenty-one

Sylvie could do nothing to change the pattern of the past. She had no choice but to let the tide of life carry her along. What had been acceptable as a temporary measure was a good deal less so after a month in Endicott Street, however, and Sylvie felt it was time to give herself a shake before she slipped into total apathy.

She had not been entirely idle, of course. She had bought clothes and shoes, napkins for the baby, a tin bath from the market. She had also uncovered a little fireplace in the apartment that had been boarded over. It was comforting to have a fire in the room, less comfortable to have to haul coals from the bunker in the hall, tote water from the tap in the yard or sneak downstairs to the lavatory with a chamberpot splashing in your hands. Fran Hagarty's tenement was unusually clean and quiet, though, for there were no families in any of the upstairs rooms and only on

Friday and Saturday nights was there a bit of a racket on the stairs.

Unlike her mother, Maeve recovered quickly from the shock of her father's death and within a week or two knew all about their neighbours.

'Who's that man we passed on the stairs?' Sylvie, mildly curious, asked.

'Which man?'

'The big dark-haired chap on the second floor.'

'Mr O'Rourke, you mean.'

'Is that who I mean? Comes in late every night.'

'Docker,' Maeve said. 'Likes his drink.'

'Oh! He's not married, I take it?'

'None of them are,' said Maeve. 'Fran wouldn't take them in if they were married.'

'Except Pauline.'

'Pauline!' Maeve snorted at her mother's naïvety. 'Pauline ain't married. What's she been tellin' you, Mam? If she told you she was married to Fran then she's spinnin' you a fanny.'

'Maeve!'

'Well, she is.'

Lunchtime, around half past twelve: Maeve was tucking in to a plate of broth and Sylvie, with Sean at her breast, was still too sunk in on herself to press for information.

Two or three days later, in the evening, she took the matter up once more.

'Is Algie Pauline's boy?'

'Nup.'

'Whose boy is he then?'

'Nobody's boy. His own boy,' said Maeve.

'What age is he?'

Maeve shrugged. 'Ten or eleven.'

'Who pays for his keep?'

'Fran does. Fran did.'

The room was wreathed in smoke from the coal fire, for the chimney had not been properly cleaned yet. The paraffin stove on which Sylvie cooked gave off a rancid odour and Sean, growing larger every day, had filled his nappy only minutes before and was having it changed. His wails grew louder and more petulant, for he did not take kindly to being turned on his back like a turtle and having his bottom wiped. Sylvie raised her voice. 'Why did Fran do that?'

'Hmm?'

The novelty of having a half-brother had almost worn off and although Maeve was still loving and considerate towards Sean she had lost interest in the sordid mechanics of child-rearing. She was lying on the bed reading a tattered copy of the *Irish Times* and at that moment looked less like a girl on the threshold of womanhood than a gawky half-grown boy.

'Maeve?'

'Whaa-at?' She rustled the newspaper irritably.

'Why did Fran take in those children?'

'I don't know, do I?' Maeve said. 'Why don't you ask Pauline?'

The question was perfectly reasonable but Sylvie had no ready answer.

She lifted Sean from the mat on the floor and dropped the cloth into the bowl. He was naked save for a neatly pinned napkin and in the wand of sunlight from the window reminded her of one of the cherubs in an Italian painting she had seen in Glasgow when she was a schoolgirl. His hair had already begun to thicken and curl and he snatched at the mischievous sunlight as if it had been put there just for his benefit.

'Pauline knows everythin',' Maeve said. 'All you have to do is ask her.'

'Perhaps I will,' Sylvie said. 'Perhaps I will at that.'

She was reluctant to communicate with the woman in the ground-floor apartment, though, for she resented Pauline Rafferty's position as counsellor, arbitrator and rent-collector. It seemed to Sylvie that she, a proper landlady who had once managed a proper hotel, should be given her place and that it was up to Pauline to ask for her help rather than the other way around.

Pauline was smart in some ways, naïve in others. She seemed blissfully unaware of the irony of the situation, that both she and Sylvie had been Francis Hagarty's lovers and were stuck together in the same house now that Fran was gone. Sylvie suspected that there might be more of Fran's 'wives' and children running around Dublin, but she had no intention of asking Pauline to confirm her suspicions. She wanted Fran and all Fran stood for to drift off into the mists of time and leave her with Sean and her memories and none of the guilt, pain and responsibility that being one of Fran's 'wives' had entailed.

Unfortunately, Pauline refused to accept that Fran was really dead and Sylvie didn't have the heart to force the truth upon her. ''Merica. Fran's in America,' Pauline would say. 'He always comes back. He gives me money, an' then he comes back.' Meanwhile, she continued to stand by the door of her apartment every Friday night and count the shillings that the tenants put into her hand and, so Maeve told her, record the amounts in a skinny black notebook. Sylvie found it difficult to believe that the swaying creature in the hall below was numerate and literate enough to keep an account book but that, so Maeve told her, was just snobbery on her part.

Although she had been a dozen years in the city, Sylvie did not know Dublin well. She had seldom ventured far from Sperryhead except to window-shop in Grafton Street, take a turn around the park with Gowry or visit one of the theatres. She had no real sense of the city's nuances and distinctions. She regarded Dublin as the Dublin that came to her door, a town peopled by the commercials, priests and rebels. She had turned a blind eye to the rest, to Dublin's coarseness and delicacy, its pace and pulse and vigour. Now that Gowry was dead, and she was sure that he was, she had every excuse for returning to Glasgow but she wouldn't capitulate and kow-tow to fate. For Maeve's sake, she would stick it out in Dublin.

May gave way to June. The sun lay like a waxy ball in the sky over the mountains and the evenings were wonderfully long. It was breathlessly hot and stifling, though, and from her window Sylvie would look down into the street at the women seated on the pavements while their men sheltered in McKinstry's cool, brown interior and little girls trotted to and fro carrying jugs of porter – just toddlers some of them, hardly bigger than the jugs they carried – and the children all barefoot to save on shoes and the boys, most of them, stripped down to their trousers, bare-bellied and bare-chested.

Maeve was among them, prominent because of her height, racing about, chasing and being chased, skipping rope. Her breasts had developed enough to have shape and mobility and the older boys eyed her with sly speculation, her hair and breasts bouncing and her long gawky body going up and down, up and down, nimble as an antelope or a kangaroo as she hopped across the rope.

In slanting sunlight, in the dust between the tenements, Sylvie almost expected to catch sight of Fran strolling out of the twilight in his long black overcoat, or Gowry, her lovely, unappreciated Gowry, jaunty in khaki, marching home from war. Then she was smitten by loneliness and a sudden longing to be at one with the women below, part of the texture of this funny, fair, furious city.

Sean was fast asleep in his basket, dew on his brow, eyelids flickering as if he were dreaming of things too remote to be other than dreams. She got up from the chair by the window and went to the fire, hardly a fire at all, just a bridge of ash and a frail finger of smoke. She gave it a stir with an iron poker then plucked her shawl from the hook and went down the spiral staircase into the street.

Pauline was seated on the top step. She wore a dirty white dress and was barefoot and bare-legged. Sylvie saw then what Fran had found attractive in the girl, a fey quality, but sexual too, and slightly cruel.

'Hoh!' Pauline said, glancing round.

'Hoh yourself!' said Sylvie, and sat down.

The letter was typed on brittle brown paper and headed War Information Office. It was signed by the Hon. Secretary, Catherine M. McPhail.

It said:

> In addition to information which you may have received from the Department of War I have to report that it is believed that your husband, Private G. McCulloch, 2nd Battalion, Sperryhead Rifles, was one of a party on detachment to a position near Heuvert and did not return from a night attack upon a German emplacement in a sector where casualties were abnormally heavy.
>
> As you will appreciate identification is no easy matter and so far it has not been possible to obtain eye-witness confirmation through the Red Cross Society,

although it appears that a body bearing resemblances to your husband was brought in and buried in a grave close to the aforementioned town along with thirty-seven other men, the site being marked with boards. So far, however, it has not been possible to obtain entry to company or battalion records or receive final confirmation from the surviving officer, Lieutenant A. J. Soames. Consequently your application for a pension form claim is being held pending further enquiry.

I am afraid, however, that there is little room for hope that your husband is alive and I therefore offer you my sincere sympathy.

'What a bugger,' Pauline said when Sylvie showed her the letter. 'Sure an' they'll not be givin' away their money without a fight. Is there nobody you could drop a line to, somebody who knew him, a chum in the ranks?'

Sylvie shook her head. 'Gowry wasn't the sort to make chums.'

'What about this fellah, this Soames?'

'I wouldn't know where to find him,' said Sylvie. 'In any case, I imagine he'll be far too busy to answer letters from strangers.'

'Maybe Dad's a prisoner,' Maeve said. 'Maybe he has magnesia.'

'Amnesia,' Sylvie said. 'I doubt it.'

'Amnesia,' Maeve went on, 'an' can't remember who we are or where he comes from. Maybe when the war's over he'll come home, see us on the street an' there'll be a flash an'—'

'How can he come home if he can't remember where home is?' Pauline put in. 'I think the Germans'll have him.'

'Red Cross,' said Maeve. 'Best bet.'

'Well, you'll not be gettin' a penny out o' them miserable beggars at the War Department until you find out for sure he's dead,' said Pauline.

'If he isn't dead' – Sylvie smoothed the paper with the palm of her hand – 'shouldn't I still be receiving my share of his pay?'

'No pay an' no pension,' Maeve said. 'That's how the government's payin' for the war, Mam, by starvin' the widows an' orphans. By Gad, we could all be dead an' gone before we get a penny piece out of them.'

'He's gone away – like Fran,' Pauline said.

Maeve tilted her head and rolled her eyes towards the ceiling.

'Aye,' she said, 'maybe my dad's hidin' in 'Merica too.'

'Maeve' – Sylvie raised an admonitory finger – 'enough.'

'If only we'd written to Daddy,' Maeve said, 'we'd have his letters to tell us who to write to now.'

'What?' Pauline said, frowning. 'Didn't you write to him?'

'No, not often,' said Sylvie.

'Tell the truth,' said Maeve. 'I wrote to him an' there was never the scrape of a pen back. I reckon he was mad at all of us 'cause of Fran. I mean, you can't hardly blame him.'

'I've got letters,' Pauline said.

'Letters? What letters?' said Sylvie.

'All sorts o' letters,' Pauline said. 'In a box downstairs.'

'Fran's letters, you mean?' said Maeve.

'Fran used to take them out o' his pockets. He carried a lot o' paper stuff in his pockets, Fran. He'd pull out the box, drop the stuff into it an' put it back.'

'Back where?' Sylvie said.

'Back downstairs.'

Mother and daughter glanced at each other. Friend though she had become these past few weeks, Pauline could still be infuriatingly vague. Maeve perched on a stool, heels propped on the hood of the fireplace, her calves kippered by smoke. She spread her knees and expertly brought the stool to rest on the floor. 'Letters from Fran? May we see them, Pauline?'

'What for?'

'To see if he ever had anythin' to say about us.'

'He never did,' said Pauline. 'They're mostly business.'

Maeve smiled her most winning smile. 'Pleeeeease.'

'It's a fair big box,' Pauline said. 'He wrote a lot.'

'I'll bet he did,' said Maeve.

*　　*　　*

The small plywood chest that Algie lugged up from the cellar had *Ceylon Tea* stencilled on one side and, oddly, *Jesus is Lord* on the other. It was filled with bills, paid and unpaid, a great many grubby *billets-doux* from anonymous women, several letters from a Seamus O'Doyle in Chicago, more from a Peter Blanchard in Philadelphia, and a series of complaints from the editors of journals and newspapers, some of which had been crumpled up then smoothed out again.

The papers had been tossed casually into the box on top of more solid objects and among the oddments that Maeve and Algie unearthed were an old meerschaum pipe carved in the likeness of Wolfe Tone, a tarnished medallion of John the Almsgiver, a big rosette of faded green flannel and a dented pewter tankard with *Oliver Francis Hagarty, 1896* engraved on the base. Why Pauline hadn't raided the box for items to sell or pawn was a mystery, but while Fran had been alive there had been no real scarcity of money and, like every other thing in this queer household, the stuff in the tea-chest had been his property.

Sylvie experienced a certain distaste at sifting through the correspondence, scanning the love letters and the letters of commitment and conspiracy that Fran's short, sad life had engendered.

Head inside the chest, Maeve said, 'Look at this.' She emerged with a batch of letters in buff-coloured envelopes. 'Recognise the handwriting, Mam?'

Sylvie took the letters and held them up to the light.

'Dad's,' Maeve said. 'Those letters are from Daddy.'

'Yes,' Sylvie said, heart sinking. 'I do believe they are.'

'Why would Daddy be writing to Fran?'

Pauline was standing by the table on which Fran's scrappy history had been spread. She had put the baby down but two of the younger children clung to her skirts. They were quite different, each from the other, the boy with the crisp, curly black hair of a Celt, the girl with hair as fair and fine as a Nordic princess's. Pauline had adopted a vague, far-away air that suggested less innocence than indifference. Sylvie slit the seal on the first of the letters with her thumbnail, dropped the page into her hand and scanned it.

'What does it say, Mam? Why did Daddy write to Fran?'

'It isn't addressed to Fran,' said Sylvie. 'It's addressed to us.'

'Us?' Maeve said. 'Daddy wrote to us?'

Sylvie groped behind her, found a chair and sank down on to it.

'Gowry didn't – he didn't abandon us. He wrote to us from Fermoy.' She fanned out the letters. 'Five, six times. He told us where he was and what he was doing and that – that he loved us.' She was conscious of Pauline swaying on the edge of her vision. 'I thought Gowry didn't care, and all along . . .'

'Give me that.' Maeve snatched the letter from her mother's hand. 'Did you know about this, Pauline? Did you know Fran had stolen our letters, my letters from my daddy?' Pauline crooned and swayed in time to music that only she could hear. '*He stole our letters, Mam*,' Maeve cried. Algie stopped rooting in the box and looked up, and the smaller children clung more tightly to their mother's skirt. 'Fran stole our letters. Why, why would he do that?'

Sylvie had no answer to give to her daughter. Perhaps, she thought desperately, it wasn't deception on Fran's part but just another manifestation of his love for her. Perhaps Fran had been afraid of Gowry, afraid that Gowry would try to steal her back. Fran couldn't have been seeking information about the whereabouts of the guns – how remote that episode seemed now, how immaterial – for the letters had not been opened. She guessed that Fran had removed them from the stand in the hallway of the Shamrock, whisked them away so she would think that Gowry no longer cared what became of her, and in so doing had cut Gowry off from the scant consolations that remained in the wake of her self-centred affair.

It was all so puzzling, so disturbingly ambiguous, like Fran himself: Fran and his women, his conspiracies, his drinking; Fran and his flattery, his charm, his generosity; Fran alone and enigmatic, cruelly condemning Gowry to his fate. And both of them dead now, both of them dead. She had no way of knowing which of them had loved her most. And no way of making amends.

Maeve gave her a shake and reached for the rest of the letters.

Sylvie yielded them without resistance.

'And the letters I wrote to Daddy, did Fran steal them too?'

'Probably,' Sylvie said. A month ago she would have dissolved in tears but she had changed, and when it came down to it, it hardly mattered who had done what to whom. She turned to Pauline. 'I'll take these letters. They're mine.'

'Aye.' Now that she knew she wasn't going to be blamed, Pauline emerged from her protective trance. 'Take anythin' you want, Sylvie. Take the whole boxful if you like.'

How incongruous, Sylvie thought; every scrap, every jot of her life with Gowry had gone up in smoke and what she had in its place were scrappy reminders of Fran. It dawned on her then that Fran hadn't intended to write an end to his own history. He had simply left her out of it, jettisoned her with the same casual cruelty as he had jettisoned the wife and sons in Huddersfield. Fran Hagarty had been master of his own destiny, nobody else's.

'Yes,' she said. 'It might be interesting to see what else is here.'

'*Mam!*'

'Maeve,' Sylvie said, quite adamantly, 'carry that box upstairs.'

On a dreary Sunday afternoon not much more than a week after her mother had found her father's letters, Maeve and Algie were playing on the pavement when a great big enormous chap whom Maeve had never seen before came striding up the street. He had a moustache but no beard, a little caterpillar moustache, far too small for the size of his face. He wore a cutaway jacket like the Irishmen in *Punch* and a bowler hat was stuck on a mop of dark brown curly hair.

Algie had been to mass with Pauline and the rest of the brood and Maeve had accompanied Sylvie and Sean to church around the corner. Now, about half past one o'clock, true blue boozers had wakened parched for a hair of the dog and, with tongues hanging out, were scuttling into Mistress Cafferty's boarding-house for young country girls which, on Sunday afternoons, somehow transformed itself into a shebeen.

Maeve had eaten dinner in Pauline's apartment. The children were still dressed in their nice neat clothes, clean and patched, and trailed the air of piety that Pauline had dinned into them out of respect for the Man on the Cross who had died for their sins and who would be waiting for them with a host of angels and a hot dinner on the day they went to heaven which, of course, wouldn't be for a long time yet.

'Look 't him.' Algie dug Maeve in the ribs. 'He ain't from round here.'

'I'll bet he ain't.' Maeve leaned on Algie's shoulders as if he were a windowsill and peered at the approaching stranger. 'I bet I know who he is, though.'

'Sure an' you don't.'

'Sure an' I do. I'll bet his name's Trotter.'

'Is he a peeler?'

'Nup, he's lookin' for me.'

Maeve's deductive powers were not stretched by the observation, for the gentleman in question had a piece of paper clutched in his fat-fingered hand and consulted it from time to time. The size of him and the length of his stride were unmistakable.

'Mr Trotter, Mr Trotter,' Maeve called out before he could be waylaid by a stray country girl from Mistress Cafferty's. 'Mr Trotter, we're this way.'

The man came lumbering up to them. He was so big that even Algie quailed and slid behind Maeve for protection.

'Are you Maeve McCulloch?' the man asked.

'I am, sir. Did Turk send you?'

'That he did.'

He was hardly Turk's double, except in size. He had bad teeth and the curly brown hair was already turning grey and there were wrinkles at the corners

464

of his eyes. He must be quite old, Maeve reckoned, thirty or thirty-five if he was a day.

'Has Turk sent me a letter?' she asked.

The man shook his head. 'You're awful young,' he said. 'Are you sure you're Maeve McCulloch?'

'I was when I got up this mornin',' Maeve said. 'An' I'm not that young.'

'Well,' the man said, 'I'm Turk's brother, Breen.'

'Brian?'

'Breen,' he said. 'Breen Trotter.'

'It's a funny lot o' names you Trotters have,' Maeve said, striving to show her sophistication. 'Is Turk still incar-incar – in jail at Richmond?'

'No, he's been sentenced,' Breen said.

'What?' She felt her bowels turn to water. 'To death?'

'Now, now, lass, no need to alarm yourself.' He put one big paw on her shoulder and patted her as he might have patted a nervous calf. 'Did you not hear the cheers from yesterday?'

'Ch-cheers?'

'From the dockside?'

'I never heard nothin' – anythin',' said Maeve.

'They shipped the first o' the prisoners away to England. Turk an' his friends Charlie an' Peter were among them. I thought you'd have heard.'

Maeve was surprised that Pauline hadn't said something about it. Pauline knew she had a sweetheart in Richmond Barracks and had visited him there.

'Where have they taken them?'

'Stafford,' Breen told her.

'Where's that? Is it on Dartmoor?'

The man still had his hand on her shoulder. The friendly gesture made Algie agitated and he was beginning to show signs of an imminent war dance by huffing and puffing and whistling through his teeth. Maeve ignored him. Breen Trotter's hand on her shoulder made her feel as if Turk were with her.

'Dartmoor's a convict prison,' Breen went on. 'Those prisoners who had a death penalty commuted – about seventy I think – were given penal servitude an' sent to Dartmoor for life. Turk wasn't one o' them, thanks be to God. There's hundreds, thousands goin' over the sea to English jails but' – Breen gave a cheerful wag of the head – 'there's nary a one o' them been tried. Officially they're all prisoners o' war. Isn't that all to the good?'

'Will he be in – where is it?'

'Stafford.'

'Stafford for long?'

'Can't say,' Breen told her.

'When did you last talk to Turk?'

'Friday. He knew he was soon to be moved.'

'Was he sad?'

'Nah, not him, not any o' them. They were singin' like larks and undiscouraged. By Gad, they were even more cheerful yesterday when they were marched through the streets to the boat. What a send-off the folk gave them, cheering and blessing their names and running out through the lines o' soldiers to press gifts upon them.'

'I wish I'd been there,' Maeve said. 'I wish I'd known.'

'Aye,' Breen Trotter said, 'it's the turnin' o' the tide, sure an' it is.'

'What?' said Maeve. 'What tide?'

'The uprising didn't fail after all,' Breen Trotter said. 'It's wakened our people, rallied their fightin' spirit. Just you wait an' see, the standard of independ-ence will be raised before much longer.'

'Really?' said Maeve. 'Really an' truly, Mr Trotter?'

'Aye, really, lass, really an' truly.' He hunkered in front of her, hand on her waist to steady himself, and looked straight into her eyes. 'Turk says I was to give you all his love. He says he'll write you soon as he can. He says you've not to forget him.'

'Forget him! As if I would!'

'Good.' Breen got up, rising up, it seemed, out of the pavement until he was half the height of the tenement above her, a huge amiable figure softened by the little moustache and the creases around his brown eyes. 'Well, that's my message delivered so I'll just be goin' for a bite to eat before I head for the railway station.'

'You'll do no such thing,' Maeve said. 'Come along inside an' we'll see if there's still somethin' in the pot.'

'Your mammy won't be too pleased at a stranger

467

landin' on her doorstep at the dinner time, I'm thinkin'.'

'No, but my friend Pauline will,' said Maeve and, taking Breen's hand, led him into the tenement in search of a spot of lunch.

Chapter Twenty-two

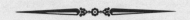

At about the time that Breen Trotter first clapped eyes on Pauline Rafferty and fell instantly in love, the devil was stalking Dublin in the shape of General Sir John Maxwell. Maxwell had been Commander-in-Chief in Ireland for some time and, while Westminster debated what was to be done about the Irish, he devoted himself to the task of rounding up insurgents with a zeal that made him the most hated man in Ireland. Sylvie shared the universal loathing of Maxwell but because she was unable to claim assistance from the National Aid Association and because her husband had fought for England her loyalties remained divided.

She was scrubbing the upper landing when the men arrived.

The door of her little room was open and sunlight streamed through the windows and new cotton curtains. It was not unpleasant to be on her knees scouring away a week's dirt with a big bristle brush. She was well aware that it was a queer old existence she had slipped into but there were many queer goings-on in Dublin and the eccentricities of one tenement in Endicott Street were nothing compared to what took place elsewhere.

Monday morning, about eleven: Maeve was at school and all the men were at work, all bar Mr O'Dowd who was a coal-heaver on permanent night shift. He was sound asleep, and snoring, in his room on the second floor.

Sean was seated in the middle of the room in his little baby-chair. Sylvie had purchased the chair at the Anglesea market, had scrubbed it thoroughly and dusted it with Lenger's powder before she had strapped Sean into it. Harry Houdini himself couldn't have escaped from the baby-chair's clutches but, scowling like a gargoyle, Sean persisted in trying to pick open the lock with his soft, inadequate fingers until frustration got the better of him and Sylvie had to appease him with milk or a biscuit.

Peaceful, almost serene it was in the tenement with just the swish of the scrubbing brush, Mr O'Dowd's snores, and Sean's contented mumbling. Then: voices in the hallway. Sylvie wondered if Pauline was at home. Most mornings Pauline took the youngest out shopping, trailing them up to the vegetable market or the wholesale butchers to buy an oxtail or a sheep head that, thickened with floury dumplings, made a grand big pot of stew.

Pauline was at home; Sylvie heard her cry of

alarm. She slipped the brush into the bucket and, on all fours, crept to the railing and peered down into the hallway. She could see little from that high angle, not Pauline or the men to whom Pauline was talking, only elongated shadows and the backside of a man in a long black overcoat. Mr O'Dowd had stopped snoring. Sean was staring at her, a wet fist stuffed into his mouth. Far away, the sound of a locomotive whistle drifted down from the Dublin loop.

Heart in her mouth, Sylvie leaned out over the rail.

'It's not a matter of whether you like it or not, Miss Rafferty,' Vaizey was saying, 'it's a matter of what has to be.'

'Fran's not here. He's the one you've got to talk to.'

Sylvie saw John James Flanagan turn and exchange a glance with Vaizey. They knew – they both knew – that Fran Hagarty would not be talking ever again. 'That, I'm afraid, isn't possible,' the inspector said.

'Fran – Fran'll be back soon.'

'Will he?' said Flanagan. 'Where, may I ask, is he coming back from?'

''Merica.'

'Merica?'

'She means the United States,' said Vaizey.

'It's just as well you speak their language.'

'I'm well practised. Now – America you say, Miss Rafferty?'

Some women reasoned with their hearts not their

heads and when it came to squaring up to men like Flanagan, let alone a slimy lickspittle like Vaizey, Pauline had no powers of resistance.

'Fran's visitin' 'Mer . . . A-merica.'

'Did he tell you that?'

'He – he did.'

'Did he indicate when he would return?'

Vaizey spoke in a jocular, almost teasing manner. Loathing flamed in Sylvie. Her cheeks grew hot. Anxiety turned to resentment, resentment to hatred. She had no idea if Vaizey knew that she had taken up residence in Fran's apartment, but sense told her to keep her head down.

'He – he'll be back soon,' said Pauline, shrilly.

'What if I were to tell you that Hagarty will not be returning to Dublin?'

'He will. He will.'

'What if I were to tell you that he, ah, intends to remain in America?'

'He won't.'

'What if I were to tell you, Miss Rafferty, that Hagarty is selling off his properties in Dublin and that this building has been purchased by Mr Flanagan.'

'Pur-chased?' said Pauline. 'What?'

'Bought,' John James Flanagan explained, indulgently.

'Transfer of ownership has been arranged,' said Vaizey. 'In the very near future you'll be obliged to pay your rent to Mr Flanagan's representative.'

'It's my house,' said Pauline. 'Fran's house. I don't pay rent.'

'The girl's clearly not up to it,' Flanagan said.

'Fran's comin' back. You're not sellin' his house.'

'I regret to inform you, Miss Rafferty,' said Vaizey, 'that Francis Hagarty is deceased.'

'Nah he's not. He's – he's . . .'

Sylvie craned over the railing and shouted, *'Fran's in America, Mr Vaizey. Where else would Fran be?'*

The men peered up at her, their features flattened and foreshortened.

'Who is that?' Flanagan called out.

'Oh, I know who it is,' said Vaizey. 'Show yourself, Mrs McCulloch.'

She glanced in at Sean, hesitated, then gathered up her damp skirts and hurried down the rattling staircase into the hall.

'Who are you?' Flanagan said. 'Do I know you?'

'You should,' said Sylvie. 'If you don't know me now you'll certainly know me next time, Mr Flanagan.'

'Gowry McCulloch's wife,' Vaizey said.

'Widow,' Sylvie said.

'Widow?' Vaizey said. 'Really now?'

'Really now,' said Sylvie. 'Didn't you know? I thought you knew everything.'

'When was he killed?'

'Last month.'

'I'm sorry to hear it.'

'Never mind all that,' said Flanagan. 'What the devil's *she* doing here?'

'I imagine she lives here,' said Vaizey. 'Am I correct?'

'You are,' Sylvie told him.

'Good God!' said Flanagan. 'More trouble.'

'Oh, yes indeed, Mr Flanagan,' Sylvie said, 'more trouble.'

She crossed the hall and joined Pauline in the doorway of the apartment. The small children within had been schooled in persecution and knew when to lie low. They would probably be hiding under the table, Sylvie thought, the elder hugging the younger. Pauline groped for Sylvie's hand.

'How long have you been resident here?' Vaizey asked.

'Since the Shamrock went up in smoke.'

'Both of you here together. How curious.'

'What's curious about it?' Sylvie said.

'All Hagarty's eggs in one basket,' Vaizey said.

'Waiting,' Sylvie said, 'for his return.'

'Oh, come now,' Vaizey said. 'You of all people know the score.'

'Do I?' said Sylvie. 'What is "the score" then, sir?'

'You can't stay here,' said Flanagan. 'I won't have McCulloch's wife in one of my houses.'

'You know that Hagarty isn't coming back,' Vaizey said.

'Is he not?' said Sylvie. 'Why is that?'

'Because he's – no longer with us.'

'You mean he's dead,' said Sylvie.

'Of course he's dead.'

'Then where's his body?'

Vaizey blinked.

'If Fran's dead, where's his grave?' Sylvie pressed. 'If he's dead, why did you tell my friend Miss Rafferty that he's selling his properties in Dublin?'

'He left debts,' said Flanagan, quickly.

'Debts? Really! And when did an officer of the Special Branch of the Metropolitan Police become a debt collector?'

'Oh, this is nonsense,' Flanagan said. 'Utter nonsense.'

'I trust you're not going to be spiteful, Mrs McCulloch?' Vaizey said.

'Spiteful? After what you put me through,' Sylvie said, 'what reason could I possibly have for being spiteful?' She took a pace forward. 'I suppose you might say you were just doing your job when you murdered Fran, but what sort of job is this, I wonder? Is it your job as a policeman to lie to poor widows and rob them of what's rightfully theirs?'

'Hagarty cheated me,' Flanagan said. 'Tell her, Harold. Tell these stupid women just how their hero came by his cash. He cheated everyone who trusted him. It wasn't his money that purchased this house. It was mine.'

'Yours,' said Sylvie, 'or his friends' in America?'

'What do you know about our American friends?'

'He stored guns here,' said Sylvie, 'so if Fran chose to put the funds he received from American sympathisers into property, I see no harm in that.'

'You're out of your depth, Sylvie.' It was the first

475

time Vaizey had used her Christian name. 'This house was used for the storage of arms. Consequently I can have a court order drawn up within a couple of days and have you and your friend and your children tipped out into the street.' He raised a finger. 'Don't tell me I can't, because you know dashed well I can.'

'Has the owner of the property no say in the matter?' said Sylvie.

'The owner of the property is dead.'

'The owner of the property is not dead,' Sylvie said. 'Francis Hagarty is alive and well and on business in America.'

At last she had ruffled Vaizey's implacable self-assurance.

'You won't get away with this,' he snapped.

'No,' said Sylvie. 'It's *you* who won't get away with it. What can you do to me now, Inspector? Drag me out into the yard and have one of your thugs shoot *me* in the head? No. Not now. Now there's law in Ireland. It might be military law, but it's law none the less. There are too many witnesses, too many folk to vouch for my innocence for you to get away with another murder. You'd have far too much explaining to do if the poor widow of a British soldier vanished from the face of the earth.' She stepped closer. 'I'm a British citizen, Inspector. I've proved my loyalty by sacrificing my husband. Let me ask you again, what can you possibly do to me that hasn't already been done?'

'Plenty,' Vaizey said.

He rubbed her skirt with his knee just as he'd done all those months ago in the nook in the Shamrock. Sylvie did not back away.

'Show me the body,' she said.

'Pardon?'

'Show me Fran's body. Take me to his grave.'

'I certainly will not.'

'Why not?'

'It's outwith my jurisdiction.'

'Of course it is,' said Sylvie.

'What's that supposed to mean?' said Vaizey.

'You can't show me Fran's body because he isn't dead.'

'Come now, you witnessed—'

'I witnessed nothing,' Sylvie said. 'The last I saw of Fran he was being bundled into a police wagon outside the Shamrock. If Fran's dead, it's up to you to prove it.'

'I could have you summoned, make you swear under oath—'

'That I saw an unarmed man murdered in cold blood?' said Sylvie. 'Are you so desperate to please your friend Flanagan that you'd risk a coroner's enquiry into the circumstances surrounding—'

'There are no circumstances,' Vaizey said. 'Hagarty was trying to escape.'

'So you shot him at close range in the side of the head?' said Sylvie. 'That isn't martial law, that's just plain murder.' She was aware of Pauline's presence behind her but would not back down, not even to

477

save Pauline's feelings. 'Where is his body? Have you buried it where it won't be found? Did you put it in quicklime – isn't that what you do with criminals, bury them in quicklime? – or did you have it dumped at sea?'

Vaizey grunted. 'I'm beginning to think I under-estimated you.'

'I know what you're doing: you're trying to obtain ownership of this tenement so that Mr Flanagan can add it to his other slum properties. Now either the owner of this property is dead and the property is part of the estate, or the owner of this property is on a visit to America and will return in due course. If he's dead then it's up to you to prove it. If he's not dead then you'll have to wait until he comes back before you can charge him and grab his property.'

'Is what she's saying true, Harold?' Flanagan asked.

'Not entirely.'

'Some of it, enough of it?'

'Yes,' Vaizey admitted. 'Some of it.'

'How long will *that* take?' Sylvie went on. 'Years, years waiting for Fran to come back to Dublin so he can be charged. And then,' she said, 'there will be his heirs to consider, their legal entitlements.'

'Heirs?' said Flanagan.

'He had sons to a wife in England,' said Vaizey. 'Three sons.'

'I wonder if his wife knows where Fran is?' said Sylvie. 'I wonder if he's gone to visit her perhaps.

You never can tell what Fran will do next, can you, Inspector?'

She waited for Vaizey to lay hands on her, bully her, but that wasn't his style. She sensed that she had him where she wanted him, at least for the time being. She wondered what hold Flanagan had over him, if it were simply a matter of money, of bribes, back-handers, and feathering the inspector's nest.

She had one more card up her sleeve, but would not play it just yet.

She said, 'Will you answer a question for me, Inspector Vaizey?'

'What question is that?'

'Don't tell her anything, Harold. Don't say a word,' Flanagan put in. 'It's a matter for the lawyers now.'

'Your question, Mrs McCulloch,' Vaizey said.

'If the owner of a property is alive, can the authorities take possession of the house – this house, our house – in his absence?'

'Not without a court order,' said Vaizey.

'How difficult would that be to obtain?'

'Not very,' Vaizey said, 'but since you and I both know that the owner is dead surely the point is moot.'

'Yes,' said Sylvie, smiling to herself. 'Of course, the point is moot.'

It was a fair old ride on the train from Wexford to the capital, but Breen Trotter didn't seem to mind.

Up he charged every Sunday forenoon. With a bunch of wild flowers in one fist and a parcel of Wexford bacon in the other, he headed straight from Harcourt Street station to Endicott Street to spend three or four hours with his honey, his enchantress, Miss Pauline Rafferty.

Breen had been in love several times before. He had pursued the daughter of a factory manager for several months before she'd sent him off with a flea in his ear. Next he'd courted the daughter of an auctioneer who'd refused to squander her youth and beauty on a cattle dealer's son and had threatened to summon the constables if he didn't stop loitering at her gate. Finally he had been smitten by the widow of a blacksmith who had been kicked in the head by a horse – the smith not the widow – undeterred by the fact that two of her seven children were older than he was. That awkward passion had remained unrequited too, for the object of his affection had been too stupid to realise what a fine catch Breen would make and had married her cousin instead.

Breen was well rehearsed in falling head over heels in love and it didn't take him much longer than half an hour to fall for Pauline whom he'd encountered in what he considered all her glory with stew pots bubbling on the stove, children clinging to her skirts and a lovely wee new babby nestling against her breast.

He was aware that at least one of Pauline's children

had been fathered by Turk's renegade friend Fran Hagarty, had heard all about Fran Hagarty from Turk. He regarded the man as a bit of a hero and was excited by the prospect of following in the great man's – ahem – footsteps and taking on the great man's – ahem – burden now that the great man was no more. The only problem was that Pauline seemed unwilling to admit that Fran was no more. She puckered her lips and frowned whenever Fran's name was mentioned, but otherwise she was as sweet as honey and made Breen welcome when he happened to drop by at Sunday dinner time.

By mid-summer she was flirting with him quite openly and trusted him enough to let him hold the baby while she served stew, sliced lumps off a flank of boiled mutton or dispensed the floury potatoes that had been slyly nudging each other in the pot for a half-hour before his arrival.

'He's infatugated with her,' Maeve said. 'What a clown!'

'Why do you say that?' Sylvie asked, surprised.

'He can do better than Pauline.'

'I thought you liked Pauline?'

'I do,' said Maeve. 'But . . .'

'But what?'

'Well for one thing, she has all those children.'

'I think Mr Trotter likes children.'

'Imagine comin' all the way up from Wexford just to see Pauline.'

Maeve was a good deal less cynical than she

pretended to be. She was probably a little jealous of the woman downstairs, Sylvie thought, for although she had received a letter – just one – from Turk in Stafford jail, she was dependent on Breen for up-to-date news and felt that Turk's brother should be giving her more of his attention.

'Would you not go all the way down to Wexford to see Turk?'

'That's different,' Maeve said, hotly.

'What's different about it?'

'I don't – I haven't had babies.'

'You're too young to have babies.'

'I am not.'

'Yes you are,' Sylvie insisted. 'Any man who gave you a baby would be arrested on the spot.'

'For what? Oh, for *that*. Really?'

'Really,' said Sylvie.

Maeve's precocity had its limits, it seemed, and she was quiet for a while after that, brooding on the mysteries of conception. Out in the street playing with Algie, Maeve was still a child. Indoors she demonstrated shrewdness and shyness in equal measure. What Maeve needed was a father, a strong man at the centre of her life, Sylvie thought, just as she needed a husband to protect her from her own cleverness.

When she saw Breen Trotter hastening up Endicott Street she was tinged by concern that one day she would be driven to take on a man like that. She wondered about the bachelors in the rooms round about, though, why they remained uninterested in getting to know her better. True, they were quiet men, wrapped up in earning a living and Fran had chosen them for their rectitude. Even so, when she came upon one of them on the stairs, she couldn't help but wonder why they didn't flirt with her.

On Sundays she sat on the bed with Sean at her breast, listening to Breen's booming laugh and longing for a man – not any man, not Fran, but Gowry. How odd that when she had been married to Gowry she had yearned for other men, but now that Gowry was dead she wanted him back. And at night, with Maeve asleep beside her, she would pinch her nose with thumb and finger and weep for the green times that were gone, for Gowry, Gowry and Fran, in a spiral of sorrow that seemed to have no end.

Sunday evening: Breen had gone loping off to the railway station to catch a train back to Wexford and Maeve had taken Sean out for a breath of air. Sylvie had prepared supper – a pork pie and cold potatoes – and was seated at the little table at the window, where Fran had so often sat. She had taken the hood from the typewriting machine and had it in mind to write another letter to the authorities asking for information about her husband, but she had lost the inclination to chase false hopes and when Pauline knocked on the door she was doing nothing more constructive than feeling sorry for herself.

For once Pauline did not have the baby stuck to her and her distant eyes had width and brightness. She slipped into the room and stood before Sylvie in a spotless white dress to which someone – Breen, of course – had pinned a little posy of wild flowers.

'He wants me to marry him.' Pauline pursed her lips, frowned, then laughed. 'Asked me to marry him. Just now. Downstairs. In front of everybody. Came right out. Said it. Got down on his knees. Gave me these flowers. Said he was in love with me. Said he'd take me away from here. Take me an' the kiddies to live with him an' his mammy an' pappy in Wexford.'

'Oh!'

'If that fellah comes again, that Mr Finnegan . . .'

'Flanagan,' said Sylvie.

'Him, an' the peeler. What a surprise, eh! I'm not here. I'm gone away to Wexford with Mr Trotter. He says he's in love with me.'

'If you marry Mr Trotter,' said Sylvie evenly, 'what will happen to this house and all the people in it?'

Pauline had obviously given no thought to that problem.

'They can stay here,' she said, airily.

'What happens when Fran gets back?'

'Fran's not comin' back, you said.'

'You didn't believe me, though, did you, Pauline?'

In spite of having borne a child, Pauline retained a virginal quality that Breen Trotter had obviously been unable to resist. He was Turk's brother and from what Sylvie had heard the Trotter boys were well known in Wexford for being wild, though Turk's father ran a profitable dealership in cattle, his mother was a good God-fearing Catholic woman, and, so far, Breen had given no indication that he was involved in rebel politics.

'What if I'm wrong?' Sylvie said. 'What if Fran does come back? How will he feel if he finds you've married someone else?'

'He'll know I done it for the kiddies.'

'I'll have Fran to myself then, won't I, Pauline?' Sylvie knew she was being unkind.

'You told me Fran was dead.' Pauline sank down on the bed. 'I never had a pappy before.' She shrugged apologetically. 'I want a pappy.'

'Yes,' Sylvie said. 'I've no doubt Mr Trotter will make a very good pappy once he gets used to the idea, but will Breen make you a good husband?'

'Algie likes cows.'

'All children like cows,' said Sylvie. 'Pauline, where did Fran find you?'

'Mammy was ill. Long time she was ill. Fran came with the priest one time. He took me out when Mammy went to heaven. I stayed with the nuns in Kingstown for a while. Then Fran came and took me away. Brought me here.'

'What age were you when he brought you here?'

Pauline shrugged.

'Did he – did Fran . . .' Sylvie said. 'Were you his wife then?'

'He had another wife then.'

'What was her name?'

'Maureen.'

'Was she kind to you?'

'Aye, she was. Kind to all of us.'

'Did Fran stay with you, with Maureen?' Sylvie said.

'Aye, when he wasn't visitin' 'Merica. He left Maureen money.'

'To look after you?'

Pauline nodded. 'Then Maureen went away. She tooked the money an' went away with Mr Weekes.'

'Did Mr Weekes live here too?'

'One down,' said Pauline, tapping the floorboards with her toe.

'What did Fran say when he got back from America? Was he angry?'

'Aye, he shouted.'

'At you?'

'Shouted at everybody. We all hid.'

'How many of you were there?'

Pauline held up one hand, fingers spread. 'Nine. When they growed up, he took them away.'

'Took them where?' said Sylvie.

'To A-merica. He had jobs for them.'

'What sort of jobs?'

'Just jobs. He paid their fares on the boat.'

'Did he take the girls too, or just boys?'

'Three girls: Margaret-Anne, Ellie, Nuala.'

'Do they ever write to you,' said Sylvie, 'from America, I mean?'

'They wrote to Fran.'

'I wonder,' Sylvie said, 'what he did with those letters.'

Pauline had already lost interest in the fate of the orphans.

'Mr Breen asked me to marry him,' she said.

'So you told me,' Sylvie said. 'Do you think you'd like to marry Breen Trotter? Do you think you'd be happy in Wexford?'

'He says he'd care for the children, even the baby.'

'How . . .' Sylvie hesitated. 'How can you marry Breen when you're already married to Fran?'

'I'll ask the priest,' said Pauline, nodding. 'He'll tell me what to do.'

'Pauline, dearest,' Sylvie said, 'why won't you believe me? Fran is dead. He has no claim on you now, no hold.'

Pauline offered no denial, made no protest. She stared past Sylvie at the patch of dusty blue sky that showed above the tenement roofs and the skeins of pink-tinted cloud entangled in the chimneypots.

'Do you know where Wexford is, Pauline?'

'No.'

'Were you frightened by the men who came here?' Sylvie said. 'Is that why you want to run off with Breen?'

'Algie likes horses too.'

'You don't have to be frightened,' Sylvie said. 'Really and truly you don't. Take my word for it, Vaizey can't harm you.'

'I never had a pappy,' said Pauline, wistfully. 'Breen says he loves me. Do you think it's true, Sylvie?'

'I think it might be,' Sylvie said. 'When does Breen expect an answer?'

'Next Sunday,' Pauline said.

'That doesn't give you much time to make up your mind.'

'No,' Pauline said. 'I think I'll have to ask Fran. Yes, that's what I'll do. I'll ask Fran.'

Sylvie felt the hair on the back of her neck rise.

'How, Pauline? How can you possibly ask Fran? Fran's dead.'

'Sure an' that doesn't matter,' Pauline said, eyes wide and shining. 'Madam Lomborosa knows where to find him.'

'Madam who?' said Sylvie.

Chapter Twenty-three

'The dead,' said Madam Lomborosa, 'are always with us. The ego, as I hope to demonstrate tonight, is no mere secretion of the nervous tissue as scientists would have us believe but a link to our loved ones in the spirit realm. Our loved ones' existence in the world beyond is personal and unbroken. They know what's happening to you even if you cannot comprehend what has happened to them.'

The woman reached for an ebony cigarette holder that rested against a green glass ashtray the size of a soup plate. She lifted the holder between finger and thumb and inhaled smoke from its amber mouthpiece. When she let her breath out smoke rose like ectoplasm into the circular lampshade that hung above the table. The corded tassels around the shade, Sylvie noted, oscillated as if the spirits of the dead were already there and chafing at the bit to get a word in edgeways.

Sylvie was not taken in. In spite of her fancy

handle and polished speech, Madam Lomborosa was no more Italian than she was. The woman was probably the daughter of a fishmonger from Bray or a publican from Galway who had rehearsed her act in the halls and who, with a hundred thousand war widows to exploit, had gone into the more lucrative business of personally consoling the bereaved. At the cost of two guineas for a private sitting, small wonder Madam Lomborosa could afford to live in a splendidly furnished apartment in Kearns Court and employ a servant to greet you at the door and show you into the drawing-room.

Resentment not anticipation made Sylvie tense. She wished she had heeded Maeve's words of warning. 'Rot!' Maeve had told her. 'It's all rot. If you go anywhere near that place with Pauline then you need your head seen to.'

For all her cynicism, a grain of longing lay deep in Sylvie's heart, longing not for reassurance, not to have the empty void filled by false hopes, but to see what Pauline had latched on to and to make sure that by some miraculous contrivance Fran wasn't still alive. Far, far down within her, below the level of conscious thought, there also lurked a faint hope that Pauline's naïvety might be infectious and that by accompanying Pauline to a séance a little of the young woman's optimism might rub off on her.

'Are we all here?' Madam Lomborosa pinched out her cigarette and detached it from the holder. 'Is this the lot of you?'

'It is,' said Pauline, reverently.

'Have you been in communication before?' Madam Lomborosa enquired.

'I have,' said Pauline. 'She ha'n't.'

The apartment was lit by electrical light but the bulb was dim and the room, even on a summer's evening, shadowy. The maidservant – tall as a guardsman and gaunt – had drawn heavy velvet curtains across the windows before she left the room. A coal fire burned in a marble fireplace and the atmosphere was stuffy. Sylvie dabbed little globules of perspiration from her brow with her handkerchief and carefully studied the woman who sat by her at the oval table.

Madam Lomborosa was about sixty, sallow-skinned, olive-eyed. Her hair was dyed jet black and worn in a style that Sylvie thought of as Parisian. She had small, tight-set ears, like an otter's. Her hands were freckled with liver spots, her fingers weighted with big silver rings and one plump ruby in a gold setting. She had a mobile little mouth and a delicate, dark moustache on her upper lip accentuated the movement of her lips. She wore a loose dress in a dark blue arabesque pattern fastened just below her breasts with a pale blue sash as broad as a cummerbund. The chair she occupied was well upholstered but tall and the firelight made a strange sort of wavering halo behind it.

The oval table was enormous and could, Sylvie reckoned, have accommodated fifteen or twenty diners in comfort. Pauline and she were huddled at one end close to the medium, and the collection of vacant chairs that ringed the shadowy surface to her right seemed as if they might already be occupied by guests unseen.

'I saw you down the Ockram Hall,' Pauline said. 'Been three times.'

'Ah, I thought I recognised you,' Madam Lomborosa said.

'You got a callin' from a man friend o' mine.'

'Did I? A soldier? Wait. I remember: a sad soul who died a violent death.'

'Is he here tonight?' said Pauline, looking round.

'That remains to be seen,' said Madam Lomborosa.

'Can you bring him down?'

'Patience, child, patience. This ain't – isn't an exact science, you know. It's one thing to mediate in a crowded hall when the anterooms are filled with clamour and many are waiting to come through but here – well, I'll do my best to contact your loved one, though I can't make no guarantees. There are laws governing the spiritual empire that we know nothing of.'

'What sort of laws?' Sylvie chimed in.

'Laws, like the laws of nature – a different sort of nature.'

'Why don't you ask them?' Sylvie said.

'Pardon?'

'About the laws. The spirits must know what the laws are. Why don't you ask the spirits?'

Madam Lomborosa was quiet for almost half a

minute, her expression not one of annoyance but of melancholy.

In the lull Sylvie could make out the grinding of tramcars in Grafton Street and the rattle of a van going by just under the window. She had forgotten that she was close to the heart of the city, the fashionable heart, and wondered if smoke, beer fumes and bustle in the poorer area round by the Ockram Hall might not be more appealing to ethereal travellers than this sober, almost sepulchral setting.

'Well,' Madam Lomborosa said, at length. 'I think we should begin, don't you? By the by, you do understand, ladies, that I cannot promise a materialisation. My powers are not at the beck and call of every random spirit and I am not attuned to everyone who waits in the anteroom. Besides, the person you wish to contact may not be with us this evening.'

'If that's the case,' said Sylvie, 'do we get our guinea back?'

'Oh dear! Dear, dear, deary me!' Madam Lomborosa sighed. 'Here, take my hand, will you please.' She lurched forward from the chair and grabbed Sylvie's left hand. 'Reach across the table and take your friend's hand so we make a ring, a circle, then we'll see what I can do for you. Right?'

'Right,' said Sylvie.

Obediently she stretched her arm across the polished surface, found Pauline's hand and clasped it tightly.

'Now,' Madam Lomborosa said, 'you mustn't be

alarmed at anything you hear or see. I'm not a trance medium. Do you know what I mean by that?'

'No,' said Sylvie.

'I do not go into a trance,' said Madam Lomborosa. 'I will be entirely conscious at all times.'

'Will you be doin' the voices, though?' Pauline asked.

'I will be a conduit for whoever might wish to communicate,' the medium said, 'a mouthpiece for anyone who wishes to speak. You won't be able to communicate with the spirit – the loved one – except through me and I would ask you not to cry or shout out. The spirits are remarkably sensitive and dreadful easy upset. If we are fortunate enough to witness a manifestation—'

'Is that like a ghost?' said Pauline.

'An appearance, an apparition,' the woman said. 'If we do happen to see something I implore you not to start up or break the circle. Do not let go my hand or attempt to reach out and touch the person.'

'Has anyone ever done that?' said Sylvie.

'Yes, on several occasions.'

'What happened?'

The medium's grip tightened, crushing her knuckles.

'You mustn't challenge them,' Madam Lomborosa said, crossly, 'nor must you challenge me. I'm not here for the good of my health, you know.' Then suddenly she stiffened, looked up and away to her right, up past the tassels of the lampshade into a corner of the room.

'*What?*' she said loudly. '*What?*'

In unison, Sylvie and Pauline repeated the medium's question.

'There's someone here,' said Madam Lomborosa. 'Yes. Speak.'

Pauline said, 'F–Fran, is it you?'

'Yes,' said Madam Lomborosa, speaking very rapidly. 'Yes yes, there is a presence with us tonight, a determined presence, I feel him tugging at my throat, I feel him within my mouth, I hear the voice, a strong voice, a man's voice, an Irish voice, I hear his utterances, he is love, he is not angry, he is love, he is here with us, he is crowding out . . . *Oh! Oh my!*'

She jerked her arms from the table, carrying Pauline's hand and Sylvie's with her until their arms seemed to take on a life of their own, to become as boneless as garden hoses, slapping about.

'Jaysus! Oh, Jaysus save us,' Pauline said in a barely audible whisper. 'Is it Fran? Is it Fran come down on us again?'

If it was Fran then he had learned a thing or two in the great hereafter for Madam Lomborosa suddenly burst into a chorus of 'The Soldier's Song' in a deep bass voice, a voice so hollow that it seemed to come from below her navel.

She sang a snatch of the verse as well as a chorus and then, with a chuckle that turned into a high childish giggle, said, 'What a naughty boy you are, whatter naughty, naughty boy.'

'Is that my Fran?' said Pauline.

'No.'

'Who is it then?'

'Ronnie.'

'Ronnie? I don't know nobody called Ronnie.'

'Ronnie's a bad boy. Ronnie's a naughty boy.'

Sylvie was unaccountably afraid. She knew full well it was a trick, a performance, but she was drawn in spite of herself. Ronnie! There was no Ronnie in her life and, as far as she knew, no one of that name in Pauline's.

'He won't let Gowry through, the naughty, naughty boy.'

'What?' said Sylvie. 'Who did you say was . . .'

'Gowry-powry, Gowry-wowry, Gowry . . . *Oh my, my!*'

'Gowry?' said Sylvie, under her breath. 'Is Gowry here?'

'Hmmm.' Madam Lomborosa nodded. 'Hmmm.'

'It's your man, Sylvie.' Pauline straightened and squinted up at the ceiling. 'Speak to us, Gowry. Speak to us.'

'For God's sake,' said Madam Lomborosa, 'will you leave it to me.'

'How did you know about Gowry?' Sylvie said.

'He . . . he . . . he . . . is . . . here,' said Madam Lomborosa.

And he was.

Rising up from behind the medium's chair was a tall gaunt figure clad in a soldier's tattered uniform, the face swathed in dirty bandages, one visible eye glazed like that of a fish. The fire blazed up behind the apparition, creating an aura about him, a bleary, almost blinding aura that Sylvie could not quite penetrate. She swallowed, and said, 'Gowry? Is that you?'

'Yes. It is me.'

'Are you dead?'

'Yes.'

'I mean, *are* you dead?'

'I am happy, happy. Do not shed tears for me, my love.'

The voice came from Madam Lomborosa not the figure behind the chair but at that moment it seemed that Gowry was speaking to her from beyond the grave. 'Wh–where are you?'

'At peace. At peace. I am happy. Everybody here is happy.'

'Where's your bod— I mean, where were you – where do you lie?'

'In the mud of Flanders. I am happy now, my love. I must go, must go.'

'Gowry, are you really, really dead?'

'I am spirit now, spirit pure and unalloyed.'

'Wait,' Sylvie called out as the figure sank down and, in another flash of firelight, vanished behind the medium's chair. 'For God's sake, wait.'

Madam Lomborosa gripped her hand like a vice.

Sylvie rose then fell back as the little giggling voice came pouring out of the medium's mouth once more, 'Gowry-powry, Gowry-wowry, Gowry-towry. *Bang!*' Sylvie and Pauline jumped. '*Bang. Boom*.

Bang.' Then Madam Lomborosa, in her normal, clipped, Anglified voice, was saying, 'It's the guns. The guns trouble the child. Do you hear the guns? Ah, the guns are everywhere, even beyond. Was that your husband?'

'Yes,' Sylvie confessed in a tiny, chastened voice.

'He loves you, see, he still loves you.'

'Can't you bring him back?'

'No, he's gone. Gone for tonight at any rate.'

'What about Fran?' said Pauline. 'Can you do Fran now, please?'

'Fran isn't with us.'

'Ask Ronnie about Fran?'

'We're not running a blessed telephone exchange,' Madam Lomborosa snapped; then with more control, said, 'We've been terribly privileged tonight. It ain't – isn't every sitting I receive a visitation. Materialisation takes a lot out of them, you see. He must have loved you very much, Mrs McCulloch, to wait so long and make so much effort . . .'

'Try again,' said Pauline. 'Try again for Fran.'

Madam Lomborosa sighed. 'I'm sorry, my dear, but the room is absolutely empty. Perhaps next time we'll be more successful with Flan.'

'Fran. You got him down before, in the Ockram Hall.'

'And I'm sure we'll get him down again,' said Madam Lomborosa. 'But all my spiritual energies are drained and my powers depleted for this evening.'

She released Sylvie's hand then Pauline's and sat

back in the tall, well-upholstered chair. She laid her small, ring-laden hands on the arms of the chair, and closed her eyes.

After a moment's delay the door of the dining-room opened, the maidservant duly appeared and obsequiously enquired if everything was all right.

'Yes, Maddy, thank you,' the medium answered.

'Was there an appearance, Madam?'

'There was.'

'I can see it took a lot out of you.'

'It did.'

'A sad occasion?'

'Sad, so sad – but joyful too,' said Madam Lomborosa.

Then with a little nod, she indicated to Maddy that the ladies – one of them in tears – had had their money's worth and should quietly be ushered out before the next batch of grieving widows arrived for the nine o'clock show.

They sheltered in a shop doorway, waiting for a tramcar to appear over the brow of the hill. It wasn't dark yet but mist lay low on the hills, the sea was veiled by rain and even for a wet Monday in mid-summer, the city was uncommonly quiet.

Although Sylvie had recovered her composure soon after they'd left Madam Lomborosa's, she still clung to Pauline's arm.

'What did you tell that woman, Pauline?'

'Tell her?'

'About me.'

'Nothin'.'

'She knew my name. Did you tell her my name?'

Pauline squinched up her face, concentrating hard.

'Nup,' she said.

'When you made the appointment perhaps?'

'Made the 'pointment at the Ockram Halls, with the big woman.'

'I see,' said Sylvie.

'Don't you think it was Gowry?'

'I don't know.'

'Did it look like him?'

'It might have.'

'I think it was him. It wasn't Fran.'

'No,' Sylvie said, 'I could see it wasn't Fran. She knew Gowry's name.'

'Aye, an' she knew he was a soldier.'

'One soldier looks much like another,' said Sylvie. 'The bandage covering his face was very handy, wasn't it? Still, I admit it gave me a shock to see him. How did Fran materialise at the Ockram?'

'He didn't materialise. He just spoke.'

'What did he say?'

'Said he loved me. Said it was grand on the other side, a very happy land.'

'Did he ask about Turk or Charlie, or the children?'

'Nup.'

'Did he ask for you by name?'

Pauline, discomfited, leaned forward and peered up the street.

'I wish this tramcar would hurry up,' she said.

Maeve had been left in charge of the children. If the night had been fine they would still be playing in the street but in this sort of weather they would be running about the hallway and fetching up to all kinds of mischief.

'I wonder,' Sylvie said, 'if it's been in the news-papers.'

'What?'

'Notice of Gowry's death.'

'I thought he was only missin'?' said Pauline. 'Oh, I see what you mean. If he's a ghost, he must've passed on. Is that why you were cryin'?'

'It caught me by surprise, that's all.'

'Done that to me at the Ockram, first time.'

'Why didn't you tell me you were attending spiritualist meetings?'

'I thought you'd just laugh.'

Pauline was calm tonight, rational; halting speech, blank gaze – there were no signs of mental disarrangement. She seemed to accept at face value the existence of the dead and the surety of an afterlife. Sylvie was less certain. There was something too clumsy about Gowry's appearance in the medium's drawing-room, something too convenient to be wholly convincing.

Once she was out in Grafton Street, she realised that Gowry had said nothing personal. He hadn't even uttered her name; 'Ronnie' had come between them, Ronnie and a chorus of 'The Soldier's Song' sung in a deep, lyrical voice far removed from Gowry's tuneless tenor, and that there had been no spiritual rhetoric or oracular pronouncements.

Even so she felt curiously light, as if a weight had been removed from her shoulders. She was more mystified by the manner in which the trick had been done than comforted by its relevance; yet there were elements that she'd missed, clues concerning not Gowry but Fran. She couldn't be rid of Fran, it seemed; Fran and Gowry, Gowry and Fran entwined together, ghosts who would haunt her for the rest of her days.

'Here's the tramcar,' Pauline said. 'I'll be glad to see home.'

'You're not the only one,' said Sylvie.

Endicott Street was almost deserted. Lights burned in McKinstry's but the pavement was devoid of the usual loungers and there wasn't a kiddie to be seen between the lane and the canal. Some tenement windows were lit, little postage stamps of colour in a grey rain-washed landscape. There were no lights in Fran's building, however, and when Sylvie and Pauline entered the hallway they found it empty, the door to the ground-floor apartment firmly closed.

Sylvie glanced upstairs.

Gas-mantles hissed blue and yellow but there was more shadow than light on the landings.

Pauline rattled the door handle.

'Algie, Algie, what're you doin' in there?'

'Who is it?' Maeve asked from behind the bolted door.

'It's us,' said Sylvie. 'Who did you think it would be?'

The door opened a half-inch. Maeve's pale face peeped out at them.

Sean was in her arms, kicking and grizzling. Backing his friend, Algie brandished an old chair leg in lieu of a weapon. You could smell the room, not dank but fetid, feel the heat of the fire, taste coal smoke in your throat and hear the younger children whimpering within.

Sylvie said, 'Maeve, what is it? What's wrong?'

Maeve hissed, 'The peeler's waitin' for you, Mam.'

'Which peeler? Vaizey, with the moustache?'

'Yes,' Maeve answered. 'He came about a half-hour ago.'

'Did he frighten you?'

'Yes,' Maeve confessed.

'Open the door, open the door,' Pauline cried. 'By Jaysus, if he's touched one hair on your heads, I'll kill the soddin' bastard, so I will.'

Maeve stood back and Pauline rushed into the room.

Sylvie did not follow. She knew that Vaizey

wouldn't harm Pauline's children, that he had come here not to wreak vengeance but to negotiate.

'He told us to keep out the way,' Maeve said. 'Is it a raid, Mam? Are they still lookin' for Fran's guns?'

'No,' Sylvie said. 'Where is Vaizey? Is he upstairs?'

'I think so.'

'Did you tell him where Pauline and I had gone?' said Sylvie.

'I told him nothin',' Maeve said.

Algie, braver now, repeated, 'Nothin'.'

'Stay inside,' Sylvie said. 'Stay with Pauline and keep the door closed.'

'What're you goin' to do, Mam?'

'Settle this thing,' said Sylvie, 'once and for bloody all.'

She took off her wet overcoat and hat on the landing and held them on her arm. She was more nervous than afraid. She knew what Vaizey wanted and what she was prepared to give. She pushed open the door and stepped into the room.

Vaizey was seated on the end of Fran's bed – her bed – hat in one hand, a cigarette in the other. He had lighted the candle on the whatnot and most likely he had rifled through the papers in the drawers and poked about among the clothing in the cupboard. The fire was still smouldering in the grate and the room was stiflingly hot.

'Still raining?' he asked.

'Worse than ever,' Sylvie answered.

She hung her coat behind the door and placed her hat on the little table by the typewriter. There were three cigarette stubs in the ashtray and thin fronds of tobacco smoke clung to the windowpane.

'There's a front moving in,' Vaizey said. 'We'll be in for a wet spell, I fear. Are you soaked?'

'Just damp.'

'Dry yourself,' he said. 'Don't mind me.'

'I do mind you,' Sylvie said. 'What are you doing here?'

He shrugged.

'I take it this isn't a social visit?' Sylvie said.

'Call it what you like,' Vaizey said. 'Did I scare the kiddies?'

'Yes.'

'I didn't mean to.'

He rotated the hat, round and round, then lifted the cigarette to his lips and inhaled while Sylvie pulled a towel from the rack above the tin bath and, with her back to the window, began to dry her hair.

'I could do that for you,' Vaizey said.

She knew he was going to say it and it didn't jar. The offer reminded her of Fran, of what Fran had said and what Fran had done to her right here in this room all those months ago. She dabbed the towel to her throat, unfastened the hook at the collar of her blouse and dabbed the towel across the top of her breasts. She still had milk, would have milk for ages yet.

'I think I can manage,' she said.

He placed his hat on the quilt, reached for the candleholder and ground out his cigarette on the rim. He returned to his original position, knees apart, and hands – idle now – cupped on his thighs.

Sylvie rubbed her hair with the towel. She knew he was watching her, eyeing the shape of her under the blouse, under the skirt. She was still thick about the middle and her legs had fattened since Sean had been born. She had thought little enough of it. Sean was Fran's child and if Fran hadn't much liked how pregnancy had changed her then Fran had just had to lump it. But Vaizey's scrutiny made her aware that she was no longer lithe and attractive. She felt only contempt for the man for desiring her.

'Where were you, you and the girl?'

'What business is it of yours?'

'I'm just making conversation,' Vaizey said.

'We went to a séance.'

'Did you now? Where?'

'At Madam Lomborosa's house.'

'That old charlatan,' Vaizey said. 'Who did she have on show tonight, the Indian in feathers and war-paint, or the African witch-doctor?'

'Neither,' Sylvie said.

'They're all just the other woman, Amanda Crowe. She used to be a male impersonator on the variety stage until they teamed up together. They're Sapphos, you know.'

'Are they indeed?' said Sylvie.

'Don't you know what that means?'

'Female poets?' said Sylvie.

Vaizey laughed, a soft purr in the throat. 'I've always been curious as to what Sapphos do, how they achieve — satisfaction?'

'I have no idea,' said Sylvie. 'My posh school education didn't stretch quite that far.'

'Did Hagarty put in an appearance?'

'Alas, no.'

'It's probably just as well,' said Vaizey.

'Why do you say that?'

When he stood up she did not jump back. He did not have to stoop to kiss her. He did it tentatively, shyly, like a young boy with a first sweetheart. He touched her only with his lips, the moustache feathery against her cheek, then, to Sylvie's surprise, he sat down again.

'I'm not up for this,' Vaizey said. 'I thought I would be, but I'm not.'

'Would you prefer me to resist?'

'I'd prefer you to button your blouse.'

'Oh!'

'And sit somewhere else. Over there by the window.'

'By all means,' Sylvie said.

'Flanagan wants his money,' the inspector said.

'His money? What money?'

'You don't know what I'm talking about, do you?'

'No,' said Sylvie. 'And that's the truth.'

507

'I don't doubt it,' Vaizey said. 'Your friend Hagarty was never one for letting the right hand know what the left was doing. He was going to leave you, Sylvie, leave you and the girl, and the wife and the other family . . .'

'Other family?'

'He has yet another family in Cork.'

'I find that hard to believe.'

'Two sons to a priest's housekeeper.'

'How did he find time for all of them?'

'I wish I knew,' said Vaizey.

'You didn't shoot him on moral grounds, did you?'

'No. Hagarty was no innocent bystander like some of the others who went to the wall,' Vaizey said. 'He was a money source for the brotherhoods and linked to a network of spies and gunrunners. He refused to trade with the Germans, I will say that for him. He dealt with us instead, with the British. He bought guns and ammunition from sources in England.'

'How do you know so much about Fran?'

'We had a very well-placed informer.'

Sylvie could feel the coldness of the window glass against the back of her neck. The secrets that Vaizey dealt in were not the same as her secrets. She understood now why he had refused to press his advantage over her.

'John James Flanagan?' she said.

Vaizey did not answer.

Sylvie said, 'If Flanagan's your informer why

didn't you arrest Fran long ago? Why did you have to shoot him? No, wait, I think I understand. You're protecting Flanagan. You have to protect an informer as important and well placed as John James just to keep him out of the limelight. The only way you could be sure of doing that was to be rid of Fran once and for all?'

'Hagarty wasn't the charming fellow you took him to be.'

'Did he believe in what he was doing?'

Vaizey sighed. 'Perhaps. Probably. In the beginning.'

'Why are you telling me all this now?'

'Because Flanagan wants the house, this house. He feels he's entitled to it and, I admit, I tend to agree with him.'

'Of course you do,' said Sylvie. 'When he whistles, you dance.'

'That's harsh.'

'Harsh, is it?' Sylvie said. 'It'll be harsher still when your bully-boys arrive to evict us. How are you going to explain that to your superiors?'

'My superiors won't be involved. Hagarty was in partnership with Flanagan in the ownership of property. Hagarty's American sponsors insisted on it and Flanagan had no option but to comply. We knew that the houses were used as arms dumps, of course, but the guns were harmless provided they weren't distributed.'

'Is that why Fran came to the Shamrock?'

'Part of the reason.'

'And the other part?'

'He needed somewhere safe that Flanagan didn't know about. I don't think he entirely trusted John James by that time.'

'He didn't bargain on meeting my husband, though?'

'No, and he didn't bargain on meeting you.'

'Me?'

'Hagarty saw no harm in mixing business with pleasure.'

'Unlike you?'

'Yes,' said Vaizey, with another little sigh, 'unlike me.'

'I was more than a fling to him,' Sylvie said. 'I gave him a son.'

'Hagarty had children everywhere.'

'What do you want from me?'

'I came to give you warning. I don't care what you think of me, really. I'm used to being disliked. But there are children downstairs and you have a baby and you aren't to blame for what happened.'

'Am I supposed to grovel and say thank you?'

'You can't stay here, Sylvie, none of you.'

'Can we not?'

She leaned on the edge of the table. She could feel the typewriting machine behind her, the hood pressing against her buttocks. The machine was a symbol of all that Fran had stood for. From it had poured articles and reports, lies, half-truths and prevarications, all the perceptive warnings that he had thrown before the Irish people and to which they had turned deaf ears.

'I've persuaded Flanagan to find a place for you, to give you and the girl a room in a building in the Liberties. Your widow's pension will tide you over and in time – though I don't know when – you may get some money from the compensation board.'

'Flanagan doesn't have a partnership document, does he, Inspector?'

'Flanagan doesn't need a partnership document, not with Hagarty gone.'

'You've come here tonight to make sure I don't have it either.'

'It doesn't matter whether you do or not . . .'

'Well,' Sylvie said, 'I do.'

'Pardon?'

'I do have your precious document,' she said.

'Where is it?'

'Hidden away safely. You don't think I'd leave it lying around, do you?' Sylvie said. 'However, the existence of a partnership agreement will only become an issue if Fran's dead.'

'You're not going to start that again, are you?' Vaizey said.

'I know he's dead and you know he's dead, but his wife – his legal wife in Huddersfield – doesn't and she might want a share of the proceeds of his estate. I imagine it wasn't your intention to inform her of Fran's death. After all, from what I gather Fran hadn't been in communication with her for years.

She'll assume he's decamped to America and taken his cash with him and that she isn't going to see a penny of it. He has brothers, and a mother still alive, though I don't know where they are.'

'Galway,' said Vaizey. 'They want nothing to do with it. As far as they're concerned dear Francis has been dead for years.'

'Because he was a black sheep, a renegade republican?'

'Yes,' said Vaizey. 'Now, where's this document?'

'With a lawyer.'

'What are you telling me?'

'I placed it in safe-keeping with a lawyer,' Sylvie said.

'What's the lawyer's name?'

'Now that would be telling.'

He came at her suddenly, plunging across the room from the bed. His reaction took her by surprise. He clasped both hands around her waist, lifted her and held her, struggling just a little, above him.

'Do you know what I could do to you?' Vaizey said.

'I know what you'd like to do to me,' Sylvie said.

'I could make you vanish,' Vaizey told her. 'I could make you disappear. And what would your daughter do then? Who would take care of your son? That girl downstairs? She can barely take care of herself.'

'You're hurting me.'

'I'll hurt you a blessed sight more if you don't tell me . . .' He lowered her, but did not release her. He leaned into her, pressing and aroused. 'How did you come by the document? Did Hagarty give it you?'

She lied without a blush. 'Yes.'

She was not about to blacken Fran's name further by telling the peeler that she had found the deed and its codicils in a box in the cellar. It galled her to think that Fran had been as careless in handling property as he had been with his women. She would not acknowledge the failing, though, no matter what Vaizey did to her.

'When?' Vaizey said.

'Three days before Easter.'

'Why, why did he give it to you of all people?'

'I think he trusted me.'

'Oh, you're a smart piece of work, Sylvie McCulloch, perhaps a bit too smart for your own good. Oh, I could . . .'

'What? Kiss me again?'

'Smack you,' said Vaizey

'It would do you no good,' Sylvie said.

'Flanagan has to have that document, you know.'

'So he can destroy it?'

'Yes.'

'It's too late.' Sylvie broke his hold on her. 'I've read it. Now here's a wee surprise for you, Inspector, and for your friend the informer: Fran gave away his half-share in the partnership, signed it away on

513

a witnessed document attached to the property deeds and the partnership agreement.'

'Signed his share to whom – to you?'

'Oh no, not me,' said Sylvie. 'Fran might have been trusting but he wasn't stupid. He left his share to the Catholic Church. Your friend Flanagan is therefore in partnership with His Holiness the Pope, or his Dublin representative. If he wishes to challenge the validity of the documents then I reckon he'd better employ a very sharp team of lawyers.'

'You're making this up?'

'I'm not,' said Sylvie. 'I might just be a heathen Protestant but I feel a whole lot better being under the wing of the Catholic Church right now.'

'I – Flanagan – we'll need to see these documents.'

'Of course,' said Sylvie. 'I'll have the lawyer deliver notarised copies within the week; unless you wish me to put you in touch with the archbishop who, I imagine, will be dealing with the matter personally.'

'Send them to Flanagan,' the inspector said.

'Not to General Sir John Maxwell?'

Vaizey let out his breath in a whistling sigh, then, not entirely to Sylvie's surprise, laughed. 'By God, you *are* a smart one. When did you waken up, Sylvie McCulloch? Tell me, just when *did* you waken up?'

'The day you murdered Fran,' Sylvie said and, stepping past him, lifted his hat from the bed. 'Does that answer your question, Inspector Vaizey? Does that answer all your questions?'

'It does. Alas, it does,' the inspector said, and, with a little shrug of resignation, gave up his pursuit of justice.

The babies were asleep. They lay side by side across Pauline's cot, a light blanket drawn over them. Maeve was seated at the table nursing a cup of tea and scanning a copy of the *Mirror*. Algie stood by her side, the chair leg still clenched in his fist like a cudgel. Pauline knelt by the mattress in the corner, soothing the children's fears and feeding them, each in turn, one pink fondant cream to bring sweet dreams.

'What did the bastard want?' Maeve asked. 'What did he have to say?'

'Are – do we . . . ?' Pauline began. 'Turned out?'

'No,' said Sylvie. 'What the inspector wanted, he didn't get. It's settled, or nearly so. Now, Pauline, I need you to give me the name of the priest.'

'Priest?'

'The priest Fran worked with, the priest who brought you out of the nuns' house? Do you know who he is and where I can find him?'

'A priest?' Maeve said. 'For God's sake, Mam, what next?'

'Pauline?'

'Father Macken. His name's Father Macken.'

'And his parish?' Sylvie said.

'I can take you there now, if you like,' said Pauline.

'Not now,' said Sylvie. 'Tomorrow will do. Tomorrow, first thing.'

In darkness you would have walked past the little church in Maul Street with never a second glance. Stunted trees shrouded the front and the brickworks at the rear crowded so close that it was difficult to tell where the brickworks ended and the church began. Hard times had fallen on the parish when thorough-fares that had once swarmed with well-to-do Catholic merchants had ceased to be residential. Clerical staff had been reduced to two curates and one parish priest, Father Cornelius Macken, who was known to all and sundry as Father Mack.

Some folk thought him an interfering old goat, others considered him a saviour, still others – a shifty handful – believed him to be the mastermind behind the schemes that delivered charity to the indigenously disreputable.

The tumbledown church was the key to the good father's success as a scrounger. With no well-heeled toffs to tap for charitable contributions, he had been forced to find other means of raising the wind, ways that were a shade less than orthodox and that wouldn't please the archbishop if that august gentleman ever found out about them. The archbishop was rather less

dim than Father Macken believed him to be, however, and on more than one occasion had discreetly
covered little Father Macken's hindquarters without
Father Mack being aware of it.

It wasn't the fact that Father Mack was so adept at
fund-raising that gave the Church authorities sleepless
nights, but the fact that after ten years of fund-raising
not one dollop of plaster or one lick of paint had found
its way on to the church walls. All the cash that the
father had raised for improvements was spent instead
on the poor, the needy and the absolutely dissolute; a
rabble of souls who lay beyond the reach of the broad
arms of the Church's own societies, a rabble of souls
whose politics did not bear too close an inspection.

'Well now,' said Father Mack, 'if it isn't the lovely
lady Pauline come to pay us a visit. And who's this
you've brought with you?'

'My name's McCulloch,' Sylvie said.

The father gave a little bow and offered his
hand.

The elbows of his jacket were threadbare, his shirt
cuffs frayed. He smelled not of alcohol but of beef tea,
and cracker crumbs were sprinkled on his vest. His
eyes were the soft grey colour of rain on the streets.
He was small in stature but had a large head, the brow
domed and shiny as porcelain. His hand encompassed
Sylvie's completely.

'I'm pleased to make your acquaintance, Mrs
McCulloch. I know who you are, of course, since
Fran – our mutual friend – used to talk of you.'

'Not disparagingly, I hope?' said Sylvie.

'Oh, no, indeed not. He was never disparaging about his ladies.'

'He kept his spleen for the British, I suppose.'

'He did now, he did.'

'I take it, Father, that you know Fran is deceased.'

'I heard that thing, yes.'

'May I ask who brought you the news?'

'A friend of mine, a fellow-cleric,' Father Mack answered. 'He was summoned by an officer in the Crime Branch to administer last rites, though I'm told poor Fran had departed before he got there. My friend also presided at the burial.'

'So there was a burial?' said Sylvie.

She glanced at Pauline who had obviously reached an accommodation with Fran's death, aided, no doubt, by Breen Trotter's proposal of marriage.

Even at ten o'clock in the morning it was dark in the chapel, for the narrow windows admitted very little light. Sylvie felt uncomfortable in the presence of the crucifix that hung above the gnarled little altar. She was wary of the trap-like confession box and the statue of the Virgin with a bowl of holy water at her feet. They were seated on a bench under the altar, knee to knee with the priest. He patted Sylvie's hand, then Pauline's.

'Have they not told you where Fran lies?'

'No, Father, they haven't,' Pauline said.

'They dumped him in a grave in the yard at the rear of the old debtors' prison. Consecrated ground to be sure, but neglected. It does for those who die in custody, the nameless, unloved souls who pass away in prison and who the British don't know what to be doing with.'

'Is there a stone?' said Sylvie.

'No, no stone.'

'He should have a stone,' Pauline said. 'Fran should have a stone.'

'Fran should have a monument,' Father Mack said, 'a monument at the top of O'Connell Street just to remind the good folk of Dublin that there are more ways to be a martyr than are dreamed of in their philosophy. Is it for news of Fran you've come to me?'

'Not exactly,' Sylvie said, 'though I'm glad to hear he had a Christian burial, even if it was in a dismal and deserted place.'

'God did not desert him, be sure of that.'

'Fran did not desert you either, Father Macken,' Sylvie said.

She unbuttoned the top of her overcoat and took out the papers she'd unearthed from the box from the cellar. She handed them to the priest.

'What's this?' He patted his pockets, found a pair of spectacles with bent frames and fitted them to his nose. 'Is this a will? Sure an' you're not telling me our Francis was thoughtful enough to leave a will?'

'It isn't a will, Father,' Sylvie said. 'As you'll see from the codicils, though, you are now the proud owner of half a tenement in Endicott Street.'

'He can't do that,' said the father, peering at the paper. 'He can't leave me a tenement. I mean, what am I going to do with a tenement?'

'Half a tenement,' said Pauline.

'Half a tenement.' Father Mack glanced up. 'Who owns the other half?'

'John James Flanagan.'

'That rogue!' Father Mack said. 'I see it now. It's the bargain Fran struck with Flanagan come back to haunt us, is it? Oh, now, yes, I knew about it, of course I did. I warned Fran against doing business with Flanagan, but Fran went on his headstrong way. Expedient, he called it. Everything with Fran was always a matter of expediency.'

'Our home,' said Pauline. 'Flanagan wants to throw us out.'

'He has Special Branch behind him,' said Sylvie. 'One officer at least.'

'Vaizey?'

'Yes,' Sylvie said, and went on to explain what she had learned of the twisted relationship between the police officer and the businessman.

Father Mack listened attentively. He put the papers on the bench beside him and when Sylvie had finished speaking, took her hand again. 'Where did you find these documents?'

'In a box of letters and other rubbish in the cellar,' Sylvie answered. 'It was just good luck that we stumbled on them.'

'Fran didn't think he was ever going to die,'

said Father Mack. 'That's why he was so careless. If he'd thought for a moment that he wouldn't be dwelling somewhere in the world, he'd have given the documents into safe-keeping, to a lawyer, say, or . . .'

'Or to you.'

'Huh!' the priest said. 'Flanagan and old Father Mack, eh! What a strange partnership that is. There's a bit of wit in what Fran has done. I can't take share in ownership of a tenement, of course. I'll have to be handing the papers over to the archbishop for the benefit of the Church.'

'You could sell it to Flanagan and nobody would be any the wiser.'

'He would rook me, that villain.'

'I think it would take a sharp man to rook you, Father Macken.'

The priest laughed. 'I'll be taking that as a compliment, Mrs McCulloch. However, the fact remains that drawing rent from a tenement is not allowed. It will become Church property and it'll be up to the archbishop's financial advisers to decide what to do with it.'

'Throw us out?' said Pauline. 'If it's throwin' us out they'll be doin' then I'll be marryin' Mr Trotter.'

'Turk Trotter?' said the priest. 'I thought he was in prison in England.'

'She means his brother,' Sylvie said. 'Breen. From Wexford.'

521

'Is this a match made in heaven?' the father asked, quite seriously.

'It's a match made in Endicott Street,' said Pauline. 'He asked me sudden. I hardly know the fellah but he says he loves me an' he'll take the kiddies too, all o' them. There's no hope for them now, with Fran gone.'

'Of course there's hope for them.'

'Not in A-merica,' said Pauline, glumly.

'I don't understand,' Sylvie said. 'Why did Fran take these children in? Are there no organisations to care for orphans like – well, like Pauline?'

'He had a soul, had our friend Hagarty, a soul and a conscience. He had more money pouring in from supporters in America than he knew what to do with. You're not Irish-born, Mrs McCulloch, are you?'

'I'm a Scot, from Glasgow.'

'Ah, you see,' Father Mack said, 'that's why you don't understand. We are divided, we Irish, collectively and individually. We have our passions, our pride, our own songs to sing, but unfortunately we're more caring than cared for. Our consciences have been fed by a deep knowledge of suffering, and that knowledge makes us what we are.'

'You helped him, didn't you?' Sylvie said.

'For my sins, lass, I did.'

'Where do the children go?'

'To America, of course,' said Father Mack. 'Into decent lodgings in Irish houses, to jobs in Irish-run factories, into Catholic service a few of them, to college as well, to enjoy a better life than we can offer under foreign rule.'

'And they in turn . . .' Sylvie did not complete the question.

'Support us here at home, if and when they can.'

'It's not over, is it?' Sylvie said. 'You won't let it end.'

'No, we won't.' Father Mack lifted the documents, folded them carefully and slipped them into his inner pocket. 'Our history has changed direction, though, and it will change again and again until there's nothing much left for you or me to recognise, only memories of men like Francis Hagarty.'

'What happens now?' said Sylvie.

'I'll be having a quiet word with Mr Flanagan, just him and me, and then we'll see, we'll see. Be sure, though, that you're safe where you are for a long time to come, both you and your kiddies.'

'Fran saw to that, so he did,' said Pauline. 'Him, I know it.'

Father Mack rose from the bench and put his hand on the young woman's shoulder. 'You've grown up well, Pauline. Are the babies healthy?'

'Aye, Father, they are.'

'Algie too?'

'Full of fight, he is,' Pauline said. 'He'll be a soldier some day.'

'I'm glad to hear it,' Father Mack said.

'Algie won't be goin' to A-merica, will he?'

'No.' The father smiled. 'I think we might have more need of him here.'

'An' me?'

'Is Breen Trotter an honest man?'

'Aye, Father. He says he loves me,' Pauline said. 'He's got a pappy.'

'Well, there you are, lass,' Father Mack said. 'A nice young man from Wexford with a pappy at home and a brother in jail; what more could you want?' He gave Pauline's cheek a tender little tap with the flat of his hand and turned to Sylvie, not smiling now. 'And you, would you like to light a candle before you go?'

'A candle? May I?'

'Of course,' the father said. 'A candle for Fran Hagarty.'

'No, for my husband.'

'The soldier?'

'Yes,' Sylvie said. 'He was killed in France a month ago.'

'Well then,' Father Macken said, leading her towards the rail where the votive candles spluttered in the gloom, 'may he rest in peace. Would you like me to say a prayer for his soul too?'

'Please, Father,' said Sylvie, softly. 'Please do.'

PART SIX

Gowry

Chapter Twenty-four

Gowry had a bad feeling about it from the moment he learned that the 16th Division was being pulled out of the Hulluch sector. He had been in the thick of things too often to be frightened but there was something different about this one. He was haunted by feelings of insubstantiality, of not belonging to anyone, and wrote a number of farewell letters prior to being entrained.

He wrote once more to Maggie, to his mother, to his brother Forbes and, of course, to Rebecca, but he received no word from anyone, not even Becky, before the battalion left for the Somme.

Guillemont was the objective. Gillymong, the lads called it. Guillemont, like guillemot; Gowry remembered how the seabirds had skimmed across the water south of Howth Head that morning when he had taken Maeve to see the battle boats, how she had held his hand and how he had loved her more than anything in the world. He loved Maeve because she was so much like Sylvie, because she didn't doubt that he would always be there for her. Now here he was in a landscape without landmarks, in a village pounded to matchwood, cowering in a shallow trench hacked out of cold French sludge, watching the little aeroplanes drone overhead – and waiting for zero hour.

Somewhere to his right the Connaughts were preparing to storm the quarries. The Rifles had assembled with the Leinsters for an attack south of the railway line and were lying in extended order in the gridiron three hundred yards north of the village. How far away was Amiens? Gowry wondered. Forty miles, fifty miles? Where was Becky, and why hadn't she replied to his letters?

Last night he had taken the sacrament. Father Dillon was battalion chaplain. Fathers Cope and Doyle had assisted: Cope and Doyle and Dillon, a litany unto itself. He had queued for admission to the canvas confessional. The chaplains and those Rifles who knew him for a Protestant hadn't protested. Hidden by a flysheet, he had told the priest about Becky and had received a little penance and the relief that went with it, and had gone into the big tent to taste the wafer and be united with his little heathen Catholic girl. Later he'd cried, helmet held across his face, cried not just because he missed Becky but for Maeve and Sylvie too. Then gradually he had fallen asleep, dreaming of lakes and islands and a cottage close to the mountains, a cottage where they could accumulate and be at peace together, all the living and the dead.

The sunken road south-west of the village was the first objective.

English riflemen would move in behind to consolidate ground taken. Brigadier Crozier had explained it in detail. Crozier was a small man, almost dwarf-like. He strutted through the shallow trenches, undetected by the enemy, to remind each man that this was the chance they'd all been waiting for since training days. Gowry wished he could be more like the brigadier, a bred-in-the-bone soldier, defiant in the face of death.

The road lay five hundred yards beyond the Germans' front-line trench. There were several concrete strongpoints and dugouts among the ruins. At noon a salvo from the heavy artillery would signal the beginning of the attack. You could hear nothing through the infernal racket of German shelling. When you pulled yourself to your feet the sound of the bombardment seemed as dense and all-enveloping as fog. The morning was fair, though, cloud high and puffy, like shell bursts frozen in the stratosphere.

When the signal came Gowry scrambled to his feet. One man, quite far along the grid, went down immediately, then another. There would be no attack for them, no glory. Gowry heard the chant of Irish pipes, thin and fragile in the uproar, saw Crozier raise his arm, heard the crack of a revolver. He clawed at the earth and hoisted himself over the parapet.

The shelling was hard ahead. Squalls of machine-gun fire. He walked forward, a nice, neat, steady pace. He felt as if he were walking into a sea of absolute sound. Then he was running. They were all running. From the corner of his eye he could see the little brigadier running too, fat legs pumping, mouth wide open. Gowry opened his mouth and yelled. The chap beside him buckled and fell. Another chap a half step ahead flung up his arms as a little palmate explosion of dirt blew him off his feet. Gowry shouted louder and ran faster. Jerries were swarming out of the trench like rats from a trough. He went at them with the bayonet, all detachment gone, just another wild Irishman, swept along on the skirts of the pipes, stabbing and butting and running with the pack.

Jerry was surprised and disorganised. Jerry fell back. Jerry fell down. Jerry lay dead on the ground, dead in the rubble. Jerry bled and squealed and sur-rendered. Jerry begged for mercy – *Kamerad, Kamerad* – or sullenly surrendered his arms. Jerry was passed over, passed back, funnelled away into the ranks of the riflemen, into shell holes and shelling and bullets from Jerry machine-gunners behind the quarries north of Trônes Wood. Shot, bayoneted, brained, poor old Jerry got the worst of it in that mad Irish rush on Guillemont in the half-hour after noon.

When he reached the top of the road Gowry walked on corpses as he might have walked on cobblestones.

'Good man,' said the brigadier.

'Stand firm,' said the sergeant.

'Dig in,' the corporal told him.

'Bugger off,' said a voice in Gowry's head.

In his excitement he would have gone on running, alone at last, away along the road to Ginchy if someone hadn't dragged him on to the slope of the sunken road and shouted in his ear: '*Stop.*'

Panting, sweating, splattered with blood, Gowry obeyed.

The objective had been achieved, it seemed.

Yes, the objective had been achieved.

He was working with the others, strengthening the parapets in expectation of a German counter-attack when a Connaught sergeant came up and tapped him on the shoulder.

'You McCulloch?'

'Yes, Sergeant, I am.'

'You that pal o' Maurice Leonard?'

'Yes.'

'The bus-driver?'

'Who told you I was a bus-driver?' said Gowry.

'Maurice. Said you had a shine for his old mother. Said you drove the bus out for to see her whenever you could. Thought it a great joke, old Maurice.'

'Maurice – Sergeant Leonard's dead.'

'Sure an' he is, but I'm alive an' kicking an' I got a job for you.'

'Job? What sort of job?' Gowry said.

'Spot o' the old drivin'.'

'I'm not Transport.'

'You are now, son,' the sergeant said.

The nut had been cracked. Guillemont had been taken. The Irish volunteers had written their name in the footnote of history. Now, just an hour after jump-off, the Munsters were passing through the Connaughts and by two or two thirty the 6th Royal Irish would advance on Wedge Wood. The victory had not been achieved without heavy loss, however, and when Gowry was led down a chain of captured German trenches he saw why the sergeant had been sent out to find a driver. The trenches were littered with wounded, more wounded than Gowry had ever seen in one place before, many dead among them, many dying. The medical orderlies who had come up from the rear were few in number, for they had been caught in crossfire off the quarries. Evacuating the wounded would not be easy, for the casualties would have to be carried across open country to a clearing station a thousand yards beyond Trônes Wood.

Gowry leaned on the side of the trench and looked through the battered periscope that the sergeant had commandeered.

'See it?' the sergeant asked.

'See what?' said Gowry.

'The tin lizzie.'

'Where?'

'Big crater, left of it, on the bridge.'

'Bridge?'

'You thick?'

'No, no, no,' said Gowry. 'I see it – I think.'

The little field ambulance was a Ford Model T, purchased from the Americans by the Red Cross. It should not have been there but the drivers of the vehicles were brave to the point of recklessness and made it a point of pride to get as close to the fighting as possible. He had seen wrecked ambulances often enough, torn apart by a single grenade or tipped over and burned out in the bottom of shell holes. The image in the mirror of the periscope was blurred by smoke and dust but the Ford, sitting perkily on the breast of the wheat field, seemed to be intact.

'What do you want me to do about it?' Gowry said. 'I'm not a fitter. I don't know how these things work. You need a Transport johnny.'

'I know I do,' said the sergeant, 'but what I've got, son, is you.'

'Jesus!' said Gowry, peevishly.

'Don't blame me,' said the sergeant. 'Blame old Maurice's big gob.'

Gowry peered into the slot at the base of the periscope.

There seemed to be a heck of a lot of activity among the shell holes, men crawling about and waving. There was no one within two hundred yards of the ambulance, though, and that was worrying.

He pulled away from the mirror and blew out his cheeks.

The sergeant, leaning on his shoulder, handed him a lighted cigarette.

Gowry took it and looked up at the sky.

Flimsy paste and paper aeroplanes continued to circle overhead. He watched the planes for a moment, dragged on the cigarette, then applied himself once more to the periscope.

The bombardment had eased but the punch-bag slap of mortars continued and the sharp, stinging snap of trench torpedoes – whatever Jerry could find in the dumps behind the bunkers that ringed Ginchy and flanked the battlefield. Gowry saw shells exploding and vertical plumes of dirt rising, and in the distance, more than half a mile off, the relic of Trônes Wood.

'Who's in the ambulance?' he asked.

'None o' your business.'

'Big-wig, is it?'

'Big enough,' the sergeant admitted. 'Can you bring it in?'

'Is it stuck?'

'How do I know? Can you drive it?'

He had dug out Flanagan's charabanc one wild March day when snow had filled the pass at Raynor and he had rescued Des O'Neill and his little bus with a winch and a towrope from a flooded road near Ardee. He knew about engines and axles and towropes and had heard that the Model T was so tough you could bounce it along on three wheels for ten or a dozen miles over rough terrain. The lizzie looked so lonely and vulnerable, like a child lost in the wilderness, that Gowry felt a strange urge to rescue it.

'I can drive it,' Gowry said, 'if I can get to it.'

'It's behind our front lines, you know.'

'Is it? Then what's makin' that bloody racket on the flank? Pixies?'

'None o' your lip, McCulloch. Grab what you need an' fetch—'

'Where's the crew?'

'No crew. The crew's had it.'

'I see,' Gowry said.

'I'm givin' you an order, McCulloch.'

'Sure an' you are, Sergeant,' Gowry said. 'An' I'm obeying it.'

Stripping off his webbing, Gowry rolled up his shirt-sleeves, tightened the strap on his helmet, and went over the top once more.

It was a beautiful afternoon in the Ecole de Saint-Emile. Patients were out in force on the lawns. Some were playing boules, a couple had even ventured on to the tennis court, but the majority were resting in the shade of the trees or, still bed-ridden, enjoyed the late-summer breeze that drifted through the cloisters. It seemed a shame, Becky thought, to be leaving

France on such a pretty day, putting all this behind her for rainy old England.

Morphine had taken the edge off her reasoning and under its influence she had become a dreamy optimist, half in love with the progress of her illness and unaware of its seriousness.

The bleeding had started suddenly and dramatically. She had staggered back from the operating table with blood pouring down her legs. Her first thought as she slumped to the floor was that she had been pregnant and that God was punishing her for loving Gowry by taking the baby away. Silly, of course; she was a trained nurse and would surely have known if she'd been pregnant.

Bobby Bracknell had peered down at her. A surgical mask covered his face and he had a retractor in his hand. On his gown, she'd noticed, was a very neat, very large splodge of fresh blood, like a map of Australia.

'Oh, damnation!' the captain had said crossly. 'Will someone please get her out of here. Women! I don't know!' and had gone back to his work while two orderlies had eased Becky on to a stretcher and carried her out.

That same night, very late, Mr Sanderson had performed surgery.

The right kidney was diseased beyond treatment, a little smooth blackened bullet of a thing that the surgeon had dropped into an enamel basin and covered with a strip of gauze. Timorous manifestations were already apparent on the left kidney. Mr Sanderson had expressed amazement that Becky hadn't complained or suffered more obvious symptoms, but, as Angela pointed out, Becky was a modest person and had been ailing since Christmas.

Surgery had been extensive and destructive. Becky had been very ill afterwards, too ill to be shipped out to recuperate or – though nobody dared say it – to die in transit. Here in Saint-Emile she was among friends and had lain for three weeks in a screened bed in a cloister ward.

Morphine had taken away the edge of her pain and dulled her fear. She had slept when the pain allowed and had demanded no prognosis from her colleagues. She seemed not so much defeated as resigned, as if all that had happened while the disease was taking root had been part of a pattern, war and love and sacrifice all linked together.

When Angela read Gowry's letters aloud to her, Becky smiled and nodded but when Angela offered to write to Gowry on her behalf Becky had become quite angry and refused to burden her poor Irishman with her woes. Raising herself from the pillows, straining at the drainage tubes, she'd told Angela in no uncertain terms that she'd be furious if anyone informed Gowry of her changed circumstances, for she only wanted his love, not his pity.

She had, however, dictated letters to her mother and to her sister in Portsmouth, informing them that she'd been knocked out by an infection and would be coming home to recover. She told them no more, not that she'd fallen in love or had undergone surgery or that her days in the sun might be shorter than anyone had ever anticipated.

Then she was ready, ready and wrapped up like a soldier. She had her belongings with her; her uniform too, packed in a brand-new kitbag. The flowers that Mr Sanderson had picked and fashioned into two small posies rested on the blanket, together with fruit Angela had brought and three large bars of chocolate that Captain Bracknell had saved from his last parcel from Fortnum & Mason. Becky had no appetite for chocolate, for anything. She was as thin as a rake, her sturdy little body so emaciated that she looked frightfully pale and interesting, Angela said, like one of the debutantes in *Tatler*.

'When you're well, you'll come back to us, won't you?'

'Of course I will,' said Becky, in a whisper. 'If you're still here.'

'Oh, we'll be here,' said Angela. 'We ain't going nowhere for a long time yet and if we are moved on, you'll catch up with us.'

'Are you comfortable?' Mr Sanderson enquired.

'Yes, I feel like a lady, being carted about in style.'

'Cleopatra,' Bobby Bracknell said, 'Queen of the Nile.'

They were not themselves, Becky thought, not the people she had known. Already they had become strangers. Awkwardness had altered them; time and distance would change them even more. There would be a few letters, cards at Christmas, a small celebration when the war finally ended, then they would fade into memory. She would remember them all with affection, though, even despicable Bobby Bracknell, who probably couldn't help himself.

Sister Congreve said, 'Your records have been forwarded to Rolleston Hospital in London. You'll be met at the docks by an RAMC officer, someone who knows who you are and what sort of treatment you require.' She glanced round at Mr Sanderson, who nodded gravely. 'After that, it'll be off home to that Scottish island for you, my girl, and a lot of fresh air and porridge to build you up and make you well again.'

'Meanwhile, take care of your label,' Captain Bracknell told her.

The label was tied to a button of her overcoat. Scribbled on it, in the cabalistic script that only nurses and doctors understood, was a record of her treatment. She had no interest in reading the label. She was in their hands now. The MOs would see her safely home. She had nothing to worry about, nothing. Gowry wouldn't know what had happened to her, how she had changed, how she had let him down. She would become *his* dream, *his* memory, as poignant and mysterious as Robbie had been for her.

She began to cry with gentle regret for all that she was leaving behind.

'Oh, God, Becky, I shall miss you,' Angela said, sobbing too, and, leaning over the stretcher, gave her a hug.

On Sister Congreve's signal, the orderlies lifted the stretcher and slid it into the ambulance. Becky looked out into the sunlight, at the green lawns and pale stone facings of the Ecole, at the little group of friends and colleagues who had come to see her off, then the doors closed and the ambulance drove off.

Gowry was fifty yards from the captured German trenches before he realised that Jerry hadn't been beaten back after all. Only the front lines had crumpled; stout pockets of resistance remained on both flanks, and snipers and machine-gun nests were still hidden in the rubble.

When he looked back he could see staff cars and armoured vehicles approaching along the road from Albert. He had no map. Officially this was no longer occupied territory – only nobody had told the Germans that. He had absolutely no idea who was doing the shooting or why the motor ambulance had become a target. There might be no rational explanation. Jerry was no more sensible than Tommy when it came to picking targets and the Ford, sticking up like a toy, just begged to be blasted to kingdom come.

The excitement he'd experienced during the rush to the sunken road took hold of him once more.

He was curious to discover who was in the motor
ambulance and why the Connaught sergeant had been
sent to find someone who could drive the damned
machine instead of waiting to haul it in after resistance
had been mopped up and the village finally secured.

He looked down into the shell hole at a tangle
of bodies. A year ago the sight would have turned
his stomach but now it affected him hardly at all.
He glanced behind him again and saw the sergeant's
bloody periscope sticking up above the parapet. He
waved and set off for the little tin target on what
passed round here for a hill.

Three men lay dead near the ambulance. One had
been shot through the chest. He had fallen backwards,
hands raised. The other two were huddled a few yards
from the rear door. They had been caught by a burst
of machine-gun fire. Gowry turned them over just to
make sure they were dead. As he did so a machine-gun
opened up. He threw himself to the ground behind
the corpses as bullets strafed the side of the Ford,
pitting the metal.

The door at the rear of the vehicle swung open.

An arm groped out and tried to pull it shut.

'Hoy,' Gowry shouted. 'Hoy, you in there? How
many?'

The arm continued to wave about until another
burst from the machine-gun chased it away. A shell
came over, high, and exploded about sixty yards away.
The machine-gun fire ceased. The instant Gowry
raised his head, however, three or four shots from

a rifle flicked up dust close by. He tucked his chin into his fists and lay flat on the ground like a lizard.

At least he knew there was somebody in the ambulance and that he wasn't risking his neck just to retrieve an empty vehicle. He lay motionless, covertly studying the machine. The offside was badly scarred but there was no stink of spilled fuel and the tyres seemed to be intact. The driver's door hung open and Gowry thought he could see a leg sticking out of the cab.

He lifted his head and yelled: 'Hoy, you? Are you deaf? How many of you are there?'

'Two.'

'Alive?'

'Yes, but barely.' An Irish voice, high register, squeaky with fear. 'Have you come to get us out of here?'

'I have,' said Gowry. 'So your worries are over.'

'Praise be to God.'

The face that appeared in the open doorway was familiar: a small, pinched, middle-aged face, white with fear.

'Padre?' Gowry said. 'Father Coyle, is that you skulkin' in there?'

'Who is that? Do you know me?'

'Sure an' I do.' Gowry grinned. Sheer chance had stuck him with poor Father Coyle and it felt as if Becky were with him too. 'Who's your passenger?'

'Colonel Rayboult.'

'Ah!' Gowry said. 'I see.'

The sniper was still potting away but he was on the limit of his range and not particularly accurate. Gowry put his head down and rested for a moment.

Now he understood why he had been sent out to rescue the lizzie and why the sergeant had been so secretive. Rayboult was a battalion commander, a much-respected veteran who had insisted on coming out of retirement to fight with his old regiment. He was a bit of a figurehead, an icon. What puzzled Gowry was why the Connaughts hadn't sent out a heavily armed team to reel the old boy in. Surely someone in the Rangers' ranks knew how to drive a motor vehicle. He wondered if fate had manipulated him into this position, if that blunt, demanding sergeant was destined to be his nemesis.

Stealthily, keeping low, he began to crawl towards the ambulance.

The ambulance men were very attentive. She was treated with so much consideration that she did indeed feel like a lady. Morphine flowed in her veins. She could feel its soothing warmth in every particle of her being. It felt like warm milk. It felt as if her brain were bobbing in milk. It was all rather spectacular in a misty kind of way, the orderlies so kind, and the stretcher-cases on the platform waving as she went past. She was conscious of their interest and the voices of the orderlies shouting, 'Gangway, gangway,' while they eased her up the ramp and entered the dim interior of the hospital train.

Where was she exactly? Heuvert? Albert? Perhaps she was in Amiens and Gowry would come hurrying along the platform with poppies in one hand and champagne in the other to see her off properly.

The posies that Mr Sanderson had given her had a sweet scent and the chocolate bars that Bobby Bracknell had parted with were heavy in her pockets. She remembered the lovely taste of chocolate, but had no desire to eat. Memory was sweeter than reality in any case, especially her memories of Gowry: Gowry in Amiens, Gowry kissing her in the lane behind the cathedral, Gowry holding her close after they'd made love. She was glad that they had made love, glad that she had given herself to her Irishman before random chance separated them.

The stretcher was strapped to a rack at the end of the corridor. She was probably the only woman patient on the train. She could hear the groans of the wounded and how they clamoured for attention, for relief. She had no urge to tend them. She had done all she could for them and there came a point at which duty became pointless and all you were left with was a fretful little echo of responsibility.

The MO leaned over and drew down the green-painted shade to keep the sunlight from blinding her. He was a young man, younger than Captain Bracknell, and had no smiles for anyone.

'All right, Nurse Tarrant? All right for now?'

She managed to nod. She was very sleepy.

The racket from the platform, the cries in the corridor were like sounds from a seashore. She thought of the island where she'd been born, of her mother's cottage and the great blue-green Atlantic stretching out to infinity, of her aunt's house on the headland and her cousin Robbie coming down the slope of the hill towards her. Then it wasn't Robbie at all, but Gowry. She gave a little laugh and tried to wave to him, but her hands wouldn't move.

She felt the train move.

She was bleeding again, bleeding within.

It wasn't morphine but the slow turbid oozing of blood that soothed her. Her mouth was dry. She thought of calling out, but didn't want to make a fuss. She wondered where Gowry had got to. The strip of light at the edge of the green-painted blind darkened as the train shuddered and the iron wheels beneath her began to beat out a rhythm, a sleepy rhythm like the lapping of waves on a seashore.

'Nurse Tarrant?' said a voice. 'Rebecca?'

The train was rolling freely now, rumbling along. She had a headache, not much of one, quite endurable. It was all quite endurable, really.

'Becky?'

She imagined that her eyes were open. She imagined that Gowry was with her, for the priest looked so much like him. One thing she had always dreaded was pain but there wasn't much pain. There was no pain at all now that Gowry was here and the sound of the seabirds crying and the waves on the shore by the cottage on the bay and the bay so wide and the sea blue-green with the light upon it.

She felt someone touch her, heard anxious, murmuring voices.

The train jerked and there was a weight on her chest and Gowry was leaning over her, his arms about her, trying to lift her up. She yielded to him, let herself go. The green-painted blind detached itself suddenly and clattered up and she was looking out into the sunlight that bathed the plain and the words the stranger murmured meant nothing and the plain looked unbelievably white, and the weight went from her chest.

'Gowry,' she said, 'are you with me?'

'Sure and I am,' he said.

Father Coyle caught him by the hand and yanked him into the ambulance. The floor was puddled with blood. Colonel Rayboult was propped against the canvas that backed the cab. He had a tourniquet around his thigh and his tunic had been cut away and there was a dressing on his chest, a huge pad of flesh-coloured lint, heavily bandaged. There had been a dressing on the thigh too, Gowry reckoned, but someone or something had ripped it off.

The colonel was fully conscious.

When Gowry made to stand up he shouted, 'Get down, man. Get down.'

Father Coyle groped for the door-handle while bullets whined off the panels. Gowry reached around the padre and pulled the door shut.

'Who the hell are you?' The colonel's face was filthy, but dirt and blood did not diminish his authority.

'I'm the driver, sir,' Gowry told him.

'Jesus Christ! Are you the best they could find? You're not a Ranger?'

'Sperryhead Rifles, sir.'

'Well, whoever you are, you'd better get us out of here.'

'I'll do my best, sir.' Gowry glanced at Father Coyle who looked scared and sheepish. 'How're the boils, Padre?'

'What? Oh, very well, thank you. All gone.'

'Boils!' the colonel exclaimed. 'Oh, for Christ's sake!'

'Where were you headed?' Gowry said.

'The clearing station at Trônes Wood,' the padre told him.

'Why did you stop?'

'I don't know. Something happened. They all went out to help and they didn't come back. Are they dead, do you think?'

'Of course they're bloody dead,' the colonel roared. 'We've been squatting here for the best part of forty minutes. Do you think they'd have left us high and dry if they hadn't been dead? Where's Watson? Where's that bloody oaf of a sergeant? I'll have his balls for breakfast when I get out of here.'

'It's the femoral artery,' Father Coyle said. 'You know what that means?'

'It means I'd better get moving,' said Gowry.

'Of course it bloody does,' said the colonel. 'Here, take this.' He groped about in the puddle of blood, found a jack-knife and held it up. 'Cut through the canvas and climb into the cab. See if you can get this blasted contraption moving again.'

'Yes, sir,' Gowry said.

'Take the padre with you. He's no use to me.'

Spleen had kept the colonel going. Spleen would keep him going for another half-hour, longer if it took longer. Temper made the old boy seem vigorous but he had lost much blood and his strength was waning. Surely the medicos hadn't sent him off in this state. Something must have happened on the way. It didn't matter what, for, like a lot of things in this war, the situation was so farcical and improbable that it might have been the plot of a pantomime.

The colonel tightened his grip on the tourniquet, screwing it so tightly that his arm shook. His cheeks were scratched and blood matted his moustache.

Gowry took the knife, wiped it on his shirt and thumbed open the blade. He stabbed at the canvas, pierced a hole, worked the knife blade up and down and then ripped a hole large enough to climb through. He put his foot and leg through the opening, then his arm and shoulder and finally his head.

The driver was sprawled across the seat. He had been shot through the mouth and there was nothing much left of his face. Gouts of blood clung to the windscreen and smeared the steering wheel.

Father Coyle stuck his head through the tear in the canvas.

'Oh dear, poor chap.' He murmured something in a language Gowry didn't understand. 'Can we take him back with us?'

'Sorry, Padre,' Gowry said and, easing his arms under the dead man, lifted him into a sitting position and heaved him out of the cab door.

'Oh, dear, dear God!'

Gowry seated himself behind the wheel. The seat and the wheel were slick with blood. Oddly enough, he had never been in the cab of a Model T before and was astonished at how basic everything seemed, a far cry from Flanagan's limousine. He tamped the gear pedal and manipulated the stick.

The padre leaned over his shoulder and watched him jiggle the switch to test the starter motor. Gowry was just beginning to wonder if the lizzie had a starter motor when the engine turned over. He jiggled the switch again, praying that he wouldn't have to go out into the open and use the crank. He dabbed at the pedal and coaxed the engine to turn over again. Then, abruptly, it roared and caught. He released the spring-loaded handbrake, threw the vehicle into gear and tapped his foot on the accelerator. The rear wheels dug into the dirt. The note of the engine rose to an ear-piercing shriek and the Ford crept forward.

Gowry wiped blood from the windscreen and peered out.

They were moving in a lumpy fashion towards the crest of the hill.

'Where are you going?' the padre asked.

'Trônes Wood?' said Gowry. 'Isn't that where you want to go?'

'Wouldn't it be easier to drive back to our lines?'

'An' risk having the colonel bleed to death?' said Gowry.

He was beginning to feel confident now, almost cocky. The lizzie wasn't all that difficult to handle. He peered through the windscreen again.

'Which way, Padre?'

'To the left, I think. Yes, there's the village. The wood must be—'

A mortar bomb exploded. Earth rained down on the cab. The vehicle canted up on two wheels, hung there for a moment then fell back with a bone-jarring crash. Gowry pressed on through the curtain of debris, though he was dazed by the explosion. He could no longer hear the colonel cursing and wondered if the old boy had lost his grip. He glanced behind him and drove carelessly over corpses – he hoped they were corpses – and a litter of the stuff that polluted every battlefield. He spotted a bridge, not the bridge he'd spotted through the periscope but another just like it: four planks across a drainage ditch with three or four dead Germans draped on the verge. At least Gowry supposed they were dead until one of them reared up and started shooting.

The windscreen shattered.

Gowry punched out the glass that remained in the frame and there was glass everywhere, glass in his lap, glass on his bare arms, glass clinging to his shirt. He knew he was bleeding and had a terrible, shocking pain, but he didn't know where. He fought the wheel one-handed, trying not to pass out. He swerved broadside to the Jerries and swung away in an accelerating arc. He could no longer see the approach road, couldn't see much of anything. A grenade went off, lifting the back of the Ford like a kick from a mule.

The padre reappeared.

'All you all right?' he said. 'Look, you've been hit.'

'Never mind me,' said Gowry. 'What about him back there?'

'I fear he'll lose the leg, whatever happens.'

'Is he still with us, though?'

'Of course I'm still bloody with you,' came the colonel's shout. 'I've been through worse than this with better men than you, Sperryhead. Stop bloody dithering and get me to a quack.'

Gowry said, low-voiced. 'Have you given him last rites?'

'He refused to accept them,' the padre answered.

Gowry said, 'I went to mass, Father. I made a

confession and took the sacrament. Was it wrong of me to do that?'

'Did it give you comfort?'

'Aye, it did.'

'Did you go to mass in Amiens with your young lady?'

'How do you know about Amiens?'

'It's a very nice town,' the padre said. 'Beautiful cathedral.'

'That's not what I meant, Father. Did Becky tell you—'

'What have you done to your hand?'

'What?'

He had driven the last fifty or sixty yards without conscious thought. When he glanced down he saw what the padre meant. His left hand had been reduced to a mess of bloody tissue by the bullet that had splintered the windscreen. He tried to clench his fingers. Couldn't. When he tried to clench them again pain leaped up the length of his arm, searing every sinew and muscle. He would have screamed if the padre hadn't been with him. He moved the hand to the gearstick and tried to grasp it. Couldn't. Looking up, he saw a horse and gun carriage directly in front of the wheels. Tried to swerve. Couldn't. The front wheels lifted and the lizzie tilted. He wrapped his good arm around the wheel and leaned against the sway. The horse, all swollen up, was coated with black flies. They rose from the carcass and flew in a buzzing cloud into the cab.

Gowry thrashed from side to side to keep the flies out of his mouth. The ambulance bucked and somersaulted. He shot forward, smashing his nose and mouth on the steering wheel. The padre came over the top of him and they thudded against the roof of the cab and hung there together, upside down.

Bleeding from nose and mouth, Gowry tried to focus.

The padre's eyes were open. One arm was looped behind his neck and his legs were folded up to his chest. Gowry politely turned his head and spat out blood. He thought: if this sort of thing goes on much longer I won't have any face left. He spat again and probed the jagged edges of broken teeth with his tongue.

He rotated his neck and peered at the priest.

'Pah . . . pah . . .'

'I think,' the father said, 'I can just about reach the door.'

'Pah . . .'

Cheek by jowl with Father Coyle, belly pressed against the father's buttocks, all he could feel was embarrassment.

'Soh . . . soh-ly,' Gowry said.

'No, I really can reach the door,' said the father.

Gowry's nose and mouth were filling with blood. He couldn't spit it out, couldn't spit on a man of the cloth. He had always been fastidious. Charlie used to jeer at him for being so fastidious. He had been fastidious with Sylvie, even more so with Becky. He had been gentle with Becky, more so than he had ever been with Sylvie. He wondered where Becky had got to. He should have asked Father Coyle while he'd had the chance. He thought: imagine Father Coyle knowing about Amiens. There was something spooky about Father Coyle knowing about Amiens. He wondered if you could drown in your own blood and if he was injured badly enough to be sent back to Saint-Emile.

Cheered by the prospect, he eased himself away from the clergyman and gave the priest room to wriggle out of the cab.

The vehicle shifted, tilting again. He wondered where Becky was right now and, come to think of it, where he was. How far were they from the clearing hospital? Had they left Jerry behind? Were they safe?

Still pondering these difficult questions, Gowry passed out.

He opened his eyes. Father Coyle was pouring water on his face and wiping it with a handkerchief. The handkerchief was pure white and spotless. Gowry stared upward. Sky above him. Two little aeroplanes flying round and round, like a dance, a mating dance. He puffed out his cheeks and blew and saw that the planes weren't planes after all but flies, filthy black flies. He tried to speak. Couldn't. The shape of his nose, a huge nose, marred the view.

Father Coyle trickled water into his mouth. He swallowed blood.

'I'm afraid we've lost the colonel.'

'Lho . . . lho . . .'

'He's dead. I'm sure he's dead. I think the tumble broke his neck.' The padre seemed calmer now, not at all scared or sheepish. His cheeks were ruddy as if he'd been slapped. He tucked away the little glass water bottle and sat back on his heels. One arm trailed behind him like a broken wing; otherwise he seemed to be intact. 'I can see the road. It isn't far. I don't think the Germans are in this sector. I do hope not. I'll have to fetch someone to take care of you.'

Gowry tried to hoist himself into a sitting position. He was eight or ten yards from the upturned ambulance, lying on dry yellowish earth. Through a little forest of wheat stubble he stared at the horizon and its wreath of smoke.

'I think I'd better head for the road. I'm really not sure about the wood.' The priest leaned over him. 'Don't try to move. I'll bring help.'

He wetted his fingers, touched them to Gowry's forehead and made the sign of the Cross. Then he sat back and rolled away.

Gowry lay on his side. He felt broken beyond repair. Saint-Emile would be the best place for him, yes. He would tell them: send me to Saint-Emile, to Becky. Yes, my lovely Becky will take good care of me.

He watched the padre darting across the plain, an

ardent little figure, full of tadpole energy, darting and flickering through the strange afternoon half-light. He watched the priest become smaller and smaller, then vanish altogether.

He looked up at the sky, blue and infinite, at the two flimsy little aeroplanes dancing among the clouds.

'Becky?' he said. 'Rebecca?'

There was no answer save the distant mutter of the guns.

Chapter Twenty-five

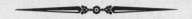

The wedding in Wexford had been a whiz-bang affair that had lasted the best part of a week and it wasn't the drink that had dragged Sylvie down – she was after all a nursing mother – so much as the unremitting jollity. Eventually even Maeve had wearied and on the train back to Dublin all three McCullochs, including Sean, had slept. Meeting the Trotters explained where Turk got his energy, for all the family members were massive in size, hearty in appetite and filled with inexhaustible enthusiasm. It seemed to Sylvie that they had discovered a means of cramming forty hours into each day and ten days into each week, for, in the midst of all the drinking, eating and singing work had gone on uninterrupted, a round of cattle purchase, cattle shifting and selling, each transaction settled with a spit and a handshake and a glass.

If she'd been concerned that Pappy and Mammy Trotter would be leery of Breen's bride and her father-less children then all her fears were put to rest. There

Jessica Stirling

was no scarcity of cash and no scarcity of affection and the children, even Algie, were welcomed as ambassadors for the spirit of goodwill that prevailed in the farmhouse out on the Crossabeg Road.

The wedding itself was held in the new church near the Abbey of St Sepulchre. Pauline looked lovely in a bridal gown of corn-coloured silk that one of Breen's sisters had worn some years before and which, after a lot of work with needle and thread, had been reduced to fit Pauline's trim figure. She was modestly veiled, of course, and had behind her a train of perfect little pages in spotless white shirts and well-sponged trousers and flower girls in almost-matching dresses. The moment had been very decent and solemn indeed, though the solemnity was reduced just a mite by Algie shouting out, 'Mammy, I need to pee,' as Pauline came up the aisle from linking her name with Breen's in the parish register.

Afterwards, there had been speeches, some funny, some long-winded, toasts galore, toasts to groom and bride, to Mr Brendan Trotter, the father of the groom and father of the feast, and to all the brave men who were prominent by their absence, Turk number one among them. Even so, Sylvie felt sure that Pauline and her lost children would have a good life in Wexford, as safe as any life could be in the troubled times ahead.

On Friday morning Pauline accompanied the McCullochs to the railway station. Breen had gone off to do business in the glens and had taken the younger children with him in the back of the horse-van.

She looked well, looked younger did Pauline. The innocent naïvety had gone from her eyes and the faint, startled anxiety too. She stood under the wooden archway out of the rain and took Sylvie's hand.

'I've you to thank for this,' she said. 'If you hadn't come to Endicott Street then Breen wouldn't have come lookin' for you an' wouldn't have fallen in love with me.'

'Nonsense,' Sylvie said. 'You owe me no thanks for anything, Pauline.'

'Fran then,' the young woman said. 'Perhaps it was Fran lookin' out for us all from above. He would do that, Fran would, if he could.'

'Do you miss him?' Sylvie asked.

'Aye, but not so much as all that. You?'

'Yes.' Sylvie was relieved to see the train approaching. 'I miss him.'

'You'll get over it,' Pauline said.

But Sylvie was not so sure.

The tenement in Endicott Street had been 'looked after' by two of Father Mack's parishioners while Sylvie was off at the Wexford wedding and if there had been any trouble in the house then those stalwart volunteers would surely have sorted it out. They had also collected the weekly rents, for Father Macken's superiors hadn't yet decided what was to be done with the tenement and in the muddled way of administrators, even Church administrators, did nothing at all. Little had changed, except that profits were now divided between John James Flanagan and Father Macken's church restoration fund.

Sylvie, Maeve and Sean exchanged Fran's tiny room for Pauline's ground-floor apartment, which, in their absence, had been cleaned and repapered by the stalwart caretakers. The rent was modest but Sylvie had spent much more than she anticipated during the past few months and returned from Wexford more worried about money than anything else.

She tried to convince herself that it would only be a matter of time before some good honest man came along, and waited eagerly for the arrival of a tenant for Fran's room in the hope that some miracle of love at first sight might happen to her as it had happened to Pauline. The room, however, was let to another dour bachelor old enough to be her father. He gave her barely a second glance and, like so many of his generation, seemed more interested in drinking than courting and spent most of his evenings at the bar in McKinstry's.

Nine days after her return from Wexford, though, a miracle did occur.

Sylvie had written to her mother-in-law at Brunswick Crescent in Glasgow where Forbes and his family lived. She had written to Kay McCulloch not because she wanted anything – not yet – but because she had learned that burning your bridges wasn't a good idea and because . . . well, because she missed Gowry and regretted that she had let him down. She was awaiting a letter from Glasgow, then, and perhaps a letter from the Red Cross or Widows' Welfare, though she had virtually given up hope of hearing anything from any of the aid organisations. She had all but reconciled herself to the fact of her husband's death but, late at night, when Maeve was asleep, she would fish out the letter from the War Information Office and read it again and again, as if it offered the possibility of multiple interpretations instead of that one irrefutable sentence: *I am afraid, however, that there is little room for hope that your husband is alive.*

She was out on the steps in the autumn chill waiting for the postman when it came to her that something beneficial was about to happen. It was as if there were an aura in the street, a wave of light sweeping down from the railway and the canal, like sunlight peeping under cloud: absolutely no accounting for it, for she, unlike Pauline, had never been superstitious and there were no wise women hanging from her family tree and if there had been her father, an engineer, would surely have cut them down.

Even so there was a feeling within her that something unexpected was about to happen when she stepped down on to the pavement to receive the bundle of letters that the postman, with a rueful shrug, handed her.

She took the bundle into the hall, sorted out three or four addressed to other tenants and put them carefully on the scarred table that lurked under the staircase. She glanced at the great wad of letters that remained, surprised and intrigued by their uniformity: *War Department. War Department. War Department* – fourteen in all, each franked with an identical postmark, each addressed in the same cramped script.

She ran into the apartment where Sean, strapped into his baby-chair, was determinedly gnawing on a bone ring that Maeve had bought for him. He looked up when his mother entered, his dark brown eyes round and his mouth crimped into a little questioning O as if he sensed her excitement and didn't approve. She swept away the breakfast dishes and shouted for Maeve who had gone out to the water closet in the back with the chamberpot and who, still sleepy and grumpy, stumbled back into the room, scowling.

'What?'

'Letters,' said Sylvie. 'Look, dearest, lots of letters.'

'Open the blessed things then,' Maeve said and, kicking the empty pot back under the bed, sat down and reached for a knife.

It was all very ordered and correct, all completely crazy. Some clerk in some gloomy office had carefully post-dated fourteen postal orders, had signed and stamped them and put them in separate buff-coloured envelopes, had addressed the fourteen separate envelopes and fed them into the postbag, presumably one at a time. Fourteen payments; fourteen weeks since Gowry had been reported missing; fourteen weeks during which time he had all but dwindled out of existence. Fourteen times three shillings and sixpence came to forty-nine shillings which was not a very great deal but might be a lifesaver if work proved difficult to find or if some kind, caring man didn't come along soon.

Sylvie was so stunned at first that she didn't realise the significance of the fourteen hand-printed envelopes and fourteen three-and-sixpenny postal orders. Then Maeve raised her hands, spread like an angel conferring a blessing, and shouted, 'He's alive. Daddy's alive.'

Sylvie sat down. 'No,' she said. 'How do you know?'

'Look,' said Maeve, chattering with excitement, 'it's back pay. It's all back pay. Fourteen weeks of back pay. He never was dead, never was missing. They just lost his pay book or whatever they call it an' now they've found it they're coughing out what's due as if nothin' had ever happened. No letter of apology, just fourteen weeks of soldier's pay right up to . . .'

'Last week,' said Sylvie.

Maeve rose, a lark ascending, plucked up her half-brother, baby-chair and all, and whirled around the room with him.

'Daddy's alive, Daddy's comin' home. Daddy's comin' home. Ay-hay, ay-hay, ay-hay,' she chanted while Sean, deprived of his bone ring, bellowed in frustration and alarm.

The clear tonic sunshine of autumn had begun to dim and thicken into the first misty days of winter and the leaves, which should have gone out in a blaze of glory, had withered to a lifeless brown. Though he stood for hours at the fence on the breast of the hill above the Usk staring across the river valley, Gowry had never watched the changing seasons with such disinterest and if it hadn't been for the teeth, might have sunk irredeemably into melancholy and despair.

The teeth gave him more trouble than the hand. The hand – or, rather, the lack of it – was something he could almost put out of mind. It bothered him only on those occasions when some stupid little chore had to be done, like buttons, bootlaces, buttering bread or opening a letter or a tin.

For the most part he kept the hand buried in his pocket, itching, scabrous and leaking a little serous fluid into a light gauze dressing.

Easy to ignore the hand, the stump that the surgeons were so proud of and the thumb that stuck up in a permanently cheerful gesture. He couldn't ignore the teeth, though, not even when the wire was removed from his jaw. The teeth, like his fingers, were no more; gone, vamoosed, left behind with a million other grisly trophies that would surface one day in the wheat fields of France.

All that would have been fine with Gowry, just dandy, for, much of the time, he felt that all that was left were the missing fingers and teeth, that the rest of him just wasn't there at all; until, that is, they came to make him presentable again and began fiddling with plaster casts and moulds and to their satisfaction, not his, stuffed his mouth with vulcanite and porcelain, a great ugly wedge of vulcanite that thrust his upper lip into his broken nose and trapped every grain and seed that entered his mouth.

The nagging, salivating discomfort of false teeth constantly reminded him that he had survived and that Becky had not, that Becky had left him behind.

The letter from Father Coyle offered little comfort, the letter from Angela even less. It had taken five weeks for the letters to catch up with him. He had been in a bad way before the letters arrived and in a worse way afterwards. He hadn't shed tears, though, not even when he learned that Rebecca was dead. She had died on a hospital train somewhere along the line that led to the coast. She had been ill for months, so the padre informed him, and had died with Gowry's name on her lips. How the padre had obtained that information Gowry had no idea, given that the padre had been with him in the field near Trônes Wood at the time or, to be absolutely accurate, had been zigzagging away into the strange half-light of a sunny September afternoon.

He liked to believe – the one fallacy he allowed himself – that Becky had passed on at exactly the same moment that he had passed out and that in the ether above the battlefield, a little to the north of Guillemont, his soul and hers had crossed for an instant, spinning and spiralling like those damned little aeroplanes in a blue and empty infinity.

Father Coyle was resting in a Catholic hospital in

Antrim. He had a broken arm, a clean break apparently, clean as a whistle. He hoped to be back 'in service' in four to six weeks. Father Coyle did not offer to visit him and Gowry was thankful for that. He wanted nothing to do with the father or what the father offered, wanted none of what Angela offered either: that smooth, plump, chimerical creature who had shared more of her life with Becky than he had done and whose expressions of sympathy were so cloying that they almost made him sick.

He replied to neither the padre nor the nurse, though by then he had learned how to press the upright thumb on to a slippery sheet of notepaper and write with his good hand. It was, the nurses said, quite an achievement. They were very keen on achievements, the staff at Maidenhall, praising every small triumph of dexterity and every small triumph of the will. They wanted him to will himself well again, to pretend that he was as good as new, that the skill with which they had patched him up was reward enough for what he had gone through and what he was going through now.

It would have been a calm and healing time in the South Wales military hospital if it hadn't been for the vulcanite and porcelain plate that rubbed his gums raw and made his upper lip so stiff that his nose hurt and his eyes watered.

The nurses thought he was crying. He wasn't crying. He had deliberately chosen grief over nothingness and, like many another survivor, daily rehearsed the terrible explosive patience that was necessary to put up with all the fussing and busyness with which the doctors, nurses and welfare organisations insisted on filling his days.

They drove him out with other walking wounded to visit Tintern Abbey and Monmouth Castle, to concerts in Newport and, once, to a Chaplin film in a picture house in Cardiff. Every evening there was a brass band to listen to or a singsong or a male voice choir. He went on excursions and sat through concerts without complaint, complying with the rules of recuperation as he had complied with the rules of war, except that there was no meekness in him now, only a soft suffusion of anger as he came to realise what he had really lost.

Only when he leaned on the fence at the foot of the lawn and looked out on the Vale of the Usk in the winter-coming gloom was he forced to acknowledge his true situation. He was an Irishman who had loved a Scots girl, imprisoned in Wales and attended for the most part by the English – the blessedly efficient English – in a unity of nations that reeked, that stank of irony.

It was not yet four o'clock, but dusk was already sifting down as he walked back up the slope to the conservatory where the wheelchairs were and the legless practised hopping among the potted palms. Lights glimmered wanly in the wards and he had no sense of what was to come, no warning. He let himself in by the side door. He could smell cabbage and the burnt-toast odour that the tea urns gave off. He was on his way into the dining-hall to draw a cup of tea when he first caught sight of his mother.

She was seated on a bench in the corridor that led to the hall. At first he thought he was seeing things, that grief had finally affected his brain but as he walked towards her and saw her steely little eyes fixed upon him he realised that she had come to berate him and he felt much as he had done when the ambulance had turned over and buried its snout in the earth.

'What's this you've been doing to yourself?' Kay McCulloch said. 'Are those supposed to be teeth? I've seen better teeth on a horse.'

'Who let you in, Ma?' Gowry said. 'There's no visiting today.'

'I happened to be in the neighbourhood.'

'In the neighbourhood – in Wales?'

'I was up seeing your brothers.'

'Where are they?'

'Frongoch.'

'Where the hell is that?'

'Merioneth.'

'That's miles away, miles an' miles away.'

'I know. I can't stay long.'

He stood before her, sheepish and unaccountably ashamed. It had been weeks since he had spared a thought for his family. He had been preoccupied with Becky and the shattered dreams of what might have been, of a future no longer linked to the past. He had thought of Sylvie, of Maeve, of the time just before the war, but that other period in his life, his time in Glasgow, seemed like someone else's story, not his.

He looked around, found a chair and pulled it up to the bench.

He seated himself before her, the stump tucked into his lap.

'What are they doing in Frog – Frongoch?'

'Haven't you heard?' his mother said. 'Frongoch's an internment camp for Irish prisoners. Didn't you get my letter?'

'Aye, I got your letter.'

'They were in Stafford jail for a while but then they were moved to this camp in Wales.' She laughed drily. 'They're billeted in an old distillery.'

'That'll suit Charlie.'

'Eighteen hundred of them locked up there, out in the wilderness at the back of beyond. Peter's not well.'

'Is that why you were allowed to visit?'

'Forbes pulled a few strings,' his mother said. 'Are you well?'

'Well enough,' said Gowry. 'Better than I look, I suppose.'

'Will they send you back to the front?'

'No.'

'Why not?'

He held up his hand, thumb cocked.

She stared at it. 'Well, that's your driving days over and done.'

He had almost forgotten that the same forceful molecules that had made her family so successful in the shipbuilding business thickened his mother's blood too. He remembered his grandfather's huge house high above the park and his brother Forbes's mansion in Brunswick Crescent and thought how he might have become rich and respected and spared the grief that had come upon him. But he wouldn't have chosen another path even if it had been possible, for if he'd stayed in Glasgow he wouldn't have known Becky.

'What are you going to do with yourself, Gowry?'

'I haven't decided yet.'

'The Shamrock's gone. The British blew it up.'

He felt nothing, not surprise, not regret.

'The man's dead, her fancy man.'

'Is he?' said Gowry.

'Shot during the Rising, murdered in cold blood – so they say.'

'Did you ever meet him?'

'Thank God I did not.'

'Tell me about Peter,' Gowry said. 'How sick is he?'

'The wound he got in the fighting won't heal properly. It's not right for him to be in that dismal camp, not with winter coming on. Fortunately he's got Charlie to look after him, and the Trotter boy.'

'How long did you stay in Frongoch?'

'An hour.'

'It's a long way from Dublin to North Wales for a short visit.'

'I didn't sail over from Dublin. I came down from Glasgow by train.'

'Ah!' Gowry said.

He could hear the clink of teacups and the cheerful cries of the nursing staff. The dining-room would be crowded, for food and drink offered comfort. He would have settled for a parboiled tin of bully beef if he could have his own teeth to eat it with.

Conscious of his mother's stare, he put his hand to his mouth.

'Are they going to be leavin' it like that?' she asked.

'Yes.'

'What a mess.'

'Ain't it, though?' said Gowry.

'You haven't asked about her yet.'

'How is she? Maeve, I mean. She must be nearly grown up.'

'They all thought you were dead.'

'What?'

'We all thought you were dead.'

'I'm not dead. You can see I'm not dead.'

'Word came through that you were. Missing believed killed.'

'Oh, for Christ's sake!' Gowry said. 'That's ridiculous.'

His mother had changed not at all, not in appearance or character. She had never been a typical tradesman's wife, of course. She had always had a certain style, a certain class. She had her Franklin upbringing to thank for that. And she had Forbes to look after her, Forbes, her darling son. Come to think of it, his grandfather had been Welsh. Gowry had all but forgotten that the old man, old Owen, had been born in Wales and had learned his trade in a Cardiff foundry. Now, two generations later, he, Gowry, had returned to within sniffing distance of Cardiff's docks and blistered chimneys; another grim irony, he thought, to add to his collection.

'Did they stop my pay?' he asked.

'Yes,' his mother answered. 'They were considerin' signing her on for a widow's pension when a sheaf of postal orders turned up and she knew by the dates that you weren't dead. Then she had a letter from the War Office saying you were wounded and in hospital in Wales.'

'That must have been a shock.'

'It was. Why didn't you write to her?'

'Why didn't she write to me?'

'Well, we both know the answer to that, don't we, son?'

Kay looked up as a couple of soldiers in dressing-gowns swung past on crutches. They glanced at Gowry, nodded amiably and went on into the dining-room. From upstairs came the scratchy sound of dance music from a gramophone in need of a new needle.

'If the Shamrock's uninhabitable, where's she staying?'

'Up near the Mountjoy in a tenement he used to own.'

'Hagarty?'

'Yes, Hagarty. It seems he had property.'

'Is the baby with her?'

'It's his baby, you know.'

'I know it's his baby,' said Gowry. 'Is it all right?'

'Why would it not be all right?'

He shrugged. 'I mean, is it healthy?'

'Aye, a big, healthy lump of a boy.'

'What did she call him?'

'Sean.'

'Not Francis?'

'No. Sean – Sean McCulloch. Can you imagine?'

Gowry smiled as best he could. 'Tell me about Maeve.'

'She's fine.'

'What about the brewery?'

'Closed up, at least until the boys are released.'

'I see,' Gowry said. 'Dad didn't feel like keeping it open?'

'He's not capable, Gowry. He's – gone a bit funny.'

'Is that why you've taken him to Glasgow? Out of harm's way?'

'It was Forbes's idea. We're lodging with him. He likes having us there.'

'I'm sure he does,' said Gowry.

Resentment stirred within him. He was tempted to tell his mother that he had achieved more than Forbes had ever done, that the king's shilling had purchased more than a shipbuilder's fortune could ever do; that he had met a girl, had fallen in love, and that she had died.

No, he told himself, closing his lips on the rubberised wedge. He wouldn't boast about Becky and he wouldn't use her as an instrument of revenge. He would never tell anyone about Becky, not his mother or his brothers, not Maggie or Jansis or Maeve, certainly not Sylvie. Becky would remain his secret.

'You'll get a pension, won't you?'

'Probably, but it won't amount to much.'

'Well, you won't be driving for Flanagan again, not with that hand,' his mother said. 'Can they do anything about it?'

'Sure an' they'll fit me with an ornament.'

'A what?'

He lifted his arm and displayed the stained bandage.

'They'll fit me up with a wooden hand with little hinges to give me some sort of grip. That's the important thing, Ma, to restore my grip. That's why they're so pleased they managed to save the thumb. Doctors tell me it's what makes us human. This' – he waggled the thumb painfully – 'is what separates us from the apes. I've exercises to do to free the knuckles but once they loosen up I'll be able to hold things. With a nice wooden hand and a glove, by God you'll hardly know I'd been in the war at all.'

Now that he had started talking it was difficult to stop. Only by concentrating on the inconsequential details of his treatment, however, could he prevent himself from revealing the things he didn't want her to hear.

He rattled on. 'There's a workshop in Bristol where they make these things: glass eyes, false teeth, wooden legs and arms. Crippled ex-servicemen are being trained to turn them out and thousands of ex-soldiers are queuing up for jobs there. Funny, isn't it? All those one-armed, one-legged soldiers sitting at benches making artificial limbs for other crippled soldiers.'

'Is that what you're going to do with yourself?'

'No, Mother,' Gowry said. 'That isn't what I'm going to do with myself.'

'You can't work in the brewery.'

'I know.'

'Forbes said he'll look after you if you're stuck for work.'

'I don't need looking after,' Gowry said.

He still couldn't fathom why she was here or what she wanted from him. He doubted that mere motherly concern had brought her to Maidenhall.

'She'll take you back.'

'Who?'

'You know who.'

'If you mean Sylvie, I'm not sure I want her back.'

'Don't you want to see Maeve?' his mother asked.

'Of course I do.'

'Can't you let bygones be bygones?'

'Oh, for God's sake, Ma, stop interfering. You never liked Sylvie. You never approved of Sylvie. Just because Forbes and she—'

'Forbes?'

'Don't pretend you don't know.'

'I have no idea what you're talkin' about.'

'All right, all right,' said Gowry. 'Let's just say I'm not ready to forgive anyone for anythin' just yet.'

'I told her to get rid of the baby.'

'Why should she get rid of it? The baby's done nothing wrong. He didn't ask to be born any more than I did. Is that why you've come to see me, Ma, to talk me into helping you get rid of Sylvie's baby? Why?'

'It's a mark of shame, that's why.'

'Jesus!' Gowry said.

Anger broke through his indifference, rising like something from the depths of a deep, dark, icy ocean. Becky had been a virgin until she'd lain with him in the hotel bed in Amiens. Becky had given him what every husband should have, her love and her devotion. He would have given her what every loving wife desired, a child of her own, his child, and the security that went with it. But those promises, like so many others, had been broken through no fault of his. He was alone now, without role or purpose. After what he'd seen, what he'd done, how could his mother talk as if the world had been standing still all this while, mired in the old moralities.

'A mark of shame!' he said. 'You don't even know what shame is. I'm not sure I do either any more but, by God, I know what it isn't.'

'She deceived you. She cheated you.'

'Out of what?' said Gowry. 'Sylvie never belonged to me.'

'You gave her a child, you gave her Maeve.'

'Maeve?'

He had never spoken of it to anyone, not even Becky. He had never dared express his doubts that Maeve was really his and not his brother's child. God damn it, what did it matter now? He had raised the girl, had loved her more than anything, and had given her away as lightly as he had thrown away his marriage.

He raised the stump of his hand and stared at the cocked thumb that the doctors claimed distinguished him from the apes. He pressed down on the knuckle joint and felt pain scissor into the sinews of his wrist. He would have movement, pronation they called it, articulation; the rest would be mere ornament. He pressed down on the joint until sweat came on his brow and the faint serous stains on the gauze were tinted with blood.

His mother watched impassively.

'Gowry,' she said, 'you'll hurt yourself.'

'What if I do?'

'Stop playing the fool.'

He loved it, loved the pain. He could feel knots of gnarled tissue beginning to crack and delicate bones creak under pressure. He cupped his good hand over the thumb and closed his fist, crushing the thumb into his palm, ridding himself at last of that farcical gesture of resignation; then he sat back, grunting, and unfolded his good hand. The thumb was bent, not supple, not healed but bent as it should be, folded across the remnant of his palm. He sucked saliva from under the vulcanised plate and wiped his mouth on his sleeve.

'See,' he said, 'I'm not a monkey. I'm not an ape.'

'Gowry, what's wrong with you? Why are you sayin' these things?'

She leaned forward, glowering, genuinely concerned now. He knew what concerned her: irrationality suggested madness, and madness too was a mark of shame. He'd learned a lot in the past year, how to obey, how to rebel, how to cope with being in love and, the hardest lesson of all, how to embrace grief in preference to nothingness. It had taken his mother to drag him back to reality, to the pettiness and spite that tainted all family matters.

'Nothing,' he said, with a wheezy laugh. 'Nothing's wrong with me, Ma.'

'Why are you laughing? Are you laughing at me?'

'No,' he said. 'No, no.'

'It's no laughing matter, Gowry, none of it.'

He tucked the hand into his lap again, hiding it. He cocked his head and regarded his mother, that old strait-laced renegade who in her day had been a black sheep too and had run off to Dublin to marry an Irish brewer.

'Why didn't Sylvie go back to Glasgow?' he said.

'I asked her to, I begged her to.'

'Why didn't she go back to Forbes?'

'She wouldn't.'

'You mean she refused?'

'Yes.'

'After Hagarty . . .'

'Yes.'

'What was she waiting for?'

Kay hesitated and in her eyes he could see something that he had never detected there before, some quality, some soft ineluctable measure of admiration.

'You,' his mother said, reluctantly. 'I think she was waiting for you.'

'She's with you, isn't she?'

'Yes.'

'Where?'

'Down in the town, in a hotel in the town.'

'The Fortress Hotel?'

'Aye, that's the one,' his mother said.

There had once been a Roman garrison close to the town of Maidenhall. There were no baths or amphitheatre as there were at Caerleon but you could still see the foundations of the barracks stretched on the narrow plain between the river and the first uprising of the hills. Gowry came down to the little town quite often, not to pop into a pub or the saloon bar at the rear of the Fortress Hotel but to wander along the stone lines of that long-gone Roman garrison and wonder at the nature of the men who had served there. He wondered whether they had longed for home or if, in time, this had become their home and they had taken wives from among the dark-haired, dark-eyed natives and fathered children and, when time was up and arms laid down, had claimed an acre or two of rich bottom land or green grassy hillside to farm away their days in peace.

Wales was not his land either, not his home, yet he felt an affinity with the place through his grandfather Owen Franklin who had chosen to emigrate to Scotland to fashion a better life for himself. He could have chosen Scotland too, Gowry supposed, could have been snug in some protected trade that Forbes would have conjured up for him, safe and whole and married to some girl – not like Sylvie, not like Becky – some plain, unexceptional Glasgow lassie whom he would have loved and looked after without ever realising what he had missed.

He came down in the dark, following the pavement that led from the back of the hospital, down the steep hill past terraced houses, past new cottages, past the first of three public houses, past the Methodist hall and the railway station, past the yew hedge that surrounded the remains of the ancient garrison, and saw ahead of him the lights of the Fortress hazed with a mist that was not quite rain.

He had put on his greatcoat – he was still a soldier after all – and his cap and had wound a muffler round his throat. He had his bad hand in his pocket, his teeth in his pocket too, wrapped in a clean piece of gauze. He had shaved twice to make his haggard features smooth, and standing on the pavement across from the old hotel felt so nervous, so unsure that what he was doing was right that he almost turned tail and fled back to the hospital.

She had travelled a long way to see him. The crossing from Dublin had been rough, so his mother had said, and the baby had been sick and the train journey from Fishguard slow and lumbering, and he could not in all conscience ignore her, no matter what she had done. He wished, though, that it could have been Becky who was waiting for him in the big, high-ceilinged lounge under shabby chandeliers and whispering fans; that when he opened the door and looked into the room Becky, not Sylvie, would be there, eager and understanding in the light of new love, and that he might begin again, begin anew, to repair and redeem the happiness that he had lost somewhere along the line.

He took a deep breath, crossed the street, climbed the three shallow steps, stuck out his good hand, pushed open the heavy, glass-panelled door, crossed the foyer under the fans and went straight into the residents' lounge.

She was dozing on one of the knobbly leather sofas, the baby drowsing on her lap. She looked pale, pale and fat, not healthy. He felt a little stab of anxiety, a fear that she too was ill. He stepped across the worn carpeting and peeped down at the sleeping child, at the quiff of black hair and the little pursed Sylvie-mouth on him and the dribble wet on his baby cheeks.

Reaching into his pocket Gowry took out the vulcanite wedge, stuck it in his mouth and bit down.

Then, softly, he said, 'Sylvie. Sylvie, it's me.'

★   ★   ★

She sat up, hugging the baby to her breast, and her first words – out before she could stop them – were, 'Oh, Gowry, what have they done to you?'

He had changed so much he seemed almost like a stranger. The handsome chap she'd run off with half a lifetime ago had been stripped to skin and bone, his nose misshapen, his mouth filled with artificial teeth. He smiled not at her but at Sean who, waking, stared cross-eyed at the creature and blew a few derisory bubbles. Sylvie propped her son on her knee, adjusted his woollen jacket and wiped dribble from his cheeks with her handkerchief.

'Did Ma not tell you what to expect?' Gowry asked. 'Where is she?'

'Gone back to Glasgow,' Sylvie said. 'She left just after six.'

'Why didn't you go with her?'

'I decided to stay in case – in case you wanted to talk to me.'

Gowry seated himself on the sofa. He glanced into the recesses of the dining-room where four Guards officers were gathered at a corner table. From the saloon bar came the faint strains of male voices chanting one of the hymn-like battle songs of which the Welsh were so fond.

'Why didn't you just come up to the hospital?' Gowry said.

'I wasn't sure you'd want me to.'

'Why did you have to use my mother as a go-between?'

'There was no one else,' said Sylvie. 'Charlie's in prison.'

'Yes, Ma told me.'

'What else did she tell you?'

'That Hagarty was murdered. Is that true?'

'Yes. I was in one of Vaizey's cells when it happened.'

'I'm not surprised Vaizey wanted rid of him.'

He spoke in a strange pedantic manner, not slurred but clipped, the porcelain teeth clicking a little. He sat back, pressed into the box end of the sofa as if he might suddenly start up and leave at any moment.

Sylvie adjusted Sean's little jacket once more, praying that he wouldn't start fussing. What she had to do was difficult enough without having to wrestle with one of her son's tantrums. He was quiet for the moment, though, not drowsy but attentive, staring intently at Gowry as if he were envious of those fine, big, adult teeth.

'Tell me what happened,' Sylvie said. 'Where were you wounded?'

'Guillemont,' Gowry stated.

If she'd hoped for an account of heroism and endurance she was disappointed. Gowry closed his lips over the awkward rubberised wedge and said nothing.

'Your mother tells me your hand . . .'

'Aye, my hand,' Gowry said, shrugging.

'Don't you want to talk about it?'

'No,' he said. 'I'd rather talk about Maeve.'

She told him about Maeve, Jansis and the downfall of the Shamrock, how she had fared in the uprising and what had occurred afterwards. She spoke quietly, not fishing for sympathy. When she told him about the missing letters and how she had tricked Flanagan he shook his head, and when she told him how they had all supposed him to be dead he shook it again. He hardly seemed to be listening, though, and refused to look at her. He gazed into the depths of the room beyond the archway where the Welsh officers were gathered round a white tablecloth. She wondered if he felt more affinity with them than he did with her, if he had left a part of himself in the trenches, the way a bee leaves its sting.

She told him about Pauline, Breen Trotter and Father Mack: names new to him, folk who had no role in his life. And she told him a great deal about Maeve, for only when she spoke of Maeve did he give her his full attention.

'So where is she?' he asked.

'I sent her to Wexford to spend a few days with Breen and Pauline.'

'Doesn't she want to see me again?'

'She was desperate to see you,' Sylvie assured him. 'But she wouldn't have been happy just seeing you. She would have wanted to go with her grandmother to the camp at Frongoch to visit her sweetheart.'

'She's too young to have a sweetheart.'

'Her friend then, her friend Turk Trotter.'

'Trotter!' Gowry said, with another little shake of the head. 'Why did you write to my mother of all people?'

'To tell her you weren't dead after all.'

She waited for him to ask why she'd brought Fran's child with her. If she was asking Gowry's forgiveness – and she wasn't at all sure that she was – then she would have to ask it on her son's behalf too.

Gowry said, 'You made a mistake, Sylvie.'

'I know I did.'

'You shouldn't have trusted her.'

'Her?'

'My mother.'

'What do you mean?'

'She only agreed to help you because she wants rid of the baby.'

'Rid of . . .'

'A mark of shame, she called him.'

'Oh that!' Sylvie said. 'I told her to say that.'

'But why?'

'To see how you would react.'

'You haven't changed, Sylvie. You're just as devious as you always were. What are you doing here? What do you want from me?'

'I want you back.'

'Second-hand?' Gowry said. 'Second-best?'

'I admit I was taken in by him.'

'I know you were.'

'Fran wasn't the man I thought he was.'

'In bed,' Gowry said, 'or out of it?'

'I'm not going to beg, Gowry.'

'I'm not asking you to.'

'We really thought you were dead. We thought we'd lost you.'

'Perhaps you have,' Gowry said.

'Is there someone else?'

He hesitated. 'No, no one else.'

'I heard you had a woman friend in Tipperary.'

'Who told you that?'

'Vaizey, I think. He said you had a woman on the road.'

'I didn't have a woman on the road; I had a friend. Her name's Maggie Leonard an' she's old enough to be my mother. I lodged with her when I was down at Tipperary. She was never more to me than a friend, Sylvie, though why I should have to justify myself to you because of some lie Vaizey told . . .'

'Do you want to go back to her?' Sylvie put in.

'No.' He hesitated. 'Besides, I don't think she's there any more.'

'Isn't there?'

'Her son was a sergeant in the Connaughts, killed at Heuvert. I wrote to Maggie but she didn't write back. I think she might have sold up and gone away. She has daughters in America.' He put out a hand, his good hand, scooped Sean from her arms and dandled him on his knee. 'She was only a friend, Sylvie, and by God I needed a friend at that time.'

'I don't blame you for wanting someone else.'

Sean wriggled, stretched out his arms and punched his tiny fists into Gowry's chest, not in temper but in play.

'There's no one else,' Gowry said after a pause.

'Then come back to Dublin,' Sylvie said. 'There's room enough in Endicott Street for all of us, at least until you get back on your feet. Maeve still needs a father.'

'An' you, what do you need, Sylvie?'

'Whatever you're prepared to give.'

'How do I know there won't be another Fran Hagarty? How can I be sure some other smarmy seducer won't come along and sweep you off your feet?'

'You don't.'

He held the boy against his chest and, patient as always, let him poke and pry at his mouth with inquisitive little fingers.

'You're asking a lot, Sylvie.'

'I know I am.'

'I don't have a lot left to give.'

'I'll take whatever you have,' she said.

Still he would not or could not make himself meet her eye. It wasn't guilt or embarrassment that prevented communion between them but something else, something she couldn't put a finger on.

She had read that the war affected soldiers in odd ways or she might have played up to him, flirted with him, even shed a few pathetic tears. How many pals had he seen die, though, how many Germans had he killed? She couldn't imagine her husband killing anyone, not even a German. Whatever his experience in France, apparently it hadn't made him callous, only distant, unreachably distant. She was too astute to force herself upon him when he was occupied with Sean. She watched him tickle Sean's nose with his bandaged hand, the wrecked and ruined hand, and let the boy wrestle with the ugly, upright thumb.

'Ow,' Gowry said. 'Ow, what a grip. What a grip you have, wee man.'

Sylvie said, 'When you're well again will you come home?'

'I might,' Gowry said.

'What does that mean?' Sylvie said.

'It means I'll have to think about it,' Gowry said and, handing Hagarty's son back to her, got up and walked out of the Fortress without another word.

'What did he say about me?' Maeve asked. 'Did you tell him I want him to come home? Did you tell him about the mix-up with the letters? Did you tell him we've room enough here for—'

'I told him as much as he wanted to hear,' Sylvie said.

'Then he just walked out?'

'He – he isn't himself.'

'Well, I could have told you *that*,' Maeve said, grandly. 'He's been fightin' in the trenches for months, never mind gettin' blowed up. How does he look?'

'Awful,' said Sylvie.

'Has he really only got one hand?'

'He's waiting for a new one.'

'They can't give him a new hand,' said Maeve. 'Can they?'

'They saved the thumb. Apparently they can do all sorts of things if they save the thumb, so he told Gran McCulloch. She didn't believe him. She thought he was raving. Even so, I think she got more out of him than I did.'

'It's your own fault,' said Maeve. 'You should've took me with you instead of Sean. Did Gran get to see Turk?'

'She got to see Peter. He isn't well.'

'If he dies it'll be another murder,' Maeve said. 'Breen says the British are worried about what's happenin' in the camp. Breen says he's heard the prisoners run the place an' they've appointed new leaders.'

'I didn't know Breen was interested in politics.'

'It ain't politics,' Maeve said. 'It's revenge.'

'Whatever it is,' said Sylvie, 'you'd best keep out of it.'

'Uh-huh!' said Maeve with just a hint of scorn. 'Sure an' I will.'

She was seated in the tub chair that Pauline had left behind, a nursing-seat with torn upholstery that Mam had covered with an old travelling rug. She had Sean on her lap, feeding him his nightly bottle. He seemed none the worse for his trip across the sea or his brief sojourn in Wales. The home crossing had been easier than the crossing out and there had even been a patch of blue sky over the Irish coast, so her mother had said.

There was no ambivalence in Maeve, no division. She was reconciled to life as a changing process, a seesaw of fortune and misfortune. It wasn't constancy she hankered after, just the presence of men to act with and react against in whatever role she chose for herself. It would not be a man like the man her mother had been taken in by, though, not a smooth, complicated chap like Fran Hagarty, for she was immune to charm now and the conceits that went with it. Breen had told her a lot about Turk and the manifest destiny of the Irish – though Breen hadn't put it quite that way – a lot more than she'd ever learned in class from poor martyred Mr Whiteside. Five days with Pauline and Breen Trotter in Wexford had been, she felt, the beginning of her education. She was more assured and more determined than she had been a year ago, even with Turk in jail and her daddy in hospital.

She watched her half-brother guzzle at the teat, wondered what sort of babies she would have when her time came, if they would be gigantic Trotter types right from the start. She had told Pauline of her plans and Pauline had encouraged her to marry Turk as soon as she was old enough. They would live in Wexford with the other Trotters and if Turk wanted to join a new rebel army to fight the English then she, Maeve, would stand with him, shoulder to shoulder.

'Why did they send Daddy to a Welsh hospital?' she asked.

Mam was propped up in bed, sipping a glass of stout. The journey had tired her, or, Maeve thought, perhaps the shock of seeing Daddy so changed.

'It's where they do the best repairs,' said Sylvie.

'You make him sound like a motor-car.'

'Well, perhaps there isn't much difference, not to the doctors.'

'Talking of motor-cars, he won't be able to drive one, will he?'

'I doubt it,' Sylvie said.

'What'll he do for a living then?'

'I expect he'll find something,' Sylvie said.

'If he comes back here at all.'

'Yes.'

'Do you think he will?'

'Will what?'

'Forgive you,' Maeve said.

'I don't see what else he can do,' Sylvie said with a sigh. 'I mean he has nowhere else to go, really.'

Maeve took the teat from her half-brother's mouth and let him grope for it, his gaze hostile.

'He might come back because he loves us,' she said.

'You know,' said Sylvie, sitting up, 'I never thought of that.'

'Then it's high time you did,' said Maeve.

★   ★   ★

On the ninth day of November 1916, the 2nd Battalion of the Sperryhead Rifles was disbanded. There had been too many casualties and too few recruits and the remnants of that gallant fighting force were merged with the Irish Brigade. By coincidence, on that same day Private Gowry McCulloch received both his new wooden hand and his discharge papers and, within a week, was standing, aching, in the rain in dear old dirty Dublin. He felt neither joy nor relief at being there. He, like Dublin, had changed, had become older and wiser and that little bit more decayed.

Even in the rain, in grey afternoon light, he saw how broken the city was and that gangs were still working on clearing debris from the streets. There was dust in the air, a thin muddy dust that caught in the throat. He was no longer in uniform, no longer distinguishable as foe or friend. The haversack he'd bought in a shoddy shop in Cardiff contained everything he valued: Becky's letters, wrapped in canvas. He knew he should destroy them and that he was clinging to something that no longer existed, to memories that would only bring him pain, but pain was better than nothing and grief was his only consolation.

He walked slowly along the City Quay, over the Butt Bridge to 'his' side of the river, the side of the river where the Shamrock had stood and which, against all logic, he still expected to find just as it had been, with Jansis grousing in the kitchen and Mr Dolan sulking upstairs.

He crossed the back of the station, entered a pub

and bought himself a whiskey and a Guinness. He didn't know why he did such a thing for he wasn't celebrating and wasn't keen on company. He kept his left hand in his overcoat pocket and drank with the right for a while then extracted the heavy, black-gloved object strapped to his forearm with a cigarette packet pinched between thumb and wooden forefinger.

The new leather, dampened by sea air, gave off a faint smell of cat's pee, but at least the black dye hadn't started to seep out of it yet. He held the cardboard packet lightly, clicked his right hand over his left and felt the clever little hinges slide and the joint close in on his palm. Lo and behold, he was holding the packet securely. He removed a cigarette and, glancing up, noticed that the chap behind the bar was watching him. He gave the chap a wink. There was nothing jolly in the wink, nothing spontaneous. He put the cigarette into his mouth but didn't light it.

The publican shifted along the counter, absently polishing a glass. His expression indicated that he was about to ask questions and, depending on the answers, offer sympathy, for not even a Dublin publican could tell a brave Irish rebel from a brave Irish soldier in the gelid light of a November afternoon. Provided he kept his mouth shut, he, Gowry McCulloch, could be anything he wanted to be: a traveller, a docker, an emigrant returning home, a seller of holy trifles or ladies' undergarments, a liar or a lout or a leader of men. He was none of these things, of course. He was merely a nonentity, a man without soul or identity, nursing the memory of what he had left behind.

When he brought up the haversack and dumped it on the polished counter, the publican's curiosity became tinged with alarm.

'An' what's that you have there?' he asked.

'What does it look like?' Gowry said.

'A bag, a haversack. Have you been far then?'

'Far enough,' said Gowry. 'An' this, what does this look like?'

He linked his right hand with his left, pressed down on the hinges hidden in the oak and then, stiffening his elbow, held it up.

'A fist,' the publican said.

'There you are then,' Gowry said and sweeping up the glass finished his stout in a swallow, plucked the haversack from the counter and went striding out into the rain, heading not for Sperryhead Road but for Endicott Street and all that was left of the life he had lost on the plains between Albert and Baupaume.

The rain had eased by the time he reached Parnell Street but he could see nothing of the hills. It felt clumsy to be moving on pavements again without a rifle and a pack. Buying a haversack had been a stupid idea; it made him look like a postman. He came up into unfamiliar territory at the mouth of Endicott Street and saw the four tenements rearing up in the gloom ahead of him. Then he caught the inimitable sound of a school bell and the sudden starling-chatter of children exploding from the gates of a schoolyard. They flooded out of a side street and were suddenly all around him.

Behind the youngsters older boys and girls strolled more sedately, feigning self-assurance. They were all just children, of course, stained by the classroom, ragged, rumpled and untidy. The girls walked in twos, the boys in packs; Gowry, in the midst of them, so adult and uninteresting as to be almost invisible. He had fought for them, though, had plunged his bayonet into German bellies just to give them a future – or so he had been led to believe. He questioned that noble ideal now, for he had come around to the view that he had been gulled into fighting for nothing more worthy than the vanity of nations.

Then there she was – Maeve. He hardly recognised her in her shabby black overcoat, short and tight about her long frame, her beret at a jaunty angle, swinging her satchel as if it were filled with feathers. She walked with another girl, trailed by four scruffy boys whose sly comments the girls casually ignored.

Gowry had a quite unreasonable urge to knock the lads' heads together and tell them to leave his daughter alone or to learn a few manners and a bit of respect. He sucked in a deep breath, and another. He could hardly breathe – the gas again, the wave of sticky green fog – and his eyes were wet. He tucked his chin into his collar for fear that she would see him weakened or, worse, that she wouldn't recognise him at all. He loitered by the corner lamppost. He couldn't move, couldn't advance or retreat.

Maeve glanced up. She was smiling at something; he didn't know what. The girl beside her was smaller and less robust than Maeve and she was laughing and when Gowry heard the girls' laughter he felt a catch in his throat and his eyes fill. He lifted his arm and wiped his nose on his sleeve. The movement drew Maeve's attention to him. She frowned. When she frowned she looked like her mother, prettier than ever with that soft crease in the middle of her brow and her lips parted. If he had been a young man he would have walked behind her too and felt the awkward pitter-patter in his chest that he couldn't put a name to yet or do much about.

The satchel checked in mid-air. She caught it and pressed it against her breast, the beret cocked over one bright, startled eye. He heard her say, 'My God! My God!' and then she was running towards him and, a moment later, flung herself into his arms.

'Daddy!' she cried. 'Oh, Daddy!'

And at that precise moment Gowry knew why he had returned to Dublin and what had brought him home.

PART SEVEN

Maeve

Chapter Twenty-six

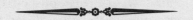

By Christmas the gilt had gone off the gingerbread. On the surface all was as well as could be expected and her daddy, though changed, was less moody than she remembered him to be. The fact that he didn't look like her daddy might have had something to do with it. She soon became used to his altered appearance, though, and wasn't daunted by the detachable wooden hand or the crumpled, pink-skin stump at the base of his thumb.

When she first caught him with the hand unstrapped he'd tried to hide the injury from her but she had said, 'Let me see,' and he had obediently held out his hand like a schoolboy awaiting a stroke from the pandy-bat.

'Does it hurt?'

'Yes.'

'Does it hurt more when you wear the strap?'

'Yes.'

'It's not infected, is it?'

'No.'

He had peered down at the thing as if he too were seeing it for the first time. He bent the thumb experimentally and released a puff of breath as the tendons tightened, wrist and forearm rubbed hairless by the broad, buckled straps that held the hand in place. It was, Maeve had to admit, ugly, almost as ugly as the dental wedge that pushed out his lips. There was something distinctive about his ugliness, though, a battered quality that made him seem more of an individual. When she asked her mother what she thought of Dad, however, Mam answered only with a shrug and Maeve wondered if that was why Dad slept upstairs and she still slept with Mam.

She had offered to swap, to sleep in Fran's room on the fourth floor, though she didn't fancy the climb up the spiral staircase in the dark, but her mother would have none of it. So Dad occupied Fran's old room and the man who had lodged there – Mr Dunnigan – was found lodgings in another Catholic house and lurched away with two bottles of Powers in his cardboard suitcase to compensate him for the inconvenience.

Because she had never been in the room when Fran was alive, Maeve didn't think it odd that her father should be sleeping in a bed that her mother and Fran had shared. It was such a neat little room and the coal fire made it cheerful on cold November evenings and if Dad felt uncomfortable there then he didn't complain. In fact he didn't complain about anything.

When she clumped upstairs to see how he was faring she would find him seated in the chair by the window staring out at the chimneypots with a far-away look in his eyes. When she asked if she was interrupting him he would shake his head, not irritably but as if he were bringing himself back from some colourful land that only existed inside his head, like a jigsaw with jumbled pieces that needed sorting out.

For two or three weeks he kept himself to himself. Mam told Maeve to leave him alone, for he needed time to adjust. Then one very cold afternoon he went out and didn't come back for supper and Mam became very tense and when she heard the outside door rattle handed Sean to Maeve and ran out into the hallway.

'Are you all right, Gowry?

'I am. I am.'

'Would you like a bite of supper?'

'Aye, that would be fine.'

He came into the room, grey with cold, chafing the wooden hand with his good hand as if the frost had made the artificial joints ache. He sat down in front of the fire, slumped, then glanced over at Maeve and gave her a wink.

'I've found work,' he said.

'Where?' Mam asked.

'Watton's.'

'Watton's!' Maeve heard herself exclaim. 'Not drivin'?'

'Storeman.'

'Can you – I mean, with the hand?' said Sylvie.

'They put me to the test.'

'What sort o' test?' said Maeve.

'Dexterity. I'm to be employed as a checker. I'll keep tally of what comes in an' what goes out. I've a board an' a pencil, an' my own tally book. It's countin' mostly, so I can manage it well enough. The pay's miserly, but beggars can't be choosers.'

'You're no beggar,' Sylvie said. 'They're lucky to have you.'

He nodded, looked into the fire for a moment. 'Know why I got the job? I got the job because I fought in France,' he said. 'First question the boss asked me. An' when I said I'd served with the Sperryhead Rifles the post was as good as mine. They have a policy there: no republicans. They don't care for republicans.'

'Huh!' said Maeve, scornfully. 'Tell that to Turk.'

'I don't have to tell it to anybody,' her father said.

'Turk fought for—'

'Maeve, that's enough,' her mother said.

She put her half-brother down on the floor. He was crawling now like a little tank and would be walking before he was much older. He went off across the floor like a rocket, heading straight for the hearth and the firelight. Her daddy reached down and scooped him up, held him one-handed and let him swim in the air, plump legs and arms flailing, then stood him on his knee, upright with an arm about his middle.

'I start on Monday on the back shift. Four o'clock

until midnight. Saturday too. I'll be on the docks when the cargoes come in for unloading. If the boats are late, then I'll be late.'

'What does it pay?' said Sylvie.

'Enough,' he said.

'Enough for two rents?' Sylvie said.

'I wondered when we'd get around to that.'

Sean was dancing on her father's knee. His front was bathed in firelight, his plump little face ruddy. He seemed oblivious to the tensions in the room. The tension stemmed from her mother, for her father was still calm and patient, and pleased with himself.

'It's not right,' Sylvie said. 'That's all I'm saying.'

'One room isn't big enough,' Gowry said.

'One bed you mean.'

Maeve flushed. Talk in the schoolyard in Endicott Street was a lot more informative than it had ever been in Mr Whiteside's class. She had learned more than was good for her, she supposed, and the knowledge had thrown her mother's affair with Fran into a different light. She had spoken tentatively to Pauline about it but Pauline had not been very helpful; no more had Breen. She had thought of asking Father Macken for advice but he was a priest and would hardly know what she was talking about.

She opened her mouth to say, 'I'll sleep upstairs if you like,' then thought better of it and looked down at her darned stockings and worn shoes.

She couldn't help but listen, though, for she was appalled by the thought that her mother might chase her father away again, or that his quietness was really indifference and that he was only putting on an act to get himself a clean bed, a couple of hot meals a day and his washing done free of charge. She had always been led to believe that the important thing for a husband and wife was to sleep together in the same bed, but her mother had disabused her of that idea by sleeping with Fran Hagarty.

Why Mam didn't share a bed with her father now was something Maeve couldn't quite understand. She wondered if it had to do with the artificial teeth and detachable hand, if he was embarrassed by the dismantling process that went on every night before he slid under the sheets. It appeared that Mam wanted him back in her arms and Daddy would have none of it. Perhaps it was the baby; perhaps it was the wound; perhaps it was something that even the older boys and girls in the playground didn't discuss. Perhaps it was all just money after all; three and sixpence a week rent on Fran's old room, though cheap even for Endicott Street, might soon become a luxury they could ill afford. Ears pricked, eyes averted, Maeve listened in the hope of finding an answer.

Gowry was quiet for a while, staring into the fire, while the baby danced and pranced on his knee.

At length, he said, 'I see they've demolished the Shamrock.'

'What does that have to do with it?' Sylvie said.

'There's nothing there,' Gowry said, 'just a gap.'

'If you're thinking we'll get compensation . . .'

'No,' Gowry said. 'There's no possibility of compensation. I'm just wondering what they'll put there now the old place has gone.'

'Whatever it is, it'll be more than we can afford.'

'I can do it. I can handle the job. We'll be all right.'

'How long are you going to keep up this charade?' Sylvie said.

'Hmm?' he asked, mildly puzzled. 'What charade?'

'I don't know why you bothered coming back. Did you do it just to punish me?'

'Punish you? No,' he said. 'Oh, no.'

'Well, you are, Gowry,' Sylvie said. 'You are punishing me.'

She began to cry, elbow on the table, cheek resting on her palm, her hair spilling in little wisps across her brow.

She looked, Maeve thought, like Pauline, innocent and knowing at one and the same time, blue eyes wet with tears, tears splashing on to the dinner plates. Her father moved stiffly, like the hinges of the wooden hand in frosty weather. He turned towards Maeve, then towards the door, then, finally, towards Sylvie. He let her cry, head on hand, for almost half a minute before he swung Sean from his knee, lowered the little boy on to Maeve's lap, turned to the table and put an arm about his wife's shoulders. He leaned against her, his cheek brushing hers, almost sharing her tears.

'Why are you crying?' he asked. 'Because I'm not dead? Because you lost Hagarty an' are stuck with me instead?'

'No, damn you, Gowry McCulloch.' She slapped both palms on the table, making plates and cutlery jump. 'No, you fool, you don't see it, do you? I love you,' her mother said. 'I want to love you, and you won't let me.'

'Sure an' I don't think that's it at all,' her father said. 'I think you want *me* to love *you*, Sylvie, just the way I used to – and that's impossible.'

'Why? Because of – of what happened? Because I kept Sean?'

'Sean has nothin' to do with it,' Gowry said. He was still close to her and his arm had tightened and he seemed, at least to Maeve, to be holding her mother down now, pinning her against her will. He spoke softly, though, very softly, so softly that she, Maeve, could hardly make out what he said. 'If you're askin' me to love you, Sylvie, the way I did before I went away then' – he gave an almost imperceptible shrug – 'no, I can't; and you can't expect me to pretend that nothing's changed.'

'If you hate me so much—'

'I don't hate you.'

'Is it her?'

'Who?'

'That woman in Tipperary?'

'God, no,' Gowry said. 'No, no.'

'Go to her, see if I care.'

'I can't go to her,' Gowry said. 'She isn't there any more.'

'If she was, I suppose you'd . . .'

He leaned closer still, pressing her down, covering her. To Maeve, they looked like one thing, one entity, bulky and not beautiful. Although he breathed the words into her mother's ear it seemed to Maeve that he was speaking to no one but himself, that what she heard was a secret voice, an inner voice, like thought itself. 'Perhaps,' he said, 'yes, perhaps I would.'

'You slept with her, didn't you?'

'That hardly matters now.'

'You did, didn't you?'

He drew away, lifting his arm high, letting Sylvie slide out from beneath him. There was pain in his eyes, a kind of suffering that Maeve had never seen before and when he squeezed his eyes shut she wondered if he would ever open them again. She wasn't looking at her stockings and worn shoes now. She was staring at her father, at a man whose principles she had spurned, whose intelligence she had doubted, whom she had loved only when she had been young enough to know no better. Now she had an inkling that he was more man than father, more man than husband, more than a provider and that what he had done in coming back to them was bravery itself. She saw her father then as clearly as she ever would; saw into him and through him to the struggle that was in all men. He was a good man, her father, as brave in his own way as Turk.

'No, Sylvie.' He let out a wheezy sigh and opened his eyes. 'No, I did not.'

It was not the denial, the lie, that brought her mother down but the manner of its delivery.

She was suddenly as fussy and feathery as a hen, and as helpless. She reached out, wrapped her arms about him and laid her head against his chest.

Still as a stone, Maeve watched, hoping that all would be well now and that she would never again have to see the sort of pain that she had glimpsed in her father's eyes, promising herself that Turk, her Turk, would never have to suffer in that way, that she would never give him reason to doubt her loyalty.

'I'm sorry,' her mother said in a tight, constricted little voice. 'Oh, Gowry, I'm sorry,' and reached up to kiss his mouth.

There had been talk of going to visit the Trotters to celebrate Christmas in Wexford but her father had a late shift on Saturday and that had put the kibosh on that. Besides, he was none too struck with the idea of meeting Turk's family, and even Father Mack, who had called round to visit the hero, had been unable to convince him that the Trotters were anything but wild-eyed fanatics who would blow up a pillar-box as quick as look at you. So there she was, stuck in Dublin over Christmas but being a very obedient young woman just at present, she heeded her mother's pleas not to rock the boat and to let Daddy have his way.

In later life, when Maeve cast her mind back to those disastrous months when her mother had taken up with another man, her father had gone off to war and the Shamrock had gone up in smoke, she found that she could only really remember the little, individualised moments when love in one of its many manifestations had touched her. She remembered, for instance, the gloomy morning when her father had left to enlist and had come to her room in the wee small hours and kissed her; remembered too the night when her half-brother had been born and her mother, worn out, had insisted that she take the tiny, shawl-clad bundle in her arms and hold him; remembered how Turk had looked at her through the barbed-wire fence in Richmond Barracks and how she had known then that he was the man for her.

Of all the wayward memories of that difficult time, however, the one she cherished most was of Christmas Eve morning in 1916 when her father came into the room on the ground floor and stood above the bed, dark and gaunt, his overcoat freckled with sleet and the smell of the cold sea air coming off him, and how she had wakened an instant before his lips touched her brow, surprised but not alarmed to find him there.

There was still a flicker in the coals in the grate and a hint of light from the street outside and she could see the transient shadows of the snowflakes drifting against the glass.

He kissed her on the brow and, leaning over, said, 'They're out.'

She sat up, and her mother sat up.

She said, 'How do you know?'

'It's the word on the quays.'

'Is Turk with them?'

'I don't know.'

'Is it Wales?' her mother said. 'Is it Frongoch?'

'It is.'

'All of them?'

'All of them,' her father said. 'Lloyd George let them go.'

Maeve felt a great wave of gratitude to her father, as if he had personally signed the release order. She loved him for coming to tell her the good news in the half-dark dawn of a winter's day just before Christmas.

For weeks she had been scanning the papers for news from Westminster. She was well aware that certain factions in the government were concerned that the risk of detaining internees was becoming greater than the risk involved in letting them walk free. The change of heart for which Maeve, and the whole Irish nation, had been waiting had taken place by fits and starts: General Maxwell had been recalled in November and in early December Asquith had resigned as Prime Minister and Lloyd George had taken the helm. Now, at last, release orders had been signed and Turk and her uncles would be coming home.

'When?' she said.

'Tomorrow,' her father said. 'Today.'

Cold air nipped at her shoulders and breasts as the warmth seeped out of the bed. She didn't care. She was hot with anticipation and the excitement of seeing Turk again. Daddy sat on the side of the bed and pulled the quilt over her. He said, 'I don't know whether they'll be in time to catch the steamer from Fishguard. If they are, they'll land at Rosslare. I think, though, that if they have enough cash, they'll head for the late-night steam packet from Liverpool, and dock at Rogerson's Quay early tomorrow morning.'

'How early?'

'Eight o'clock.'

'I'll be there,' Maeve said. 'I'll have to be there.'

'We all will,' her father said.

'You too?'

'Me too.' Then he kissed her, and Mam too, and slipped out into the hall and clambered upstairs to snatch a few hours' sleep.

Maeve snuggled down against Mam, heart beating like a drum at the prospect of seeing Turk again. 'Will they know, will Breen have been told?'

'I doubt it,' Sylvie said.

'How can we let them know?'

'They'll find out soon enough.'

'Telegraph, we could send them a telegraph.'

'No, dear,' Sylvie said. 'Don't spoil the surprise.'

'Charlie an' Peter too. Will they reopen the brewery?'

'Yes, I expect they will.'

'An' Gran'll come back an' everything will be like it was before.'

'No,' her mother said, stroking her hair, 'not like it was before.'

It was still pitch dark and bitterly cold when she wakened. She heard her half-brother breathing in the darkness but saw nothing except a faint line of light under the door. She was too excited to go back to sleep and, not knowing quite what time it was, dressed herself and stole out into the hall.

She had no idea what she was doing out in the hall, for at that early hour all the other residents in the tenement would still be dead to the world. She was bursting with excitement, though, and needed reassurance, someone to keep her spirits high. She peered up the spiral staircase and wondered if the alarm clock had gone off yet and if Dad would mind very much if she wakened him a little bit early. She crept upstairs to the top landing. Light spilled from under the door of Fran's old room, a flicker of firelight that warmed the boards of the landing. She knocked on the door, heard him stir within.

She knocked again, and entered.

He was kneeling by the tar-blackened fireplace. He wore a striped flannel nightshirt, his pea jacket draped over his shoulders. She could see the wooden hand, ungloved, and the bite of the straps in the flesh of his forearm and the stoop of the shoulders that war and age had given him.

He looked round guiltily when she stepped into the room and the flare of burning paper in the grate angrily illuminated his face.

On the table by the window were a half-pint bottle of whiskey, an enamel coffee mug and the ashtray – Fran's ashtray – brimming with cigarette butts and spent matches. The alarm clock ticked loudly, firelight gleaming on its tinplate face and round brass bell. He had lighted the oil lamp, though, and by its light she could see the haversack on the bed and the trinkets that he had taken from it spread out on the quilt: a battered tin cigarette case, an oilskin-covered matchbox, tarnished German buttons and the Shamrock badge he had torn from his cap – and letters, a shoal of letters written on blue or buff-coloured paper.

'Daddy?' she said. 'Are you cryin'?'

'No,' he said, wiping his nose with the back of his hand.

Instinct told her not to venture further. She sensed that she had interrupted a ritual, a vigil, that there was something here that it was better for her not to know about. She was too selfish, curious and happy to heed the warning voice, however.

She stepped to the bed and look down at the letters, all written in the same precise, manicured hand, some in pencil, some in ink: *Dear Gowry . . . My Dearest, Dearest Darling . . . To My Darling. My Love . . .*

She reached out a hand, and he said, 'No, Maeve, please don't.'

He was standing now and looked ridiculous with the nightshirt hanging below the pea jacket, the strapped hand dangling by his side, hair tousled and eyes puffy, a letter, one page of a letter, crumpled in his fist.

Deliberately she turned her back on the bed.

'Who is she?'

'No one.'

'What's her name?'

'Rebecca.'

'Are you goin' to see her again?'

'She died.'

'Oh!' Maeve said.

She experienced a queer mingling of awe, protectiveness and pity and longed to reach out to him, hug him and tell him that everything would be all right, but she had reached the age when that lie would no longer hold.

'Oh!' she said again, softly this time. 'What time is it?'

'Ten after six.'

'I'll start the breakfast then, shall I?'

'Yes,' he said.

'Will you . . .'

'I'll come down for it.'

'Soon?' Maeve asked.

'As soon as I've finished here,' he said.

★   ★   ★

Sleet was thickening into snow as they climbed down from the tramcar at the O'Connell Street Bridge and set off along the City Quay.

Across the Liffey the Custom House stood out against a brown canvas sky, Britannia, Neptune and the roof of the portico draped with wet grey snow, the dome capped. It was a fair walk to the quay where the Liverpool steamers docked but the cold was less intense now and lights in the shipping offices glowed in the gloom. Word had leaked out that the boys were expected home and relatives were gathering on the North Wall and at the boat-train terminus and a small but raucous crowd was trailing out to the British & Irish berth on Rogerson's Quay.

Strange to be on the river front at that hour of a Sunday morning; Maeve felt as if she were floating in grey space, as if the long quay were moving and she was standing still, caught in this hurrying moment but not part of it. Boys ahead of her, a group of eight or ten, were singing and cheering, giving every peeler they passed the sign of the fist and the folded arm; not a soldier to be seen, though her dad said the platoons would be marshalled behind the offices, very rigorous, very disciplined, and not looking for trouble.

Daylight seemed a long time in coming and the air was heavy enough to catch the flicker of the lighthouse below the Basin. The British & Irish steam packet looked small with the sky and the sea, smeary with sleet, behind her. The peelers had put up ropes, for the Christmas boat would be packed with Liverpool Irish and from what she had heard of the Liverpool Irish there would have been more drinking than sleep on that cold crossing.

She watched the boat grow larger.

The fretwork along the rails solidified into heads and shoulders, into men and women. Maeve pressed anxiously against the sagging rope.

Mam had insisted on bringing the baby. Sean was cocooned in a huge, warm shawl, nothing much of him showing but a pink nose and alert brown eyes. He had been unusually quiet during the tram ride and on the long walk along the riverfront, absorbing every sight, sound and smell, adding, Maeve supposed, to his experience of the queer world he lived in. Her father had carried him most of the way, holding him securely against his shoulder, the artificial hand under his bum and his good arm wrapped round to keep him snug.

When they reached the ropes, however, her father passed Sean to Mam, pushed hard behind her and gripped her arm tightly.

She sensed his tension and suspected that it had more to do with the letters than with his brothers' return from prison. She wondered if he was thinking of her, of the woman – Rebecca – who had written those love letters or if he was still caught up in the war. So far he had refused to speak about it – wouldn't talk, wouldn't tell – as if the war were his secret, the war and the woman he had met there, one small secret contained within the larger.

They were cheering wildly now, those on board and those on shore.

Some lads had lit a pine torch and were waving it about, spattering globules of blood-red fire on to the sleety quay. Then the cheering turned to chanting: an anthem, a hymn, so wonderfully joyful that Maeve felt it in the pit of her stomach like an ache.

Ropes were coiled and flung out and fastened to bollards. The steamer creaked against the quay, shuddering. Bow-legged quay-masters and pursers of the shipping line rolled out the gangways while the peelers watched impassively, big and whiskery most of them, pompous in their uniforms.

The passengers were piling against the deck rail, fighting to be first down the gangway. Maeve heard the cries of the women in the crowd, the yelling of the men on deck, names and prayers and joyful tears all entangled in the celebratory whoop of the steamer's whistle and the gritty black smoke that billowed from her funnel. She pushed forward, searching for Charlie, Peter, for Turk. She didn't even know if he would be on the Liverpool boat. Might be on the train, or still in Fishguard or Rosslare. Might be seated at home in Wexford stuffing his lovely big face with bacon and eggs.

Then she caught sight of him, tall above the press, taller than ever, she thought, bigger than ever, clean-shaven now but just as wild and woolly as he had ever been, bouncing up and down and waving his hat.

Uncle Charlie and Peter clung to Turk's coat

tails; Peter, scrawny and crabby, scowling down at the crowd as if he hated them all.

She had no eyes for Peter or Charlie.

She raised herself on tiptoe and yelled at the pitch of her voice, '*Turk, Turk. I'm here. Here I am. Here.*'

She felt her father's hand tighten on her arm.

She turned and looked up at him, questioningly.

'She was a nurse,' he said.

'What?'

'The woman who wrote me those letters – she was a nurse.'

'Was she in love with you?'

'Yes.'

'An' were you in love with her?'

He didn't answer, not then, not ever.

Maeve's question drifted in the still brown air then melted away, like a fleck of sleet on wet flannel, as Turk came jolting down the gangway.

She could see him now, see that he had found her, could hear him shouting, as he rushed towards the rope with arms wide open, '*Maeve, Maeve. By Gad, ay-hay, my sweetheart. I'm home. I'm bloody home.*'

She felt Gowry's hand close on her arm once more.

He held her only for a moment, though.

And then he let her go.